I0741260

The Perfect Side Piece

A NOVEL BY

Nanette M. Buchanan

Copyright 2016 by Nanette M. Buchanan

All rights reserved.

This book is a work of fiction. All the events, places, and characters are products of the author's imagination or used fictitiously. Any resemblance to actual events or locales or persons, living or dead, is purely coincidental. No part of this book may be replicated, stored in a retrieval system, or transmitted by any means: electronic, mechanical, photocopying, recording, or otherwise, without written permission from the author.

Type of Work: Fiction- Suspense
Creation Date: December 6, 2015
First Edition: January 14, 2016
ISBN- 978-0-9793883-9-2
ISBN- 0-9793883-9-2
Cover Design: Fideli Publishing

I Pen Books
www.NanetteMBuchanan.com

Acknowledgements

This page is always difficult to write. Who do I thank? Will I forget someone who has indeed been there in the shadows giving me the necessary push? Novel after novel I write this page praying that I have not forgotten to thank that individual who will read my work and wonder why they weren't acknowledged or thanked.

Now you can understand why I have not addressed particulars when it comes to my audience, my readers, and my followers. There are so many of you that have touched me during this journey. Many of you who have connected with my writings have given me your voice, kept me focused and led me to the last chapter with confidence. It is you that I want to thank.

Without an audience, readers, or supporters this "hobby" would have found a way to my shelves to collect dust. I thank you, family, friends, Facebook followers, book clubs, and literary companions. You have become important to me. Page after page I think of what reading means to you. It's imperative for me to touch your emotions and link you with my characters. Your response has been overwhelming over these years. Thank you.

To my husband, look where we are now, it has been a journey, and I thank you for your support and love. The hours I spend writing, promoting, and working are your hours. Thank you for the sacrifice you've made. Tynicia, Katia, and Aaron, thank you for being the backdrop to my writing. I can always count on you, and that's important to me. I love you all.

Aaron, this is your thought and from you to the pen touching the pad. *The Perfect Side Piece* is now complete. I hope this is close to what you envisioned. I thank you for the root of the story that I believe is another "Can't put it down" drama.

Chapter One

Mona listened to the news broadcast for the third time. The story was "breaking news" on the five o'clock report that repeated at six. Now at eleven, the report revealed, the police had no new leads regarding the unidentified body found at the Pine Ridge Resort. There were no names, no suspects, and no definite location; just a report that there was another homicide.

"This makes the third killing within the last two years at the resort. The police won't say, but there's been talk that a serial killer is targeting men." The reporter looked to his co-anchor for his thoughts.

"Well Bob, if there is, this would be devastating for the tourist season. Many would change their vacations if they felt they may become a target for a killer."

Mona changed the channel and sighed. While surfing the channels for an updated report, her phone rang; the caller ID indicated the call was from Kendra. Mona forgot about their monthly outing.

"Hey girl, you okay? We waited for you, almost starved, until seven thirty. What's up, you didn't even call?"

Kendra was always in high-energy mode. Her voice, only a notch below soprano, was quite annoying, but her personality made up for it. Over the years, Kendra Lewis and Candice Miller had become Mona

Mandell's only true friends. They met once a month, a tradition they started to ensure they took time out for themselves. The three women were self-employed, self-sufficient, and single. Qualities they wouldn't relinquish for any relationship be it business or pleasure.

"Today seemed like it would never end. I worked on contracts until noon and sat waiting for that asshole to call. He never did. I don't know Kendra; you say he may not be cheating but what else is he doing? He doesn't return calls, stands me up for dates; it just seems as though I'm the perfect side piece again. I don't want to be played. He could at least admit it and let me state my rules."

"Well, you said you thought he was cheating. Do you have any proof?"

Mona looked at the pictures on her table. She had the proof. Leon, his wife, and children smiled at her, as though they were posing for the family photo again. She brushed the pile of pictures around and picked up another image of his children and wife.

"I have proof. He never mentioned a family, or being married. I'm sure he doesn't think I'm on to him. We were to have lunch today, and I was going to tell him I knew."

"So why didn't you join Candice and me later. You could have had a few drinks, forgot about Leon, and glanced at the eye candy we watched for a few hours."

"Well I had my drinks here, and I've put Leon on the back burner. Eye candy is a temptation for me. That's how I got involved with Leon. I'll just sit back awhile."

"Are you watching the news? They found another man dead at the Pine Ridge Resort. I thought those resorts were couple friendly. What single person goes there? The cops are so dumb. It has to be a woman or someone she's hired."

"What makes you think it's a woman?"

"Who else would kill a man at a couple's resort? Either couples or groups of couples go to those resorts. It's a woman, a scorned woman at that. I don't know about those other murders, what was it two more?"

"Yeah, they mentioned two others…"

Kendra cut her off. "Oh my God Mona, it's Leon!" Mona stopped surfing the channels when she caught a glimpse of Leon's picture. His name was there next to the faded image. She kept quiet as she waited for Kendra to speak.

"Girl, they said there's no obvious evidence other than the blood from his head….wow, Wow, it looks like he was hit while sleeping."

"Sleeping with who? It sure wasn't me. He was playing me all the time."

"Mona, I'm so sorry, I don't know what to say. Are you okay, do you want me to come over and sit with you?"

"No, no, I'll be fine. After all, his wife is the one who needs consoling."

Mona changed the channel again looking for more information on the murder.

"Well, you did have a thing for him, for what, three months? I'm sure you have some feelings for him. I'm here for you girl if you need me. Don't get all caught up over this and seclude yourself."

"No, I'm good. I was a little hurt when I found out about his family. I wanted him to tell the truth. Hmmm, maybe I wasn't the only one that knew he was playing the game."

"Yeah, maybe his wife knew too. Who knows, men that play eventually pay. Do you think the cops will question you?"

"I doubt it. How would they know we even dealt with each other? His wife doesn't know. Who else would? You and Candice are the only two I told about us dating. There's not much to tell even if they did question me. He stood me up again today. I doubt they'll even consider me."

"Consider you as what?"

"Girl, I have to go. This mess on the news and talking to you, I won't be able to function tomorrow."

Mona put the phone in the cradle gently. She didn't want Kendra to think she needed her shoulder to cry on. She put Leon's pictures, credit cards, and identification together. It wouldn't take long to shred them and take out the trash.

Chapter Two

St. Paul's Episcopalian Church was filled with the friends and family of Leon Bates when Mona arrived. She hoped Kendra and Candice would have met her in the parking lot. After seeing the size of the crowd, her nerves settled. No one would recognize her or assume she was out of place. Candice made a point of reminding her that the police would be interested in those who didn't attend the funeral. Mona didn't quite understand her reasoning but didn't argue the point. The trio decided to go to the latter of the two wakes and skip the funeral. Mona agreed, but she would be at the funeral. She needed to witness his coffin being put in the ground.

She stood in the church foyer nodding to people as they passed by, wondering who they thought she was. She was dressed conservatively in all black. She wore darkened shades to hide her straight face and tear free eyes. She pinned her shoulder length braids into a neat bun, something she rarely did. She kept the handkerchief in her hands as a prop.

Candice spotted her first and pulled Kendra in the right direction. "She's in the lobby; c'mon."

The two excused themselves as they made their way through the crowd that seemed to prefer gathering outside.

"Your hair is cute. Hey, are you okay?" Kendra whispered hoping not to attract any attention.

"I'm fine, but can we find a seat before everyone comes inside?" Mona led the way not waiting for an answer.

They walked down the aisle and took a seat in the middle of the church. The procession was doubled to view the body and give their condolences to the family. An usher handed each of them, a program and a fan.

"Did you view the body earlier?" Candice hoped they didn't have to get up.

"No, I don't think I want to, maybe during the last viewing."

"I'll walk with you if you'd like Mona. I know this is stressful for you." Kendra was becoming a pain. Mona gave her a pat on her hand.

"No, I don't want to." Mona watched the reaction of the family. Leon's wife, a woman she would never imagine him dating, had a complexion that was shades darker than the pictures reflected. She thought for a moment that maybe the woman wasn't the image in the pictures. The woman and two children sat huddled together. The boy had his father's features and color. The girl kept her head buried in her mother's breast. She couldn't have been more than four years old. There was an elderly woman, sitting next to them, but she seemed distant as though in her world.

Leon mentioned his mother often. He said there was no one left in his family but him and her. His brother died at a young age. Mona watched as the woman interacted with those offering their condolences, she had to be his mother. She felt sorry for her. She couldn't help but be curious about his wife. He never mentioned her or the children. His mother, he said, lived with a roommate, a woman who cared for her over the years. Mona looked at those seated in the pew but saw no signs of a caregiver.

There was a noticeable distance between his wife and the rest of the family as well. Maybe he was separated, perhaps on the verge of a divorce.

Neither seemed to matter now; he didn't believe in a committed relationship nor marriage, that was obvious.

The choir began to sing. Mona said a silent prayer of thanks; her attention now was directed to the pulpit. The prayer and dedications didn't take long. The last viewing began after the minister reminded the audience not to wait to find God. Mona closed her eyes and sighed. "Let's go," She said as she stood avoiding the ushers, who were leading those seated in the front of the church.

"I don't think it's appropriate for us to stand in the middle of the final viewing. Mona wait, we can leave right after we go to the front." Kendra whispered tugging at her dress, "I'm not…"

Before she could continue, the usher was extending her hand for their pew to proceed to the front of the church. Mona had no desire to look at Leon's poised face. She had nothing to say to his wife, children, or mother.

As they got closer, she could feel his mother's stare. She had been watching as each person stopped to view her son. A chill went down Mona's back as she glanced at Leon lying in the casket. She tried to walk past him totally, but the pulling at her sleeve by Kendra made her pause as though in prayer. She rolled her eyes closed to keep from looking at his serene face. Kendra gave her a slight push, an indication to move on. Leon had on the suit he wore when they first met. Mona remembered the shirt and tie. She pictured his smile as he approached her at dinner that night, the night before their first weekend together. Candice shook his wife's hand and mumbled her condolences. His mother's stare never changed. Mona wondered if, in her elderly wisdom, she knew or had Leon told his mother about her. Had he told her there was another woman?

Kendra extended her hand for Leon's mother, and she smiled grasping it softly. Mona's nerves weren't prepared to meet his family. She smiled, uncertain of the response his wife would give. Leon's mother began to have a coughing spasm. His wife turned to attend to her in-law, no longer focusing on those who wanted to express their sorrow. Mona didn't offer any assistance. She stepped away allowing the church nurse to come to their aid.

"I bet that's his mother," Kendra commented as they descended down the stairs of the church.

"His wife was handling it pretty well, don't you think?" Candice questioned.

"Hey Mona, are you okay?" Kendra asked. Mona was walking at a slower pace.

"Yeah, just thinking, karma is a bitch."

"Karma?"

"Yeah Candice, karma, you know what goes around, comes around. Like you said his wife was handling it well. I wonder if she knew he was cheating."

"You think his wife found out? You think she could have killed him?" Kendra's imagination was painting the murder scene.

"No, not at all; but, I bet his mother knew," Mona replied softly.

"Oh my God! Did she recognize you?"

"How would she Kendra? She didn't know you, did she Mona?" Candice put her hand on her chest dreading the answer.

"We've never met, no. Listen it wasn't that serious. We dated a few times. Did our thing, you know, and that was it. I wasn't about the 'meet the family' thing."

"Well, you couldn't have been. I mean seeing he had two kids and a wife."

"Candice, you don't know Mona too well. Girlfriend will get with a husband, or two." Kendra turned her lips up giving her words emphasis.

"Oh, please you will too," Mona stated as she scanned the parking lot.

"Look, Candice, the man, ain't in the ground good. What are you looking for Mona or should I say who?"

"I thought maybe the police would be looking the crowd over. I swear they ain't worth a damn. Man gets killed, and they don't suspect the murderer would be around the funeral?"

"Police, at the funeral, please. The police in P-A did that investigation. Why would the police here give a damn?

"Humph," The ladies harmonized.

Mona told them she would call later. She opened the door of her Lexus as she admired the 'eye candy' as they approached their cars.

"That's right, boys. Another one bit the dust. Just know, you need to come right or don't come at all. Who's next?" Mona's thoughts took over as she slammed her car door.

Chapter Three

The continuous chirping of the birds woke Mona the next morning as they had since the beginning of the warmer weather. She sighed deeply wondering why she put a feeder on her deck in the first place. She checked the program she placed on her nightstand for the time of the service.

"Home Going Service for Leon Bates," she read aloud. Candice and Kendra didn't think twice about her saying she didn't think she would be seeing any clients for the next few days. They offered their availability, and she graciously declined, certain they would ask her to "just let go." They had no idea that her relationship with Leon had been longer than three months, more like a year. After being baited by the other broken relationships, she wouldn't be on the sideline again. She explained that to Leon during their early morning, late night, pillow talk. Candice and Kendra wouldn't begin to understand; she didn't have any tears for a man who couldn't; no wouldn't commit.

Leon's words were, *"What else do you want? You've got the best of me, baby. It's just my time doesn't always connect with yours."* His words soothed her into his arms time after time. Mona rearranged her appointments to make more time for them. It was then she understood that her married lover had other obligations. She never questioned him. She never mentioned the nights in the middle of the week that he couldn't stay over or the trips he cut short. She never spoke about his late arrivals after she checked into her choice of hotels. He made excuses and called her that stupid nickname, *Mimi.*

"*Who the hell is Mimi?*" She asked after he called the name during their lovemaking.

"*You baby. You have that Spanish look. My Mimi that's who you are, aren't you?*" He asked and kissed her gently.

She pulled away from him resisting his passion. "*What does Mimi mean? And for the record, I am not Spanish; my family is from Puerto Rico. I'm Puerto Rican and African American.*" She didn't like the game he was playing. It was dangerous.

She went to her closet and began putting an appropriate outfit together. The service was to begin at eleven. The internment would follow. She would meet them at the cemetery. There was no need to sit and listen to prayers for his soul. Hearing the minister say, "*Ashes to ashes, dust to dust*" would be enough. The burial would close another chapter in her life.

She started her journal two years ago hoping her life had changed after Raymond. She didn't enter information daily. It wasn't a diary; just the notes filled with lies and excuses she was told time and time again. When they started dating, when she confronted them about commitment, and when the relationship ended. The headings were by date, as though they were a part of the epitaph, the beginning, and the end. She'd write another prayer after the ending date. She had words to add to the eulogy, and she wouldn't miss the burial.

Chapter Four

The drivers followed the hand signals of the funeral director as they parked one behind the other near the prepared plot. No one opened their doors awaiting the nod of the professionals who assembled them in a column of two.

Mona spotted Leon's immediate family as they proceeded to the front of the other family members and friends in formation. Their empty seats sat in front of the coffin and the opened earth. Mona placed her shades on her face hoping no one noticed her roving eyes. She looked over the audience of approximately seventy people or more. There was no sign of the police or anyone who she met while in Leon's company.

Leon's wife, mother and the children sat in their designated seats. There seemed to be more relatives in attendance than at the wake. They all positioned themselves near his mother. Everyone moved in closer. Mona focused on the dirt wall she could see below the coffin. The roots of the grass, flowers that bloomed, when in season, were visible. The darkened dirt and the roots gave her a grim glimpse of what Leon's surroundings would be for eternity.

Mona came out of her trance when she heard the words from the minister requesting the family and friends to pray with him. He began reciting the Lord's Prayer. She bowed her head and prayed for her soul as she had done over the past two years. She prayed that Leon would be the last man to push her to the edge. She prayed that she wouldn't have to return another child of God's to the earth again. As she had at each funeral, she said "Amen" and meant it.

Everyone took a step back, allowing the caretakers to pass out a rose bud to be tossed, or kept in memory of Leon Bates. Leon's mother was helped to her feet when she began to weep aloud. Leon's wife remained seated, staring at the coffin as the top began to fill with red roses. When touched on the shoulder by those who passed her chair, she would tap their hand never taking her eyes off the coffin.

Mona plucked the petals of her rose as she followed the others. She mumbled, *"He loves me not"* as she released the petals in the air over the casket. She stepped off the green turf, careful not to trip over the unleveled ground.

She never looked at the faces that watched her pass. They mumbled about the petals and who was the woman who tossed them in the air. The crowd waited for Ms. Bates to stand before they began to walk toward the parked cars.

Mona opened the door to her vehicle and stood to watch the funeral director as he ordered the caretakers to lower the casket after the family left. The procession of cars exiting the cemetery took no more than five minutes to clear the area. Mona hadn't moved. She avoided having to circle the cemetery by being the last car. She watched Leon's casket as it was lowered into the ground. She remained in her car until they moved onto their next burial site for the day.

Mona walked to the gravesite that was still surrounded by green turf. She took off her shades and looked at the dirt that was packed down by the shovels.

"He loves me not!" She spat, "He loves me!" Her voice raised in intensity, "He loves me not!"

Mona kicked the dirt loose. She kicked the dirt until her shoes, and ankles became discolored with the soil from his grave. She bent down, touched the disheveled covering, and cried. As the tears dampened her face, she wiped her eyes. Smearing the dirt over her face, she began to laugh hysterically.

Two hours later, Mona turned her attention to business. It was best to work herself into a better mood than open the bottle of Hennessy that was calling her by her full name. She didn't have time for reality to speak to her emotions. The connection would cause anger, frustration, and irrational decisions. She felt better after a shower and now sitting in her robe, she could focus on the clients she had neglected to call over the past few days.

She was currently dealing with five new prospects. A couple from the West Coast representing an independent firm and three men, business partners, who happened to stumble upon her name on the Internet. Commercial land to build on wasn't much of a commodity, but foreclosures made it possible to level the land. The money on each finalized sale proved to be lucrative, and Mona didn't miss working at Fosters Real Estate. After discovering she could make more as an independent agent, she went to school immediately.

It was her work that introduced her to most of the men she dated over the past five years. There hadn't been many she could brag about, and it seemed there was always a trust issue. In the last two years, it seemed the dating scene had changed drastically. The men were looking for a woman to take care of them; they still lived in their parent's home, or they were cheating and hadn't mentioned the wife or the girlfriend. Mona never dated a man who couldn't take care of himself, most held prestigious positions. She hadn't met their family or visited their homes, and there had been little to no conversations about past relationships. There was no reason for them to be losers. There was no reason for them to assume she would accept being their part-time love.

She often asked herself if it would have saved them. Could she understand if Leon, Raymond or Kevin had mentioned they were dating other women? Leon was the only one who was married. She put too much into her relationships. She would have to change. After all, she had no reason to act desperate. A side piece was desperate, unaware, and deserved what she got, or so Mona thought. She didn't fall into that category.

An hour passed before she began to return the calls. Clearing her mind and making entries into her journal took longer than she expected. She promised Kendra she'd go out with her for drinks. She wasn't in the mood. She stretched the length of her couch and put down her pen.

The faces on the television were becoming a blur. She deserved a nap. Mental stress was catching up with her, but sleep would bring on memories. She refused to give the three men who brought out what years of therapy suppressed another minute of her time. She entered her thoughts in her journal as her psychiatrist suggested that was enough.

Mona reached for her portfolio that held the two business cards she needed. After dialing both numbers on the cards, she found it had been a waste of time. She could only leave messages.

She turned off the radio that had been playing since she walked into her apartment. Kendra would be calling soon. She didn't have any excuse not to go out other than the desire to lie down.

There was never anything on the television when she had time to watch it. No movies she hadn't seen and the sitcoms didn't hold her interest. HBO offered a better lineup starting at eight.

She went into the kitchen and found she still had a little salad left. She would eat, watch the television, and sleep soundly. She hoped her entries in the journal would rid her subconscious of any lingering thoughts.

Chapter Five

"There's no evidence that the three crimes are connected, other than location." Damien Tyson spoke into the phone as he moved the folders around. "Yes, I have them here on my desk. They called my unit this morning." He paused looking at the picture of Leon Bates. "Hey, this last guy Bates, where did he work? Maybe there is a connection." He listened as the answer gave him no clue. "No, no that doesn't link them either. Well, I'll be sure to contact you if we dig up anything. It may be a cold case, though. I don't want to take more time with this than necessary."

Tyson, as he was known in Moorestown, Pennsylvania's Homicide Unit, listened to the Captain's reason for requesting him for the case. He was what the unit considered the best. Tyson, a twenty-year veteran started on the unit as a detective younger than most. Now after fifteen years in Homicide, his job was to prevent cold cases. He would review the case evidence, read over case notes, and if necessary take a team and investigate again.

The first two cases of what was now called, The Resort Murders, Raymond Murphy, and Kevin Styles, raised the eyebrows of the police who responded. The third murder at the resort raised suspicion; it may have been the same killer. A disturbance of any kind at The Pine Ridge Resort was unheard of. Leon Bates tipped the scale, and they immediately turned over the cases to the Homicide Unit. Tyson laughed when they handed him the folders in the morning briefing. After watching the news broadcasts, he knew his next assignment would be the murders that had everyone whispering. The Leon Bates murder was clean, just like the others. He would have to dig deep to get a suspect.

"Well Chief, I'll give it my best. I don't think it is as simple as you think. If it was I wouldn't be holding these folders; yeah, I understand. I'll call you."

Tyson hung up the phone and took a sip of his coffee that still had steam rising from the cup. He leaned back in his leather high back chair holding Leon Bates' picture. There was something about the picture. Although he didn't know the name, he thought Leon looked familiar.

He'd have to run a report on the three men. He set up his desk preparing to work on the computer most of the day. Along one wall, there were posted pictures of the victims with labels indicating where the bodies were found. A map with colored pushpins marked the distance between each killing. He posted the news articles and requested the first news broadcasts to be sent to him. The folders he had in hand contained the additional information he requested from the initial police report.

Raymond Murphy was thirty-five, single, and a resident of Morristown, New Jersey. He worked for a real estate agency located in the same city. He was employed there for three years. There was nothing unusual about his background. The police questioned his neighbors and the staff at the resort. No one remembered him checking in with anyone, although he said he was checking in for two. One of the servers remembered seeing him with a woman at dinner. She couldn't describe her, and no one else remembered seeing her.

Tyson wrote notes on his pad and moved the folder labeled Kevin Styles closer to him. Kevin was thirty-seven and divorced four years before his death. He was the father of a boy, age eight. His ex-wife and son lived in Texas. Celeste Styles was listed as the next of kin. She and her son flew in the night before the service. They didn't attend the repast. Tyson noted that she had changed her name to her maiden name,

"Summers." He wasn't sure it would have any relevance, but he underlined it. Styles worked in construction, commercial buildings.

Tyson leaned back in his chair. Maybe there was a connection between the first two. He scribbled on his pad again, marking the assignments for his secretary and officers who would be available to him as needed. He'd have them check the last job, and real estate deal Styles and Murphy were handling.

Leon Bates didn't seem to connect with either of them. He was self-employed as a consultant or it seemed that way according to the reports from various companies that hired him. Tyson would let Kai, his secretary, delve deeper into the backgrounds. All the other information about Bates proved he was no more than the average guy. Bates was married, had two children and took care of his mother. Tyson would handle talking to the Bates family himself.

The intercom interrupted his thoughts. "Tyson, I've got the second reporter on the phone. I guess they found out you have the Bates case. I tried telling them they had it wrong, but you know how they are. Any comments you want to relay?"

"Yeah, is it the Ledger or the Village Post?" Tyson smiled. He enjoyed talking to the news reporters. He wanted to know who was covering the story. They would help him dig up information without realizing it.

"It's that fine red bone. What's her name?"

"Jeff, get professional, man. That's Ms. Fine Red Bone to you." The two laughed. "Transfer her over; she's from the Village Post."

Jeffrey Porter was Damien Tyson's partner for more than ten years. They worked long hours, case after case and understood each other most times without a word or communication between them. Damien knew Jeffrey liked Ms. Sayers. She was a beautiful woman from head to toe, and she knew it; a turn off for Damien. Jeff backed up once he saw he couldn't hold her attention. They both agreed she was high maintenance, and neither needed the drama she would bring.

"To what do I owe this honor, Ms. Sayers?" Tyson teased.

"I should say the same Detective. I feel honored that they asked me to question the great mind about these serial killings." She answered with a sexy overtone.

"Serial killings, what, or who gave you that idea?"

"Detective, they don't call Tyson and Porter unless there is a serial killing."

"That's not true. Cut off the recording and I'll tell you the cases we really handle."

There was a pause. Tyson listened, as it seemed Ms. Sayers shut the door to ensure privacy. "Tell me Tyson, exactly what kind of cases do you handle."

"Ah, I said we, not me. We handle cases just before they're considered cold. Yes, we do work on serial killings, the cases that take some extra attention, those you love to report. However, for the most part, we are the last stop before filing the cases until more evidence or time reveals something that may have been overlooked."

"That can't be true in these cases. I mean it hasn't been a year."

"Doesn't matter, the evidence appears to be cut and dry. I've just started to look at it, though. You may be right."

"So you're telling me I don't have a story?"

Tyson could hear her smirking, and it brought a smile to his face.

"I'm telling you that you'll have to call back, stop by or whatever you want to do. What is that name they have for you? Ms. Newsworthy, yes, there's got to be other stories brewing. I don't understand why you're on this story. There's not much to tell."

"There will be, and you know it. There's a scorned woman out there, and if you don't stop her detective, she'll do it again."

"So you know about scorned women, from experience or?"

"C'mon, Tyson, why would I be a scorned woman? Scorned women are desperate. If a man doesn't want you for who you are, one simply needs to move on."

"So you're saying you could just move on if a man told you that he wasn't interested any longer?"

"Yes, how long were they dating?"

"Who?"

"The woman who killed them."

"Who said a woman killed them? Now I see why you're a reporter. Listen if you're working on this story, don't print what you think. Print the facts. I'll give you the facts. Once you print that inquiry mess, I'm done."

"I know your rules, Detective Tyson. I was just asking what you thought."

"Not my thoughts Ms. Sayers. For the record, any woman can be hurt and be scorned including Ms., what is your first name?"

"Samantha. No, Samantha Sayers would not be scorned. Do you know how much you would have to be thinking about someone to do something like this? There's a thin line between scorned and crazy. It's almost the same as the line between love and hate. It takes a lot of emotional regrets to get there. Fortunately, I've never regretted any of my relationships."

"Hmm, well maybe you have a point. I just don't see a woman doing this. Not to say one couldn't. I don't have any answers yet."

"So you think it's a man?"

"No, I can't say that for certain either. Let me work at this for a few days. You're the first to call so, as you said, you know my rules you've got the story."

"That's the reason for my call, thank you."

"Ms. Sayers, I'll call you when I get information that would be worth reporting."

"Detective, you and I both know that won't happen. I'll call you. Do you think I could pick up a few pictures from you to get the report started?"

"I saw pictures in the Village. What about those?"

"Tyson, please I'm trying to get my own story."

"Porter will give them to you. They'll be ready tomorrow for you. That's the best I can do."

"Well, um, okay. I guess I should thank you."

"You don't have to, later, Ms. Sayers." Tyson disconnected the line without the thought of avoiding her.

Chapter Six

Kendra turned the key to her apartment door, happy to get out of her shoes and clothes. She'd have to do something about her sudden schedule changes and appointments. As a Program Director for the Youth Now, Professionals Later leadership program, she made her hours but she couldn't cancel appointments. Appearance was a necessary evil in the summer. She preferred flat sandals, shorts, and a halter top, but she often pulled the girls in the group into her office for that type of attire.

Candice called as Kendra was parking. She promised she would call her back after she showered. They were meeting Mona at seven. It had been a month since Leon's murder. Mona declined their other invitations to get out of her daily routine. She seemed paranoid, assuming she would be recognized as Leon's girlfriend. Kendra finally reminded her that no one knew she and Leon were dating. Kendra didn't understand why, and Candice didn't care. They both shrugged their shoulders at her response and changed the conversation.

They went on a spontaneous shopping spree earlier in the week and had lunch. Kendra and Candice agreed they were looking forward to the night out. Mona was hesitant but finally gave in.

Kendra turned on her television selecting the news channel as she chose a light summer dress with matching flat sandals. She came out of her walk-in closet when she heard the commentator mention Leon's name.

"The Resort Murder Case is still being investigated according to authorities. There has been no new evidence. However, detectives have found there may be a connection in two of the murders. A spokesman for the Homicide Unit told reporters at today's meeting with city officials that they would not let the case go cold."

Kendra sat on her bed and adjusted the volume on the remote. She dialed Mona's cell while the commercials aired.

"Hey, what's up?" Mona answered sounding better than she had in the past week.

"Have you seen the news? They're still investigating the murder. I wonder what connections they could have made between them. Did you know those other guys?"

"No, who are they? Should I know them?" Mona stood in her bra and panties facing the mirror in her room. She had the television on watching the same broadcast. Neither Kendra nor Candice knew Raymond or Kevin had dated her. She was glad she never introduced them. Now she could see it might have been a mistake for them meet Leon.

"I was just thinking about the connections. They're saying that two of the murders are connected in some way."

"Hmm, police work. You love that mess. Maybe Leon knew them, maybe not. It's all guesswork. Maybe this, maybe that." Mona felt relieved as she realized her friend hadn't put any of the pieces together; no one would.

"I guess you're right. I do love it, though. It runs in the family. I've got a few relatives that are police, detectives, or work closely with them."

"So what made you work with those bad ass kids?"

"To keep them from getting locked up, and they ain't that bad. Just curious, and—"

"Bad! Look if I'm going to meet you guys I've got to hang up. Are we still meeting at seven?"

"Yea girl, it's almost 5:30. You're right, see you there."

Kendra remained seated listening to the reporters as they discussed the evidence that was disclosed.

"The detectives are reaching to connect these murders, Howard. Seems the victims may have made contact with the suspect; they may have worked together."

"Yes, Rob, they have not identified a suspect in the case. Leon Bates was killed at the same resort. Do you think the same person murdered them?"

"The detectives are looking into that. That question was brought up, but no clear answer was given."

The report went to a prerecorded interview with the manager of the resort. Kendra sat back and put her legs up, engrossed in the broadcast. The phone rang, and she grabbed the remote cutting the television off.

"Yes."

It was Candice. "What are you doing? You sound funny?"

"Girl, I almost forgot what I was doing. They're still investigating the murders."

"Whose murder?"

"Candice. Leon's, and the other two at the resort." Kendra responded annoyed the cases didn't hold anyone's attention.

"Oh, wow I thought they weren't looking for anyone."

"It's turning into a big thing. I guess 'cause it happened at the resort. Hell, it probably put a damper on business. I know I wouldn't want to be staying there."

"I know that's right. Is Mona still coming?"

"Yeah, she'll meet us there."

"I'm leaving now. I'll get our table."

"Cool."

Glancing at the time, Kendra had to rush and get dressed. It would take her at least thirty minutes to get to the restaurant. She looked at her hair and shook her head. If she didn't get to the beautician in the next few days, she would be the "hot mess" talk for the teens. She laughed and brushed her hair into a ponytail. She could just hear them saying, "Stop letting Sha-naye-naye do your hair."

Kendra met traffic on the Parkway. The exit was minutes away, but she was already ten minutes late. Candice and Mona sat sipping wine and eating the appetizers they ordered. The friends grew accustomed to someone being late.

"If Kendra had moved away from the television she would have been here before us," Mona said as she looked around the restaurant.

"They were talking about the murders; or something like that. When I called, she was wrapped up in it. She loves that stuff. She should have been a cop." Candice added as she reached for a dinner roll.

"Hmm … well if they find the killer, she'll be the first to know. I'm not that interested."

Taken aback by Mona's comment Candice tried to hide her expression. She reached as far across the table as she could.

"Can you pass the butter?"

Kendra arrived with the server at her side. Eating at Porto Leggro near the Waterfront in Jersey City was her favorite. She loved Italian food and was glad they hadn't ordered without her.

"You are the best," She said greeting them both with a kiss on the cheek and a hug. She sat and patiently waited for them to place their orders before ordering her favorite dish.

"And more wine please. Right, you guys want another glass?"

Mona and Candice nodded in agreement. The server removed the used napkins preparing the table for their salads.

"This place always looks different, don't you think?" Candice asked adjusting her seat.

"I think it must be the décor.' Most restaurants don't change their basic colors. The last time we were here I think everything was gold."

Mona answered quickly hoping Candice would forget her comment. She didn't want Kendra bringing up the investigation details. They both would wonder why she had no interest in the new evidence or the connections in the murders.

"Maybe so, so what's up? How did your week go? Those kids got me going through hell, you know? Every teen there must be raising their siblings, parents never home, it's a mess."

Mona smiled. She was glad Candice was hungry. Candice was busy filling her plate from the large bowl of salad they ordered.

"Well, I've just got back to working. I've got five clients and three prospects; so things are picking up."

"I guess that's why the news about the investigation didn't faze you huh?" The question caused Mona and Kendra to look at Candice as she continued to chew. "You said you weren't that interested."

"Candice, you misunderstood. I don't want to become depressed over this mess. I'm hurt more by the fact that he never said he was married. I was devastated when I saw he had a wife and two children. What woman would put herself in that position over and over again?"

"You've dated married men before?" Candice's question gave Mona an opportunity to make them her emotional supporters.

"Only to find out later, I never knew. I seem to be attracted to men who always have someone at home or have a girlfriend they can turn to. It's been a rough year and it's only June. I'm thinking about becoming celibate. Maybe if I wasn't so horny, I would pay more attention to who I'm dating. I mean I get caught up in the physical thing and forget to do the thorough background check. How did he date me for months and I not know he was married?"

"I know girl. Dating is like finding an employee. You have to check them out before giving them the position. Candice what's up with that guy you went out with last week?"

Mona's plan worked, the conversation changed. No one mentioned the murders again until after dinner. The television flashed the earlier report promising to have an update at eleven.

"You know, they didn't have to work together for it to be the same suspect. It could have been someone who wanted to ruin the resorts status in some way." Candice shrugged her shoulder and waited for a response.

"Candice, I don't think so. Three men at a resort and no women to come out and say what they saw or what went on while they were there? Seems strange to me, I think it's a woman. The same woman killed them. I don't know why, but it's a woman, I'm sure of it."

"That would mean that Leon had a wife, Mona and another woman? Sorry Mona, but I'm just trying to understand Detective Kendra Lewis here."

Mona laughed, trying to cover her mounting anger. She wanted them to leave the dead alone. "No harm done here, I wouldn't put anything pass him. Did they say the others were married?"

"One was divorced, and the other was single I guess, or they didn't find out yet. I don't remember which one was divorced. They didn't talk much about the families. Anyway, they're still looking, and I'm sure they'll get her."

"How can you be so sure?"

"Mona, women are emotional creatures. She'll make an emotional mistake. Hell, killing three men is an emotional statement."

"Hmm…" She hadn't thought about that. Kendra was right she had made a mistake already. She was done and this time she meant it.

"Oh, before I forget. I've got tickets for you two. I bought three, but I can't go. It's a networking event for Networking Opportunity Corp. in Newark. I've got an event with those crazy teens that night. You guys go and have a good time. It may be good for your business Mona."

"I don't like mixing business with pleasure. I'll go, though if you want Mona, but I'll be going strictly for pleasure." Candice continued chewing as she buttered her bread.

"I'll handle the business end then. I'm not ready for any pleasure; I'm still grieving remember."

Candice couldn't help but laugh, and Kendra joined in.

"My ass you grieving, are you preparing a statement for the police? C'mon Mona, we know you. Leon was that hit and miss guy, and I guess he missed more times than he hit it."

Mona smiled and replied, "Yea, you're right. This is so crazy. How does a married man date or cheat on his wife and no one know it? I mean I can't believe that no one knew about me."

"Be glad they don't. The police would be questioning you and maybe looking at you as a suspect."

Kendra said what Mona had been worried about over the past few weeks. How long would it be before the police were knocking on her door? Every time she thought the case wouldn't point in her direction, they would air another piece of evidence. Now they were looking for connections. She couldn't remember what she left in each room. She hoped none of it was obvious.

"Well go to the NOC event and enjoy. I wish I were going with you. I'd be hanging with you, Mona. I'm satisfied with Jay for now."

"Jay." Candice and Mona chimed in together.

"I know, yes I took him back. I love him. You'll understand when you get to that level."

"I don't want that level. At least Jay is not married and even if he is a nerd, he's all yours."

"Thanks, Mona yes he's all mine, and we understand each other."

"So this thing is Saturday. Mona, you and I will have a great time I'm sure."

Mona nodded her head in agreement and downed the rest of her wine.

Chapter Seven

Jeff tapped on the desk with his pen to no particular beat. He was reading the evidence reports for the Resort Murders. He highlighted what he thought might lead to witnesses or questions they hadn't asked. He had given his opinion regarding the case. There were no other questions or witnesses. The case was dry, the suspect had got away, and there was no reason to give the families hope. They didn't have any idea who killed the victims or what had been the motive. He and Tyson were known to be thorough, but Jeff was ready to box the files and move on.

"Alright look, both Styles and Murphy were doing business in Jersey. Now that may not sound like much but so was this Bates guy. Last use of their credit cards just happened to be the same restaurant. I checked with their offices, and it seems that the companies paid for what was thought to be a business lunch."

Tyson waited for Jeff to stop tapping his pen before he continued.

"All we need to know is who they had lunch with."

"And what will the lunch prove? Okay, I'm with you. There may be a connection between the people due to business, but how does that prove murder?"

"May not prove murder but suppose the lunch was with the woman who was with them at the resort?"

"Okay, I see where you're going now. So what did the staff at the restaurant say?"

"Going there now, then I'll stop and see Ms. Bates. I want to talk to Ms. Styles too."

Jeff stopped tapping completely. "Road trip, you know she lives in Texas."

"I'll call her. If we have to go there, we'll go. I think it's a woman Jeff."

"Are you serious? I can't see a woman killing three men and not breaking down. What do you think is the motive?"

"No clues yet, I thought about the spouse of Leon Bates, but then that would ruin our speculation about a connection. I just don't see a man killing another man at a resort. She waited until they got to the resort. Maybe to show the wives what the husbands were doing."

"But what about Murphy, he wasn't married." Jeff leaned back in his chair. "Look Styles was killed almost two years ago; Murphy six months later, and Bates almost a year after that. If we go with your theory, it would mean that the suspect was a date or a girlfriend.

"Yeah, check and see if there was a fiancée or a girlfriend that showed up at the funeral for Murphy or Styles. Find out who claimed the bodies."

Jeff sighed and wrote down the request on his legal pad. His partner left him heading to the restaurant in Montclair.

The lunch crowd was small; Tyson was surprised it was near empty. He sat at the bar waiting for the bartender to come to the end where he took a seat.

"Hey there, what's up?" The young man spoke as though he knew Tyson wasn't interested in an afternoon drink.

"Coke with lemon, I need to know who works here weeknights," Tyson replied flipping open his wallet to his badge.

"I do most times, depends on what night. The waitresses vary though we have a schedule in the back. What night you interested in?"

The young man continued working as though it was the norm for a detective to be questioning the staff. Tyson paused before answering waiting for him to return with his beverage.

"You're the manager?"

"You could say that. My dad owns the place."

"Is he here or is there somewhere we can talk without you working?"

"Sure, he's not here; give me a minute."

The young man, not much older than twenty-three, waved Tyson on as he exited the end of the bar. A female replaced him bringing a smile on the faces of the customers they left behind. The door to the office muffled their conversations and laughter. Tyson appreciated the seclusion.

"Have a seat, can I get you, uh…freshen up your soda?"

"Nah, man I'm okay." They both laughed at the sarcasm.

"So is this about an employee, disgruntled customer, or what?"

Tyson made a mental note of the young man's demeanor. He didn't come off as arrogant as most that managed business while their fathers were out. A characteristic the detective could appreciate. It made his job easier. Often young boys would give him a problem with simple questions. He never got answers until he called them into the station.

"What's your name?"

"Scott Bearman. My dad owns the place, and I'm here most of the time. So I'm probably the one you would have to talk to anyway."

"Did you work here in March, April, or May?" Tyson watched Scott's reaction. He thought he would say he was still in College.

"Again, that depends on the night. You are questioning a night right?"

"No, in fact, I'm questioning lunch hours. The customers were frequent eaters here, and I need to know if the waitress or someone remembers them."

"Oh, I see. Do you mind?" Scott asked as he pulled out a pack of cigarettes. He readjusted himself after retrieving an ashtray and lighter from the desk across the room.

"Do you have the pictures? I can get you a schedule for that day, but I may know them."

Tyson opened the folder with the separate photos of Raymond and Kevin. He passed them to Scott and waited for him to reply. The picture didn't capture the full face of the woman, but it was all they had. He was sure that Scott knew them, but he began to shake his head no.

"Those were two of the men that were killed a few months back right?"

"Yeah, so you don't recognize them?"

"No, uh let me look at the schedules. Maybe the waitress may recognize them. I don't know detective, but if they had seen either of them, it would have been a conversation here. Someone would have mentioned it. First time I heard anyone say anything was last night."

Scott left Tyson thinking about his observation. He scribbled a few lines on his pad as a reference. He wasn't certain he wouldn't have to ask any of the night staff about the photos.

"Last night they aired a report about the murders. There were people talking at the tables about it, nothing more than that. Some even made bets that you guys wouldn't catch her."

"Her? What made you think it was a woman?"

"Talk, just listening to what everyone at the bar and the tables said. Detective, this restaurant jumps at night. Most of our customers get along with the staff and come here frequently. If these two came here, someone saw them. Ah, look here, this is who you need to talk to, she's off today, she'll be in tomorrow." Scott was pointing to the waitress in the background of the picture. "That's Jess; she's here most days."

"So do you have any contact information for her?"

"Here, take this business card. You call back, and I'll tell her you need her help. Call early on Friday."

Tyson shook the young man's hand, glad to have something to go on. He walked out the door and waited until he got outside to read the business card, Porto Café, Scott Bearman, Staff Manager.

Chapter Eight

Janelle Bates had cleaned her house thoroughly. She got rid of all her husband's belongings immediately after the funeral. She hadn't had visitors nor had she spoke to anyone other than her sister. She couldn't explain to the rest of her family and friends that she was not the grieving widow; she was relieved. Their marriage had been over shortly after the birth of their second child.

She told his mother as they made the funeral arrangements, there should have never been a marriage. She explained the feelings she held within for years. She and Leon made an effort after the unexpected pregnancy of their son to rekindle what she thought was love. It was a strained marriage, and as his needs led him to the arms of others, they held on for the typical reasons.

She played the role for her two children and Estelle, his aging mother. Janelle owed no explanations, there was no need for apologies, and she wouldn't pretend now that he was dead and gone. Estelle Bates didn't argue the point. She waved her hand at the children and her daughter-n-law as she got in the family car after the funeral. Janelle hadn't seen her since that day.

Janelle met Leon while working for Stanley and Sons Contractors. She was their bookkeeper and Leon brought the company business. He became a regular part of the office on Friday afternoons and lunch dates for the couple soon followed. Janelle, a smaller woman then, didn't have much of a social life and Leon wooed her with his interest in the arts, music, and travel.

She sat on the deck surrounded by photo albums. She was sorting through the last remnants of the earlier years of their marriage. The books marked with title and date made it easier for her to decide which photos she would discard.

Since the death, funeral and the repeated calls from the police and reporters, her sister volunteered to keep her children. Their school would be ending in a few weeks. Under the circumstances, Leon Jr. and Melissa wouldn't be expected to return until September. Shortly after the burial of her husband, Janelle bid her eight-year-old son and four-year-old daughter goodbye. There wasn't much to talk about; her sister understood her needs. She promised to call her about their summer activities and set a date for their return.

Now in the empty house, Janelle could work through her emotional breakdowns. She would wean herself off the nightly dose of pain medication. She could admit to her doctor that there had never been any pain; at least not one a pill could cure. She asked herself often if she still loved her husband. There was never an answer. The pill would take over her conscious state and render her sleep until the next morning. Her depressed demeanor would return the next morning, and she would continue to deny the emptiness she felt each day.

Leon was better at pretending than Janelle; she attributed that to his ability to lie. The problem was he lied at the altar. He lied to his family, including his mother. Janelle believed he would have gone to his grave with the lie. Leon Bates had a child with another woman. The child was born the night before they married.

Leon made excuses to his friends during his bachelor party and left. Using his mother's illness, no one questioned him. Over the years, his mother, brother and others celebrated the child's birthday with the mother of the child behind his wife's back. Janelle separated herself from his family and vowed Leon would suffer through the rest of their years together. She wouldn't discuss or consider a divorce or separation.

Janelle filled her need for love with the birth of each child. She gave them all her attention while ignoring Leon's attempt to be an attentive husband. He pampered her with gifts, paid all the bills, and spoiled their children. Leon paid child support, but couldn't have the older child visit him or her siblings in the Bate's home. Janelle played the depressed wife between the births of the children. She went to counseling, therapy, and took her medication, which prevented her from working. She quit her job and became a permanent fixture in their five-bedroom home. Leon couldn't please her, and he dared not tease her. He sought affection and attention elsewhere. Janelle didn't care. He was no longer her concern.

After trashing his clothes and selling what had worth, Janelle felt better. She had the insurance payment in full. She took out two extra policies when she found out he was still cheating. She thought about meeting the mother of his eldest child, or speaking with the other women, especially the last one, Mona Mandell. She changed her mind after the Private Detective she hired assured her none of them knew he was married.

She took the envelope with the photos of each of the women, the images of the encounters that would have proven adultery, and began to shred them. She pulled deeply on the cigarette she lit enjoying the menthol as though she finally had an orgasm. A feeling she hadn't had since hiring the detective. She made a mental note to call him before the children returned.

She stubbed the cigarette and picked up the next album. The pictures went back to the days when they dated. Most of them were from vacations; overnight stays in other states, and holiday celebrations. There were pictures of his brother, Lance. His image brought tears to her eyes. He was the only family member, hers or Leon's; that understood her depression. They spoke often and during his last few months she visited him regularly.

She begged him to hold on, but cancer had taken over his body and eventually his mind. She would keep his pictures.

Janelle got up to make herself a cup of tea. The house was cleaner than it had been in years. She had stopped cleaning and refused to allow Leon to hire a woman he would likely bed in their home. There was no more mention of having anyone in the home after Janelle threatened to leave and never return if any other woman darkened their door.

Leon cleaned and she cooked, remaining silent for months. He was a homebody until he found someone to remind him he was a man. Now he was dead, killed at a resort, proof to Janelle that his manhood was still functioning.

The call from the police didn't surprise her; the location of the body caused a rise in her emotions. She thought he would die on the side of the road. She often watched the news looking for a collision on the Parkway, his daily route. He never came home before the early morning hours. She would leave his plate on the stove certain he would eat it.

The doorbell rang, and Janelle quickly closed the sliding door, which would separate her visitor from the memoirs and mess she made. She had prepared for Detective Tyson's visit. She opened the door certain her expression would reflect the pain of a heartbroken widow.

They both were surprised looking at each other before they spoke. Janelle was not as he imagined she would be. Short in stature, beautiful skin, and shoulder length hair, nothing like the television news reports, without the black veil he could see her beauty. She had lost what he would imagine had been a shapely figure. It was possible that after the marriage fell through she no longer had a desire to keep her girlish look. Although, he wouldn't make light of her grief, she didn't appear to be depressed at all. The signs of fatigue coupled with the lack of sleep showed on her round face.

Detective Damien Tyson softly spoke as he introduced himself. Janelle was impressed by his appearance. His tailored suit and accessories were more than the actors who depicted his title on many of the television shows. She expected the "Columbo" type with a pad and pen ready when she opened the door. His cologne teased her senses, a smell she recognized but couldn't call by name. He was tall and proportionate. She couldn't help but think of him in his entirety. She didn't let him wait long on the porch. Inviting him in, she led the way to her living room.

"Can I get you something to drink? I was having a cup of tea. Maybe coffee, tea, juice or water, I also have soda, if you like."

"No, no thank you. I appreciate it, though. I hope I haven't interrupted you, or anything."

He knew he hadn't stopped her from anything as he scanned the room for unfinished tasks.

"As I said I just made myself a cup of tea. I've been cleaning a bit and, of course, packing my husband's things for charity and family that can use them."

"Forgive me. I should have said first that I am sorry for your lost. Please accept my condolences as well as my apology."

The room was large. The house seemed small. There were no signs of her husband. No picture display of the family with or without Leon. He could see the corkboard in the kitchen near the refrigerator. It held no postings, pictures, or any of the expected memos that hung from family note boards. He made a mental note that the house was thoroughly cleaned. She didn't want him to notice anything that reflected the life she lived with her husband.

"I understand. You have a job to do, and that's first and foremost. Do you have any leads on who may have killed Leon?"

Tyson heard the question, but the subliminal message was heard as well. "Leon" not "my husband" stung as the words lingered in the air. He looked at her as she sat back in the winged chair. She made herself comfortable with her tea in her hand.

"We've got a few leads. A few other detectives and I are looking into them. I wanted to tie in your statement and those who may have seen him the night before the murder. Can I ask you a few questions? And please stop me if you feel uncomfortable."

Tyson leaned forward placing the folder on the coffee table that contained the same photos he showed at the restaurant.

"Ms. Bates, do you recognized either of these gentlemen?"

Janelle put the cup down and lifted the photos to get a better look. "No, other than seeing them on the news I wouldn't know them. Aren't they the other victims? I believe the news said they were killed at the resort before Leon was killed."

Again, she referred to her husband as Leon.

"Ms. Bates, were you and your husband on good terms at the time of his death?"

Janelle put the pictures down slowly. She knew his questions would lead to their relationship. Why would a married man be at a resort without his wife? Over the past few days, the question was repeated, and she gave the same answer each time.

"Our marriage was doomed from the start. I thought we were in love, but Leon had other loves. He never let go of his work, his hobbies, or his fantasies."

"I don't want to speculate. What type of work did Mr. Bates do?"

"He was I guess you could say, a head hunter. He hired the contractors according to CDC's needs. CDC is a large company that works across the United States building industrial plazas. They would call Leon in, and he would get the specs from the main office. He'd travel wherever necessary searching for the property and then he'd hire the contractors to build."

"I see, so he traveled often?"

"At least once every two to three months. It depended on the job. So, yes I was used to him being away from home."

Tyson wrote on his pad, but he knew her disposition was changing. She was becoming defensive. He'd have to get her to relax.

"Ms. Bates, can I trouble you for a glass of water, please?"

"Certainly." She rose from the chair and went to the kitchen. Tyson put the photos back in the folder. Again, he scanned the room for normality. No photos of the children no signs of the family. The room was too clean. The air was fresh, no odors that he could detect, not even hers. She returned with the glass and a coaster.

"How are the children, Ms. Bates?"

"What do you mean?"

"I mean have they had any concerns, fears, questions since the death of their father?"

Janelle was thrown off. There had been no questions about her children. She felt her emotions rising. Her children cried all night after the funeral. They had questions, fears, and unlike their mother, they were still grieving. Her sister stepped in and consoled them. It didn't take much to convince her that the children didn't need to be around reporters and police.

Tyson could see he stumped her. She lowered her head hoping the detective would sympathize with her and abandon the questions about her children. He waited patiently.

"Melissa hasn't said much, you know, other than asking where Leon was. She asks for him more at night. Detective they were used to their father being away. Jun that's my son's nickname, understood more and, of course, it bothered him more. His introduction to deaths and funerals, shouldn't have been his father's."

She wiped her eyes and continued. "I explained as much as I could to a child. What do you say? Your father was killed by who? That's what he asked, who killed him? How could I say his lover? How could I say he deserved it? I don't even know that whoever he was with that night killed him. What do you tell them? I know that the questions will come back to haunt me later. They're children now, what about when they get older. How do I explain what happened?"

"We're going to get you answers."

"I don't care who killed him. Do you understand?" Janelle blurted. "He got what he deserved. He can rot in hell!"

Tears flowed freely, and she got up from the chair. "He cheated throughout our marriage, and I prayed he would stop, get caught by husbands, or just drop dead. I stayed with him for the children. Do you understand? I wasn't in love anymore. He loved someone else!"

Tyson stood and walked to the distraught wife of Leon Bates, wondering if she would be offended if he touched her when he consoled her. It was definitely beyond the call of duty, but she needed someone who understood.

He turned her to his body and pulled her in close. She sobbed loudly. Tyson could feel her trembling as she tried to control her tears. Responding naturally, he rubbed her back gently. The detective held her until she was able to speak again.

"I don't know who the woman is, or why she felt the need to kill him. I wanted to kill him too."

Tyson had no response to her muffled confession. Janelle Bates wasn't the killer, and that's what he needed to know.

Chapter Nine

Tyson left Janelle Bates promising to do what now seemed hopeless, find the killer. Before turning the key in the ignition of his Durango, he looked into the other folders that blanketed the passenger seat. Placing the notes from the meeting with Scott Bearman and Janelle Bates in the folder, he pulled out the information for his next stop.

The Moorestown Police Department didn't have much on Raymond Murphy. The Desk Sergeant informed him that it was an open and shut case. Just as in the other cases, the murder was investigated by the Pine Ridge Mountain Police Department. The information forwarded to them was a summary, forwarded only as a courtesy. Tyson knew most of what was on the computer-generated report the Sergeant was happy to provide him. Raymond Murphy was single and worked as a contractor. His cause of death was noted as blunt force trauma to the head. There wasn't much of the remaining information he could use.

They discussed the possibility of the three victims working together and knowing their killer. The Sergeant made a valid point; they had no proof, it was all speculation. The Detective thanked the Sergeant and left no more than twenty minutes after his arrival. As he left the building, he called Jeffrey from his cell.

"Glad you called. There's no reason to go to Texas. Kevin Styles wife or ex is here still. She called asking to meet with whoever was investigating the murders. I guess the news got out that the case is still being investigated. I took her information; don't know if you'll have time to deal with her today."

"Man, Porter this case is done. I'll talk to her, but I doubt if she'll have any information we can use. The only thing I've got left is showing the pictures to the waitress. I'll be at the office in another fifteen minutes. Call her back and tell her this afternoon is fine."

"Hey that thing at the NOC is this weekend, you going?"

"Hanging out with you and Amir could be a problem."

"He's not going so you're stuck with me."

"I'll think about it."

"Look it will give your stiff ass a reason to shake a leg, or at least do the two-step."

"The hell with you man. I'm on my way."

Not needing the chill from his air conditioner, Tyson let down the windows in his truck and turned up the volume on the radio. The upbeat tunes from WBLS confirmed what Jeffrey said; he needed a night out. The ride to the station would be longer if he drove through town, but a ride on the highway wouldn't allow time for his thoughts. He took the long route, giving himself the time to think through the case.

Tyson loved the streets, the traffic, and the people he and his co-workers served. Foot patrol had been a bore but the Homicide Unit, his choice, kept his adrenaline pumping. His love life suffered because of it and his close friends Jeffrey and Amir often sought to satisfy his needs by buying tickets for him to various events.

The three men were single, each having distinct characteristics most women found intriguing. Amir Stands, the youngest of the three, took exercising to another level. Spending most of his free time at the gym, his body told stories of the sweat he released in the gym and the bedroom. His physic spoke long before any introductions.

Jeffrey, quite different from Amir or Damien, didn't work hard at keeping fit. In fact, he only went to the gym when he couldn't find an excuse to do something else. His pastime included reading and research. Porter, the name he preferred to be called, was a workaholic, and most of the females he dated were cops. He said only another officer could understand his passion and his hours. The females at the precinct called him their sweet surprise. His good looks were bestowed upon him from his father's side of the family. His height, deep voice, and nonchalant attitude made him an easy target for one-night stands, and he preferred not to stay around for commitments.

Damien was older, settled and most could tell he had been married. His military shine was in part from his high school ROTC training. The death of his father deterred him from fulfilling his dreams of being a soldier. Damien was a sports fanatic, a college basketball jock. Time in the gym was a deliberate release of frustration. Cases like the Resort Murders caused longer gym hours. He loved his family, but spent most of his time like Jeffrey, working. His relationships were long lasting and seemed to end just as they begun without his input. Damien had been a model for a few recruitment posters, so his face was known. He didn't brag about it much, but it didn't hurt his opening lines whenever the guys went out. His sharp features, small eyes, and even-toned skin made his appearance more subtle than most detectives.

Jeff and Damien were a team, and Amir was their sidekick. Amir would often tease that Tyson and Porter were like Batman and Robin. They didn't need another man on their team. They lived up to their names. Amir worked for the DEA Unit, and although he wanted to work in homicide, he thought the Cold Case Prevention Unit was as dead as some of the cases that landed in his unit. Cold Case investigations required time and officers. Amir declined the Chief's offer to being transferred.

Tyson's thoughts wandered between the notes he made for his discovery wall and what was causing so much traffic. Neither held an obvious answer. He tapped his horn hoping to move the Honda, whose driver refused to drive faster than five miles per hour. As the traffic moved on, he hoped the waitress or Ms. Styles would add some life to the case.

Damien was certain Jeff hadn't found any other evidence to go on. They would have to start looking for missed information. The light changed and a horn blared for him to move on. He could only smile in the rearview mirror.

"C'mon man, chill."

His prediction of a fifteen-minute ride went out the window. Damien was still sitting in the traffic twenty-five minutes later. He hit the speed dial on his steering wheel.

"Porter, did she get there yet?"

"No, but she said she was coming so I guess she'll be here any minute. Where are you?"

"I'm on Watchung Avenue."

"You took the streets. Man you and your thought provoking drives. You would have been here…."

"I know, I know. Look I can see where the hold up is. I can't turn around here, though. I'll throw on the overhead if I need to. Call me if she…"

"Throw 'em on man, she just walked in."

"Listen, don't question her without me."

"I've got my questions for her," He whispered into the phone pointing to the chair across the room.

"A looker huh?"

"Right, I'll let her know you'll be delayed."

"Not delayed, I'm on my way."

The dial tone answered. Porter hung up before hearing Tyson's response.

"Ms. Styles, that was my partner Damien Tyson, I'm Jeffrey Porter. He's caught in traffic; he'll be here shortly. Can I offer you something to drink?"

The woman sighed displaying her aggravation before answering. Porter hoped she wouldn't openly display her attitude. It would take away from her natural beauty. All reports indicated that she handled the questioning during the investigation of her husband's death well, almost better than expected.

"Am I to assume that Kevin's case won't close because of this new murder?"

"I'm not sure I understand your question?"

"They haven't closed the investigation on my husband's death. I've been waiting for the final findings so my son and I can move on. Now there's another murder. Will this delay the insurance payment?"

"Uh, I don't know if this will delay anything as far as your husband's case is concerned."

"They're not being investigated together?"

"Ms. Styles, I'm going to ask you to wait just a little while longer before I give you answers that may be wrong."

Celeste Styles crossed her legs and gave him an unpleasant smirk. There was nothing left to say.

Chapter Ten

Tyson walked through the busy waiting area paying no attention to the woman who stood complaining to the Desk Sergeant.

"I was waiting in Detective Tyson's office until Detective Porter decided my presence was too tempting. I want to see someone in charge; first to complain about his arrogant ass, and then to complain about the Styles investigation."

She wasn't ranting, but her tone was agitated. An indication she would be ranting in the next few minutes. The Sergeant noticed Tyson walking by and smiled. Tyson would want to talk to Porter before seeing Ms. Styles.

He open the door stenciled Homicide Unit and closed it quickly before anyone else could enter. Porter looked up at his partner and shook his head.

"Where do we find these people? We're trying to help her pretty little ass, and she's here to read us the riot act. Did you see her out there?"

"She's got the right to be mad I guess. She wants to go home. Probably tired of the whole thing, I can't blame her."

"She came in saying she wanted the investigation over. You want to know why? She wants to collect the damn insurance! What the hell is that about? She didn't even want to know if we found out who killed her husband. That's fucked up man."

"Listen, Porter, they were divorced. Did you expect her to have some love left for the man she divorced and moved away from?"

"So why stay around for the money? Don't tell me about the money being for her son. She may be the killer. Like you said, Murphy and Styles had a connection. Maybe she did them both."

"Did you ask her something personal, ask her out or something?"

Porter turned his attention to the papers on his desk, shaking his head. Tyson stood expecting an answer. Porter shook his head again and waved his hand.

"Man, she's not my type. No, I told her to wait and get the answers from you. Now she's out there making a case because I didn't give her any answers? She's looking to cash in. We need to check her out."

"And that we will. Listen, I got nowhere with the police reports. Check the forensic evidence. Maybe they got some prints somewhere in the room."

"Man that's crazy, it's a resort. There could be thousands of prints."

"Yeah you're right. Check the cell phones again. Any numbers that match make a note of them. That will be our primary list."

Tyson sat at his desk and moved the papers that Ms. Styles would find interesting. He called for her to come into his office.

Porter didn't look up as she walked past his desk. He waited until she got to Tyson's office to shake his head in disgust. She knew what she was doing, and he could see she was a tease. Tyson watched her actions as she approached. Celeste's conceit stepped into his office before her body did. The atmosphere seemed to change as she looked at the seat that was available in front of his desk. Tyson passed her the box of tissues.

"There's nothing wrong with the seat but here, use a tissue."

His comment caught her off guard. "Oh, no I wasn't inferring that … well…"

She took a few tissues and wiped the leather seat. Her soft butter colored suit would show the faintest stain. She wouldn't take the chance. Tyson stretched his hand to retrieve the used tissue. He wasn't ready for the fake beauty that sat before him.

"Would you like something to drink Ms. Styles?"

"No, I'd like to know that the investigation is over. Detective Tyson, I live in Texas, and I would like to go home."

"Has someone told you not to leave?"

"I don't want to make two trips. There were some loose ends that needed to be handled. Kevin and I had a business together, accounts, and, of course, his insurance. You do understand don't you?"

Tyson listened as he examined her. She was a petite woman standing about five foot eight inches. He assumed she was in her mid-thirties, but he would be sure to check the records. He could tell the way she sat and spoke, she wanted to display her confidence. However, as she spoke, her eyes roamed a sign of nervousness. Being straightforward would be the best way to handle her.

"No, I don't understand. Ms. Styles if no law enforcement official has told you to remain here for questioning. You are free to go back to Texas. We have no control over the insurance, your businesses, or anything else you and your ex-husband may have shared."

"Who killed him, Detective Tyson? I guess I need closure. I've waited for months. The insurance company seems to think there was foul play. They won't release any of the funds until the investigation is complete."

"Ms. Styles, I assure you, we've given them the necessary information to release any monies due to you. The case is with my unit to ensure we've done everything before officially stating it as a cold case. At this time, we don't have the killer, nor do we have a suspect. Unless the investigation has re-opened, I can't see a reason for anyone to hold you here."

"So that's it? It wasn't bad enough that he was cheating, wow … that's it? I can't believe it. At first they thought I was a suspect, and now it's dropped."

"How long had you been divorced from your husband?"

"It's been two years, no three. What difference does that make?"

"Your relationship with him was cordial after the divorce?"

"Yes, we both agreed it was best for my son and the business."

"What type of business is it?"

"We, well the business is, contracting. We refurbish, build, whatever. There were families involved. If we dissolved the company, those families would lose out. We didn't want that so we kept the business as it was."

"Why didn't he buy you out?"

"I didn't want out. It was our sole means of support. I moved to Texas to be with my family after my dad got sick, last year. This mess, his cheating, the business, it's too much."

"You can handle it from Texas, why are you still here?"

"Detective Tyson, someone killed my husband. Whoever it is, I think is tied to my business. Suppose they killed him to sabotage the business. I want all of this buried, just like Kevin, before I leave. Now there's another murder. Is there a connection or not?"

"Again, it has nothing to do with your insurance. Your case has been pulled for further review. We have not contacted any insurance company, and I don't think we will."

"An emotional roller coaster Detective, that's where you and your unit have placed me. How will I be able to move on if the investigation is not closed? If there is nothing there Detective, bury it!"

Celeste took another tissue from the box and sat back, indicating that was her final statement. Tyson watched as she dabbed her tear-filled eyes. Another wife, more tears, and still no closer to who killed the three cheating men.

Chapter Eleven

The crowd at the NOC Theatre was diverse. The Times Square Grill was perfect for a networking event. Tyson needed the night out and appreciated his partner's invitation. The two took seats at the bar for the first half hour after their arrival. Jeff nudged Damien and motioned for them to move toward the lobby. Although neither of the detectives exchanged information about their career, they listened as others exchanged business cards and experiences.

The lobby was packed. There was another event in the upper rotunda. Jeff and Damien stood watching the people mingle before they both realized they weren't on duty.

Mona and Candice came through the door laughing. Candice made the mistake of bumping Jeff and tipping his drink onto the carpeted floor.

"Better the floor than that beautiful dress of yours. Excuse me for being so clumsy." Jeff responded immediately.

The four of them backed out of the entrance making sure no one's outfit caught the Hennessey that was in his glass. Candice smiled allowing Jeff to steer her away from the door.

"I don't think it was you. Thank you, I'm sorry I wasn't looking."

Mona looked past the two men getting a view of the crowd.

"Is our event in here?" She asked Candice pretending the men didn't interest her.

"I believe so. Do either of you know where the after-hour networking event is being held?"

Candice was obviously beginning her night of pleasure. Jeff smiled and as a courtesy allowed the two women to enter the Grill first. Damien knew too well what his intentions were.

"Can I offer you ladies, a drink, since I'll be refilling my glass?"

"Really, I am so sorry about that." Mona moved over giving Candice the room she needed to perform.

"I'll have a Cosmopolitan, please." Mona waited for Jeff to ask her to repeat her order. Jeff looked at Candice.

"I'll have Chardonnay on the rocks. Thank you." Jeff left the ladies with Damien.

"So, are you ladies in business together?" Damien felt strange asking the question. He always did when first meeting women. He tried not to interrogate them, but it seemed any question sounded like he was on the job.

"No, we're friends. What about you and your friend?" Mona questioned. Damien's cologne caught her senses. She decided Candice wouldn't be flirting with both of them.

"We're friends too." Mona smirked and looked across the room. "Hey, did I give you that look when you cut it short on me?"

The question opened the door neither of them wanted to walk through. The conversation softened. When Jeff returned with the drinks the trio were talking about people they knew weren't possibly in business. The unprofessional cards were tossed carelessly on tables.

"So did I miss the introductions? I'm Jeffrey Porter."

"We didn't formally introduce ourselves. I'm Candice Miller, and this is my friend Mona Mandell. Your friend Damien…"

"Damien Tyson" Damien added as he paused in the middle of his discussion with Mona. Mona shook her head, realizing Candice drew the attention to herself again.

"Your drink Mona, well it was a pleasure bumping into you lovely ladies. Damien, I think I saw Amir on the other side. Let's make our rounds."

Damien understood the signal but didn't know the reason for them leaving the table. He followed Jeff's cue, smiled at Mona telling her he hoped to talk with her again. The two men walked off leaving Candice and Mona at the table with their drinks.

"What the fuck was that about?"

"Mona, you said you weren't interested in any pleasure. I figured maybe he was bending your ear. You had your own little conversation going on."

"And…?"

"And there were three of us sitting here. Damn, make up your mind. Are you grieving or what?"

Mona forgot she told Candice and Kendra she was still feeling some out of sorts.

"You're right. He did make me feel better, though. Hmm…Damien Tyson, he wasn't bad on the eyes either."

"He was packing too. I sneaked a peek; brother has a package for sure."

"Oh, girl for a minute I thought you were talking about a gun. He probably couldn't shoot if he had one."

"Hell, for you, all he needs to know how to do is unload."

The two laughed as they looked through the crowd. Jeffrey and Damien spoke to a few of the officers they knew who had entered The Grill. Jeffrey had done the right thing by moving away from the two ladies before greeting the uniformed officers.

"Detectives, how are you?" Officer Jones and Brooks shook the detective's hands.

"Everything's good. How's things with you; this your area now? Jeff questioned. He and Jones had been partners years prior.

"Some nice honey's here tonight. I hope no one gets stupid." Brooks commented watching the women walk by in groups. "They always have a nice crowd for these events. It's the ones that come out after eleven that start the shit."

"Well, that's why you're here my man. You know, to keep the hounds at bay." Jeff and Damien laughed knowing they didn't have to handle the nonsense the night might bring.

"What's up with that serial killer, they say it's a woman. You think so?"

Jeff started to talk but was cut off by Damien's response.

"Let's just say unless they were gay, a man could care less about another man cheating on his wife at a resort."

"I don't know man. If a man took my wife to a resort, I might want to kill him." Brooks gave the detectives a questionable look.

"Nah man, we've got three murders. What, you saying the man is a pimp, he's got three women? And if she's the same woman; nah man, that's why they got you on this beat."

Jeff's comment made them all laugh. The detectives moved on. They took a seat on the opposite side of the room on a circular sofa and ordered more drinks.

"So what's up with the abrupt departure? I was beginning to enjoy the lady's conversation."

"Tyson you and I both know they were looking for someone to buy them drinks all night. I ain't about that shit man. She bumped me on purpose."

"They were just getting here."

"My point exactly, man women are always looking for someone to do it for them. They probably don't even have a business. What are they here for...to catch a brother like you or me and drink all night with no return?"

"So if they gave you something in return it would be cool? Jeff, you're crazy man. And what business do we have?"

Jeff laughed. "One we can't tell them about, check this out."

He pulled out a business card and passed it to Damien.

"Security? That's your business. You could have done better than that."

Damien passed his card only to be intercepted by Mona.

"Funny, I came over here just to get your card, Mr. Tyson. I was wondering what type business you were in. Tyson Security Consulting Firm, so what type of consultation do you provide?"

Mona took a seat on the couch next to him. Jeff saw the need to get a refill.

"Most of it deals with personal problems, getting them through hard times. You know home and business protection. I talk with them to determine if they or their business would need security. It can include escorts, finance, and even personal security. Things I'm sure a pretty lady like you wouldn't need."

"Hmm…sounds like something you made up. I don't see you as a consultant."

"Really? Well, you're right I did make it up. I saw there was a need, and I got with others, and we help a lot of people."

"So what makes you think I wouldn't need your help?"

"You seem to be well organized. I'm sure you have a means of support. Like I said, things you wouldn't need."

"You'd be surprised at what I need. Here, I wanted to give you my card as well. It doesn't say what I do. You'll have to call and find out."

Mona stood and left Damien, who was baffled looking at the professional business card, with a smile as she walked away. He stood wanting to beckon her back to the couch. He put the card in his wallet and agreed Jeff was right. She was on the prowl.

Chapter Twelve

Mona flipped the business card between her fingers as the phone rang. She was making an attempt to get back to her daily routine.

"Yes this is Ms. Mandell, I'm calling to confirm your appointment to see the property. Yes, two o'clock is fine. Yes, I look forward to it. Thank you."

She met a few prospects at the networking event. At the close of the evening she was glad she accepted Kendra's invitation. Damien Tyson's business card held her interest among the others she collected. Tapping her manicured nail on his card, she smiled, tempted to call him. She and Candice left without her having a chance to say goodbye. Their conversation ended when Jeff returned. Mona didn't know if it was her, but Jeff seemed a bit conceited and a tad bit jealous about her interest in Damien. Candice remained in the opposite corner of the room, arranging to meet an old friend for lunch. Mona excused herself hating to leave Damien on the couch, but she was sure he would call her. He hadn't, it had been two weeks and she pretended she didn't care.

She kept his card in her hand tapping the table in thought as she dialed the client who booked the last appointment for the day. When there was no answer, she knew her afternoon would end after her two o'clock appointment. She wondered what time Damien would be ending his day.

Kendra and Candice wouldn't be a part of her agenda for another week, so she was free to ask Mr. Tyson if he would care to meet for a drink. She could take the rejection, but the possibility of him accepting to meet her racked her nerves.

There was time to make the call and prepare the paperwork for her new clients. Mona hated to be rushed, especially when there was a chance she could hook a man with Damien Tyson's charisma. She reminded herself that she wouldn't take it to heart if he rejected her invitation.

Damien's cell phone rang, startling him as he read the newly prepared evidence files on the Resort Murders. He received the files after two weeks of requesting the previous evidence be reviewed. It was his first break of the day. Jeffrey had gone to pick up their lunch from the nearby deli.

"Hello."

"Wow, I was expecting the professional answer," Mona replied.

"Good afternoon. It's my personal phone, so there's no need for that. How are you?"

"Do you even know who you're talking to?"

"Your number was put on my phone the night you gave me your card. Keeps me from having a file that I can't carry around and caller ID is a good thing." Tyson leaned back, turning the leather swivel chair away from his work.

"Why do I feel your smile through the phone?" Mona put her index finger to her mouth. She could feel more than that but enjoyed teasing him.

"Maybe I am smiling. I'm glad you called. You were on my mind."

"On your mind and you didn't call? I don't understand. Maybe you could explain that later today, about six?"

"Well Ms. Mandell, I happen to be free this evening. Would you like me to pick you up or would you rather we meet?"

Mona liked his manner. She adjusted herself and gave a sultry reply. "I'll meet you at Jazzin'. Do you know where that is?"

"Yes, ma'am. I will be there at six with my explanation." Damien replied. He knew she was flirting. He was willing to play along.

"Mr. Tyson don't make me wait, you hear?"

"A pretty woman like you; why would I have you waiting in a place like Jazzin'?"

"I don't know, just don't. I don't take kindly to being stood up. If you can't make it, call. A little courtesy goes a long way."

Damien listened and made a note on a post it. Separating it from the pad he stuck the yellow paper on his computer. It was something about the statement. He did understand her; most women would be pissed after being stood up. He looked at his wall of notes. He removed the paper from his computer and tagged his wall with it. The statement could clearly be a woman's motive.

"Not a problem. I don't foresee any reason for standing you up. If anything should cause a delay or interfere with our plans for this evening, I will call. My mother raised a gentleman."

"Well, it's a date then. See you at….."

"Six. I'll be there."

Tyson laid his cell phone on the desk. Mona's comment led him to the files. He had gone through the files so many times, he had memorized some of the information. There was another question he may have missed. The jealousy, the anger, or the fear of each wife put them at the top of the suspect list. He was so convinced that they had no reason to kill the husbands. They seemed to have separated themselves from their husbands and the marriages long before their deaths.

Tyson would be meeting Jess, the waitress from Porto Café. Scott Bearman called to apologize for overlooking her vacation on the schedule. Tyson would meet her before his six o'clock date with Mona.

Porter took another angle in the investigation. He was checking the employment connections, phone calls, and appointments. After three days, he found the men worked in the same field, but there was nothing connecting them to each other. They did use some of the same realtors, and referrals. A small lead but anyone who remembered anything about the men became helpful. He called in his findings, but all seemed to lead to a dead end.

The office phone rang catching Tyson off guard. It was buried under the pile of papers on his desk. He tossed items aside, trying to catch the call before it went into voice mail.

"Hello."

"Detective Tyson, please." The voice on the other end was barely audible, barely above a whisper.

"Yes, speaking." Tyson listened closely.

"This is Jess. Scott told me you wanted to talk with me about that guy that got killed. I don't know him. Why do we need to talk?"

"Actually, I need to show you a picture of a woman, hopefully, you can tell me if you saw her with him. Do you remember him being with someone the last time he was at the restaurant?"

"Detective, I'm not comfortable talking with police. I don't think I can help you."

Tyson could tell there was something she was hiding.

"Jess, I'm not interested in you or what you may be into. This is a murder investigation if you didn't commit the crime you have nothing to worry about. It won't take long; we can meet somewhere else if you like."

"Oh, okay, yes can we meet somewhere other than the restaurant? I can't meet you until my shift is over, about eight?"

"Eight will be fine. Where would you like to meet?"

"There's a Starbucks a few blocks down from the restaurant. Can we meet there?"

"Sure I'll see you there about eight fifteen. Is that okay?"

"Yes, and thanks, Detective Tyson."

Tyson hung up the phone. He forgot about the possibility of being with Mona after their dinner.

Chapter Thirteen

Mona had a sudden burst of energy. It was six o'clock, and she couldn't control the adrenaline rush. Two new contracts and a date with Tyson; maybe she would have more than a few drinks. She could stand for him to put her in the mood.

She hadn't given dating much of a thought since Leon's funeral, and she vowed it wouldn't be a client ever again. Candice and Kendra didn't need to know she was dating again. She had made a huge mistake by sharing that information with them. There would be no need to talk about Tyson until she was sure.

The atmosphere at Jazzin' allowed its patrons to decide their mode of dress. Mona decided a wrap with a low neckline would be simple but enticing. She would add her favorite necklace and earrings. Putting her braids up gave her a sophisticated natural look, one that caught the eye of many. She'd be sure to highlight her eyes and features with a touch of color added to her makeup.

The news was broadcasting the "Resort Murders" latest report from the police when she deliberately turned the channel. The police had no clues. Stringing it along, they hoped to get details from anyone who could remember anything about the victims. The vague coverage was a sign that the story and the investigation would soon be history. Mona had perfected her steps, covered the evidence, and had no need to boast as they fumbled over probabilities.

She did think about following the stories of the families. The questions asked by the media in the days after the burials were questions she asked herself. The investigation by the police did spark a few nights of airtime for Janelle Bates and Celeste Styles. Neither of them seemed to care whether the police found the killer. Solely the media kept the story alive. There was no outcry from the families or community. Mona didn't quite understand their feelings as widows, but after all their husbands were cheating. She prayed each night for her soul. She needed forgiveness from God. No one else mattered.

The murders were behind her. She could move on, love and be loved. She'd be careful not to fall for another's husband or lover again. Love was the only thing missing in her life, not including her friends and family; she was sure they loved her in their way.

Her thoughts were beginning to overshadow her premonition of a pleasurable night. It was too late for a writing session in the journal. She went to the refrigerator and grabbed the remains of the wine she'd been drinking all week. There was enough to take off the edge. She was riding a sentimental roller coaster filled with mixed emotions. She hated roller coasters.

It would take fifteen minutes to get to Jazzin'. She didn't want to seem anxious, but time seemed to be moving too slow. She sipped on her drink while thinking of the reasons anyone would deceive the one they claimed to love. Tears began to fall from her eyes. The aftermath upset her the most. Asking herself questions she could not answer, and grieving for men she thought loved her.

Mona sat longer than she expected, wiping tears and caught in memories. She jumped up, realizing the time and the need to redo her makeup. The wine took the edge off but left her a mess. She mumbled to herself as she applied new mascara and lip-gloss. One last look in the mirror and a wink of confidence was all she needed.

Her purse and keys were sitting on the end table. Mona checked for her cell phone and smiled. It was six fifteen; she was sure he'd be wondering if she stood him up by the time she arrived. She'd keep him interested and wondering until she was sure he was single.

Tyson arrived early, not wanting Ms. Mandell to sit waiting. The restaurant was crowded but not filled to capacity. Damien had not been at Jazzin' in over two years. Although he enjoyed the mature atmosphere, the entertainment, and the food, he felt out of place sitting at a table or the bar alone. It wasn't a place for Amir or Jeffrey. They preferred the club scene, the scene Damien let go years prior.

Visually scanning the setting, he spotted an empty table for two. The DJ was playing, meaning the band had not begun the first set. He excused himself bumping pass a few couples standing around the bar. After looking for someone to stop him from sitting, he took the seat. Damien nodded to the waitress, who passed with an empty serving tray. He was hoping to get a drink in before being the perfect gentleman.

"Hennessy on the rocks please." He smiled seeing Mona walking toward him.

"I'll have an Apple Martini, please," She ordered winking at Damien. She placed her purse on the table and took her seat.

"Would you like a menu?" replied the waitress, apparently annoyed by Mona's arrival. She walked away from the table, not waiting for an answer, hoping to attract Damien's attention.

"I see if we're to keep dating it won't be here." Mona teased.

"What would make you say that? Are you going to restrict every restaurant we go to?"

"Are you insinuating that I would need to?"

Damien smiled. He liked her sense of humor. She was well put together, not like the women he dated recently, who seemed to need a man in their life.

"So Mr. Tyson, after meeting you, I had so many questions."

"What is it you'd like to know?" Damien held his breath. Most women wanted to know more about his job. The job he never discussed and kept out of his relationships for obvious reasons; the job that caused him to lose his wife and family. That had been ten years ago and the reality still stung.

"Okay, children or a wife?"

"Yes, both." He hesitated to wait for her reaction. "Divorced for more than ten years, two daughters and yes I pay child support. I don't see them much. They've moved to California with my wife's parents.

"They…you mean your wife and children?"

"No, just my children. I don't know where my wife is."

"That's strange. She's not lurking in the shadows, is she?"

Damien was sure Sonya wouldn't be in the shadows, but lurking sounded like something she would do.

"She's not the motherly type, so the children are with her parents. My parents are deceased. That was one of the reasons we couldn't be together. I wanted a wife, a family, a home… you know — the entire happily ever after. She wanted the spotlight, and the magazine spreads. She was or is a model. She'd come back whenever her money was low, or she remembered we existed. I grew tired of it and filed for a divorce."

"No regrets?" Mona didn't understand his sincerity.

"No, I thought I would try to convince her. After a few trips to meet her, discuss us, the girls and our so-called love, I gave up. Guess I wasn't that into her." Damien laughed to lighten the conversation.

"So you said that was ten years ago, what about now? No special lady?"

"Wow, you get right to it, huh? No, I go to work. Hang out with Jeff, the guy you saw me with, or a few friends. I date, but nothing serious. What about you?"

"Just getting out of a bad relationship, so be gentle." She laughed and sipped on her drink. Looking over the glass, she tried to read his expression.

"I'll keep that in mind. So you and the Mr. are done?"

"Let's just say he won't be knocking on my door or looking for me."

Damien nodded and called the waitress to the table for another drink. He looked at his watch without Mona noticing. He wished he didn't have to end their evening in little more than an hour. They shared an appetizer and talked freely over dinner.

"When can we meet again? I've enjoyed your company." It was ten minutes to eight. "I promised someone I'd meet them at eight."

"Client's in the evening?"

"Not really a client but the meeting is about business. So is it okay to contact you say, tomorrow or the next day?"

Mona hadn't anticipated ending their evening so soon. On a Friday night, she was sure he wouldn't be working in the morning.

"I could give you my address, and you stop in on your way home." Her eyes finished the sentence. Damien felt the heat rising from his neck.

"I'll call you. If I had known about us getting together …."

"I'm sorry, I don't want to seem forward or desperate."

"No, Mona you don't sound that way at all. That's not what I was getting ready to say or imply. I've got a better idea. How about tomorrow? I'll pick you up, and we can ride to the city. Let's stick to your time, say six?"

"My time is now your time. I'd love that."

Chapter Fourteen

Jessica sat waiting, watching the traffic through the window. She hadn't noticed Tyson's vehicle pull into the parking lot or the door open for him and two other customers. The Starbucks was crowded for a Friday evening, and she chose the seat near the window hoping no one would notice her talking to a cop. She was surprised when the casually dressed man put out his hand to introduce himself.

"Jessica, I'm Detective Tyson. Sorry, if I've inconvenienced you."

She smiled, hesitant to shake his hand. "I'm sorry I expected a uniform or something." He reached for his wallet. "No, no, I believe you. Please, you don't need to flash your badge."

"I want to make sure you're okay with this. I am who I say I am." Tyson responded wondering what she had to hide. He looked around following her eyes searching the other tables close to them. "Are you okay?"

"Yes, it's just my boyfriend is very jealous and…"

"He doesn't like cops. It's okay. I don't think we'll be long."

He watched her reaction. Jessica was young, not much older than twenty if that. Her mixed heritage was noticeable. Full lips frizzled curly hair, and her caramel skin tone caused him to guess one of her parents was African American. She smiled noticing her appearance took him by surprise.

"My dad is black; most people question my genes. I am used to it. Guess you couldn't tell by my name. Jessica Wright, definitely doesn't say Puerto Rican."

Her smile showed more of her character. Tyson put the folder on the table hoping the child that sat in front of him could help connect the dots. He doubted it. Jessica seemed to relax more as she continued to talk about her family and her boyfriend.

"He's really not that bad of a guy. My father scares him off when he tries to visit, so I don't see him often. Scott doesn't like him hanging around the restaurant either. So he thinks I'm cheatin' or something."

"I see, well I'm right there with your dad. I don't know if I would want you dating if you were my daughter either. How old are you?"

"Nineteen. I don't serve alcohol or anything at the restaurant, and I work the tables well. Scott says I'm better than most of the workers there. I make good tips. My dad thinks my boyfriend gives me money. He's crazy. I'm good with the customers that's all, a lot of them come back because of me." She laughed putting herself at ease.

"I'm hoping you can identify a customer for me. The case I'm investigating may involve customers you may have served or seen in the restaurant. Scott thought you might be able to help. I have these pictures; they're not that great but take a look. Do you remember seeing any of these people?"

Jessica turned the folder toward her and flipped through the pictures. She paused, in thought, and continued to turn the last two over. As she passed the folder back to Tyson, he knew he was at a dead end.

"I recognize the man here." She reached for one of the photos. She picked up the picture of Kevin Styles. "That lady with him has been to the restaurant with another man, though, a few times. I think her husband was the one that was killed at that resort."

Tyson looked at the photo. Neither Janelle nor Celeste was in the pictures. "Which man is her husband? Here let me show you another picture." Tyson pulled another folder from his leather case.

"This is him." She pointed to Leon Bates. "He introduced me to her. This man is Mr. Bates; he came to the restaurant often."

Tyson looked at the picture. Janelle Bates bared no resemblance to the woman in the photo. Jessica just added mystery to the case.

"Have you seen her with the other man here in the picture?"

"No just Mr. Bates and that guy."

"Did he tell you her name?"

"Yes, Janelle."

"Jessica, look at this picture again. Are you sure this is the same woman he said was his wife?"

"Yes, they came to the restaurant a few times for lunch. I think I saw her once with that other guy. He never introduced himself. She waved when she saw me, so I guess she wasn't cheating on Mr. Bates. I was shocked when I saw he was killed at that resort."

"Okay so you saw Mr. Bates a few times, and he said this woman was his wife, Janelle? Did this other man have lunch with Mr. Bates at any time?"

"No, just her, I don't remember seeing this other guy." Jessica took the picture of Raymond Murphy in her hands. She was looking at the people in the background. "Hey, here she is again. Look, she's right here at the bar."

Tyson took the picture and looked closely in the background as she had done. The woman was seated at the bar talking to Scott. He'd have to go back to the restaurant. It was obvious the woman was a connection he needed to explore.

"Is Scott at the restaurant tonight?"

"Naw, he left early today. He won't be back until Sunday or Monday. He doesn't work the weekends."

"Well, thanks, Jessica. You've helped a lot. If I need to talk to you, I'll have Scott reach out for you. Is that okay?"

"Sure. I hope you catch her."

"Her? Why do you say her?"

"The same person that killed Mr. Bates killed those other two men, right?" She didn't wait for his reply. "I think it's a woman and she was dating them. I guess Mr. Bates was the one cheating."

Tyson asked Jessica if she needed a ride. She politely declined. She said she was returning to the restaurant. She'd wait there for her boyfriend. He gave her his card, and she promised to call if she thought of anything else that would help him with the case. Tyson told her he'd see her Monday when he stopped by to talk with Scott.

It had been two months since the last murder. Tyson hated dragging out a case with no leads. He would have to change the papers he intended to submit closing the Resort Murders. The waitress gave a little life to the dead file. He and Porter would have to probe deeper with the hope they would find the killer.

Chapter Fifteen

The date with Mona went well and as comfortable as Tyson felt with her; he was determined to take it slow. It was his experience that taught him dating a detective was challenging for most women. Mona presented herself as the type of woman who would want all his free time to be with her. He'd date her again, as they planned, but he wouldn't expect her to accept his unorthodox schedule.

Jeffrey didn't think much of the waitress' remarks. He didn't see the connection or where it would lead if there were one. Tyson left him in the office checking for Raymond Murphy's wife. Tyson was sure Murphy was married. Jeffrey didn't argue as he jotted down his partner's thoughts and request. The identity of the woman in the picture bothered Tyson the remainder of the weekend. He decided to make one more stop before talking to Scott Bearman again.

Scott asked if he could stop by before or after the lunch crowd. Something about him being short for the shift, he'd be too busy to talk during lunch. Tyson picked after lunch, hoping the morning would hold a few answers. He listened to his partner as long as he could. He wasn't sure there wasn't more to investigate. He left the office to think. He hadn't shown the pictures to either of the wives, and now two months later

Celeste had returned to her home in Texas. He pondered the possibility of either of them knowing the woman in the picture.

Celeste left after being told her husband's insurance would be settled without any further delays. Her snappy responses during their phone call made him aware she wouldn't be willing to help him identify the woman. Janelle Bates, the more cooperative of the two, told him she would look at the pictures if he brought them to her job. He would see her before going to the restaurant.

"He's bringing a picture for me to see this morning. I'm not sure who she is; she may be the one we're looking for." Janelle typed the message and waited for an answer to appear on her computer screen.

"Why are you still looking for anyone? Leon's dead and you've handled all of his unfinished business haven't you?"

"She may have been hired to handle a few things with both of them. The job may have been given to her."

"Yes, but what difference does it make?"

"Celeste, are you certain we won't be accused? This detective is still looking for the killer."

"Listen, whoever she is, she did us a favor. Kevin and Leon are gone. We didn't know how to get rid of their cheating asses, and the problem is solved. You got Leon's stocks from the business, and I have Kevin's insurance. Prayer does work. I'm done Janelle, their dead and I'm done. They can't tie us to a murder we didn't commit. We can't be charged for wanting our husbands dead. We didn't make any attempts or complete the transactions; I thought the price was steep. Did he call you back?"

"No, didn't he call you? I didn't hear from him until after Leon's funeral. Once the deaths were reported he called and said, job done."

"So he didn't say he had a woman do it, did he? He didn't call me at all."

"No, but if he didn't arrange this he could use it to blackmail us. He could say we hired both of them. I've been sitting on pins and needles. We need to know who she is and if she was hired to kill them."

"You're paranoid girl. If he didn't ask for any money two months ago, he won't now. Call me when the sexy detective leaves. Better yet send him my way."

"Stay by your phone. I think I'm gonna call our friend to make sure he didn't hire her."

"Leave it alone. What's done is done and like I said killers don't wait months to be paid. Whoever killed them had another agenda. I don't care what it was. We're not involved, let's keep it that way."

Janelle shut down her laptop, without typing goodbye, just as her phone rang. She pressed the intercom and waited to hear the secretary announce Detective Damien Tyson had arrived.

Damien stepped into the small office. It wasn't much, but it was more than he expected for a construction company. He was surprised there was a front desk, a waiting area with plasma televisions mounted on two of the walls, and a conference room. Janelle led him into the adjoining room, which was much more accommodating in size and décor.

"Detective, can I offer you something to drink?"

"No and you can call me Tyson or Damien, I don't care about the title thing."

Janelle smiled; pleased it would be a relaxed conversation even though she knew he would be making mental notes of her responses and reactions.

"I promise I won't take up much of your time; seems I'm running in circles with your husband and the others." He continued to make small talk as he opened his leather case. He laid the three pictures on the table.

"Seems that they all ate at the same restaurant, and maybe they shared clients." Damien pointed to Leon and the unidentified woman and showed her the woman at the bar again with Kevin seated at a table. The third picture was of Raymond and the woman in what seemed to be a heated conversation.

"Well, that certainly isn't the best picture of Leon. And you say this woman is who you're trying to find?" Janelle was annoyed, thinking about the decision to get rid of the photos given to her. She could have made a comparison to the pictures that now seemed familiar. The woman hid well in each photo. She was careful not to look at the cameras monitoring the restaurant and bar area.

"Yes, she may have been the last to see your husband and Mr. Styles for that matter."

The woman had on large framed dark shades and a beautiful teal scarf around her head and face. The picture didn't reveal much. Janelle looked closely at her features; she wasn't sure if she had seen her before.

"I don't know many of the clients here, but I know his contracts for the last few months listed male contacts. Is she Muslim? Seems she has to cover in the pictures, you know like the Muslim women wear; I don't know, you're the detective."

Janelle laughed as her guilt tickled her conscious. She was sure this woman didn't kill her husband. Damien marked the copies of the pictures with her questions. The woman's mode of dress was an observation that he and Jeffery noticed.

"Are most of your clients men?"

"Yes, you know owners, investors, some realtors. A few of them are women, but most of them are men. Not many are husband and wife companies. Tyson, I wish I could help you, but if this woman had anything to do with the murders, I wouldn't know how."

Damien looked at Janelle. She seemed relieved, more relaxed than when they talked in her home.

"How are your children?"

"Uh, well you know children they just started their vacation for the summer. They haven't been home since his death, so for now, they're okay."

"I see and how are you holding up?"

"Day by day, but I hold no regrets. I hope that doesn't sound cold, but Detective, Leon didn't deserve me or my love. It's obvious he crossed someone else. I don't need to know who." She used the same words as Celeste. "Whoever killed them had another agenda."

"Really Ms. Bates, what do you think that would be?"

"Detective, Leon cheated, and he paid for it, one way, or another."

Tyson knew there would be no need to ask any other questions. Her last remark would stick with him. She didn't kill him, but there had to be a reason she didn't leave him. Celeste Styles made it clear. She wanted to collect her husband's insurance and anything left for a grieving wife. He would have to see what was left for Ms. Bates and the Murphy family. If either of the wives was involved in the murders, they hired someone to seal, wrap, and dispose of the evidence. They left the bodies to confirm the job was complete. He'd check each estate to see if any lump sums were missing.

Tyson got in his truck and made his notes in the folders. After turning the key in the ignition, he called Porter.

"Hey Jeff, did we check to see if the wives knew each other?"

"Yeah, I was gonna wait until you came back. Seems like Janelle and Celeste became acquainted after Kevin was killed. They've been talking quite a bit since Leon's death. I don't know what you'd call it, shared sympathy, or I don't know man. I can't find any other connection before Kevin's death. Then, of course, a few months later Leon's dead. I think when Celeste came to town she stayed with Janelle. I can't find any hotel that housed her and her son."

"Didn't she say she was staying with family?"

"I don't remember. I don't think we thought much about it, you know, with her attitude."

"Yeah I got a piece of that again today."

Jeff moved papers on his desk into a neat pile and thumbed through them. He pulled out another printed sheet and leaned back in his chair.

"Now, this Raymond Murphy guy brings another dead end. I'm telling you this thing is a merry-go-round. We keep coming back to the beginning." Tyson could hear his frustration.

"C'mon Porter, what about him?"

"Like I said square one, he's dead. You were right. He was married, not long, but he was married. Her name is Diane. The marriage was over before it got started good, annulled four months later. Can't find his ex and no connection with the family. I talked to both his sister and his father. They said they hadn't seen or spoke to him in months. The wife moved after their separation. She didn't even return as requested by a court order for their divorce."

"Is she living?"

"Nothing to prove she's not. I've got a few calls in records and a search. I can only wait and see. Probably won't give us a damn thing. Can I say it…..it's a cold case."

Damien told his partner about his visit and after giving his thoughts, he hadn't convinced Jeff he would find much more at the restaurant.

"Man, talk with Scott, and I'll meet you later for drinks. We'll toast the closing of another case."

Damien hoped Jeff was wrong. He had the feeling this case would be one for the records. He'd seen the jealous woman assaults and murders; most didn't take the time to cover their tracks. Often their emotions became entangled with the evidence. There were no indications that the woman returned to the scene of the crime, another characteristic of a serial killer. He'd seen many crime scenes but few as perfect as these. If there was a message sent, no one had interpreted it.

It was obvious the lunch crowd didn't have a taste for Italian cuisine, the parking lot held less than ten vehicles. Tyson's timing was perfect. He didn't want to order lunch or nurse a drink waiting to speak with Scott. His eyes adjusted to the dimmed dining room as he glanced over the area placing the men and the unknown woman in the room. Jessica said she recognized the woman and with the closeness of the tables he understood the introduction. If anyone questioned Leon Bates dining with this woman, the employees would simply say it was his wife. *Could she have been the other woman? Could she have been the killer?*

Scott approached Tyson with a handshake and a smile. "Can I get you something? A beer, sandwich, did you eat lunch already?"

"Nah man, I'm good. Thanks. This won't take too much of your time. I've got a few questions."

"Alright no problem, we can sit talk at the bar if you don't mind. I'm covering for my bartender." Scott led the way to the bar. Tyson handed him the folder with the pictures.

"Take a good look at these pictures. Do you remember the lady in the scarf and glasses? Jessica seemed to remember her being here more than once. She may be a person of interest."

"Jessica is a lot better with these customers; you know she gets to talk with them at the tables." He wiped the counter before placing the folders on the cherry oak rimmed bar. Scott took a long look at the image of the woman at the table with Leon before flipping it to the next picture. "Yea, Jess would know more than me, but this guy is Ray. I think him and this guy here did have lunch together a few times. I don't think Ray knew the woman, though. Let me say it this way. It didn't look like he knew her."

"What do you mean, didn't look like he knew her?"

"Well, the date on the back of the pictures is when the security cameras took them. If I remember right, Ray died before this other guy, and this picture is of him and that woman after she got loud at the table where he sat. I thought they were arguing or something. The dates are a few months apart. I don't remember her being here with this other guy, but pictures don't lie. So I guess she knew him too. I can't remember what they were arguing about or if Ray just said something smart, you know trying to talk to her. I don't think he knew her."

Scott put the photos back in the folder slowly as though he had an afterthought. "Wait, can I show this to the bartender? He does the afternoon, early evenings with Jessica. Maybe he'll recognize her." Before Tyson could answer, Scott called over a stocky man who could pass for an Italian opera singer.

"This is Lenny, Lenny this is Detective Tyson. Do you remember this lady in the picture with Ray?"

Tyson watched the expression of the older man. He remembered that Scott told him he didn't know any of the people in the picture the first time he presented them to him. There had to be a reason he now let on that he knew "Ray." The man cocked his head to the side and frowned.

"This woman, isn't she the one that was yelling at him the last time he was here?"

"That's what I'm asking." Scott looked at Tyson whose eyebrow raised as he spoke. "See I came in after the, I guess, the argument. I didn't remember that the other day when you asked. I just glanced at the picture and, you know, figured Jessica could be of more help to you."

"Okay, let me ask both of you. Do you know the men in the pictures?"

"Yeah, we both know Ray," Scott stated as Lenny nodded in agreement.

"Do you know this other guy or the woman?"

Neither man answered.

"So what does that mean? You know them or not? Look you already said you know Raymond. Were they all friends, enemies, business partners, what?"

Lenny hung his head. "Look man they were seeing the same woman. Leon claimed she was his wife. I never believed him. Raymond found out and came here one night I guess to get proof. She never came here at night. I told him she stopped by earlier that day with Leon. I thought they had business to settle. The last time I saw them was the day him and her argued. After Ray's death, she was in here again with Leon. Next time I saw Leon, he was on the television with Ray, and you guys were looking for a killer. I don't know if her name was even her real name."

"What did she say her name was?"

Lenny seemed relieved to tell what he knew. "She never said her name and Raymond never introduced her. I asked him about her later, and he said her name was 'Diane.' I found out after his death he lied. He was married, and his wife's name was Diane." Lenny became visibly upset. "Me and Ray go back a ways, you know, we grew up a few blocks from here. I saw his wife on the television and thought to myself, why would he lie? Do you think this woman had something to do with his death?"

"That's what we're trying to determine. The pictures are the first connection we've made. So, to be honest, you've given us another angle to investigate." Tyson put the pictures into the folder watching Scott as he put his arm around the shoulder of his employee. The whispers of the men held a story. Tyson knew there was more to tell, the question was, who would tell it?

Chapter Sixteen

Mona sat comfortably on her couch sipping her favorite herbal tea. The aroma put her in a relaxed mood, definitely, what she needed after a day of disappointments. Two of her clients canceled and the others, potential pains, wanted her to jump through hoops. No one understood that the market was tight, and although the contractors were willing to move on, the banks were in control. She made her last calls at two and was glad to kick off her shoes ending her business for the day.

She'd been trying to close deals for the past two weeks. It put a strain on her mentally and she could only hope it hadn't caused Damien to step back completely. She spoke with him daily, but she also asked him to give her time to finalize her workload. He seemed preoccupied himself, never mentioning what he did or who he consulted. She was pleased with their dates, the few they had. She found him to be open, but she still wasn't sure she could trust him.

Open that's what the others lacked. The ability to be open with her; instead they chose to lie. Mona was careful not to ask Damien too many questions about his past romances. He didn't seem to be interested in hers. He promised to take her to his favorite getaway, and she promised herself she'd know more about him by then. Mona made an entry in her journal each day, *"Take it one step at a time … follow his lead, not yours."*

It seemed to be working, and that's what she needed a stable, workable, relationship.

Candice and Kendra would find it hard to believe since she often dumped a man who was slower than her heightened sexual needs. Nothing deflated her sexual fantasies more than the thought of getting less than she expected. Mona couldn't stand the wait, and she would be satisfied one way or another. Lately, it had been another. Candice told her during one of their sex toys shopping spree that she didn't give her partners enough time to explore. Kendra chimed in as she paid for her goodies, "Mona, get the toys, girl. There's nothing that's more frustrating than having to give a brother a map to the treasure each time."

That was the problem. None of the men she dated needed a map, a guide or a toy to satisfy her libido. Mona considered herself sensual, attractive, and willing to please. She just couldn't see herself sharing; not her man, or her love. Why would they assume she would? Damien Tyson was different. She had said the same about Kevin and Leon after her freaky nights with Raymond. He turned her on to the toys. They enjoyed each other and the toys. She couldn't get enough of both his favorites and hers. The sight of him brought chills to her inner thighs until she caught him with another woman.

She confronted him, and he felt it was time for the truth. He gave her places, dates, and reasons. All of which Mona felt were excuses for a quick lay when she wasn't available. They often argued about his roaming eyes. During one of their sex only dates that followed, she found mail from his wife. Raymond told her to control her anger, after all she was more than a wife; she was the other woman. He explained they were separated, and she called now and then. He had a list of attributes that the "other" woman had; those a wife just wouldn't, no couldn't have. As he talked, she thought about killing him. She was sure he hadn't counted on her having a killer's instinct. He was right; his wife just couldn't kill him. She could and did.

She tossed her planner on the table and used the remote to turn on her favorite jazz station. Sitting up, she felt the need to use one of her toys for instant pleasure. She was sure she'd be able to doze off afterward but remembered she wanted to watch the HBO Special. As she surfed the channels, the news caught her attention.

The reporter was at The Pine Ridge Resort rehashing the murders and the latest information. Hearing that there may be new leads caused her to turn up the volume.

"We're here talking to a few of the guest about the resort. None of them seemed worried about their stay here. According to the management, who declined to talk with us on camera, the reservations are as expected for this time of year. Cathy, there has been no cancelations because of the murders."

Cathy, the news correspondent at the station, seemed concerned. "Well Matt, that's surprising considering the police said they'd be interviewing people again following this new lead. Let's hope they find the killer before he strikes again."

"Cathy, they're asking anyone who may be able to identify this woman here in the picture to contact them. She may have been the last to see two of the victims. There may be a tie in the cases, as we get more information we'll let you know. Viewers, please contact the authorities at the Police Hot Line number on the screen with any information."

A toll-free number flashed on the screen next to a woman's picture. Mona looked at the picture closely. She thought it would have been Janelle or Celeste. They had been on the television all week, pretending to be devastated. Mona stated more than once that they deserved awards. Candice and Kendra laughed not knowing how serious she was.

The television gave an out of focus shot of the photograph. Mona was shocked. There she was in the restaurant with her teal scarf and large framed glasses. Knowing the restaurant had cameras she attempted to avoid the angles. She was sure her fashionable attire camouflaged her features. She sat in fear waiting for anyone, no everyone who knew her to call.

The time quickly passed as she watched every news report from seven to eleven. Mona held tightly to her journal. She found the date of her entry when she decided to confront Raymond at the restaurant and read it again. Her plan went well, and she thought there was no other evidence that would connect her with Raymond Murphy. She was wrong. The eleven o'clock news flashed the photo again. She stared at it throughout the airing. If she couldn't tell it was her, no one else could.

Mona picked up the phone and called Kendra. She needed another opinion. The phone rang again. She looked at the clock frowning at the time, wondering where Kendra would be at eleven-twenty on a Thursday night.

"Hello!" Kendra belted into the receiver.

"Hey, you okay?"

"Hell no, I mean I will be. Girl, this some shit. What the hell? Look, Mona, can I call you back? I'm on the other line with this asshole."

"Uh, sure, don't worry about the time, just call."

The line went dead without Kendra saying another word. Mona touched a few numbers on the phone but changed her mind. Candice wouldn't be any help. She'd wait for Kendra's return call.

Chapter Seventeen

Kendra hung the phone up. There was no call on hold. Jay hadn't called, and she wouldn't answer if he did. There was nothing left to say. He always said she wouldn't understand, and she didn't. They had been in an off and on relationship for five years. Kendra thought he had finally matured leaving the games of a "playa" to the younger brothers in the neighborhood.

Kendra loved him, and as Candice often told her, he wouldn't love her until she loved herself more. Neither Mona nor Candice faulted Kendra. Jay Rands was a good catch who made it clear he wasn't ready for marriage. He had a career; he wanted stability first. He struggled through his last two years of college and flirted through his first three years as the Deputy Mayor's assistant in Bloomfield. After their meeting, he described her as a chocolate dream, he and Kendra seemed to be inseparable.

It wasn't long before they were regulars at city functions and events. Kendra worked with various inner city programs and kept the Mayor's office informed with the details. No one would suspect that they weren't married or at least cohabitating. They drove to work together, went to lunch together, and quickly became frequent bedmates. Kendra loved the freedom of her apartment but whenever she found herself alone at night, she'd wonder who was in Jay's bed.

There had been phone calls, and e-mails that Jay explained were business related. There had been gifts and notes left on his desk which he explained were returns for favors he granted. Then there were the whispers and rumors, which Jay laughed about making light of the conversation and the persons involved.

Kendra sighed deeply as the tears fell from her eyes. It was over. She couldn't possibly forgive him. The girl had been working with him to complete a city project for months. Kendra assumed they would be working late again and stopped by Jay's condo to bring them dinner. She couldn't believe she fought with herself about including the woman in the food order. She was determined to get next to Jay, and since he spent most of his evenings working, dinner was a great excuse. Jay told her there was nothing to hide, and he couldn't talk long because of the work they were doing. She'd surprise them; they were working at his home because she lived on the other side of town. Kendra couldn't remember the last time she had been invited to his place. It seemed he always had an excuse. She hoped Talia Simmons wasn't the reason.

Kendra balanced the box from Tony's Pizzeria as she searched for the keys. She still had the set Jay gave her the last time she watched his apartment while he was away on vacation. She didn't think there would be a need to ring the bell. Jay's place was away from the street and the noise of the traffic. She could hear the music from the adjoining home that muffled the noise she made as she entered the front door.

There were no lights on in the living room or the kitchen. Kendra paused as she walked into the den where the television was on, but no one was there watching it. She thought about her four o'clock conversation with Jay. She was certain he said he had to work another night with Talia so they could finalize the reports before the weekend.

She didn't bother to cut on the lights leading up the stairs. She could see there was light coming from one of the bedrooms. As she reached the top of the staircase, she heard Jay say her name.

"Kendra is nice and all but she just doesn't understand. I'm glad you do. It's easier to love someone when they understand you."

Kendra froze in her place as she watched his legs cross the opened doorway. He didn't have on any pants. She waited. The conversation faded to whispers. Jay continued to compare Kendra with whoever was entertaining his fantasies. Kendra wanted to leave, but she needed to know. The room was silent. She could hear what she concluded were kisses and movement across the sheets. She needed to get closer to be sure.

She crept up the stairs and stood near the door peering into its opening. Jay was on his knees, positioned between the woman's legs. Her legs were around his neck. It was obvious his tongue was at work. She'd wait longer before breaking up the position he loved the most. As she suspected, he turned her over and mounted her. As his movement increased, the woman began to moan.

"Deeper baby, I want it all."

"He ain't got enough left to give you. He gave most of it to me bitch, this morning!" Kendra blasted profanity from the end of the bed. "Get in deep you dead ass bastard. Did you tell her I just couldn't understand how you couldn't get it up this morning for another round? I understand now, you ain't got enough for two."

Talia flipped over covering her body with the sheet. Jay slowly rolled over on his back. His disappointment was obvious. He used his arm to block the pizza box that Kendra hurled in his direction. Pizza went everywhere. Kendra felt the urge to snatch the sheet from the shaken winch that took cover beneath Jay. She could see the fear in Talia's eyes.

"Tell me how I misunderstood Jay! Misunderstood this? What is this shit? Don't call me, don't text me; don't sell me no more tickets to the playa ball. I'm done with your limp ass."

Kendra left them in the bed. She ran out the door before the tears fell. Sitting in her car, she watched his window. She imagined him explaining his mistakes to Talia. After there had been no signs that Talia would be leaving his home, Kendra sped off with another reason to be outraged. It was obvious Talia accepted him, cheating and all.

When she arrived at her apartment, the phone rang. Mona was calling. A part of her wanted it to be Jay. She wanted him to say something, anything; she wanted him to convince her that it just happened. Any pretext was better than his silence. She'd see Talia again. She had a few words for her. Talia knew he was cheating; she knew Kendra. Where was her sense of pride? She had to have led him on.

After promising Mona she'd call her back, she knew she was lying; just as she had been lying for months about Jay. Now she understood Mona's comments about her fling with Leon. She too had been Jay's side piece or maybe Talia was the side piece. It didn't make her feel better regardless to who held the title. The definition was equal to fool. No woman wanted to be a fool. She had been pretending. Whenever they were on the outs, she would simply describe herself as secure in their relationship. No need to worry about another woman, he'd be back begging by the end of the week. Now she wasn't sure why she allowed herself to be used.

Kendra couldn't take the silence in the room. It seemed to be closing in. It was twelve; Jay wouldn't be calling her, and she wouldn't be calling Mona. Her head pounded more, a plea for her thoughts to cease. Her subconscious was on overload, and her conscious mind was still in shock. She decided to take two pills for her soon to be headache. Maybe she'd pack a few of his things. She'd leave them at his door in the morning. Maybe she would pack a few of her things and get away for a few days.

That would be running; why should she run? He should be exposed for what he was, but to whom? Kendra's thoughts were beginning to sound psychotic. There was no reason for revenge. Karma had a way of taking care of things like this. She thanked God for the dose of reality and turned on the television.

As the picture spread across the fifty-two-inch screen, she shook her head. The last thing she wanted to watch was the upcoming movie entitled "Revenge". She closed her eyes and allowed the medication to take her into a deep night sleep.

Chapter Eighteen

"I thought I'd better get over here and find out why you didn't return my calls girl. You said you'd call me back two days ago, what's up?"

Mona pushed her way past her drowsy friend. Kendra hadn't left her house or returned calls from anyone. Candice called Mona and asked her to look in on Kendra after her visit with her the night before. Both knew her immediate response to Jay's drama would be isolation, but she never stayed away from them too long.

Kendra mumbled, "Whatever!" but her response went unnoticed as she returned to her couch and the television. There was a pillow and blanket tossed on the chair. As Mona looked around, she could tell the apartment hadn't been a concern of Kendra's for the last few days.

"Did you call out from work yesterday too? Are you feeling okay?" Kendra seldom took days off. Mona was glad she took Candice's advice and didn't wait until later in the week to visit.

"I'm fine. Didn't Candice tell you? My lovesick ass is fine!"

"Okay, so you took off work to sulk? Girl please, you can't be for real."

"Look, I don't need someone, a so-called friend, telling me that if I wasn't so blind I would have seen this coming. Who sees it coming? Her reply was some dumb shit about me being love sick. Candice is an airhead when it comes to a relationship; that's why she doesn't have one. Who is she to analyze mine or yours for that matter?"

"She's been analyzing my relationships? She only knows the details about Leon. You must have misunderstood her. I think she's analyzing us. You know, how we react to what goes on in our relationships."

"Whatever the hell that means, does it matter? I wanted to tell her ass off, but it would have been misdirected anger. No as an afterthought, I could still cuss her out, 'cause I want to kill him!"

"Okay, that could be arranged." Mona's thoughts hit the air abruptly.

Kendra mockingly turned her lips up; the comment did bring a slight smile. "I guess you were right. If he won't commit, you're the side piece."

"You wanted Jay to commit? I thought you weren't ready for commitment."

"Listen, we've been dating long enough for me to be able to walk into his place whenever I wanted to, unannounced you know what I mean? I could at least expect that, right?"

"You're leading up to something. What or who was in his place when you got there?"

"That damn bitch he's been working with, Talia, was there; no clothes, in his bed, with her legs wrapped around his shoulder. His sorry ass, never mind, I know my place now, and I'll get over it. That's what Candice, the relationship counselor said."

"Forget what Candice said. We can deal with that later. Who is Talia and how long have they been dealing with each other?"

Kendra told Mona the story from the beginning. She detailed her suspicions, his excuses, and the embarrassment she felt. His friends and hers now knew she had been played. She was the other woman. Talia was too comfortable. Kendra paused only to stop herself from crying.

"She answered his phone this morning. I knew he would be at work, so I called to blast that ass over the phone. My intention was to shake him up leaving a message he'd get when he got in. She was there; I hung up. Why didn't I see this shit coming? Where was I when she was calling him?

Where was she when I was at his place? Mona, he acted as though it didn't matter. He never even called. I know she told him."

"Do you really want to talk to him or you just want to vent and be over with it? Did she know it was you?"

"She knew. Candice said they always know. They are okay with the lies, the cheating, and they keep the man. So while my love sick ass sits here crying, thinking I lost the love of a lifetime. She gets to roll under him and enjoy the best sex I ever had! That's what it balls down to, shit!!"

Kendra laughed at herself, breaking the tension that had filled the room. Mona gave her a questionable look, but her thoughts drifted. She thought of those she conveniently murdered.

"There it is again."

"What?" Mona had Kendra's full attention.

"Another reason for a cheating man to die, like the killings; there is no perfect side piece. Jay ain't no better than Leon, or those other two that got killed. He's not above being bumped off. He'll get his. So what you got planned? Talking to him won't do it. Take it from me. I know more than Candice about this. You talk with them and get frustrated, aggravated, and then you want to kill the asshole. So are you trying to get back with him or just vent?"

Kendra had to replay the words she heard slowly. It sounded as though Mona could have been involved in killing Leon or she knew something about the others.

"You're probably right. I'm the one that looks like the fool. I don't want him back. I've spent the last few days trying to get a grip on this situation so I could move on. It just hurts to know I truly loved him, and he used me. I'm glad you're here. I'm gonna get it together I'll just have to buy another toy, name it Jay and be done.....or get done."

"Girl you're crazy."

"No, you're the one. Talking about bumping somebody off; you had me for a minute there girl. Are you hungry? I am. I've got some tuna salad. Come on in the kitchen."

Mona needed more information about Jay. She'd confront him. She didn't want Kendra to be suspicious. She'd have to be careful about her questions. Following Kendra into the kitchen, she barely heard Kendra's babbling about the scene that sent her home crying.

"Wait slow down. Are you saying you caught them before?"

"Well sorta, you know that bastard lied and said he had just finished making calls and arranged to meet a client. He was at my house calling that bitch on my phone. I told him I wanted to eat out. We had plans for the movies anyway."

Kendra passed the bowl of tuna to Mona. She went to the counter and got two plates. "Crackers or just the salad, I'm really hungry now. I must be feeling better."

"Salad is fine. Hand me the crackers too."

"Since he said he was meeting the client that night. I let him off the hook. I mean the arrangements changed just like that."

"So how do you know it didn't come up, just like that?"

"See now you're thinking like I did. I called his ass about thirty minutes later. No answer so I drove to his place. Yeah, she was there. He answered the door. That was when he told me they had this project they needed time to work on, together. Mona that was four months ago. Damn, how could I be so stupid?"

"Well, maybe it was convenient for them to work at his place."

"Sistergirl was supposed to live in Plainfield somewhere; nowhere near Bloomfield. Why didn't they work on the project at the job? Why didn't he go to her house? He didn't even put shade on it. That's how I know!"

"Know what?"

"That I, the lovesick chick, the dummy, I'm the side piece."

"Does he live near the Municipal building?"

"No, near Montclair, High Street that complex that sits back; it looks like an apartment building. Near the shopping mall on the avenue, you know where that is."

"Hmmm, and you say they work together?"

"Yeah, on and off the job; Mona what am I going to do?"

"You could play the role for a minute. I mean, if you still want him. She may be the side piece. Don't give in if you don't want to give up. Hell, let him sweat about it. He'd have to give her an excuse or tell you a reason she's around. You haven't talked to him right, so why not do what he expects. Let the steam blow over and get your last roll in the bed, and then drop his ass."

Kendra listened. The thought of dealing with Talia had entered her mind. She hadn't thought about playing Jay. She wasn't sure he cared. She did need closure.

"I guess I could talk to his ass again. I need to do something, sulking about it ain't working. Yes, dropping his ass after swooning him may be a nice revenge."

Mona smiled. She'd be sure he got what he deserved.

Chapter Nineteen

"I didn't get a call back from toxicology," Porter stated, never looking up from his desk. He waited for Tyson's response. Tyson stopped writing on the pad in front of him giving full attention to his partner. "I went with what we had, although it's little to nothing. We think it's a woman, right?" Tyson nodded in agreement. "Well, she had to create an advantage. My thoughts would be putting something in his drink. Drugging him was my first thought, but I don't see that angle anymore."

"Okay, so you're assuming she tainted his drink. In the evidence they collected did we get glasses, food or anything that proved they wined or dined in the room?"

"No, but if you think about it, she could have slipped something in his drink anywhere. They didn't have to eat or drink that night in the room."

"Yeah, you've got a point. Did you get anything on the wives? There's got to be a connection."

"I checked the other numbers that both of them called. Your boy at the restaurant, yeah, he knows more. They've been in touch with someone there."

Tyson pulled out the business card from the scattered pile of papers on his desk. Scott Bearmon, he knew he would have to talk to him again. Jeff laid the phone records in front of him for them to review together.

"See here, just before the murders, the calls were made from the Bates home. Seems like the calls were about the same time each day; look here's the number again. It's the same on the Styles records; the calls started a week before Kevin Styles was killed."

"What about Murphy, anything on his wife or the phone records?" Tyson was hoping his partner had found the break in the case they needed. Jeff returned to his desk leaving the reports on Tyson's desk.

"Nothing, I can't even get his ex-wife to return our calls. According to the contacts that I spoke with, at the time of Murphy's death, they had been separated for two years or more. I guess after his funeral, she was done with his side of the family. His sister seemed to be angry about her reaction, but no one has heard from her since then."

"Do we have an address for her?"

Jeff moved a few papers around on his desk. "Yeah, since the separation she's been living in Delaware. I thought someone said Murphy was single? No one seems to know about their divorce."

"You're supposed to be checking the spouses. I guess we'd need to know why." Tyson continued to look over the phone records.

"Did you notice that Celeste Styles has called Janelle Bates more than a few times since the funeral? I wonder what that's about." Tyson questioned pointing to the calls on the report.

"The problem is it doesn't add up to much. Okay, we've got two of the three widows talking to each other, and the third is who knows where. It means absolutely nothing. I thought we dealt with some dead ass cases but this beats them all."

"We've got more than we had. What kind of insurance payoffs were there?"

"Tyson, not enough to kill them, Styles had the largest pot at one hundred and fifty thousand. The others had some property and about fifty each. The insurance companies said the payoffs were mailed out and finalized without any problems." Damien frowned at Jeff's statement. "I'm saying no one bugged them about the money or wondered why they didn't get more. I think they knew what was coming to them. I don't know that the wives had anything to do with it."

"Alright, keep digging though, I'm gonna ask Scott about the calls to the restaurant. Maybe it's a lead. What else do you have?"

"Nothing, hey the fights on tomorrow, Amir mentioned the sports bar. You down with it or are you going out with your girl. He already said he won't be there."

"Yeah, I got tickets to a show in New York. Jazz performer, no big name but I've heard him on the radio. He's pretty good on the keyboard. I think she'll like it."

"So it's going well, huh, been a long time since you've been on the dating scene."

"Mona has a great personality. She's got a rough side though, I can tell. She needs a lot of attention." Jeff's expression gave him a reason to explain. "No, let me say it like this. She's that woman who would track her man, if she had to."

"So you're just, what, dating? I didn't think you would be into a woman stalking you."

"No man, don't make it into something it ain't. I just mean, listening to her conversation, I just get that feeling. I really don't know. The last thing I need is a woman tracking my time. I don't think that will happen."

"So she doesn't know you're a detective."

"No, you were there when we exchanged information. I left it like that; no need to get into that yet. I'm still trying to get to know her."

"Yeah and after that all night thing, you say what? Or when you get that call in the middle of a date, what are you going to say? Oh, that's Jeff, let me deal with this? Damien, that's how you messed up the last catch. These fine specimens fall for the line you throw and you lose them because you won't be honest? That's crazy man."

"So you just tell them what you do for a living? What's the difference, we do the same thing?"

"Yeah, you're right. Watch this chick, your observations may be right. My observations say she's a playa, and you may just get played this time."

"Well hook me up with the psych, 'cause I want to be played."

Jeff made no comment. It had been a long time since Damien even considered dating. He smiled to himself thinking about the dating lessons he would attempt to give him and Amir. Being the oldest Damien would always caution them about the women they attracted. Jeff felt obligated to give him the same lines. He didn't want to see his partner fall in love only to be hurt. Separating from his wife and children had been hard on him although Damien would never admit it. Jeff and Amir understood his silent moments, refusal to join them in public places, and secluding himself at home all of which had been the result of losing love.

Damien highlighted the phone calls made to the restaurant. He'd be sure to talk with Scott before investigating the calls between the wives. He'd talk to Ms. Bates first, hopefully he could avoid a confrontation with Ms. Styles.

His phone rang interrupting his thoughts. He continued packing his satchel as he answered, "Detective Tyson."

"So it is. Detective, I'm sure you know who this is."

"Ms. Sayers, how could I not recognize your voice? How are you?" Damien turned his chair away from the paperwork on his desk.

"I'd be better if you would give me a tease for our readers. You know this case is dragging. No one knows much, and the result of your investigation has everyone on the edge."

"Everyone, and just who is everyone? The only one who has called has been you."

"Are you serious? It would seem that the higher ups would want to close this case as soon as possible. I mean even the owners of the resort would want their prospective guests to feel at ease staying at their establishment."

"I guess business is as usual. I'm tying up the loose ends to confirm the decision and put it in the archives. I haven't found much. I've got a few leads to check but nothing more than what's already been reported."

"So you're not just stringing me along?"

"Ms. Sayers, stringing you along, me? Why would I want to do that?"

"You wouldn't? I mean giving me a story would send me on my way. Maybe, detective you want me around. Calling you every few days and almost begging you for information….."

Damien looked at the phone and rolled his eyes before laughing.

"I can assure you, I can get a lot more done knowing that you won't be calling, as you say, every few days. I can only give you the information that I have. I haven't forgotten your story. What you can do though is print that the investigation is still ongoing. Maybe that will stir some talk. You can include the number here at the office for anyone with information to call."

"So who are your suspects or what are your thoughts about the crime? I can add that with the plug you want printed."

"Let's just say that we have a few angles, and we're working those angles to find a suspect. The crime, to be honest, Ms. Sayers, looks like a crime of passion. At this time, that's all I can say. Someone was involved with these men, loved them, and then killed them."

Chapter Twenty

The restaurant was busy. Just as Damien decided he would have to talk with Scott another time, the young manager approached him at the end of the bar.

"Detective, if you're looking for Jessica, she's done for today. She usually works longer, but she's been filling in a lot this week. Can I get you a drink or a table?"

Damien felt the tension in the air the moment Scott spoke. Jeff may have been right. Scott knew something. He excused himself leaving Damien to ponder about staying. He looked over the crowd. The casual atmosphere, with broken conversations, seemed normal, but he wondered who else among the crowd knew Leon Bates or Kevin Styles. Scott returned wiping his hand on the towel tucked in the front of his pants.

"So what will it be Detective? Are you hungry, need a drink to end your day or are you here with more questions?"

Damien ignored his sarcasm. "You can give me a Coors Light. Got a pretty good crowd here for this hour huh?"

"Yeah, on Fridays we have an after work special for three hours, from four to seven. My father squawked about it, but noticed the increase in the crowd and went with it." He got the detective his beer from the tap, careful not to spill it as he placed it in front of him. Scott peered over the crowd smiling.

"My dad can't be mad about it; I mean the register proved my point."

"Does your dad come in at all? I mean does he work any of the shifts?"

"No, he hasn't in a while. I'm not supposed to notice it. I guess he figured I wouldn't take it over if he just asked me to. He's right, I wouldn't."

"So what's your plan?" Damien looked at Scott waiting to hear his frustrations.

"Well, I've learned the customers, the staff, and how to order stock. My dad's accountant comes in and does the books every week. It's really not that bad, and I make a decent buck. The old man lets me make decisions and where else would I work." Scott was beginning to be uncomfortable. "What brings you this way?"

"I wanted to talk to you." Damien continued before Scott could give him an obvious excuse. "I only have a few questions, but I wanted to save you the trip of coming to my office."

"A trip to your office, I don't understand, why am I being questioned?" Scott held up his index finger, his response to a customer who had raised his glass for a refill.

"Go ahead, I'll be here a minute." Damien watched as Scott rushed to fill the orders at the other end of the bar. He turned his back to the bar and imagined Kevin and Leon talking with the woman in the picture. He doubted if anyone would have paid attention to her.

"So, what's your question?" Scott was visibly anxious.

"Well, for one, is it always this crowded on Fridays?"

"Most of them, yeah."

"Do you remember the picture I showed you?" Damien had the picture with him if he said no.

"Yes, vaguely, you're talking about the woman and those guys who they found dead right?"

"Yes. Did they come here on Fridays? The date on the pictures we have is during the week."

"Detective, I don't know. They didn't do anything unusual; you know what I mean. They fit in, I guess that's why they met here."

"What makes you think they met here?"

Scott wiped the counter and his hands. "I don't know, man look, I work the bar. Jessica and the other staff they're out on the floor. They talk to these customers, get to know the regulars, you know. I know the ones who sit in front of me here." Scott's answer got the attention of the customers on both sides of Damien. "I don't know that woman."

Damien responded calmer than Scott, as the customers returned to their conversations.

"What about the men? They never sat here, at the bar? You made it sound like they met this woman on more than one occasion."

"Look, I don't want you twisting my words. They met for lunch or business or whatever; I don't know. What did Jessica tell you?"

"Listen, if she had satisfied my curiosity would I be here? Now you said they met here. How often?"

"A few times I guess. I didn't know it would lead to a murder investigation, so I didn't count."

"Listen, Scott, I just need help here. I'm not saying you know who, what or where, but what you do know may lead me to some answers. You help me by answering a few questions, and it's all good."

"And if I don't……"

"Let's just say it would be in your best interest to help this investigation if you can."

A customer not far from the conversation tapped his bottle of beer on the counter to get Scott's attention. Tyson turned on the bar stool getting another view of the crowd. Scott was probably right. After pulling in a few weeks of steady clientele on Friday's, he was sure his father changed his mind. There were just as many women as there were men. This was just the nine to five crowd on Friday, downing a few drinks, eating and socializing before going home doubled the weekday income.

As he surveyed the room, again he thought he saw someone he knew. The widows were together. Maybe Jeff was on to something. Tyson didn't have the picture to compare the features. He and Jeff agreed the woman wasn't Janelle Bates or Celeste Styles, now he wasn't sure. He turned quickly hoping they hadn't seen him. Scott returned hoping the conversation between them was over.

Before Scott could speak Tyson raised his hand to silence him. He leaned forward and whispered, "Look across my left shoulder. There are two women sitting at the table near the window. Do you recognize them?"

"No, should I?" His quick response caused suspicion.

"If you don't, you don't." Tyson watched Scott's actions. He returned to the cash register, a sign he was too busy to continue an interrogation.

Tyson left his payment under his glass and proceeded to make his way toward the door. He took the chance to gaze at the women as he weaved through the crowd. Janelle spotted him. Their eyes met. Neither gave a nod of acknowledgement. She didn't alert Celeste but he knew she would tell her he was there. Time wouldn't allow him to interrupt their meeting, but it was clear he would have to question them again.

Chapter Twenty-One

The moment the doorbell rang, Mona knew she would be late. Candice promised to drop off the Dsquared2 black sexy dress she borrowed months prior. The friends shared closets and accessories to save their wallets from excessive spending. Slipping the dress over her head and putting on the final touches of her makeup wouldn't take long but Mona was pacing. It would be the first real date with Damien and she didn't need to be late, even if it was expected.

Her choice of dress wouldn't have caused her to fret if she had checked to see if Candice had returned the dress earlier in the week. Candice stepped out of her heels as Mona snatched the hanger from her hand. The plastic cover from the cleaners explained her late arrival.

"I thought you had the dress at home. You just put it in the cleaners?" Mona questioned as she continued to her bedroom with Candice following her quickened steps.

"No, I picked it up today. I forgot it was in the cleaners."

Mona shook her head and decided not to respond. "Zip me up girl. He'll be here any minute."

"So how's his friend Jeff doing? We could have double dated, you know. What's up with him?"

"Why would we double date?" Mona scolded herself silently for asking the question.

"Well he is a cutie, I mean I watched from the corner of my eye. What type of work did they say they did?" Candice asked, handing Mona her earrings.

"And your reason for wanting to know that?"

"I don't want to waste my time. You and Kendra have had enough bad experiences for me to learn about the deadbeats. Well, I ain't beat. No side piece, no money, no time for me…I ain't beat." Candice caught the stare from the reflection in the mirror.

Mona caught herself before replying. She ignored her friend's honesty hoping if she stared, it would put Candice on alert.

"I'm sorry Mona. I shouldn't have said that with Leon and all. Wow, sometimes I don't know what to say, you know that saying, 'If you don't have anything good to say'…"

"Candice, thanks for bringing the dress. Let me get finished here before this man rings the bell."

"Well, you know double dating ain't that bad. I mean we can check them out for each other. You and Damien seem to be getting along."

"I'll think about it and call you. I don't know he may not want to double date. Did Jeff call you?"

"Jeff who?"

Mona paused before sliding her foot in her shoe. Again she gave Candice a hardened stare.

"Oh right, Jeff. He did, once or twice. We didn't talk long. I was answering the phones at the office. I wouldn't mind getting with him, though."

"I'll let Damien know. Now, go on girl, lock the door behind you. If you see Damien don't let him in."

"What, if he's there don't let him in?" Candice was more than confused.

"Don't. If he's here to pick me up, he needs to ring the bell."

She waited fifteen minutes before the bell rang. Pretending to be calm, she paused before opening the door. Mona couldn't explain why her nerves were on edge. As she opened the door, Damien presented her with a beautiful bouquet. She held her thought and the tears. Damien Tyson won her over with the simple gesture.

"Oh my goodness, these are beautiful. Damien, how sweet, come in please." Mona ignored her own rules and allowed him to sit on her couch. All others waited to be invited in weeks after the date. She seldom allowed male company in her home.

Damien canvased the room and caught himself before committing the details to memory. His career taught him you could tell a lot about a person by the way they kept their home. He was sure Mona cleaned the apartment before allowing his entrance.

"I'll only be a minute." Mona called from the bedroom. She glanced at herself in the mirror to be certain there were no flaws. She puckered her lips, blowing a kiss to her reflection.

"I wanted to be sure I had everything. Thank you for being patient." She said smiling as Damien stood to greet her.

"Your dress is nice. You wear it well Ms. Mandell."

"You're not bad yourself, Mr. Tyson."

"Shall we?"

The start of the evening went well. The couple wasted no time in travel. There wasn't much traffic, and the valet parking saved the time Mona lost waiting for Candice.

Mona was immediately impressed with Damien's manners. She told herself that it was the beginning of their relationship. She was sure he wouldn't show her who he really was until after the bedroom encounters.

He took the time to make reservations, a step above the others she dated. She noted that he had been there before. The servers smiled and nodded greeting him by name. There were two shows. She asked earlier about the times and Damien's reply was they would be having dinner first.

He ordered the wine without her input and assured her she would love it. He was right. She appreciated the chosen table and wondered if the reservations specified their seating.

"This place is beautiful. How often do you eat here?"

"Whenever I can, I stumbled upon it while working in the area. New York has so many places to eat, but not many that give you service and a meal you don't mind paying for. How's the wine?"

"It's good. I prefer dry wine. This is different."

"A Moscato blend. I like the brand. If you like it, I'll bring a bottle to your house the next time I stop by."

"Yes, I'd like that. So you said while working in the area. Does your work take you out of state often?"

Damien took a slow sip of his wine, thinking before speaking. The topic of the conversation needed to be changed.

"Not often but lucky for me it did. I found this restaurant, was treated to a complimentary room for a few days and loved it. The client was from New York."

"I see, well you must have come highly recommended if the client paid the bill."

"I would imagine. I never ask."

"So what does a Security Consultant do exactly?"

"Set up security. Monitors, cameras, you know the equipment that watches your property, nothing unusual."

"Has that always been your job, a chosen career? I just don't see you saying I want to be a security consultant."

"I've done other things but this is on my time and it pays more."

"Have you ever caught someone? Are you called in after the police are called?"

"No, actually it's connected to the police, and our corporate office can give them any tapes or monitoring reports. Enough about that mess, tell me about you."

"You know what I do. It's no difference in selling homes and selling the corporate property."

"Guess you're right. Tell me what I should know about you."

"I'm single, never been married, no children, but I am looking for those things in the future. I'm no different than any other woman."

"I think you're different. You wouldn't have caught my eye if you were the typical woman."

"Don't tease me Mr. Tyson you may have to fight me off you."

"I won't fight. Seriously, I consider myself lucky."

"Lucky?"

"Yes, you're free to date, no children to cut the dates short, and you're ambitious. I like that; you know what you want, and you're willing to work for it."

Mona laughed lightly. She felt a chill on the back of her neck. It wouldn't be long before the hairs would rise. She focused on her food."

"This steak is seasoned just right. How's the salmon?"

"I didn't mean to unnerve you. It's great, I usually get this or the steak. Both leave me wanting more."

"So you don't like shop talk, we'll have to create new memories to discuss." She teased.

"I'd like that, and you're right, I don't talk about my job much. Why have security if you're willing to tell everyone about it? Would you like dessert?"

"No, I think I'm full."

"We can get out seats for the show. The theatre is across the lobby."

"This place is really nice. Thank you Damien, this is one to commit to memory."

The couple proceeded to the atrium where a small crowd began to form. The décor kept Mona's attention. The beauty spoke richness, and her mind traveled into her past. Spending most of her time targeting executives she hoped for the finer things in life. None of them took the time to ask about her likes or dislikes. None of them thought to take her out without a stay at a hotel suite. The best outing with any of them was the final outing for all of them. The resort weekend was her offer. It was her final attempt to please herself, and be done with each of them permanently.

"Excuse me, Damien, I need to use the restroom before we take our seats."

"Sure, I'll be right here." Damien stood waiting. Pleased with the evening, the conversation, and the atmosphere, he began to visualize a lasting relationship.

"Tyson, what's up man?"

The familiar voice calling Damien's name, startled him. He turned quickly hoping Mona didn't hear Amir call him.

"Hey man, I didn't know you liked jazz. Where's your date?"

"I'd imagine the same place as yours, the bathroom."

"A woman's getaway. Hey, do me a favor, don't call me Tyson when I'm out. Mona doesn't know I'm in law enforcement."

"Gotcha man, no problem. Can I ask you a question?"

"Not right now, here she comes."

"Hope they didn't talk; looks like they met at the sink."

Amir's date, Leana, recognized Damien and greeted him with a smile and a hug.

"What a coincidence. I was talking with Mona about this place and she mentioned how much she's loving her date. Wow, so the infamous Damien Tyson has another side."

Leana Wilson, better known as, Officer Wilson worked with Damien and Amir. She and Amir dated off and on. Her personality was warm and always professional both on and off the job.

Mona watched as the three interacted. Leana seemed at ease, a lot more relaxed than she was in the ladies room. She'd have to find out if there was another reason for her statement. Mona didn't need a prior relationship to be held over her head. If Damien was Leana's old fling, she could be a problem.

Amir and Leana agreed to meet with Damien and Mona after the show. Damien insisted they join them for a drink. Another decision made without Mona's input.

"So Amir and Leana are close friends of yours?"

"Yes, and they've been dating a while now. I think Amir likes her a lot more than he is willing to say. They get along well together. I asked them to have a drink with us afterward so you can get to know them. Maybe the four of us could get together for a few outings."

"You're into double dating?"

"Well, not often, I mean occasionally is okay. If you're not into it though, we don't have to."

"I hope you'll let me decide before you invite them."

"I'm sorry, I just thought that before ending the night we could meet with them and have a drink. If you don't want to, of course we won't."

Candice's question about double dating was echoing as Damien spoke. She'd save the request. He was right there was a need to talk. She wasn't sure what he had to hide, but Leana could be one who could fill in the blanks.

The house lights blinked. Damien moved close and kissed Mona on her forehead.

"Whatever you want to do is fine with me. Let's make it to our seats."

The couple enjoyed the concert. Damien was surprised how many of the artist's song choices Mona knew. There were three artists and just before Dave Koz, the headliner took the stage, Damien's phone buzzed. He looked at it but never answered the call, only to get another buzz noting there was a message from Amir. Mona paid close attention to his actions. She remembered the times her past dates would excuse themselves and answer regardless to where they were. Damien proved to be different in his behavior. She wanted to be sure. Maybe Candice had a point; she needed her. At the conclusion of the show, Damien took a moment to read the message.

"A reason to check in?" Mona's question held a disgruntled overtone.

"No, it was Amir. They won't be joining us. He got a call that he had to handle."

"Oh, so he's the one on a leash."

"What does that mean? I don't think he's on anyone's leash. He had to handle—"

"No need to tell me that's on Leana. That's her name right?"

"Mona I think you've got the wrong idea. He's single, and they've been dating for almost a year. Anyway, we can have a drink in the lounge if you'd like or would you prefer to head back to Jersey?"

Mona chose the drink in the lounge. She didn't want the ride home to be in silence. A glass of Moscato would take the edge off. They sat at a small table for two and the fire from the candle centerpiece gave just enough light to dim the tension.

Damien wasn't sure what struck her nerves, but he knew it wasn't him. He'd ask Amir if Leana mentioned anything about her meeting Mona in the bathroom.

"I'm glad you enjoyed the concert or seemed too," He remarked, pretending not to notice her attitude had changed.

Mona's response was better than what he anticipated. "I did, I have a few jazz CDs but I definitely need to check out the artists that were here tonight. How about you, concerts, dinner, wine selections, you are quite different or is this the bait?"

"Why would I need to bait you? I don't believe in cat and mouse games. I'm this way all the time. It isn't always accepted, and I guess most women feel it is bait. Believe me it's not."

Mona kept her thoughts to herself. She was hooked.

Chapter Twenty-Two

The news broadcast interrupted Mona's mid-morning relaxation. The twelve o'clock news wasn't as mundane as she expected it to be. She stopped while making her lunch to listen to the reporters.

"I don't know Cathy, the police seem to think there may be a connection between this mystery woman and the murders. They have this photo of her having lunch with both Mr. Styles and Mr. Bates."

"Well Jerry, we haven't heard from any of the officials. This report is from the Village Post. They seem to have a connection with the police. The leads seem to be going nowhere according to the story."

The picture of the woman was enlarged on the television. Once again she saw her mistake on the screen. She did well with the darker make-up and accessories that served as a quick disguise. She deliberately put the cocoa foundation on her lighter skin hoping no one would recognize her behind the large glasses and scarf. Looking at herself now on the television, she knew she would receive a call from someone who thought it was her. She'd have to be prepared with an answer.

"Don't be silly, why would I be in a place like that? What is it a bar and grill?" As she ended her questioning aloud she smiled, hoping neither of the reporters would ask.

"They're willing to reopen the case. The taxpayers will wear the brunt of this expense. It may be a while before they close it again." The reporter stated continuing the on-air discussion.

"They must have something, Jerry. Here's the hotline number for anyone who may know this woman. She's not a suspect but the police do want to talk with her. She may be the last contact they made before staying at the resort. It's amazing and somewhat strange. Mr. Styles died months before Mr. Bates yet the police have found these pictures of a woman who may put the pieces together. I would imagine the family needs closure."

"Well if any of our viewers can help or think you know this woman, please contact the police at this number. Cathy, we'll be following this case closely."

Mona turned off the television. The police had to have more than the pictures. She wondered who took the pictures. She met them there weeks before the relationships, but someone took pictures of them each time. Meeting them in the same place caused problems before and after death.

"Who would be that interested in them?" she mumbled. She let her thoughts battle with reason. She continued mumbling about the possible angles sought by the police. "They know something."

Mona went to her bedroom and pulled out a pair of her dingy jeans. She'd have to follow her instinct or she would be consumed with anxiety. She pushed through the hangers and found her Penn State sweatshirt. Once she found her sneakers she would be on her way.

The phone rang causing her to pause. A conversation would be a delay. She'd be short, no annoyed, and her voice would be an indication that something wasn't right. The phone chimed again and she snatched it from the base.

"Yes!"

"Mona, it's Kendra. Can you meet me at Candice's? I'm just not feeling right. She wanted you to come, can you?"

"I've got a stop to make. I'll be on my way after that. Is that okay?" Mona's emotions went from bitter to sweet. Kendra's issue would take the edge off. Maybe she changed her mind about Jay. Mona hoped so. She'd love to arrange the setup and if necessary, the kill.

Chapter Twenty-Three

The fifteen-minute ride took thirty minutes longer. Mona turned up the radio and sighed, no need to let the traffic be another reason to stress. She changed her mind and turned at the next exit on the Parkway. She wouldn't get to Candice's apartment for at least three hours if she made the stop she intended to make. It would have to wait. She put on the signal indicator to make a left turn. There were never any parking spots on Oraton Parkway, and Mona refused to walk the block back. She decided to circle the block again.

"Candice, I can't find a space. Did Kendra get there?" Mona sat at the light waiting to turn onto Oraton Way again while listening for the answer from Candice. She allowed the car to ease into the turn.

"Kendra's not here, why, is she supposed to be coming here?"

"Candice, she called and said you told her to come and me to meet her at your place. Did she call you?"

"No. I just got in myself. Maybe she's gonna come here. I'll check my messages. She knows she should have called my cell. How did she sound?"

"Oh, there's a space. I'll be right there."

Mona put the car in the tight spot and said a prayer. She'd be upset if squeezing into the space would cause her car to be bumped by a car getting out. She grabbed her bag and slammed the door. Candice stood at the top of the brick steps.

"What's wrong?" Mona could tell by her expression Kendra left a message.

"Let's go. She's been hit her in the face with something. She's in the ER." She continued the story from her messages. "Mona I don't understand this love mess. If he loved her why cheat on her? Now hitting her, what's next?"

Mona kept the answer to herself. "Which hospital?"

"East Orange, I don't know who lives in East Orange. He doesn't and neither does she."

"I think I know. She went to talk to that chick."

"Why? I thought she was done with him. Why question her?"

"You're right. She shouldn't have questioned her or went to her house, but you said he hit her, I guess he was there."

"She didn't say he hit her, I assumed that's what she meant." Candice was listening, but she was confused.

"So was he there? Did she say he went with her to the hospital?"

"No. You can turn here the ER is on this street. Okay, so he's not defending Kendra either. I hope this is it. I hope she's over him."

"Oh, believe me, it is. I hope he's not the one that hit her. If he is, he just deposited some shit his ass can't cash."

"Right!" Candice agreed without giving the words a second thought.

The two hurried to the podium in the center of the emergency room. The triage nurse told them they would have to wait while she searched the area, partitioned with drawn curtains, for their friend. They took a seat and waited for the nurse to return.

"Ladies, here's your pass she's in the last one on the left. She's waiting for the doctor."

Neither said thank you. Their thoughts, prayers, and fears, were with Kendra. Mona pulled the soft pink curtain back slowly as the two friends braced themselves for the worse.

Kendra had been examined and was crying softly. Her left cheek showed swelling and was dressed with gauze bandages. The darkened red stains indicated there was a wound beneath the covering.

"Kendra, what did he do?"

"He didn't do this; that bitch did! I may have to have plastic surgery. He called me over to his place to return his keys. I should have gone with my first thought. He should have come to pick them up. Anyway, I went there, and no one answered the door. I called to tell him I was leaving his keys in the mailbox. He said no, to bring them to this address instead. It was her house. I didn't know it, and I went there hoping to cuss his ass out one last time. Well, she opened the door, and we argued. She asked, *"What was I doing at her door?"* I told her to bring her ass outside, and I would answer her. I know I was wrong to invite her outside and what's worse? I waited for her. She closed the door and like a fool I stood there. She burst out the door with a blade. Now here I am with half my face hanging off. I don't know where he was or why he would set me up. It was over. I let go. I wanted to talk, you know, I just wanted closure. I didn't call him and when he called I didn't answer the phone. Mona, when you said, make a decision, I did. Shit, I should have had his ass done."

Mona raised her eyebrows but remained silent. The trio waited for the plastic surgeon who agreed she would need to have stitches and maybe a skin graph to salvage her facial beauty. He assured her after her face had healed she wouldn't know she had been cut. The doctor told Mona and Candice he wouldn't know if Kendra would have surgery until he looked at the damaged area closer. He didn't recommend that they stay, but he couldn't force them to leave. They decided to wait until it was determined if she needed the surgery.

The nurses entered the curtained enclosure to prepare Kendra for the procedure. Mona and Candice told her they would be around. They left the hospital when they were informed she would have to have surgery. She'd be sleeping through the night. Mona called Jay and left a message about Kendra undergoing surgery. He never returned the call.

Chapter Twenty-Four

Scott Bearman received a call Monday morning to report to the detective's office. Neither Porter nor Tyson thought the questions would take long, but they needed the interview to be on the record. Tyson assured the young manager he would be at the restaurant well before the noon crowd.

"Its simple man, he said he didn't know either of the women. I'm sure they had a conversation after I left. He knows them, and that connection could give us the link that we need. So let him say what he does know in a documented report." Porter gave Tyson a nod as his reply. Tyson thought the caller had put Porter on hold.

Tyson prepared the paperwork, photos, and other information he needed to refer to during the questioning. Porter hung the phone up smiling and nodding his head.

"Damien, it's getting there, that was Janelle Bates. She'll be here around one and get this; Celeste Styles is still in town."

"When I saw them together I thought it was odd. They're not coming together are they?"

"No, I mentioned we might have to get in touch with Ms. Styles. Janelle slipped up and said she was in town." Porter stepped across the office looking at the paper display that was purposely set up by his partner. "Yea, we may be on to something. I'll call Celeste later and see if she'll be willing to talk as well. We may have a reason for her to stay a few days."

"Janelle will warn her before then. It should be a shock to both of them."

"It won't be. Those two and your boy, Scott, know more than they're willing to say. Maybe they were in on the killing or hired someone to do the job."

"Jeff man, where do you come up with these theories? These are nice women man, not serial killers." Tyson stated sarcastically.

"No, I can't tell. Have you ever had two scorned women, fed up with your mess? Man, they found out their husband was cheating, no, sharing the same woman. A business partner they didn't even know they had. Mad woman, scorned woman; a nice way of saying serial criminal."

"You got your theory; I've got mine," Tyson stated giving in to the debate that was brewing.

"C'mon man, don't stop now, tell me, what is your theory? I mean, I doubt that you're right but hey last week we didn't have anything that connected. Now the wives are at the same restaurant where you catch the so-called manager in a lie. Somebody there knows them, and the killer is among them."

Tyson couldn't doubt Porter's angle. He didn't want to believe women would be that cold. He stopped Porter from returning to his seat, holding his arm.

"Hey, you've got something there. This boy's father is never at the restaurant. We need to ask them do they know the owner and the son. I wonder if the old man is the connection in some way."

"Killer for Hire? You think they hired someone?"

"The scene was done like a professional. They did all their business there. Suppose the deal or contract fell through and they owed the father, Mr. Bearman money. Scott said something about the Friday crowd bringing in enough money to cover the shortage during the week. They could have been killed for it."

"And you talk about me. Listen I'm going to talk with Leana. She's got an assault case she's investigating. She said she wanted to show me something regarding the evidence. I think she'll do anything to get me in her office by myself. You know me, I'm game."

"Watch out, that's Amir's girl. I'll hit your pager when Scott arrives."

Tyson made himself a cup of coffee and reviewed the paperwork once more. It wasn't long before Scott walked through the office door visibly annoyed.

"So I guess coming to the restaurant was out of the question huh?"

"Well I've been there several times, and today I want your undivided attention. Have a seat; can I get you something to drink?"

"Oh, role reversal? I don't think I'll be here that long. You see detective I don't know anything."

"You're right, you don't. I believe you know someone that does. So let's get started. The women I asked you about, you said you didn't know them. Am I right?"

"Yea, you're right, I don't know them." Scott took a deep breath and sat back in the chair.

"Never saw them there, like you never saw their husbands?"

"What does that mean? How would I know they were married?"

"Who Scott? Who was married?"

"I don't know who or what you're talking about; they're customers that's all."

"Customers you've never seen before?"

"That's right. The men, yea they were regulars maybe two or three times a month. Then I wouldn't see them again and then they'd show up again."

"And never with either of the ladies who just happened to be there the other day?"

Scott hesitated before answering. Tyson raised his eyebrows. His silence repeated the question. Scott sighed before replying. "What does all this have to do with me? I didn't kill nobody, so why drill me every day?"

"As I said, you know something or someone who does." Tyson slid the phone records across the desk. "That the number to the restaurant?"

"Yes." Scott was reluctant to reply. He knew the next question before the detective asked it. "I never saw either of them until the other day. They called for my dad earlier, and when you saw them I didn't know….. I didn't know they were the ones calling. I swear they introduced themselves after you left."

"So what did they want?"

"My dad. He wasn't there. I told them that."

"So if your father is never there, why would they call him there?"

"They gave me the message, I called him, and I guess he returned the call. I didn't think it was any different than any of the calls he gets."

"So I've got a message for you to deliver to your father. I want to see him. Tell him make himself available or we'll come get him. Do you understand?"

"Whoaaa… Why would you involve my dad in this?"

"You involved your dad. I'm investigating three murders. I don't know who the suspect is, all I have is victims. Every step I turn it leads back to your restaurant and now your father. You know something son, you or your father knows the widows of the deceased. Which may or may not indicate you know more about the murders than you're saying, but I need to be sure."

Scott let out the breath he was holding. "Detective, my father may know these women, I don't know. Let me talk to him and I'll tell you whatever he tells me." Scott waited for the answer.

"Bring your father here or we'll pick him up. I don't have time to go back and forth with messages. If he didn't tell you about his involvement with these women before, what makes you think he'll tell you now?"

"Because his life depends on it," He mumbled barely audible.

Scott didn't offer any explanation for his answer and Tyson didn't push it.

"What's your father's name, Scott?"

"Russell Bearman … everyone calls him Rusty. Is that all you need?" The younger man stood, ready to leave.

"Just remember to call with a time you and your father will be here. Scott, you've been helpful, and hopefully this won't lead to problems for you, your dad, or your business. I'm just trying to put this crime to bed. You know give the families some closure. The resort needs that too. They've got a business that's labeled, and it's hampering their reputation. I appreciate you coming down."

"Yea well I wouldn't want you coming to get me."

Tyson put out his hand for Scott to acknowledge his apology. For the first time since they met, the detective knew they were on opposite sides. There was no handshake. He watched the young man walk out the door.

The phone rang, reminding Tyson that he hadn't paged Porter. He answered prepared to apologize.

"Tyson."

"Hey man, this report Leana has is from a DV call. East Orange Hospital emergency room called it in. You may want to check into it. "

"Someone we know?"

"Yeah, Kendra. Did she call you?"

"Kendra? One of her friends?"

"No, it's her man. She had to have surgery."

"Get the information from Leana. I still have to wait for Ms. Bates. Are you on your way back here?"

"I didn't know if you wanted to go to the hospital or not. Um, yeah I'll come back, did Scott show up?"

"I forgot to page you. He was only here long enough to connect his father to this mess. I'll explain it when you get here."

"His father? I can't believe the way this so-called cold case is running us around. Be there in a few."

Chapter Twenty-Five

Mona didn't think twice about not speaking with Damien since Kendra's mishap. She had put off her work, devoting her attention to a friend. There was no immediate need to return the calls left on her service. She had plans for Jay and Candice. Candice would have to be with Kendra to assure she wouldn't spoil anything.

The weekend was near, and Friday would be perfect for the man who loved playing on a woman's emotions. She hoped she wouldn't have to tell Damien no if he invited her out. She had grown accustomed to those dates. He hadn't called and unlike the way she felt during her other relationships, she didn't have the time to dwell on his reasons.

She checked her messages again hoping Jay had returned her call. She prayed for him as she had all her victims. Jay needed to say he was apologizing for not returning the call. He also needed to apologize to Kendra, no beg her to forgive him. After all it was his fault that she was slashed from the top of her ear to her chin, an ugly mark she would wear even after it healed. The doctor said it would take another skin graph to repair the area and bring back a beautiful blend to match the rest of her face. There was no discussion of the emotional scarring that would remind her she had been assaulted. She would be resting home until the second surgery was complete. Candice and Mona visited her daily. She wasn't talking much, and eating was painful. Her friends and family were keeping her company. There was little room for loneliness or depressive thoughts.

Mona left Candice at the hospital chatting with Kendra, who didn't say much but nodded her head in response. Mona would grant her friend's wish. After all, she had been there. Jay was another man who was unable to commit; he deserved special attention.

Jay Rands wasn't smart enough to know relationships had limits. Mona decided she'd teach him. She promised Kendra she would bring her a change of clothes. She stopped at Kendra's apartment to see if she could get Jay's address. That's all she needed. His address and his stupidity would be enough for now. The rest would be a headliner for the papers.

The clothes were where Kendra said they would be. She took the time to pack the bag with extra toiletries she thought Kendra would need. She searched through her desk for Jay's phone numbers or an address and found two cards from a florist. The cards, once attached to floral arrangements, were obvious attempts to apologize for missed dates and shortened evenings.

"Excuses," Mona said aloud. "Sorry ass excuses." The thought of Leon's apologies crossed her mind.

"I can't tell you how much I wanted to see you tonight." Leon kissed her hand as Mona sat silent at the table. The waiter poured the wine in the glasses that sat between the couple.

"Leon, can we skip the excuses tonight. It doesn't matter. I understand you're a busy man."

"Yes, anything you say. I just want us to enjoy the time we have together."

"We will. I planned something for us later tonight, and I don't want to spoil the evening. I want to apologize for my reactions. In the past, I've become angry not understanding your work, details of your life and so on. But now I realize, our relationship is not and cannot be a priority for you."

"Oh, but it is," Leon replied putting his hand on hers. Mona was hyp-notizing as she slowly licked the top of her glass, teasing him with her tongue.

"We'll see. If things change tonight, then we'll see."

That was the last conversation they had on the topic. Jay would be harder to convince. If he suspected their meeting would get back to Kendra, Mona was sure he would decline her offer. Her intention was to give him a little time to redeem himself. If he were the typical man, her seduction wouldn't make it easy. It would indeed be a challenge. Jay needed to know Kendra was off limits. His response would determine if his life had any value. Mona already knew he was like the rest, worthless.

She safely tucked Jay's information in her wallet. Near Kendra's phone, she even found Talia's number and address. Mona hoped she wouldn't have to include her. She too was like Kendra, used by a man incapable of telling the truth. She locked the doors and headed to the hospital.

Damien dialed the number again. He couldn't believe there was no answer. He hoped Kendra was alright. He disconnected the call to her cell and dialed her home. After he heard her voice asking the caller to leave a message he wondered if she was still in the hospital.

Kendra was his youngest cousin. He had been a "big brother" to her since she was a child. She had no siblings, and Damien played the role proudly. Since their family makeup included officers from both the military and law enforcement, Kendra was well guarded. He couldn't understand why no one told him about her trouble. He'd have to go to the hospital. Ms. Bates would be at his office shortly; she promised she'd be there by one.

It was close to one when Kendra finally returned his call. "Damien, this is Kendra, you called?" Her voice sounded muffled he was sure she was in pain as she spoke.

"Are you okay? Jeff told me you were hurt. Can you talk?"

"Not much. It hurts, and I want my face to heal correctly. I'll send you a text, and you can text back."

"Are you there with someone? Do you need me to come there?"

"No, I'll be here I think until tomorrow. They're sending me home. I've got another surgery when this heals. I've got friends here, and your mother will be here this evening. My mother will come with her I guess.

I'll be good. Come to the house tomorrow or the next day that will be better."

"Yeah, okay bet. Send me the details later when your company leaves. Did they get who did this? Did the cops come and pick them up?"

"No, they came and got me. I was at her house. Wait for the text. It's beginning to hurt to talk. Don't do anything before you get my text. Okay?"

Damien paused trying to hold his temper. He couldn't understand what he would have to wait for or why there hadn't been an arrest. "Okay, I'll wait for you. Love you, I'll talk to you later."

Jeff entered the office interrupting his thoughts. He threw a manila envelope on the table. Pictures of Kendra's injury became crucial evidence and were immediately added to her complaint. The pictures verified the ugliness of the crime against his cousin. Kendra would need surgery to regain her identity.

"Who did this shit, man? Did they make an arrest?"

"Not according to the reports I read. EMT's answered the call, and no one was at the location with her. She was sitting on the stairs holding her face with a towel. She didn't speak, and they thought she couldn't. They wrote she was in shock. The questioning that followed at the hospital didn't give the officers a clue. The address is the only thing they had. You know; who lived there, why was she there, what exactly was going on? Man, maybe she'll tell you. Another cop went to the house. He's to sit there until someone comes back there. No one has been there since the assault."

"She's going to text me later. Maybe we'll get more from her if she doesn't think I'm looking for a suspect."

"You think it was a robbery attempt?"

"Is that what they said? They didn't take shit Jeff unless you're counting they tried to take half her face off!"

"Alright, I got you. I don't know what they thought. They went there earlier, and no one was there. I guess they thought she stopped there."

"So who gave her the towel? Huh? They can't treat this as some neighborhood gang initiation shit."

"I'm sure they won't. I told them she was your cousin. I'm sure they'll make sure everything is done right."

"Shouldn't be man. That's how we keep getting all of these BS cases. They don't do enough to solve them. Pass them on and mark it done in the public's eye. That's—"

Damien stopped what was beginning to be a rant when Jeff pointed to the outer office.

"Ms. Bates is talking with the secretary," Jeff stated, lowering his voice close to a whisper. "Did you set up your desk for her?"

"Yeah, I'm ready." Damien shook his head as he buttoned the jacket of his suit and straightened his tie.

"What are you doing?" Jeff questioned his partner, perplexed at why he was making such a preparation to see the woman.

"Changing my mood. I don't want to seem angered, especially since it has nothing to do with this case. Call it getting into character."

"Call it weird. Okay, so I'll just listen until you ask if I want to add anything."

Jeff hated the interviews, a process he thought was unnecessary unless they were looking for definite evidence. He thought of Janelle Bates and Celeste Styles as widows after the money. They didn't have anything to add to the investigation. He was sure of it.

Chapter Twenty-Six

Janelle was asked to take a seat. While waiting for the detectives, her phone vibrated signaling she had received a call. The simple message, "He called" brought on instant anxiety. She read the message again as though the second reading would bring her clarity. She typed in her abbreviated response, *"WTH? I'm with the detectives now. Tyson asked to meet with me. He'll probably call you too. Did he say anything about payment?"*

There was no response prior to the hand signal from Porter to enter the office. She placed the phone in her purse and followed his directions. The detectives were well dressed and certainly looked the part of government officials. It may have been her imagination, but there was a slight delay in pleasantries as the officers gave her the same observation. She was sure that her apparel met their approval. Janelle didn't know the expected length of time for a widow's mourning, but she no longer looked or felt like grieving. She was sick of the sympathy cards and tired of the calls. She wanted to be free of it all, but if Porter or Tyson had evidence that pointed them in her direction, she needed to know. She and Celeste had played all the "what-if" cards. None included talking with the police again. She sat in the chair Detective Porter indicated was to be her seat. He and Detective Tyson sat at their respective desks.

"Ms. Bates, do you frequent Porto Café?" Tyson questioned, surprising both Janelle and Porter. "There's no need to pretend that you don't know more than you're telling or are willing to tell."

"Or can tell," Porter interjected. "Do you know the owner Russell Bearman and his son Scott?" Jeff followed his partner's lead.

Janelle felt her temperature rising. She didn't want to panic, but fear was creeping upon her. *'What did they know and who told them?'* Answers flooded her thoughts as she tried to respond calmly.

"Yes, I know the owner. I don't know the son. I've seen him when I've had lunch there."

"So how often have you gone there or talked to Russell?"

"I think he's retired now, so I don't see him often. It's just a restaurant where I enjoy the people, and the food."

Tyson passed the pictures to her. "You were there the other night with Ms. Styles. I didn't know the two of you were close or should I say you've gotten closer since the deaths of your husbands."

"Do you mean the murders, the untimely demise? How tacky, detective. Two widows find a connection to help each other through this mess, and you find it as a clue, a lead? A lead to what? You and your boys are still digging, and we are your lead? Well Inspector Gadget, wrong. We didn't have anything to do with the death of our husbands. My business is still functioning, and Rusty, I mean Russell, does business with me. No concern for an audit, a search, or any suspicions. Networking detective, my husband is gone. I have to pick up where he left off. It's just business."

"Okay if it's all business, may I ask what his involvement is? For that matter what does Ms. Styles do for your business? This connection may lead us to a killer who tied the businesses together."

"You're asking the wrong one. He's my client. I can't tell you what the connection is. When Leon died, was killed, he was meeting with Rusty regarding some finances paid and unpaid. That's all I'm willing to say. You want more, get a subpoena. Ms. Styles found records where her husband was dealing with him as well. I'm sure he was an investor of some sort, but I haven't spoken to him yet. I'm not denying I know him, business only."

Janelle had regained more than her composure. Tyson was sure she would ask for a lawyer if they pushed her any further. She wasn't a suspect.

"It seems strange you're not on any of the surveillance tapes. Just that night. Does he come to your office for business meetings?" Porter smiled, pleased he caught her off guard.

"You're fishing detective. Let me make this clear for you. My husband did the business and the networking. Here, there, traveling, you know? I picked up after his death because I had to. I'm tying loose ends just like you're trying to tie them. Following my lead will get you nowhere. If I knew who was involved, I would have said so."

Janelle stood, an indication the interrogation had ended. She continued as she adjusted her wrinkled skirt.

"If I find the killer before you do, I'll call. Don't call me with this hunt and peck procedure you've developed again. Believe me, my lawyers will eat you alive. Never mind the stress and aggravation you're putting me through each time you contact me. Let it fade away that's what your unit is right? Those faded cases of the past, the cold cases. Those the officers can't solve." She pointed to the files. "You just keep them hanging around only to find there is nothing in them. Funny just like Leon to still be the topic when there's nothing left to say."

Chapter Twenty-Seven

Jay dialed Kendra's number again. He had no other way to get in touch with her. The fear of the police lurking around her room kept him away. It had been a few days since he attempted to contact her. She still wouldn't answer or return his calls. He was sure she would answer now since he saw he missed her call earlier in the day. Maybe she had come around and was willing to talk without pressing charges on Talia.

Talia called immediately after the incident. She blamed him. She thought she had been set up. Jay tried to explain he planned on being there, but he got called into a meeting. There was no time to warn her and quite frankly he didn't think Kendra would show up. Talia hung up the phone as he explained how busy he was; that conversation was two days ago. He didn't know what to do. The fear of being questioned by the police for a catfight had him rattled. He had no idea how bad Kendra's injuries were. The hospital wouldn't release any details. The phone rang causing him to take a deep breath as he prepared for the worse.

"Jay, this is Mona, you don't know me, but I'm a friend of Kendra's." Mona was making one last attempt to contact him by phone. She was pleased he answered. Her next attempt would have been to meet him in his office downtown.

"Hey, she's mentioned you and—"

"Candice, I would think we'd be the ones she talked about." Mona frowned and rolled her eyes. She didn't know how long she had before Kendra would be out of the shower. She said she felt filthy and left Mona to set up the couch for her to relax afterward. A perfect time to get Jay on the phone.

"Listen, I was wondering if we could talk. Not like this, maybe meet somewhere. Kendra is hurting here mentally and physically, and I wanted to talk to you before this gets really bad."

"Before what gets bad?" Jay couldn't believe it would get any better talking to someone else.

"Well, she wants you and your little girlfriend in jail. I mean, why should you go to jail for something you didn't do?"

The silence on the phone was taking up time.

"Jay, I can talk her out of this, but I need to see you. I want to hear your side of this mess."

"Yeah, yeah, okay. Let me talk to Kendra, she can't be thinking about putting me in jail for a fight she started. She went to that girl's house."

"You sent her there. She wanted to get with you. Listen we can talk about this when I see you. How about eight at the Diner in Maplewood, tomorrow night?"

"I've got something to do tomorrow night. How about five in the afternoon?"

"Okay great. See you there. You know where it is right?"

"Yeah, Springfield Ave. How will I know you?"

"Ask at the counter, I'll let them know. If you get there first, I know you."

"Wow, okay I'll be there."

Mona hung up just as she heard the shower water shut off. She promised Kendra she would stay with her until she began to doze.

"Girl I had a ton of dirt on me," Kendra said barely speaking above a whisper. She had on her pajamas with a towel wrapped around her head. She massaged her head gently and patted her face. "The dampness feels so good on my face, the pills don't do anything for this throbbing. I have to be careful of these stitches, but I want to scrub my face too. Are you okay?"

Mona stood near the couch amazed at the jagged stitches on Kendra's face. It was the first time she saw Kendra's scars. "You are going to bandage the … stitches again, right?" She hoped she didn't offend her friend but the scars, swelling, and redness was a repulsive sight.

Kendra rewrapped the towel around her head. "The doctor said to put the medication on it at night. He didn't say cover it unless I was going out. I won't be going out with this look. Oh hell no." She tried to smile when she noticed Mona still staring. "Boo!"

Mona flinched and shook her head. "Girl put something over the scars. You don't want to rub them against your pillow, or bed. I'm sure that would hurt and yea it's a scary sight. That bitch needs his ass whopped."

"Yeah, she better not let me catch her ass. His ass? Who? Jay? I don't want to think about his ass. He'll answer to the cops. He sent me there, knowing what she would do. It was a setup Mona, and I fell for it. I'm done with his ass. He can't apologize his way out of this."

"Well, he'll pay for it." Mona didn't want to continue talking about his penance. She would be sure he'd say a prayer or two before it was over.

"I'll cover up before I go to bed. It feels a little better without all that gauze and tape. It just reminds me how stupid I was. Hell, Mona, it will be months before these marks heal."

"I know baby. Your emotions will take longer to heal. The doctor assured you he'd restore your face, right?" Mona put her fingers on her friend's lips keeping Kendra from responding. "Hush, it will all be taken care of, just promise me you won't be looking to fall for his sorry—"

"I know, excuses. There's nothing he can say. I'm done. Whew, I think I've talked too much for now. Pain is rising, and my skin is tightening. Pass me those pills and that glass of water."

The conversation ended, and the two watched a movie that lasted longer than Kendra's eyes could stay open. Mona locked the door behind her as she left.

Chapter Twenty-Eight

"So he didn't ask any other questions?" Janelle couldn't believe the conversation was as short as Celeste made it seem.

"He wanted to know had we talked to the detectives, of course. I told him I was supposed to talk with them, but I canceled at the last minute."

"You canceled? Did they ask you why? I mean that may make them suspicious."

"Janelle, they can't suspect anything, we didn't do anything. You've got to stop being so paranoid. I don't have to answer their questions unless I want to. I'm not a suspect, and they don't have enough to hold me, even if they thought I was. Girl, they would have questioned us long before this cold case detective got the files. It's an open shut case. Our husbands are dead, and they don't know who did it and neither do we."

Celeste replied hoping not to be questioned again about her fears. She contacted a friend, a paralegal who was more than willing to tell her why there was a re-investigation of the case and who was pushing to find the killers. Her fears heightened until what she knew was confirmed. The families of both men were looking to cash in. Neither Celeste nor Janelle was willing to include them in whatever the deceased left behind.

"So you told him you didn't talk to the detectives, and that leaves me where?"

"What do you mean? Look, Janelle, we didn't pay him, and he's not asking. I don't know why he asked about the detectives and at this point I don't care. I spoke with him, and that was it. That's what you were worried about right, paying him, right?"

"Yeah, yeah, you're right. I'm just worried—"

Celeste cut her off. "Too much. Listen, sweetie, we're in the clear. Like I said whoever, man, woman, lover or hater, they did me a favor and saved me money. I don't care. I'm in town to straighten out this business and then this town can kiss me where the sun don't shine."

"Humph, I only wish. I'd like to know who did it."

"For what, to thank them? You already said you wanted Leon dead. Whatever, karma heard, and it answered. As far as your detective friends, they'll have to catch me next trip. I'm leaving Thursday. Are we still having lunch?"

Janelle hung up wondering if she wanted to continue her relationship with Celeste. While enraged with her husband's behavior, she wanted him to feel her pain. She wanted him to understand what she was going through while he loved another. Over the years, the thought of setting him up was a dream. Now that he was dead she felt guilty. Someone made her dream a reality, and she was scared.

Celeste agreed to stay until the weekend. Janelle told her she didn't want a quick lunch before saying goodbye. The ladies met at a few dinners, dedications, and other business events two years before the affairs and indiscretions became their conversations. They had an instant connection that neither would admit then which took them beyond false smiles and pleasantries. Unlike Janelle, Celeste had the connections and the plan. It was her reality, and she lived it day after day.

Janelle didn't understand how Celeste could move on with her life knowing she could be a potential suspect in the murders. Janelle felt trapped. She thought once Leon was dead her fears would die with them. Now she could only imagine if it had been their hired killer how many restless nights would have followed.

Celeste was right. Their plan to have the husbands killed was handled by someone else — someone with no attachment to them. Janelle was firm with Tyson, but she feared the cold case investigation wouldn't end because of the questions she faced. Detective Tyson was relentless, and the wives were on his list of suspects. As an afterthought, she should have canceled her appointment. She said a prayer as she drove home.

Chapter Twenty-Nine

"Returning to the resort may have been a mistake." Mona wrote the sentence in her journal and stared at the words. No one acted as though it was unusual for her to be there without reservations. After the complimentary breakfast, she didn't mind the wait. The tour would start to begin soon. The Pine Ridge Resort hosted free tours for those seeking an upcoming stay.

When asked why she didn't complete the tour on her previous visit. She simply said her boyfriend got sick, and they decided she should return today for the rest of the tour. She explained she had seen the video during the previous appointment. After the charming unknowing guide, couldn't convince her to join the group, she was added to the list with no further questions. He handed her a packet and a map and let her out of the conference room. Mona had no intention of completing the tour with them. After all she just needed a reason to get on the grounds and roam on her own.

She smiled and nodded good morning to the staff she passed after the group left the spa, pool and exercise area. During this time, the group of chattering couples was allowed to browse through the area freely. Mona took the opportunity to step out into the garden. Looking across the manicured lawn, she could see the individual suites where the guest stayed. She had no idea how she would get near where she, Leon, and Kevin stayed. Her intent was to take Jay there. After all it proved to be the perfect setting. Now staring at her words on paper, she knew the murders were taunting her.

Mona continued to write as she remembered the tour guide tapping her on her shoulder. *"We're moving on, are you okay?" The young man asked. He couldn't have been more than twenty years old.*

"The grounds are beautiful. I'm not into the exercise thing, but I love walking with nature." Mona smiled, as she lied, hoping he wouldn't ask why she left the group again.

"Well, we'll be touring the grounds as well as viewing a few of the suites." His smile was infectious. Mona smiled as she teased herself with the thought of having sex with a twenty-year-old. They walked back inside to join the others.

Mona put the pen down. Her daily entries needed to change. The therapeutic resolve was no longer working, if it ever had. She still had the desire to rid the world of those that used women. She wouldn't write about Jay until the task was complete. After the tour, she was sure she'd return to Pine Ridge Resorts with him for a weekend stay. She'd tell him no one would interrupt them there. It could and would be worth his time. After all, he didn't want the police to think he was taunting Kendra by romancing her friend. They would take in the night entertainment, and she'd express her desire to stay. Booking for the weekend would be easy. She was a premium cardholder with no reason for anyone to suspect her return. She was confident they would be blind to the obvious. Pine Ridge Resorts was the perfect place for cheaters.

She closed her eyes wishing there was another way. She'd have to be careful. There were no calls from anyone thinking the woman, the feature story on all channels, involved her. Seeing her face on the news thrilled her. She had gotten away with murder more than once. Jay would be a bonus.

The phone rang bringing her out of deep thought. "Hey, are you watching the news." Candice rushed the words causing a chill to run down Mona's spine.

Mona turned the television to breaking news. The police were updating the information on The Pine Ridge Resort murders. The Chief of Police, Sal Michaels, confirmed there was no new evidence, but the Cold Case Division of the Department would continue to seek any information.

"Sounds like they're appeasing the public. Probably a demand from the resort so people wouldn't be scared to stay there."

"Candice, most people go there with someone they know. I wouldn't be surprised if they found out the wives had a hit out on them for cheating."

"Girl you think the wives did it? Kendra said she thought it was a hit, but the wives paying for a hit? Wow, something right out of the movies, huh?"

"Yep, enough drama that's for sure," Mona replied sarcastically. "How is Kendra today? I meant to call her."

"She's good. Her family is visiting her today, so I didn't bother her."

"Oh, great. I didn't know she had any close relatives."

"An aunt, and cousins, she didn't say who, just that she'd talk to me later. Mona, do you think she'll have to have another surgery. I mean, that's got to be on her mind every time she looks in the mirror. You know, that's a lifetime souvenir from her boyfriend's lover."

"Ex-boyfriend. They both need the same punishment."

"Who?"

"Candice, really? Jay and Talia. They need to pay for what they did."

"Is Kendra pressing charges?"

"I don't know. Ask her. I don't care what her answer is they need to pay for her pain."

"Mona, if she wants to let it go, what can anyone else do?"

"Karma, Candice, karma. What goes around, how you treat people, determines your fate. Let's just say that Jay's fate is sealed."

"Jay didn't do it, though."

"Well he set her up, that's just as bad as using the blade. Talia will get hers too. Karma has its way of paying unfavorable debts."

"I guess you're right. Well, what's on your agenda today?" Candice interjected before Mona could continue to rant.

"I've got an afternoon appointment."

"Well, I'm going for a pedi. So we'll talk later. If you go to see Kendra, let me know."

Mona hung up the phone and sighed. She picked up her pen again to record another thought. The staff would remember her for sure if she returned during a weekday. Check in would have to be late Friday. There would be different staff there on the weekend. She never noticed the woman at the concierge desk watching her.

She called Damien leaving another message and decided she didn't need to heighten her suspicions or her anger. He hadn't returned her call after canceling their weekend arrangements. Another weekend was quickly approaching. She told him she understood but during the tour and now as she left her apartment, she wondered was she overlooking something in their relationship.

Since Kendra's accident, she'd willingly admit she wasn't as available as she had been. Mona had become accustomed to his afternoon calls and Friday night dinners. Now no calls and no return calls. Something was up. Before she could let her, thoughts diminish her mood the phone rang.

"Hey babe, I'm sorry I didn't pick up the phone when you called. Are you home?"

"Hey, yourself. I thought I was put on a shelf or something. Where have you been?" Mona caught herself. She wanted her relationship with Damien to remain different. She could feel internal irritation building inside.

"Family drama. My cousin had an accident, and I've been dealing with that for a minute. Truly, my lady, I am sorry. I did call you yesterday. I can't say that was an everyday excuse, as a matter of fact, I don't and won't give you an excuse. There is none that would suffice. I should have kept in touch. Will you allow me to make it up?"

"I can think of a few ways."

"How about some we time? I could use a break from family and the job. Can you get away for a few hours or overnight?"

An overnight stay with Damien, she couldn't refuse. They agreed he would pick her up Saturday night about eight. That would give her time to unwind after talking with Jay.

Chapter Thirty

Rusty Bearman was older than he looked. At sixty-five he could have been mistaken for fifty. His love for the restaurant was second to his love for making fast deals. Real estate was on the top of the list, and he dabbled at the horse races. It was his choice to back away from the daily customers, but his family thought it was a medical setback. A close call one Monday morning instantly stopped his cigar smoking and drinking. Now a year later he still hadn't returned to the daily routine of running the restaurant that kept his family in New Jersey.

He shared with his wife and son his desire to leave the business but neither believed he would. After spending his time with some old friends, most who had been in and out of businesses, fast money and under the table deals, Rusty was reliving his early days. He came and went out of town on pre-determined "business" trips, and got his hands dirty most evenings settling the score for a few associates. Nancy Bearman didn't argue about his newly adopted way of life. She filed for a divorce and had no desire to "collect the benefits" from his rise to success. Rusty moved out willing to give her whatever she wanted.

Scott's knowledge of the "business" was vague. He was told to answer the phones and pass the messages. He didn't tell him about Detective Tyson's visits, but now he had to tell him about the request. He hoped this would lead to his father telling him who the women were. There was a connection between his father, the women, and now the murders, or so the police thought. Scott knew his father was well protected, but for the first time Scott was scared.

Rusty got the call from his son early that morning. He told him all he knew including the message from the detectives. Rusty laughed and told him he'd stop to see him at the restaurant. It was after lunch and his father hadn't called. Scott hoped the message didn't give his father a reason to leave town.

The voices at the bar got loud, and Scott felt instant relief hearing the customers call his father's name.

"Rusty, man where have you been, Florida?" The laughter bellowed until the next question came from the crowd. "No, he finally found his way back home, c'mon where you been man?" Laughter erupted as they shook hands and patted him on his back. Rusty made his way to the end of the bar where Scott stood smiling.

"Hey Dad, I thought you forgot about coming by."

"No, I made a few calls to be sure this questioning mess didn't include me."

"Well, does it?" Scott lowered his voice and waited for the answer.

"No, Scott, I'm good. You're good. Nothing to do with us. I'll call that Detective and get this straight. I don't know nothing about this case or the murders." The older man looked at his son and saw the worry on his face.

"C'mon, your old man ain't that dumb boy. We don't leave a mess."

Rusty smiled and waved to a few customers at the billiards table.

"Dad, do you have that kind of connection with those women?"

"Nah, that business comes and goes. Their husbands had some dealings with me, and now, well let's just say they had business elsewhere."

"Bad business. It left both of them dead. I don't know that the word coincidence would fit the situation. Looks dirty dad, dirty."

"Somebody else has the dirt on their hands." Rusty laughed as he walked to the cash register. "When it comes to that kind of business you keep clean hands. Listen, I've got another call to return, and I'm out of here. You're doing a great job son, better than me.

"Dad, handle this." He looked for his father's reaction. "Seriously."

"Seriously, I'll stop at the Detective's office before I leave town tomorrow."

The older man hadn't given a second thought about contacting any Detective. The news media gave him all the information he needed. After calling Celeste, he understood. The police were stumped. There was no one to pin the murder on, and the pressure from the resort was upon them. After all, they had paid their way with yearly campaign contributions and discounts to the Police Department. His connections hadn't been called to do the job. Rusty was impressed with the killer's work; it was clean. He told Celeste to catch her flight and enjoy the freedom she desired. There would be no need for them to be in touch until the smoke cleared. Celeste thanked him as the call ended with him promising to handle Detective Tyson's persistence.

He decided to stop by the station on his way home. He didn't want to ruin the start of his travels for the weekend with suspicions. As he pulled in the parking lot of the police station, he realized he hadn't called to inform the Detective he would be stopping in. He knew the station well. Over the years, he frequented the offices for one reason or another. He didn't recognize Detective Damien Tyson's name, but he was sure he crossed his path at one time or another. He waved at the Desk Sergeant, who smiled without hesitation.

"Rusty Bearman, how are you? Don't tell me we got one of your boys here again."

"Nah and they better not be. It ain't that easy no more. I remember when a phone call would open the gate."

"Yeah, we ain't got the key no more, that's for sure."

"Detective Tyson, where's his office?"

"Wow, cold case Tyson? Go on up to the second floor; his office is on the right. The door is marked Homicide Unit."

"Thanks, Richards, tell your family I asked about them. Call me so we can have them at the restaurant one night." Rusty started toward the elevator.

"Yeah, that'll work. Good seeing you."

The office wasn't hard to find. The gold letters on the frosted windows were more than enough assistance for lost visitors. Rusty smiled as he passed the office window that read "booking." He was pleased that he hadn't been in that office for more than a year. Avoiding the courtroom drama became his intention after his last arrest. He never did what was considered "serious time", but the process was enough. His "boys", as Officer Richards called them, hadn't been arrested either. As he turned the knob to the door labeled Records, he was startled by an officer who was exiting.

"Excuse me, sir, can I help you?"

Rusty was scanning the busy office. Continuous chatter filled the air. There were six desks outlining the room. There was no designated space, however, each Detective was obviously territorial. The office had changed since his last visit. He remembered being questioned in the same office. He answered slowly, trying to recall faces and names.

"Yeah man, I'm looking for Tyson. I got a call to see him here."

"Second door on the right. They'll help you there."

The Detective waited until Rusty moved in the direction of the office before continuing. Rusty was offered a cup of coffee and told to have a seat. It was fifteen minutes before Porter opened the office door and invited Rusty inside. The pictures that were on Tyson's desk were no longer on display. The detectives decided to see how much information Rusty had on the wives or the mystery lady before including him in the investigation.

Rusty stepped through the door and surveyed the room. It was impressively neat. Although there were stacks of paperwork and files,

Rusty concluded the detectives didn't work hard at all. There were aisles of metal files, boxes and shelves that held more "cold cases" in the back of the room. The old man assumed the job was obviously the spot for an officer who couldn't handle the crime on the streets.

He immediately recognized Tyson, the detective that often spoke on the news regarding cases that were solved years later. Porter didn't jar his memory at all. As the younger detective pointed to a seat near his desk, Rusty was sure television wasn't the only place he had seen Tyson.

"Mr. Bearman, I'm Detective Porter, and this is Detective Tyson. We're investigating a murder that happened at the Pine Ridge Resort. Now this murder may be tied to two others so our questions may also be regarding an earlier timeline." Porter suggested they question his knowledge of the three men; maybe he knew all of them. Each man seemed to be connected in some way by their line of business.

Tyson wasn't sure about Raymond Murphy's murder being tied with the others, but it was worth a try. He would question Mr. Bearman after Porter was done. He was sure he was tied to a few killings. He remembered seeing him somewhere but was unsure why he didn't remember his name.

The questioning began. Porter asked about time and places where Bearman had been on the dates of each of the murders. It took him a moment to answer, but he had places and names of people that could confirm he was there. It seemed rehearsed to Tyson, but he allowed his partner to continue with his questions.

"Mr. Bearman, let me say this, so you understand." Porter's patience was wearing thin.

"Oh, I understand. You guys don't have anyone to pin what, three murders on, and you call me? Why is that Detective Tyson?" Bearman questioned, as he turned in his seat to face Tyson.

"Sir, I assure you, with your background we would have called you first if it was a mere assumption. The wives of these men deserve to know who killed their husbands. It seems that they or someone else has or had a connection with you. Why Mr. Bearman? Why wouldn't we question you and anyone else that may be connected in any way? Detective Porter and I are doing a job that's it. If you're uncomfortable with being questioned, you're free to go, but you'll need a lawyer when you're called back."

Tyson's tone was stern. Rusty Bearman recalled where he knew Tyson from after hearing his baritone voice. He had testified and given evidence in a few of the cases where he paid a hefty fine for his connections and indiscretions. Porter continued as he placed pictures of the wives on the desk in front of them. The display included the still shot, from the television, of the woman whose face was covered with a scarf.

Rusty took his time. It was obvious he knew the wives he wouldn't lie about it. It was the picture of the woman who obviously didn't want anyone to recognize her that peaked his interest. *Could she be a person that was connected?*

"I know the wives if that's what you thought I would deny. This one is not the wife of the other guy, uh Raymond's wife. You don't have a picture of her here. Who is she?"

"Mr. Bearman did any of the women contact you?" Porter ignored Bearman's question.

"No, not until a few days after the deaths. They wanted to know about the business I had with their husband. I was, let's say a consultant for them."

"Let's say more than that Mr. Bearman. What kind of consultant? Why would the wives need to contact a consultant after their husband's death?"

"Listen, you should ask them. My son took the message; I called them back. We talked about the business their husbands had with me, and that was it. No harm, no foul and damn sure no murder. We didn't even talk before they were dead so how could I be involved."

"Did they mention they were worried about insurance, or the business?"

"Naw, man, I didn't have no connections with insurance. The business they had with me was connections with other contractors who could work on properties quickly. They flipped homes, well sometimes they did; they did renovations and sales. I invested sometimes and sometimes I would give them contractors who were looking for work. I told the wives who the contractors were. You know, they may have owed a few of them. Connections that's all."

"Yeah you said that." Porter was frustrated. It seemed to be another dead end.

"Mr. Bearman, your son indicated that you needed to come here to talk with us. He stated your life may depend on it. What would make him say that if there was no harm as you say or no foul? I mean he had me thinking that you and the wives may be in some trouble." Tyson couldn't wait for the answer. "I understand they didn't contact you until after the murder. Maybe the job was done, and you didn't need to make any connections for them. After all, you knew more than they knew, didn't you?"

"About the business, yes I did. I doubt if they knew who or what deals were made. That's it, just the business. If there was someone who had it in for these guys, it wasn't the people I know or me. Hell, we made money as long as they were making deals happen. You know real estate is a big thing, especially flipping houses. Man, you'd be surprised the money—"

"Mr. Bearman." Tyson stood and walked around his desk. "You don't have to paint a picture unless you want to erase the image I have of you and those women setting up the murders of their husbands. Look we didn't tell your son to give you the message on a mere whim. So let's not play games."

Tyson turned to his desk and picked up two papers. He handed them to Rusty.

"Those are phone records, Mr. Bearman. They've called you at the restaurant on several occasions. Mr. Bearman, before the murders. Both wives called you from their personal cell phones before the dates of the deaths. You know what that tells me?"

"It doesn't tell you who killed them; that's for sure. It doesn't tell you I had anything to do with the murders. So they called me. Business calls, I told you that. Whatever we talked about was about the business."

"Mr. Bearman, don't leave town. We may need to talk again." Tyson took the papers from Rusty's hands and returned to his desk.

Rusty stood to leave when Porter asked another question.

"You said you didn't know the woman with the scarf. What's your interest in who she is? Do you know why she was in your restaurant seeing the husbands?"

Rusty shrugged his shoulders. "I guess she had business with them. I've never seen her before. I just asked because I knew she wasn't one of the wives."

"So is there anyone that may have had business with them that turned bad. You mentioned deals were made. Did all your deals go well?"

"No problems that I know of. Listen you're spinning wheels here. Look for this pretty woman here. She may have some answers for you. Looks like she went out of her way to cover herself."

"We're on it, Mr. Bearman. You know your way out right?"

Rusty Bearman didn't wait for any handshakes. He opened the office door before making a final comment.

"I don't think they'll be another reason for me to talk to you. Gentleman, you can reach me on my cell, not my son. Leave him out of this mess. We've got a business to run, and I don't need him working scared. Our customers are just that, customers. If cops begin to show up too often, and I lose business, that could present a problem."

He closed the door behind him before Tyson or Porter could answer.

Chapter Thirty-One

Rusty Bearman left Porter and Tyson with thoughts they would share later. It was after four, a long day that ended the way it began.

"Well without going into the details, we're at another dead end," Porter stated without looking up from the paper's he was sorting through.

"You're right, but you know what? I'm going to get out of here, and we'll talk about it in the morning. My mind is going back and forth with these statements and the reactions. Somebody knows something, and I think Mr. Bearman is the center of it. Why would he worry about us just asking questions? This is not my first encounter with this dude. I've got to clear my head, though, before I say for sure, but he knows more than what he's saying."

"Tyson, they all do. He's had problems in the past with his crew. Assaults, weapons, and probably a few murders we haven't solved. This could be one. Phone calls before the murders and after that alone says something was up."

"You're right Jeff but as he said, it doesn't prove murder."

Damien cleared his desk, leaving only a few of the unlabeled folders stacked in the center.

"I'm out my brother. Listen, I'll be in after I check on Kendra. I called a few times and didn't get an answer. So I'll see you in the a.m."

"Hey, are you in town this weekend?"

"I don't have plans to go anywhere. I'm taking Mona out and hopefully she'll stay at my place."

"Well, hey, that makes a good weekend. I'll see you in the morning. Give Kendra my regards. Hope they caught whoever did that to her."

"Yeah, speak to your girl Leana and see if she knows anything or better yet ask Amir to ask her. She might give him more details."

Jeffrey didn't know what he meant by more. His non-verbal response let Damien know he would give him any new information she had. Damien picked up his keys off the desk and the phone rang. He looked at his partner as Jeff picked up the phone.

"Porter. Ms. Sayers, how are you?" Jeff smiled knowing the call was for Tyson.

Damien put down his satchel and took his seat. He waited for Jeff's pleasantries that were obviously scripted before he picked up the line.

"Good afternoon Ms. Sayers, I suppose you're looking for me."

"How did you guess? C'mon I know you have something to give me."

"The department is still investigating the case. There may be a connection between the three murders, but that's not conclusive. I will be speaking with the big wigs tomorrow afternoon and shortly after there will be a press conference. You are the first to hear this so act as though you don't know. I won't be there so don't look for me. Direct your questions to the Captain or those appointed who will give you details about the findings. Ms. Sayers, there's not much to go on."

"Will they say that or will they lie and lead the public on?"

"I hope they'll tell the truth and ask people to call the hotline with any information they may have."

"Really? The hotline? Who would know anything about a murder at the resort? Okay, you're right you don't have anything."

"I told you this one is not cut and dry."

"Are you saying that the Resort murders can be classified as murders well done?"

"Ms. Sayers, there's no such thing as a well done murder, or a perfect murder. Eventually something will break, something we didn't expect or—"

"Something your people missed detective? Can I quote you on that?"

"No those are your words. Listen, save your theory and questions for the press conference. I'm sure it will clear up a few things."

"Well, this is definitely enough to raise questions. Is Ms. Bates coming down on the department for answers? I mean she should want to know who did this. Are the other murders connected to this one?"

"Possibly, that's another angle we're looking into. At this point we don't have any evidence that connects them other than the location."

"The woman they've been showing on the television, do you know who she is?"

"A person of interest."

The reporter sighed. She hoped for more than speculations. She promised she would have a headline story for the Village Post by the end of the week.

"Well Detective, I guess I'll call you after the press conference."

"No doubt Ms. Sayers, I'll expect your call."

Tyson felt his partners stare as he cradled the receiver. His gestures were well read. Neither detective thought much of the media. Often they added problems to an investigation. It would be only a matter of time before they would use the "no comment" rule. As he headed toward the office door, he said his farewell.

Chapter Thirty-Two

Jay arrived at the diner five minutes before Mona walked in. He was glad she was on time, and he hoped she would explain Kendra's need for revenge. He tried speaking with Talia, but she was as angry as Kendra. Kendra and Talia thought they had been set up.

He needed to tell his side of the story to someone. Mona had expressed she was neutral. He would talk to her before being questioned by the police. Talia assured him that they would want to talk to him since she would include him in her statement. The conversation ended abruptly. Jay's apology was entwined with the dial tone.

Mona spotted Jay and immediately felt a chill. The prelude of another kill was taking over. He was a good-looking guy. His full lips and small eyes gave her a rush. She smiled thanking the hostess who walked her to the table. She was certain not to overdress for their first meeting. Her jeans and stilettos fit her well, and she purposely wore a blouse that accentuated her cleavage. Her make-up was flawless, and the highlights of her eye shadow drew attention to her features.

Jay stood smiling. He instantly took her hand guiding her around the table to her seat. He knew his attraction to her was sexual. The throbbing in his pants would soon be an erection. The waitress wasted no time arriving with the menus as they said "hello." They ordered sodas, agreeing it was too early for any alcohol. They decided to share an appetizer, neither feeling hungry they smiled as they stated in unison, "that will be all." Each gave the other a quick glance as they adjusted themselves in their seats.

"So, Mr. Rands, how did your day go?"

"I've been on edge all day, but otherwise okay. Have we met before? I mean other than speaking to you today on the phone, I don't remember meeting you or seeing you with Kendra."

"No, but I've heard quite a bit about you."

Jay wanted to smile but thought better of it due to the circumstances. He sipped on the glass of water as he felt his body heat rise. He couldn't understand why he was nervous. Mona waited for his response, getting none; she continued.

"I thought you and Kendra were good. I'm a little upset I didn't meet you sooner, I may have wanted to test the waters." She teased.

Jay tried not to show his confusion. He looked into her eyes and realized their meeting may have been her fantasy. He allowed his ego to take over. Maybe Kendra had shared their impromptu lovemaking episodes. Those times were filled with fantasy and pleasure. He let down his guard, and Mona read his narcissistic flaw immediately.

"Brothers like you are hard to find. But tell me what the hell happened? I mean, why would you get tangled in that squabble between two women you obviously were pleasing?"

Jay took a moment before answering. He couldn't read her motive. He couldn't contain a slight grin of confidence.

"Kendra knows me better than that…"

"Better than what Jay?" Mona injected. "You were screwing Talia behind her back. So what did Kendra know better? Certainly not your behavior."

"Whoa, I don't know what she told you. We were on the outs when, well, Talia and I got together a few times. Talia knew about me and Kendra trying to work things out. We had a project at work and—"

"And she wound up in your bed. Quite cozy, and I can see why. I mean you've got to be packing." She whispered. "Listen, I just want to know what to tell my girl. I mean if Talia cut her while in a bitch rage… Well I'm sure Kendra can handle her own, but if you set her up, man that's foul. I'd have to put my own curiosity to the side. I don't play those games."

Jay was caught between the mixed messages. *Did she come to defend Kendra or try him for herself?* He didn't want to be forward but looking across the table, her breast seemed to be calling his name.

"So why are you here? Did Kendra actually tell you to talk to me?"

"Let's just say I share her pain. She's hurting, and it's more than physical. I just want to know what your part in all this is. Kendra was in love with you and this assault was her happily ever after?" Mona's anger was mounting.

The waitress interrupted their conversation placing the Buffalo wings, celery and dressing between them. She asked would there be anything else. The pair flashed fake smiles as they said no.

"I didn't get involved with Talia to hurt Kendra. I know it sounds lame but Kendra and I just weren't making it. I knew it but she wanted to stay in touch. We were dating once a month if that and sex was out of the question if I didn't wine, dine, or give a gift. C'mon, I'm a man. What the hell was I supposed to do? I didn't set her up. I told her to bring my keys and I'd return hers. I just didn't get there in time."

Mona heard enough. His demeanor was sickening.

"So you don't feel you're responsible at all? Why have her pick up the keys at Talia's house? Do you still have feelings for her?"

Jay had asked himself that more frequently over the past few days. He felt bad that she was assaulted. Talia was wrong, but he knew Kendra. Talia could have been provoked. "I can't really say. I love what we had, but it ain't been the same. Talia and me have something different."

"So you were looking for different? Is that what you needed?" Mona decided to set the bait. "Are you still looking? I mean, you didn't call

Kendra or act like a lover with concerns. Talia has put you out so, I guess she's no longer in the picture. I wish I knew you were willing to play from both ends."

"What do you mean both ends?"

"Jay, don't play the loyal lover. Hell, we could have had a threesome. You, me and Talia of course. I don't think Kendra would have gone for it."

Jay wiped his mouth slowly. He fantasized about licking barbecue sauce from Mona's lips. He had a full erection; she had his attention.

"Before I get into trouble, I thought you were here to hear my side of the story. You said you'd help Kendra understand I wasn't involved in Talia's attack."

"Yes, but you've peaked my interest. What is it that you have that would cause such a vicious fight? I don't know a man that has brought that out in me. To be honest…" She leaned closely to whisper again. "My panties are wet thinking about you treating me to at least one night of pleasure."

She picked up her glass and licked the rim teasing him. "Kendra said you were sexy, but hell there's got to be more. Sounds like she fell for the short end of the stick. I mean Talia didn't care that you were in a relationship. You must be more than enough."

Jay wanted to pay the check and make the next move. Mona had accomplished her goal. He asked the waitress to bring the check.

"You mentioned you had a meeting. I'm sorry we couldn't get together or something…" Mona enticed him with her eyes. He was captured.

"Wait, maybe we can. I mean, you'll still talk to Kendra if we, well I mean if we arranged to meet again right?"

"Baby if you do me like you were obviously doing them, Kendra won't be your problem. She has some healing to do and she'll soon forgive and forget. You said it was over and I'll talk to her about it. She'll soon see things differently and you can move on. It would be best if you don't call her or Talia. After all you don't want to get caught up with the police."

"Yeah I thought about calling Talia again. But—"

"You said you wanted different, you call her again and you'll never know the difference. Let's meet so I can show you the difference I can make. Put this mess behind you and deal with a woman, not a side piece."

"Mona, when can I see you again?" He didn't want to sound desperate, but her teasing had him throbbing again.

"Well, you're a nine to five man. Having my own business has its benefits. Call me next week when you're free. My weekends are quite busy. I want to make our first time special. How about the resorts?"

"The Pine Ridge Resort, in Philly? First time and you want to go there?"

"No expense on your part. I'll set it up for say Wednesday night. They have a jazz special on Wednesdays. Besides, it's not close to home so we won't have to worry about you being seen with me. I don't want someone to go back to Kendra or Talia about seeing us dining together."

"Understood." Jay stood giving her his hand to assist her from her seat. He pulled her in close wanting to feel her pressed against him. She allowed him to put his hand just below her waist. He guided her toward the door. They didn't say anything as they headed to the parking lot.

"So should I call you say Tuesday to confirm?" Jay asked smiling.

"Yes, I'll be expecting your call." Mona got in her car pleased with her catch. She watched Jay walk to his car. He was well worth a one-night stand. She'd do what she did best, and he'd be another page in her journal.

Chapter Thirty-Three

Damien needed to clear his mind before going home. Taking the long route, he could think about the loose ends the case presented, Kendra's issue, and Mona. The first two were cramping his time. The time he wanted to spend building a relationship.

He and Mona had talked and dated longer than he expected. She wasn't pushy and to his surprise, she didn't ask much about his untimely business meetings or missed phone calls. Those questions and answers would cause most of his relationships to dissolve. He couldn't commit, and when he explained, most women just couldn't take a backseat to his job.

He had given up on the long-term relationships, but Mona's personality spoke volumes. She was strong willed and independent. He was certain she wouldn't hesitate to question him if his interest seemed to fade. Damien was more than interested. A revealing talk was part of his plans for the weekend. They hadn't been out even for a quick meal in two weeks. The phone conversations were hit and miss. He didn't want to think of starting over with another.

If he could tell anyone the truth about his career, he thought he could tell her. Jeff asked him when he would tell Mona; he had no answer. He wondered what her response would be and sighed deeply, knowing it was possible the weekend would be their last date.

Kendra was on his mind. As he pulled into his driveway, he thought it might have been better to stop by her house before coming home. He hadn't seen her but from their daily conversations since the attack she assured him she was healing. He wasn't sure. Her mental state was a concern of Damien's and other family members. *Would she survive another breakup?* The question was one of his concerns since her last two relationships didn't end well. He thought about the "desperate" woman that Ms. Sayers described. The thought of his cousin, Kendra, being that woman made him wonder if the others had abused her.

Women, when emotionally pushed, often became dangerous. Damien had investigated heinous crimes over the years only to find a woman was the suspect and was proven guilty. The evidence from the Pine Ridge Resort murders gave him no definite answers. The thought of a woman killing men brought on one question that remained unanswered, why? That was the link that he needed.

Walking through his front door, he immediately removed his suit jacket placing it on the back of his favorite chair. He suppressed the urge to call Mona once he pressed the button on the phone for his messages.

Kendra's voice quivered as she spoke. "Damien, call me when you get in. I'm confused by the questions the officers asked today. I'm not sure what to do. I'll be waiting for your call."

The next call was from Jeffrey. "Hey man, call me. I checked on Kendra's investigation. She hasn't been cooperative with the officers. They don't have much other than the initial reports and a statement from the neighbor of Talia Simmons, the suspect. The woman made the call for help and gave Kendra the towel. Talia Simmons hasn't been back to her place. They're checking out the boyfriend, Jay Rands to see what his involvement may be, but without Kendra's help it may be dropped. Man, the pictures from the hospital are bad. When you go to see her, convince her to press charges. Well, I'll see you in the a.m. later."

There were no other calls. He changed his clothes before dialing Kendra's number. He got her answering machine, hung up, and dialed the number again. She would know it was him. They had developed the code when she was in college. He smiled when he heard her voice.

"Hey, why are they bothering me with stupid questions?"

"Well hello to you too. Who are they, and what questions?"

"Did I know he was dating that chick? What were my intentions? Have I ever threatened his girlfriends before? Hell, I was the girlfriend! I don't think they're trying to find his ass or charge her. Why bother? Just tell me to get well soon and move on to the next case they don't want to solve. I hate sorry cops! Oooh, shit. Hold on."

Damien didn't have the answers she hoped to hear. He had the same questions. He wanted to know what sparked the argument and assault. He'd wait to hear the story.

"Are you still coming this way in the morning?"

"Do you need me to come sooner? What's wrong?" Damien was trying to read her words.

"My face is tight, and I need to put a compress on it. It hurts like hell. I guess that's why they said for me to be on complete bed rest. I'll tell you the rest in the morning."

"Okay, did you get the names of the cops?"

"No, I got badge numbers though and a copy of the police report I filed."

"Get your rest. I'll see you in the morning."

Damien looked at the desk with the paperwork scattered across it. The thought of defeat crossed his mind as he dialed Mona's number. Work would have to wait.

"Hello Damien, what a surprise. I didn't expect to hear from you until tomorrow."

"My mind was drifting, and I found a bit of peace thinking about you. How are you? How'd your day go?"

Mona thought about Jay's smile when she approached the table where they had lunch. "It went better than I thought. I hooked a new client, or at least I think I did. I'll be talking with him again next week."

"Okay business lady, looks like you've been taking the opportunity to network to the next level."

"Networking?"

"I was thinking about when we met. I guess those events bring you a lot of clients."

"You could say that." Mona hadn't thought about networking events being a business opportunity. "It helps pay the bills."

"So what time will you be ready tomorrow? I've got a few thing to handle in the office, but I'll be clear by one I'm sure."

"That's an early start. What plans do you have for us?"

"C'mon now just trust me. New York, dinner and an evening of appreciation."

"Appreciation?" Mona knew the small talk wouldn't last all night. She'd be more than happy to let her hair down. "Hmm.."

"Hmm… What?"

"Just thinking of what I appreciate about you."

"Well, then we can share our thoughts. Can I pick you up about one?"

"Sounds good. I've got a stop to make before we leave. Call me about twelve-thirty and I'll let you know for sure. It won't be much later I promise."

Damien didn't respond, allowing her words to sink in.

"Tyson, you okay?"

"I'm good, sorry reading this paperwork. Ok so call me when you're ready. I've got an errand to run for a family member myself. Listen pack an overnight bag. Saturday I want to go horseback riding, and we can get an early start if you stay here."

"You didn't have to set up an early ride to get me to spend the night." Mona laughed softly; she intended to stay with or without an overnight bag.

Chapter Thirty-Four

"I don't know what I'm going to do. I don't want Jay to be caught up in this bull, but that bitch is gonna pay one way or the other."

The doorbell rang. Damien called earlier to say he was on his way. Kendra hit the buzzer and unlocked her door without looking out. Listen, girl, my cousin is here. Have you heard from… what the hell are you doing here?"

The question met Jay's entrance and his inability to respond. Kendra didn't have her scar covered. He winced imagining her pain. The thought of plastic surgery caused him to shake his head as he whispered, "Baby I'm sorry." He couldn't imagine what it would take to restore her beauty.

"Candice let me call you back. If you don't hear from me within an hour, call me back. If you don't get an answer, call the cops and ask for Damien Tyson. Tell him this asshole showed up."

"Kendra, are you sure?" Candice questioned realizing she didn't have a direct line to Kendra's cousin. "Oh, I don't have the number. … Is Jay there? Did he hear you?"

"Yes, he heard me. Girl, just do as I ask, please." Kendra ended the call but held on to the phone. Jay began to explain his actions.

"Kendra, you've got to know that I didn't have anything to do with this. What did you say to her? She thinks I sent you there deliberately. Are you going to be okay, that really looks bad?"

Jay took steps to get closer to her. He couldn't picture the scar that Talia said would last a lifetime. She was still upset about Kendra's drop in visit. He apologized and begged her to understand. He didn't think Kendra would accept the same lines.

"Stay where you stand. What the hell do you want now? To apologize for your bitch ruining my face? No, thank you! You can't possibly think your stopping by can heal this!"

Kendra turned going to the door.

"Get your ass out of my house! Show up again and I can guarantee you won't have a job or your freedom. Jay don't call me and tell your lady friend; it ain't over!"

"Kendra, she blames me for this. You've got to tell the cops the truth. I wasn't there."

"You're a real ass you know that Jay? You didn't come here to see how I was doing. Did you come here to clear your name? You sent me there. You knew we would have words, a confrontation, shit you may have told her what to do for all I know. The two of you ruined me. How is the rest of my life, my career going to be with this Frankenstein scar? If I had a gun, I'd shoot both of your asses. Maybe that's what I'll tell the cops. If they don't pick up both of you and charge you with aggravated, no atrocious assault, they'll leave me no choice. You know what Jay, walk carefully. You never know when you'll get bumped off. This ain't over!"

Kendra opened the door as the tears rolled down her face.

"Kendra, I love you. This was a mistake. I'll leave, but please don't think I was a part of this. Close the door baby, talk to me a minute. Just a minute." He paused for her response. She closed the door and turned to listen.

"You wanted your keys. I thought I would be there to meet you. We both were angry. I wanted to talk to you and Talia. I was going to let her know that—"

"That what Jay? You sent me to her place to let her know that you loved her and me? After all, you've been telling her all about me and what I don't understand. You told her you appreciated her for understanding. What the hell did you expect? It sounds like a problem, instant drama. Did you think that we would simply shake hands and have a threesome later on? Did you think about her feelings? You damn sure didn't care about mine. Jay, I'm wearing her feelings. She lashed out because she was willing to kill for you. I don't love you like that. You deserve each other. I'm convinced, loving you is wrong—"

"Kendra." He reached for her hand interrupting her rant. "Kendra you know me. I'm not violent, and I don't like drama or confrontations. Alright, I screwed her a couple of times. I'm guilty. I never told her I loved her and yes, I told her what she wanted to hear. I told her she was different. That was the game I played and yes, for that, I am guilty. But baby, I would never want any harm to come to you. I need you to tell the cops the truth. I wasn't there, and I didn't set you up."

"I don't know that, and you know what Jay? I don't believe that. You knew she would fight, so you didn't show up. She's a hood bitch, and you know what. … Get the fuck out, Jay. Just go!"

She didn't want him to keep talking. His voice was soothing. It was what she wanted to hear before she tangled with Talia. His apology was too late. Her throbbing face was a reminder and would be for the rest of her life.

Jay walked past her and paused. "Kendra, think about it, please—"

Chapter Thirty-Five

She slammed the door leaving him pleading in the hall. She was nervous, maybe even scared. Her stomach told her so. She wanted to cry but knew it wasn't a solution. She wanted her life to return to some point of normalcy. The bell rang again, and she hoped Damien had passed Jay in the hall. She waited for the knock at the door. She wouldn't be opening the door to another unwanted visit. She sighed and cracked the door. Seeing it was her cousin, she allowed him to secure the entrance.

"What's wrong? You don't look good. Kendra, look at me." Damien closed the door as he caught a glimpse of her damaged face.

"C'mon in, close the door before that damn fool comes back."

"Who, Jay? He was here?" He did as instructed and walked to the front of the couch where Kendra had rewrapped herself with her blanket. She threw down the phone receiver she was holding, found the remote and began surfing the channels. Damien waited. He knew her actions were deliberate. She was trying to calm down.

"Damien, that ass came here to ask me if I would tell the cops he had nothing to do with it."

"Did he? Why don't you tell me what happened?" Damien took a seat in the recliner. He swiveled the chair in her direction. Having a frontal view, he took a deep breath when he saw her face. "Baby girl, what did she cut you with?"

"Box Cutter. Bad huh? That's what the surgeon said, 'Deep damage and jagged deliberately made cuts.' He said the jagged scars would take longer to heal. I'll need at least two surgeries, one to repair and one to restore."

"Damn, and he was a part of this?"

"Well, yea," She answered with a voice of uncertainty. "Maybe not directly, but indirectly yes," Kendra explained her side and Jay's reason for the visit. "He came by because he knows he's guilty, just as guilty as she is."

"And you?" Damien waited for her to think about her intentions when she went to Talia's house. "I mean, c'mon Kendra, you knew Jay didn't live there. Where did you think you were going?"

"I didn't know it was her house. You're right I knew he didn't live there, hell, I don't know. My thoughts were scattered. I wanted to confront him so bad that I didn't think. My fault. She opened the door, and I asked for him. She told me to wait a minute. We fought on her stairs; he never came out. I should have left when she went back into the house. I thought she went to tell him I was at the door."

"Was he there?"

"No. After we fought, she closed the door and left me on the steps bleeding. The cops and an ambulance showed up. I guess she called them. Jay never called or came to the hospital, and now he wants me to tell the cops he didn't have anything to do with this. Bull, she did what they planned."

"Maybe not."

Kendra put down the remote giving full attention to her cousin. His rational thinking, the detective in him, always brought her back to reality. At times, it attached to her common sense. She wanted Jay to be guilty, but she did have doubts. Maybe he didn't know Talia would attack her.

"You showed up on her doorstep demanding to see him. What would you have done if she had shown up here looking for Jay?"

"I don't think I would have attacked her with a weapon."

"Okay, but there would have been a confrontation."

"Yea, I don't think I would have left the door. She would have got it right there when she asked for him."

"Okay, why? Because she was looking for him or for having the nerve to come to your house?"

"You're right. I see your point."

"Where does Jay fit into you fighting her at your door? He doesn't. It's your reaction to the nerve of her coming to your house. I don't think he meant for you to be attacked. Yeah, he was stupid for telling you to meet him there. Now if he says it was because he wanted to talk to both of you, well."

"Damien, don't okay. He could have talked to us at his house. Why hers? He didn't call me; I called him about exchanging our keys. I didn't need his and he wasn't keeping mine. He wasn't explaining or talking about that night that I caught them in the bed together. I'm done, and the cops can do what they need to do. Let them decide whether or not he was involved. I was set up, and I know it."

"So why not answer the cops or at least give a statement?"

"If they asked what was relevant, I would. I don't think how long they were dealing with each other has anything to do with this assault. It's simple; assault is a crime, and she committed it. I told them what I thought were the reasons. I'm done, cut the hell up, and in pain. I'm the victim. If they want to know about their relationship, ask them. Jay said she was blaming him for setting her up. What does that say about his innocence?"

"Alright, so what did the doctors say about your recovery?"

Damien would have to talk with the officers to see what the angle was. If Kendra gave a statement, they'd have to talk to Jay and Talia. If Talia's statement was the same as Jay's, maybe it wasn't planned. He'd look into it later.

"Rest, heal, and then more surgeries. I don't know how many more or how long. I'm out on disability from my job. The doctor put me out. The swelling will come and go and so will the pain. Then with each surgery the process will begin all over and they want to ask about Jay? I'm hating him right about now."

"Well I'll see what they have, and I'll let you know. Kendra, they're trying to get the facts together. You know how it goes, so when you feel better call them and deal with the nonsense questions. Those answers may help them find out if Jay was involved."

"I know he was involved. She did it, and he set me up so she could do it. He could have brought my damn keys here and got his. I'm focusing on healing. I filed the charges, let the court decide. So, Mr. Tyson, you guys are busy with the Pine Ridge Resort case, right? Tell me what's up with that?" Kendra's voice changed, and so did her mood.

"I'm doing my best to keep it from hitting the cold case shelves. I've got loose ends and angles that so far have led nowhere. I'm back to dating or trying to date. That's more interesting than the case."

"Wow, you dating? I'm happy for you. It won't stop me from asking questions about the case, though." Kendra smiled and touched her face gently.

"I'm going to get out of here. All this talking is not what the doctor meant by rest. It's got to hurt."

"It does, but please, tell me about her. Who is she, where did you meet? We can talk about the case later."

"We met at a place downtown. I went out with Porter for a few drinks. I think there were a few events held there. I don't quite remember which one. She was with a friend and we exchanged cards, and she called."

"She called. Rather forward of her. What type of woman is she? What kind of work does she do?"

"Nice, really nice. She has her own business. That's what it was a networking event. Anyway, I took her being forward, as you say, to her being strong willed. I mean the qualities of a businesswoman. She knows what she wants, and she is a go-getter. I like that about her. She's beautiful. I'd like the two of you to meet."

"I'd like—" Kendra let the words fade as the tears fell. "Not like this Damien. I don't want to meet her with this face. I'm sorry. I'm so happy for you. It's been so long since you've been able to open up to someone and share who you are. I really want to meet her but not now."

"When you're ready. I don't think our relationship will be ending anytime soon if I can help it. Damn, I didn't mean to make you cry. Listen, let's talk about what you like, the murder. What do you think?" Damien didn't want to leave, but he felt like running. He couldn't wait to confront Jay, but he had no excuse to leave Kendra to deal with her unraveled emotions.

Kendra patted her eyes, careful not to touch the stitches.

"So you're looking for the woman with the scarf right?"

"She may be the last person who spoke with either of the men. I don't know what that means but, hey, she's a person of interest."

"So did your sketch artist try to do a drawing, you know without the scarf? Did it hide that much? Also did you talk with customers that frequent the restaurant, you know the regulars? Not the workers or the owners, they would ignore some of the usual movements of the men. The other customers that are regulars would notice conversations and who were there. They didn't show much of the restaurant but what about the women that come there they may have noticed that woman. Even at the resort, the workers may know her."

"Good idea. I still don't understand why you won't take the test and work with us."

"Don't care for boots without heels. Plus by the time I get to wear plain clothes, you'll be retired. No thanks. What's your girl's name?"

"Mona, Mona Mandell."

Kendra's face tightened. She didn't want to predict the outcome of the relationship, but she was sure it wouldn't be happily ever after. She kept her thoughts to herself. Mona hadn't mentioned she was dating again. Maybe it wasn't serious though they both needed a stable relationship. She'd wait to see if Mona would mention her new interest if he truly held her interest. She wondered if Damien knew Mona dated Leon Bates. Kendra decided not to give him a reason to back pedal; he seemed excited. She'd wait until they were an old item or no item at all before telling him Mona was particular about who she dated.

"How long have you been dating?"

"Not long. You know me and my work. She seems to be just as busy. This weekend will be our first—"

"You don't have to go into details. I'm happy for you. Does she know you're a detective?"

"No, I haven't told her."

"Maybe you shouldn't." Damien gave her a questioning stare. "I mean, maybe you should wait to see if you're compatible. This weekend should tell you that right?"

Damien nodded in agreement. He hadn't planned on telling Mona until Sunday morning at breakfast. Kendra was right. Spending time with her would answer a few of his questions. Mona would have to understand his work and how devoted he was to it. A relationship wouldn't work without him telling her.

"You're right my dear. Thank you. As always you're on point with your observations. I've got to meet Porter at the office. I like your angles as well. I'll check them out." He stood to leave. "Stay comfortable, I'll let myself out. I'll call you, or you call me if you need anything." Kendra turned the volume of the television up and repositioned herself.

Damien closed the door behind him. Kendra reached for the phone and then thought better of it. Damien and Mona were opposites, and Kendra could attest, opposites often attract. She'd let them find out and listen to their complaints later. She had her own drama to deal with.

Chapter Thirty-Six

The traffic was terrible, and he was nowhere near the Parkway entrance. Damien called Jeff telling him to get the picture the sketch artist drew. Kendra was good, but her skills were second to none compared to Damien and his team.

He requested undercover officers to talk with customers as they mingled with the Friday crowd. Nothing of interest had been reported. He was waiting for clearance to check all the evidence collected previously. He and Jeff called the final phase, desperation. They needed something to go on.

The ringing of the Department's cell phone brought his thoughts to the present. "Hello, Detective Tyson," He answered dryly. He hoped it wasn't the nosey reporter wanting him to praise her print in the paper.

"Detective, this is Sergeant Williams. I've got something here I think may assist you in your investigation. The staff at the Pines Resort has been cooperating with us since the murders. Well, it seems one of them thinks she has seen the woman in the photo you've put on the television. She claims the woman was there this week. I took the liberty of calling you since your unit has the case now. There seems to have been an earring left in the room also. It was turned into to the same staff member after our team cleared the room. I don't know how they missed it. Once your unit began making comparisons to the other murder, we turned our evidence over. Maybe something you can go on. I thought you might want to talk with the staff member as well."

"Have you questioned her at all?"

"No sir. Just hung up the phone from our call. I'd like to be with you when you question her, though. Her name is Mary Thurston. She works the desk and the concierge stand. She's a full-time employee and works at times with the vacation tour guides. That's where she claims she spotted the woman, with one of the guided tours they have during the week. Why do you think she would need a tour?"

"Seems strange, that's for sure. Listen Sarge, let me get to my desk. Can I call you on this number?"

"Sure can. I'll be looking forward to it." The man hung up before Tyson could thank him. He was glad the Sergeant understood that the call was important to the case. He was no longer frustrated with the traffic as thoughts of progress entered his mind. He parked in his spot glad he didn't have to fight for space each morning.

"Hey man what's up?" He yelled to the officer who got out of his car waving.

"Yo', man, what's up with that fine thing that was at your office the other day."

"Widow. Her husband is one of the men killed at the resort. She is a looker." Tyson answered hoping the chitchat would cease.

"Which one is her husband?"

"Bates."

"Really? Wow and he was seeing that other woman in the picture right?" They both stopped at the entrance. Tyson was stunned at the question.

"You know something you want me to know or you're trying to verify the gossip."

"My boy saw the dude with the woman in the picture. He didn't know her name, but talk in the bar was it was his wife. I questioned him, and he didn't know much. Nothing to pass on. So if the looker is his wife than the one in the picture was the other woman, I guess. Wow, bad way to go."

"What, what do you mean bad way?" Tyson was hoping he'd get another link.

"That other woman shit. So you guys questioning if the wives killed these dudes?"

"There are a lot of questions. You know how that goes. Some of them have already been asked and re-asked. I'm just trying to get it off my desk. Listen, tell Amir to call me when you get to the office. I've got a few calls to make. Hey, if your boy thinks of anything we can use about that woman tell him to see me. No, better yet you come with him, so he doesn't think we're trying to tie him in."

"Sure, I'll ask him and see what's up. Later man."

Tyson's mood was lifted again. He was sure that one of the leads would direct him to a suspect and ultimately a conviction. He gave nods and smiles to those who waved and gave morning greetings as he headed to his office. To his surprise, Celeste Styles was seated waiting for his arrival. Instantly, his mood changed. He didn't know what to expect. He walked past her without any acknowledgment and didn't dare look back to see if she noticed him.

Celeste was on her phone and looking into her pocketbook when he passed her. She noticed the Detective when she heard him turn the lock to his office door. "Let me call you back, he's here. Excuse me, Detective Tyson, can I see you this morning?"

"Sure, give me a minute to get settled." Tyson wanted to return Sergeant Williams' call. He feared he would miss what Celeste had to say if he put her off too long. He opened the door of the office and summoned her in. Her perfume caught his attention, and if asked he would admit it had aroused him. Tyson began to feel guilty about looking her over in a totally different way. For the first time, she was casually dressed. Porter would say she was a fake in one way or another. He smiled to hide his thoughts.

"Well, what brings you here? I'm sure there's a reason for this early visit." Damien allowed the small talk to take his mind off her fitted jeans. She wore all black, which added "sexy" to her persona. Celeste knew that would be a tease for all of the men she would pass to get to Detective Tyson.

"I received a call from Janelle; she seemed a bit upset." She paused, waiting for Damien to respond. "You see Detective, we are widows. Do you know what that means? A part of us is gone, regardless to the depth of our relationship with our husbands, they are gone. We can't fix what was wrong in our marriage, but now we can live with the memories of the good times. The problem is your team won't let the dead be dead. Every few days you pick at the core, and it hurts Detective. I'm here to ask, no plead with you, no more questions. We don't know who killed them, and you know it. Why this emotional torture? I came back to visit her; I understand how she feels. She has no one to console her. We do that for each other."

"Really? Have you invited Raymond Murphy's widow to your sessions of consolation?" Celeste felt a chill come over her. For a moment the thought of the deaths, three businessmen, and one killer, nudged at her emotions. "Ms. Styles, if I didn't do my job, you and others who seem to be certain this won't unfold, would have complaints as well. I'm sorry. I'm not here to stroke emotions. I can't say I know what you women feel like. I'm looking for a killer. Your money was released right?"

"Money, what money?" Celeste wasn't ready for his question.

"The insurance money; the last time you were here that was what you wanted to be settled right?"

Celeste didn't remember that part of their conversation, but she understood why the detective would mention it.

"Yes, and what does that prove? I was the beneficiary and may I add my husband was murdered."

"No argument from me. I just don't understand why you're here in my office this early in the morning." Tyson knew there was a reason. Celeste and Janelle were just as suspicious of his actions as he was of theirs. He hoped his assumption wouldn't lead to another dead end.

"I told you. We, as the mourning wives, would like this mess to be over. It's on the news; it's the gossip that has become whispers whenever someone recognizes us. Can we just bury this? Oh, wrong term huh?"

She stood, not waiting for a reply. "Detective do you get out much?"

Tyson smiled. It was her first attempt at being real. "I do. Are you implying this job is all I do?"

"No, I just remember seeing you the other night at the restaurant. No date, no eye contact with the women at the bar. I just was wondering who had your loving in their hands."

Tyson tried not to look stunned. "She wasn't there. It was an investigative stop."

"Well, you'd have more time to deal with your personal life too. Just seal the envelopes with your rubber stamp, 'Cold Case'."

"I do have one more question, I mean if you don't mind."

"Not at all." She smiled convinced he'd ask something personal.

"Did you and Janelle discuss how you would live after the deaths of your husbands?"

Tyson saw the change in her face. She wasn't shocked at his question. He thought he read guilt as she pretended to search through her handbag for her car keys.

Never looking up at him she asked, "What kind of question is that? She said you and you partner were fishing. I would call it insulting." She stated, allowing her keys to jingle in her hand.

"I would call it dodging the question."

Porter opened the office. Seeing the two standing in the middle of the floor, he paused in the doorway before saying, "Good morning."

"Good morning, Detective, and goodbye." Celeste snatched the doorknob out of his hands and slammed the door behind her.

"Early morning drama? I thought you were the one who stayed away from females with issues."

Tyson stared at his partner and shook his head at Porter's response. He smiled in spite of wanting to laugh.

"You know they had something to do with this murder or they knew something. She stormed out of here because I asked did she and Janelle talk about how their life would be with their husbands being dead. Man, she didn't answer. There's got to be solid evidence. I believe Janelle will talk."

"So what did Celeste want? Why was she here?"

"She came on her own. I guess her purpose was to tell me there was no need to continue the investigation. What widow wouldn't want to know their husband's killer? Jeff, it's not a cold case yet."

Chapter Thirty-Seven

Jeff agreed to take another detective with him to The Pine Ridge Resort. He would meet the Sergeant and Ms. Thurston regarding her sighting the woman in the photo. He promised Damien that he would call him if he thought the information would uncover any new clues. Damien watched the updated news report with the others in the office and spotted Ms. Sayers in the audience. It was her question that caused the other reporters to bombard the Chief of Police with their oversized microphones.

"Ms. Sayers, I assure you that we are doing all we can for the families of the victims. At this time, there is no evidence that the woman in the picture shown has done anything. We are not labeling her a suspect in this case."

"Sir, what about the other murders. Is she a suspect in those killings as well?" Sayers wouldn't allow anyone else to pose their questions.

"Again Ms. Sayers, she's merely a person of interest. We have not identified any suspects." Chief Michaels looked over the crowd hoping another reporter would interject with a comment or question.

"How long before you identify her as a suspect Chief?" yelled a reporter waving his pad.

"This is the third murder at the resort. Have you questioned any of the employees there about the woman in photos?" yelled another. The Chief tried to hide his uneasiness. He wasn't sure about the answer. He nudged the officer next to him just as Ms. Sayers saw an opening.

"Chief, is it fair to say that the department is allowing this to blow over because they have been stunned by a possible serial killer; one that may be a woman? Is the resort pleased with this type of investigation? "

"No more questions." An officer announced emphatically, staring at the annoying reporters. The officer escorted Chief Michaels from the platform. The breaking news broadcast concluded with the hotline number for viewers to call with any information.

"Tough position to be in. Ms. Sayers got her headline story huh?"

Damien turned to face the soft-spoken Leana. "Good morning lady. How's things with you?"

"Well, better than your side of the world I'm sure. Jeff mentioned you wanted to know about the officers who were assigned to question Kendra. Is there a problem?" They continued to walk toward Damien's office.

Leana spoke quietly, uncertain who might be listening. "Look, Tyson, I don't want to get into any trouble by giving you guys a heads up on this one. You know how the higher ups are. Kendra wouldn't answer any of their questions. That won't help us at all."

Damien understood. It was protocol, and he also knew they wouldn't push the complaint if Kendra didn't.

"Hey, this is family. I mean she's got to have more surgery, and she's out of work. Can you tell me if they're—"

"Assholes," Leana said what he didn't want to say. "They want whoever did it. They responded to the complaint, so they know how bad it was. They went to the hospital and again to her home after she was discharged. She won't talk to them. We got a complaint from Talia Simmons on the boyfriend, but that was it. We just need her side of the story. Maybe she's protecting him; I mean women do that you know."

"I'll call her. Maybe if I'm there when they come she'll talk. Wait, what if you went to talk to her. You're a female; you know that bonding thing."

"I'll ask. You may be right. She might not want to talk to another man about it or her feelings. So what are you going to tell the Chief? Didn't Jeff take Amir and two other guys from homicide with him?"

"Yep, I'm waiting to hear from them. The Chief knew, we both slept on Ms. Sayers, though."

"She's a tough sister. So is that chick in the photo."

"What makes you say that?" Damien paused to look at her as he opened his office door.

"She killed three men? I hope she doesn't have a long list."

Leana waved and continued down the corridor before he could answer. The picture had become a focal point. The woman went out of her way to cover up anything that could identify her. Damien pulled out the picture, placing it at the top of the pile. He didn't have much to go on but as an afterthought he flipped through his Rolodex. He found the number needed and made the call.

"Steve, look I got your report. Did you talk with Jeff regarding the photo we have?"

Steven Short was an extension of Tyson's team. He was one of the sketch artists used by the homicide unit, but Tyson labeled him the best. They came up through the ranks together. Steven like Amir didn't want to be a regular in the Cold Case Unit.

"Hey man what's up. Yea, Jeff was here with the photo. I'm working on it. Had a few interruptions but I should have it for you by Monday or Tuesday. In the initial report, I didn't include the information from any of the footage we got from the camera at the resort. It's possible that the killer is in one of those shots. I thought about your photo. If I reviewed the shots taken by the camera, we might be able to compare it with the mystery woman."

"Sounds good. Let me know what you find. Jeff is at the resort. A worker there seems to think she saw the woman again this week."

"Good stuff man. I'll call you when I'm done."

"Later, man. Thanks."

Chapter Thirty-Eight

After a productive morning, Damien was looking forward to his planned weekend with Mona. Jeff called close to twelve with his complaints about the case and the goose chase he had been on at The Pine Ridge Resort.

"This chick is crazy man. She must be on a work-release program. She talked to Sergeant Williams thinking there was some kind of reward for giving information. Williams tried to talk with her, but she ain't budging. She claims her boss would be upset if she brought an investigation team back to the resort for no reason. I guess a payment would be the reason. Anyway, no one else is claiming they saw the woman in the picture. I talked to the tour guide, young kid, said he didn't remember. Maybe this chick promised them part of the cash she thought she would get." Jeff's frustration was heard in his voice.

"Are you talking about Ms. Thurston? I thought the Sergeant had the meeting set up." Damien would have to listen to the complaints from the Chief. He blasted Tyson earlier when he found out the unit went to the Pines Resort on orders without his approval.

""Yeah, that's her. Williams is talking to the hotel manager now. Amir is still talking to that crazy broad. I stepped away to regain what little patience I had. I see why they botched this up. Have you been here? This place is laid man. They have entertainment for the guest and the public on Wednesdays everything from jazz to comedy. I guess the manager wouldn't want the negative publicity. I don't think they're receptive to us being here."

"That might be why she wants to be paid; her job may be on the line. We have the surveillance video and Steve may be able to make a comparison."

"So what do you want me to do here man, wait?"

"I'll call the manager there after you guys leave. I mean if she saw this woman that's all we need. Get the list of who was on the tour. We may need to cross-reference their records. I think they check in with ID. The person we're looking to talk to may be a member there. We've got three murders at the same location. Get the tour list and the members list. That may be another lead."

"Damien, man, I'm thinking like you. They didn't give the investigation a second thought. Business as usual."

"I'll get the paperwork ready for a subpoena, just in case they're not too happy about us digging deeper."

"Here's Williams now. I'll put him on." Damien could hear Jeff in the background talking to the others who were standing around.

"Hey Detective, Williams here."

"What's up man? I hear there's a snag."

"Man, this Ms. Thurston didn't mention she'd have an issue with us coming here. We could have arranged a meeting elsewhere. Seems the manager hadn't been informed the woman may have been here. He's following protocol, so she's suspended and mad as hell. She was looking for one guy to show up. I've got your people here and mine. We pushed her into the manager's office, and she left on suspension."

"Damn! You would have thought they'd be glad to get this thing cleared up. I'll call the manager."

"No good man. He's sent a message by suspending her. This woman is not a suspect just an interested person. Without a confirmation of who she is and if she's connected, well Detective I don't see this man budging. I asked him if we could come back to talk about it. He said he'd be in meetings all day. Dude shoulda just said no."

"I'll make a few calls. Thanks, man, I'll call you if we need to meet you again."

"No problem. I thought it would be easy. I've got Ms. Thurston's information if we need it."

"How long is her suspension?"

"A week. No pay and then a review for termination."

"Really?"

"Yep, this manager is a real ass. Told her while we were in the office. She's pissed; I don't think she'll talk to us at all."

"Well if this woman is more than an interested person, maybe we can run interference for her losing her job. Listen, tell Jeff we'll let this rest for a minute. There may be a way to help Ms. Thurston out. Something tells me this woman is key to solving this murder."

Chapter Thirty-Nine

Kendra wanted to turn her phone off, but she was still waiting for the doctor's office to call. The morning passed quickly with Officer Leana Wilson and Jay calling. Officer Wilson skipped the pleasantries and told her she was close to Damien and Jeff. She even let her know she was dating Amir.

Kendra had to admit after talking with her for more than thirty minutes she felt as though she was talking to a friend from her past; someone she hadn't spoken with in years. She agreed to meet with her after her appointment with the doctor on Monday.

The annoying conversation with Jay was followed by Candice's call saying she would stop over. Kendra started to take a shower but was interrupted when Jay called again. He started a ritual of calling in the morning, checking on her during his lunch hour and again in the evening. His sincerity meant nothing to her now, and his apologies no longer touched her emotions. She expected him to continue to beg for forgiveness. He quickly became pathetic. Jay assumed she wouldn't implicate him in the assault as long as he and she spoke daily. After slinging insults, she didn't have the energy to continue fighting she just listened. She still loved him, but she knew it was over. She hung up after he told her he would help her get through the pain. He would never understand her pain. There was no need to pretend, she had the scar to remind her. She was a fool in love.

Kendra sat on the side of her bed allowing the fragments of the conversation and her thoughts to take over. Mona was right he needed to pay for her damaged face and her lovesick heart. Maybe giving him what he wanted one last time would be enough for her to move on emotionally. He was a freak in the bed, and she loved the way he freaked her. The thought put her in a mood. She snapped out of it as her vision of Jay took her to his bedroom where he and Talia were pumping and sweating. Her conscious wouldn't erase the scene. Talia had replaced her, and Jay enjoyed her as much as he claimed he enjoyed Kendra. She remembered him lying on his back having a volcanic eruption after they got caught. His erection glistened with their passion. They didn't stop because she interrupted them; they paused. Kendra understood now after days of recall. They continued as she stormed out of Jay's home.

She allowed herself to find comfort lying across her bed. She'd only rest for a moment. Her thoughts took her back to the scene in the shadows of Jay's bedroom. She imagined him talking softly, insuring Talia that Kendra and the relationship they had was a thing of the past. As he spoke tenderly, he would find her thighs and gently touch her until he found her moist pleasure. Fondling her, he would beg her to allow his entrance and Talia would open her legs as he inserted himself once more. Instantly he would whisper his thanks for her understanding. Friction would cause their temperatures to rise, and she would wrap her legs around him tightly.

Kendra closed her eyes, feeling moist at the thought of him moving slowly, as he went deeper into her. Talia was no longer a part of her vision as Kendra remembered how she and Jay had been. She loved the feeling of his lips gently kissing her cheek. She could see his closed eye expression as he opened his mouth slightly to moan again. She moaned with him as his manhood began to take on its own rhythm. He trembled as she felt the flow of his juices. She too exploded.

She loved the new toy she now kept on the nightstand. She had to admit it took her where she needed to be. She quivered again. Kendra laughed to herself at the name 'Always Satisfied' written in hot pink letters on its velvet pouch. Her moments, as she called them, usually caught her around the lunch hour. She told Jay the best sex ever was when they both had to rush back to work. It was a midday quickie and now, without him, she decided she wouldn't deprive herself of that pleasure. Mona may have had a point. One last fling wouldn't be that bad or would it.

Candice would be there soon. Kendra got into the shower, careful not to get her face wet as she washed her hair. She felt better than she had in days and her morning escapade coupled with the shower was enough to relieve her stress. She towel dried her hair and hoped Candice wouldn't mind combing it through for her. They could talk and watch a movie. She definitely didn't want to hear Candice's "You're single now" reasoning again.

Mona's number appeared on the television screen before the phone rang its melodious tone. Kendra couldn't help but smile. She was one up on Mona's love life, the life she kept hidden. Candice and Kendra often questioned why Mona thought it was a big deal to talk about her dating. After all, she knew about Jay and a few of Candice's issues and flings.

"Hey girl, checking on you before the weekend begins. I probably won't speak with you until Sunday. Candice said she's headed your way."

"What's up?" Kendra answered, hoping Mona would say more about her weekend plans. "Yeah, Candice has been on her way since early this morning. I'm a lot better now. What's going on this weekend?" Kendra asked. She sat up hoping Mona would mention Damien.

Mona swayed the conversation. "What do you mean a lot better now? Be careful taking those pain meds."

"No, that asshole was here." Kendra allowed the conversation to put the spotlight on her problem. "Jay has been calling ever since his visit."

"What did he say?" Mona hoped he hadn't been stupid enough to tell Kendra he was meeting her. "Wait, when did he visit you?"

"Yesterday or was it the day before? I don't know I'm losing count of the days. He was begging that's all. Talia named him and me in her complaint."

"Her complaint? She cut you up, and now she's filing a complaint? Her ass is as bad as his."

"She named him in her statement and both of us in her complaint. I don't know that there's a difference, but they deserve each other. I did think about what you said, though."

"What's that?" Mona was distracted searching through her wallet for Jay's number.

"Having sex with him one last time. He's been calling here morning, noon and night. Girl, I had to turn on the teaser. Shit, I was horny as hell listening to his sweet talk. But then I'd see him and her in the bed and be mad as hell. I got off, though." She waited for Mona's response.

"I'd say you feel better. How's your face?" Mona wanted the reality to sting.

"That's cold Mona. What, you gonna remind me about the shit every time we talk? You walking on my emotions too?"

"What the hell are you talking about Kendra? I wasn't trying … never mind. Do you baby girl, that's what I asked you before. What the hell do you want to do? They already did you. Now either you fuck him or wait until he gets fucked! Call me when you decide."

Kendra had to shake her head a few times as she repeated Mona's words aloud. She'd repeat them again to Candice. She thought she heard a threat; maybe Candice would have another interpretation.

Chapter Forty

Mona threw down the pen as she wrote the word "pissed" in capital letters. She warned Jay and thought he understood. He had set off anger that the recently penned pages of her journal had quelled. She'd have to deal with him right away before Kendra changed her mind.

She'd have to convince him there was no time to waste. The plans would have to be changed. She didn't want to risk going to the resort in the middle of the week. It would have to be his place. She would convince him if he wanted to avoid the courts and the media coverage he would need her to clear up a few things.

"Jay, what the hell did I tell you?" She blasted the words into the receiver.

"Hold baby, what's wrong? What did I do?" Jay answered trying to keep his voice down. The office was busy and filled with city officials waiting for a meeting. "Can I call you back? This is not a good time."

"Listen I told you not to contact Kendra. What kinda punk ass move are you trying to pull? You didn't think she would tell me? That's how your dumb ass got in this mess, begging for her to forgive you." Mona began pacing in the middle of her living room the floor. "Meet me tonight or drown in your shit! Kendra wants to press stalking and harassment charges on your ass now! I need to know what you and Talia talked about that day." Mona lied, hoping he would understand the urgency in their meeting.

"Tonight? Talia and I didn't set her up. I was supposed to be there like I told you. Uh … Well, what are you going to tell Kendra?" He turned his back to his office door hoping to gain a bit of privacy.

"I'm gonna try to keep you from doing jail time or paying some outrageous fine. You can't be stupid enough to believe she'd fall for your lame excuses with that scar reminding her that love hurts."

"I thought I was doing the right thing. You're right; maybe she needs time to heal. I wanted her to know I was willing to go through it with her."

"What and be a reminder? Listen, you just ruined that. I told you, let me handle that, and all of this wouldn't matter. She'd get over you and Ms. Talia. Talia will too, you'll see."

"What does that mean?"

"It means you won't have to worry about court, jail, Kendra or Talia. You'll be free of the mess and able to be with who you care to play with or attempt to love."

"So that would be you?"

Mona laughed. "You're so funny, no sweetie, you won't be attaching yourself to me. You get to romp with me to settle my curiosity. I told you I can't believe Kendra and Talia didn't find treasure. Saving your ass has got to have a perk."

"Why today? I mean, baby you want to romp and play, that can wait until I see you or are you that horny?" Jay responded full of conceit.

"You want to romp and play; that's your downfall. I'll be in the parking lot when you get off. You'll follow my lead today, and we can get this over and done with. I need you to tell me the truth, and once I have what I need, we'll romp and play as you call it. I don't think this should wait until next week. Kendra will have the upper hand by then."

There was a pause. Mona didn't want to lose her catch. "Listen, if you don't want to meet, you think you can sweet talk your way back into her bed, go for it. I'm just trying to stop the legal matters."

"By fucking me? Really?" Jay laughed. "Baby you got the wrong one, I ain't desperate. Kendra, Talia, you, whoever, that won't stop, and it's all legal. I wasn't there. I don't know what happened, and I don't need your fine ass in bed to save me!" His whisper was raspy but harsh enough to sting. "So you still need that tune up?"

"Meet me or deal with it. I'll call Kendra and convince her that your ass is just like the others."

"What others?"

"The others that weren't worth saving."

"What?"

"After work or seven at the diner parking lot. It's your choice. Kendra is upset, especially now that you've been calling her daily. She said something about harassment and threats."

"Yeah right and my punishment is her friend threatening me into a sexcapade."

"You've never had me. I don't play many games. So while you've got me more than curious, say you will." Mona softened her tone. Her invitation became an arousal.

"Seven. You got it. I guess you have planned where we're going?"

"Like I said, we'll talk over a drink or two, and then we'll see. If you've convinced me, I definitely can convince Kendra you're worth saving."

"Well, sweetness I'—" The line went dead. Jay looked around hoping no one could tell he was stunned.

Mona was still pacing and had been the entire conversation. Jay was not an easy target, but he became her immediate target. His arrogance annoyed her. She readied herself for the next three hours ignoring the calls from Damien. It was six before she thought it best to return his calls.

"Are you sure you'll be okay?"

"Yes Damien, I'm sure. I've been taking medicine all day. I'm sure I'll be better in the morning. Can we begin our weekend then?"

"Sure we can. Do you need anything? Something to eat?"

"No, I've got soup and tea. I just hope I'll feel better in the morning."

"Well get some rest. I'll call later to check on you."

"Thank you. If I don't answer, I'll probably be sleep."

"No problem babe. Get your rest. I'll see you tomorrow."

Mona dimmed the lights and grabbed her bag. She had thirty minutes to get to the diner.

Chapter Forty-One

Damien decided to call Amir and Jeff. He'd find out what was on their agenda for the evening now that his plans were changed. Kendra called earlier to say she would talk to Leana on Monday. His desk was clear as well as his mind. He longed for the relaxation.

"I'll meet you at nine. Call Amir and tell him no need to bring his lady. Seems like him and Leana are inseparable. Have you noticed?"

Jeff was in his closet looking for a shirt. He told Amir to meet him at The Café, a small club that had a nice mature crowd on Fridays. Damien was always welcomed. Jeff agreed Leana had become a third wheel, the fourth when Damien joined their outings.

"Yep, you're right. Hey, maybe he's thinking about commitment."

"At work, at home and when hanging out?? Yeah, we'll have to sign the papers for his commitment. I hope the hospital isn't too far for us to visit."

"Stop man. Leana ain't that bad and if Amir loves her, what can we say."

"Leave her home tonight. We can say that as friends and say it often."

"What's up? You'd invite Mona, and I'd invite…" He paused deliberately. "Well, I'd bring somebody."

"Alright, you may need to get that piece lined up. What about that chick that was with Mona the night we met her?"

"The man-eater? Mock my words, there's a reason for Mona grabbing you that night. You may be her next meal. They both were there to set-up and conquer. No, thanks. I'll pass. I'm keeping my eyes open for you. I'll admit, she's one definition for a fine woman, but my gut feeling is she's hiding something."

"Well, I'll find out tomorrow. I hope she's feeling better."

"Well if you change your mind, give me a call. We may change locations if there's a weak crowd at The Café."

"Alright bet. See you in a few."

The trio met two hours later as planned. The Café started the first Jazz set with a local band who had been favored by the regulars. The audience added to the atmosphere as a celebration of birthdays, and a retirement was being shared with shout outs and sing-a-longs. Amir and Jeff sent drinks to a few ladies they recognized who nodded thanks as they raised their glasses in the air.

"This place jumps like this every Friday?" Amir posed the question not knowing which of his friends suggested they meet there."

"This is my first time here. Jeff would know." Damien answered as he nodded his head to the beat of the music.

"Most Fridays are like this. I don't know what it's like the other nights. Hey, your boy's restaurant jumps on Fridays too. We ought to drop by there and check out that crowd. Maybe we'll run into that fine ass mystery lady."

"I'm not trying to work after-hours man. Hey, can I get another round here?" Damien called out over the crowd to the waitress who passed their table.

"How's that going. You know the talk is the dynamic duo won't solve this one." Amir teased Jeff, nudging him for a reaction."

"Tell them we haven't given in yet. We had to call in the team, though. Did you check your e-mail?"

"Damien man, tell me you didn't put in a request for me."

"What you scared to work with Batman and Robin?"

"I guess Leana is Cat Woman huh? She told me she was checking a few things for you."

"She did, but I needed her to get with Kendra. She brought up a good point you know. Women don't want to talk to men about failed relationships or domestic abuse. So she agreed to do me that favor. We can use you to work with us on the Pines case. Check your e-mail."

Amir shook his head and began searching through his phone.

"Alright, I got it. So who is the mystery woman?" He questioned trying not to sound interested.

"That's why she's a mystery." Jeff's sarcasm caused them to laugh. She was seen again or so we think. An employee at the Pines saw her there earlier this week."

"Really? Is she setting up another hit?" Amir asked without looking up.

"And you wondered why I requested you? We thought about her involvement and yes, I thought about her being the killer. Jeff's thought was if the killer was a woman she'd have to drug them first."

"I don't know about that man. Jeff, we've met a few that could hypnotize us into an out of body experience." Amir raised his eyebrow waiting for Jeff to comment.

"Did you say that for me to feel some kind of way? We both fell under that spell as I remember that night." Jeff replied.

Damien's laughter was cut short when he caught a glimpse of Scott Bearman sitting at the bar. He recognized a few of the men he was with as customers from his restaurant, as he matched the faces to his vague memory of them around the pool table. Jeff and Amir followed his stare.

"Scott Bearman, who's the others?" Jeff asked with no explanation to Amir.

Damien turned up his beer bottle before answering. "I've seen them a few times at the restaurant. They didn't seem to be anything more than customers. Maybe I overlooked—"

"You didn't know his father was Rusty Bearman. Maybe the theory about the murderer being a woman is wrong." Amir injected.

"My thought exactly. Young boys could make good money carrying out jobs for a man like Rusty."

"The old man didn't seem to be worried, though. Amir, the dude was smooth. Pissed Damien off, I know he did."

"Cause he knows something, and that's why I sent that e-mail. For some reason, I just have a feeling, I've been around the killer."

"Well, that knocks out the theory of it being a woman. I mean unless you're going for that out of body thing." Jeff's comment brought the focus to Damien.

"Just what you need Damien, a hypnotic state. So when are you seeing this lady of yours?"

"Tomorrow, she wasn't feeling well tonight. I think I'm going to let her know I'm a detective. You're right Jeff; it's best to let her know before our relationship gets too serious. I need to say something before I subject myself to hypnotism."

"Listen man, women love that honesty thing but our job, unless she's understanding, puts demands on our love life." Jeff looked at Amir hoping he would agree.

"What, why do you think I deal with Leana? She understands, she's a cop. No explanations needed."

There was nothing more to say, and Damien hoped the conversation would change. The younger men wouldn't understand his need to be finally free of the obligations of the job when it came to his personal life.

"Well, it will be an overnight in the city, dining, dancing, and starting what I hope will be a lasting relationship."

"Or an expensive lay. Hey, here comes your boys." Jeff brought attention to the three co-workers approaching them. The detectives were also a part of the homicide unit. It was evident shortly after Damien, Jeff and Amir were chosen to work with the cold cases that there would be no love lost between them.

"Hey, it's the dynamic trio." Detective Mark Simmons smirked as he reached to shake hands. The exchange between the men was merely their silent agreement not to argue. Detective Philip Sheers and Detective Michael Boone accompanied him. The three men were close on and off the job, and their reputations for trouble had followed them throughout their careers. After being cleared of a hefty civil action suit, they became inseparable. Damien and Amir believed they were guilty, but after a short suspension and transfer from the Narcotics Unit the three thought of themselves as untouchable.

"Looking for something warmer than that dead ass case?" Sheers teased. "Listen there's two more coming your way. They're not going to look much longer for the asshole that shot that teen in East Orange."

Before Boone could throw in his dry humor, Amir added his own. "Teen murder, shooting in an alley. An alley only you would go down hoping to find the distressed girl looking for a John. Figures you found nothing. Johns in the alley is old school, my friend, unless you were the John. Teens? What's up with you guys now other than seeing prison cells in your future?"

"Hey, no harm. Why the attitude? Us going to jail gives you job security. The three of you know we should have been selected for that specialty unit. They chose the three of you because the Mayor is black. Politics that's all, but your winning streak is finally turning. I just thought I'd let you know. Sheers and Boone mentioned it earlier, and I couldn't wait to let you guys know. I mean even with the dirt thrown on us, it can't bury us like the lack of evidence in these cases will bury you. They'll close your little unit soon and see that you boys ain't shit." Simmons turned to walk away as Amir and Jeff stood blocking his passage. Damien stood up from the barstool to make his final comment.

"You're right Simmons. Shit rolls down hill and since you're at the bottom, you and your boys, you're covered in it. No need to inform us, we've been solving your cases for months now. I'm sure the department saved your asses because of "politics". It wouldn't look good on the front page for the supporters of the black Mayor. They saved you the first time; you won't be so lucky the next time. Oh and that goes for your comments in public too. Don't push your luck. We don't mind dealing with your ass in public either, remember, we know what to do with the evidence."

Sheers and Boone stood at a distance trying to hear over the chatter and the music. Simmons walked away, apparently angry. His insults brought him more than he bargained for.

The chatter that suddenly became low whispers now increased in volume. Scott Bearman noticed Tyson's stare. Excusing himself from his group of friends Scott walked over to Damien.

"Hey, uh, I can't talk to you at the restaurant, but I need to have some time with you."

"If it's about your father—"

"It is. Detective, I don't know what he's done or will do, but this afternoon there were a lot of calls and closed-door meetings. He's too old for this shit."

"What shit? What are you saying?"

"He knows something. I tried talking to him about the meeting with you and he snapped. Something about him not being involved this time. He mentioned the wives and the money he lost because those men wouldn't be a part of the business."

"Sounds legit to me. I mean if your father worked for them or had business with them, he may be at a financial loss."

"We ain't hurting for money. It's more than that. He knows something, maybe too much."

"The calls, did you answer any?"

"A few."

"Any from Ms. Bates or Ms. Styles?"

"Yes. Conference calls with the two of them most of the afternoon. Like I said, my father can't do jail time it would kill him for sure."

"He won't have to if he's not involved in either murder."

"That's just it, maybe he is."

Chapter Forty-Two

Kendra dialed Mona's number again. She couldn't find her cell phone and hoped Mona hadn't picked hers up by mistake. She knew when they got the same phone there would eventually be a mix-up. She sent an email hoping Mona was catching up on some work before she left for her weekend fling.

The news regarding the Pine Resort case was airing the updates. The reporter's speculations were like most of the reports; the police had no suspects. Kendra had her speculations after reading all of the information about the husbands and their businesses. They were definitely tied together in more ways than one. She was sure her cousin had checked those leads and found, as she had, the missing link was the woman who seemed to be a mystery.

Her phone rang, a tone she didn't often hear — no one called her home number. "Hey, girl," Kendra tried to ignore the pain in her face, "You know you have my phone, right?"

Mona checked her phone. The contacts were unfamiliar.

"Wait a minute, I think I do. No wonder I didn't get Damien's calls. So where is my phone?"

"Dig in that shopping bag you call a pocketbook." Kendra shook her head slowly trying not to laugh.

"Funny, and you can't even laugh. Girl this is a classic Coach bag. Yep, you're right. I have yours and mine. Damn, can I drop it off to you later tonight?"

"I thought you were going out with Damien."

"I wasn't feeling well. We'll hook up tomorrow. I can bring it to you. I got a business run to make."

"Tonight? I thought you said you were sick?"

"Do you want the phone or not nosey!"

"Okay, I was just thinking, if you're sick…."

"I'll bring you the phone. Anything else since I'll be coming that way?"

"No, I'm good. Just my phone. Hell, the only calls I'm ducking are Jay's. But Mona, I want to talk to him. I need closure."

"You got closure. Your mouth, your face, what you need insults and depression too? Believe me, he's not worth your healing time. Get better first. Concentrate on you and what he's left you to deal with. You'll only argue and fight right now. Give yourself time. He may see things different after a few days."

"Well, he did apologize. I stopped answering his calls. He was still sending text messages, though. I don't know Mona; maybe he didn't know what would happen."

"Heal first, then we'll talk about it."

"Alright, well I'll see you later then."

"I'll call you when I'm on my way."

Mona disconnected the call quickly to avoid being annoyed. Jay had not arrived, and it was now seven thirty. Although he called to say he would be a few minutes late. She would have to change her plans. There would be no romantic prelude. After all, he didn't expect it. She needed to rid Kendra of the pain. Mona understood it was more emotional than physical. Kendra needed the relationship to be finally over so she could move on. Mona would be sure to emphasize that once Jay could no longer visit or call.

Jay's car pulled into the parking lot, and Mona was pleased there was a space to park next to her vehicle. Mona waved from the driver's seat. Jay opened her door and smiled. Mona knew when she purposely put on the coral jumpsuit it would capture his attention immediately. She was sure her cleavage would seduce him while they ordered drinks. She would fondle him with her nylon stocking foot when they ordered desert. The plan was a simple dose of foreplay, and she was sure he wouldn't resist her invitation for more.

Mona called to cancel the reservations for the weekend at the Pine Ridge Resort. She decided not to take the suite. There were too many still seeking clues. The reports broadcasted Ms. Thurston's claim that she could identify the mystery, woman. Her arrangements and the cancelation was safe on-line. The confirmation would be emailed to her secondary account — an account that had no connection to Mona's personal or business life. She booked a cabin with fewer amenities; she wouldn't need the luxuries of the Pine Resort. They wouldn't be staying long. A midweek stay wouldn't draw much attention. She'd arrive on Monday and invite him to join her.

She accepted his hand as he helped her out of her car.

"Thank you, I thought you changed your mind."

"No, between the traffic and a late meeting, well I'm here. You look marvelous. This color, what is it called? It looks good, girl."

"Coral," She answered trying not to sound irritated.

"Coral, nice real nice."

The couple entered the crowded restaurant, and Mona could feel the anxiety building. She hoped the customers were too busy eating and wouldn't remember the entrance of the fool and the woman in coral. As an afterthought, she should have thrown on a pair of jeans and a sweater. Jay certainly would have drooled over the sight of her either way. She walked deliberately, allowing her hips to sway. She captured the attention of the men she passed and Jay quickly took her hand. Mona smiled. His actions proved he wanted to be a part of her statement. He had no idea what it would cost him.

Mona watched the time. Her appetite vanished quickly. After pretending to enjoy his narcissistic attitude, she needed to release her tension. She visualized the joy revenge would bring as she prayed for a little patience.

"So what's next, my lady?" A signature line that led to Mr. Styles' demise. Mona ignored his question reminiscing Kevin's arrogance.

"What do you mean? I call you babe, you're offended. I call you hon, you're offended. It's affection. My lady, I am learning about you, but sometimes you come across as though you just want to dabble. I'm just not into the games others play. So how do I show my affection? What term would you prefer, my lady? I never would deliberately offend you."

It was the regular weekend hook up. Kevin avoided her calls Monday through Thursday. It took Mona two months to recognize the pattern. Friday through Sunday, she would speak to him more than four times during the day. Their weekend romps often began with lunch or dinner invitations. They went to a few plays and business events. She was introduced to his clients as Ms. Wells, never his girlfriend or his lady. Mona never introduced him to anyone. Soon she didn't care about being "his lady," after all she was realistic.

"Tell me I didn't get you upset." Jay's comment brought her back to the present.

"No, no, I'm sorry. I just was thinking of the time. I thought we would have more time, you know. I hate rushing, reminds me of a prostitute and a John. Not really my cup of tea. I mean…" She rubbed her foot across the zipper of his pants. "I want you to have time to convince me you're worth the effort. I want you at your best."

"It's early, and it's Friday. We've got all night." He responded holding her toes on the bulge that rose in his pants. He leaned across the table pleading. "You can't let a brother with this knot down, can you?"

"No, I guess I can't, but what I want to give you in return," she licked her lips slowly and whispered, "is more than tonight's hours will allow."

"How about you give me that preview tonight and we can follow up before the weekend is out. I'm free. What about you?"

She moved her foot slowly, allowing her toes to move down his leg. "I'm busy this weekend." The sudden change in her voice and movements confused Jay. Mona was obviously ready to leave.

"So, what are we doing? We barely got a chance to talk."

"I didn't come to talk. You want me to get you out of a jam. I want you in the bed. It's simple baby. Please me, or else you'll face a judge."

"So when? I'm ready. We can go to my place if you like. I understand the arrangement. Let's get this settled, you might find yourself hooked to the best you ever had."

Mona slid her card with the address to the cabin written on the back of it. "Meet me there on Tuesday or call me with a day that's better for you. I'll only be there until Friday. It's business during the day, but my nights are free and lonely. Keep me company and I'll be sure to clear your name."

"How can I be sure that Kendra won't still include me in all this?"

"I'm telling you she won't. After you meet with me, I'll be satisfied and so will you. Trust me, it will be over; trying to include you will be the last thing Kendra would do."

"So can I get you to join me at Jazzin' in East Orange? It's a nice mellow spot, not a large crowd."

Mona looked at her watch. She knew where the drink would lead her.

"Wednesday, say yes and let's not spoil the anticipation with drinks and sloppy sex."

Jay agreed. He allowed his ego to deflate as the couple walked out of the diner. He walked her to her car determined to beat her at what he knew was a game.

"So, sexy, you've teased me twice. I can't do anything but accept it. I'll see you Wednesday for sure, but I need something else from you."

"What's that?" Mona questioned giving him her full attention.

"If you're pleased, let's not make Wednesday the last time. I understand your friendship with Kendra, but if you can ignore it to get me out of trouble, well we should be able to keep each other pleased. You know, off and on. Nothing serious."

"After Wednesday, ask me again."

Jay smiled and gave her a kiss on the cheek she offered.

Mona smiled. She'd be sure to enter him in her journal.

Chapter Forty-Three

Mona grabbed the cell phone from her purse. She checked for missed calls. She saw Damien's number and smiled. There were two calls from him since seven. Another number and a name she didn't recognize was listed under his. Jay's number followed. Mona scrambled to get the other phone, her phone, from her purse.

There was no call from Damien since their last conversation. The missed calls were numbers and names she could identify. It was Kendra's phone that held the missed calls from Damien. Her mind went into an immediate frenzy. It took a minute, but she convinced herself that Kendra got his number to install security equipment. *"Small world. What other reason could there be for her to have his number?"* She'd tease Kendra and Damien about it later.

"Girl, I'm pulling up to your place now. Unlock the door; I can't stay. No, don't worry about it. I'll put your phone on your table near the door. I can't stay, sorry. I've got to pack an overnight bag. Okay, unlock the door I found a spot to park."

Mona hung up the phone. Kendra didn't follow the directions given. She stood at the door waiting for Mona's approach.

"You're a rock head. You don't need to be in this night air."

"Girl, that's what I need; some air."

"How does it feel? I mean, any better?"

"A little, after I take the damn pills. I'm fine according to the nurses that call and question my progress. The cops were here again, and I have to meet with another on Monday. A woman, maybe she'll be more understanding. I don't want to talk to them. I'll get mine in court." Kendra's disappointment had her rattled

"Understood, but listen, get out of this night air." Mona insisted pulling the door close behind her to block the night wind. "We'll talk after your meeting on Monday. I'll be back Sunday night, late hopefully."

"Yeah, enjoy. You should have a great time. Hey, did you see the news? They're keeping the case for Leon and that other guy open. There's some woman saying she can identify the mystery woman."

"Really. Why are they so interested in that woman? I don't get it." Mona hoped Kendra wouldn't notice her nervousness.

"She's another lead; that's all. It's getting interesting, though. Maybe the mystery woman was there. Maybe more than once. She had to be for this Thurston lady; I think that was her name, to know she had seen her. Behind the glasses and the scarf and she still recognized her? She just wants money."

"Money, who wants money?"

"Yeah, girl the wives are putting up money for any information that leads to the arrest of the killer."

"Okay, so how does this Thurston woman collect? Did she say she knew the woman?"

"No, but she's stated that the mystery woman was the last one seen with both of the men. It's as good as the Crime Scene Investigation shows."

Mona shook her head. "Go inside girl. You need to heal and get back to work if you're this excited about a murder case." Mona gave Kendra her phone with no mention of the listed calls from Damien.

"Alright, goodnight."

Mona took a deep breath once she sat in the driver's seat. *"Thurston, damn, who is she?"* She'd have to find time to call the resort and ask who she was. She didn't need complications.

Chapter Forty-Four

"So, why are we offering a reward? This is some stupid shit. I don't have money to give, and I don't give a damn about who killed his ass!"

"Celeste, Rusty said they won't find the killer, and we won't have to pay. This will take the eyes off us and him."

"You called him didn't you?" Celeste lit a cigarette while she waited for Janelle's lame excuse. "I told you, leave it alone, and you called him anyway. Hell, Tyson and his dumb partners are twiddling their thumbs waiting for the evidence to hit them in the head."

"They called Rusty in." Janelle lowered her voice although no one was in her home to hear the desperation in her voice. "We have to go along with this or I guess he'll tell them we hired him."

"What? You can't be for real. He'll tell what; that he was hired, didn't kill either one of the assholes, and didn't get paid? Janelle, for real? Girl you need to live more. You don't have any ties with Rusty. We don't owe him a thing. It may as well have been just a thought; we're done." She took a deep pull on her cigarette and sat back on her couch. "Listen, I'll call Rusty about this damn reward. Maybe he has money to throw away. I'll call you back."

"I don't know Celeste. There's a woman who claims she can identify that woman they're looking for. Maybe she was linked to Rusty. I told you to ask him."

"Ask what? We didn't pay him. If it was his," Celeste paused in thought, "you know what? I'll call you back." She didn't wait for Janelle to respond. She hung up and dialed Rusty's number.

Janelle was scared. Rusty called her stating they needed to get his name out of the mess. There was no reason for him to be interrogated unless she or Celeste implemented him in the crime. If they did, Janelle feared, they would regret it. Janelle called the police and told them they wanted to offer a reward. The officer on the phone gave her the number to call, and she did, hoping it would be proof for Rusty that they hadn't betrayed him. She never asked him if he knew the woman the news was flashing.

Celeste dialed the number again. She heard the same annoying voice-mail. She put the phone in the cradle, and it rang.

"Hello"

"Celeste? It's Rusty, babe what's up?"

"A reward? What the hell is that about?"

"Your girl. An assurance I guess. I called to tell her I wouldn't be answering questions to a murder I had nothing to do with. I don't need the heat or the media coverage. She's scared, I know, but she's got to leave me out of this. I don't know that woman they're looking for. I told her the two of you had no worries. Janelle will talk herself into a confession."

Celeste was silent. She couldn't believe that Janelle would be so naïve. "Thank you, Rusty. I'm sorry for the trouble this has caused you."

"No trouble my dear. For all you've done for me, I would do anything to repay you."

"Once this is over…"

"Yes, baby. Once this is over we can be together without sneaking around. I have longed for this moment. Your husband is no longer an obstacle. You haven't changed your mind have you?"

"Rusty we have to be careful. The police are looking for an angle, any angle. They have nothing, and they're looking for anything. You, me, Janelle, we are all suspects as well as that mystery woman."

"I miss you so much."

"I miss you too. My love for you has never changed. It will only be until this has settled. Did you tell Scott you planned to leave New Jersey?"

"No, but I have turned the business over to him. Soon I'll let him know about us, and I'll be the next plane headed your way. Their investigation is a dead end. The police can't stop my travel without just cause."

"I'll call Janelle. I don't think she realizes she's causing a problem."

"Yes, my dear, if needed, I can settle it."

"No, she's just scared. I'll talk to her or return to see her if necessary. A great excuse to see you again."

"Well, call me if you need me."

The phone went silent.

Celeste needed a drink. She and Rusty had been lovers for more than three years. After meeting the woman Kevin left home, Rusty told her of the failing business he kept afloat for both Kevin and Leon. Celeste didn't believe him until she received a call from Janelle when her husband's books didn't balance. Kevin's named appeared several times with no dollar amounts being disbursed. Janelle unknowingly answered financial questions Kevin refused to answer. Leon and Kevin were in a joined venture that appeared to be a lost to both companies. After the women had talked on several occasions, it was determined that the money was spent on entertaining others as well. They agreed, it had to be women. The two women wished their husbands death. Celeste called Rusty for help.

Rusty separated himself; he no longer gave advice or money to either company. He reduced the frequency of his visits to the bar. He flew to Texas whenever Kevin was in New Jersey. He told Scott he wouldn't be taking calls unless it was Janelle or Celeste. He made himself scarce to everyone in preparation for the hit he would handle. Celeste trusted he would handle things his way. Kevin was dead a few months later.

Janelle assumed Kevin was killed at Celeste's request. She was frantic, not knowing when Leon would be killed brought on the pain of her guilt. Celeste kept her company, and they became close. The women never questioned who committed the crime until after Leon's death.

"Janelle, we can't afford a reward, and there is no need. Rusty didn't commit the crime, and no one knows we were willing to pay for our husbands' deaths. Why do you insist on putting yourself in the middle of this investigation? We agreed they deserved their fate. Don't let your guilt shine a light on our darkness. It wasn't meant for us to be a part of their death. You believe that don't you? Janelle, we didn't kill them. There is someone or at least another reason those bastards were killed. We didn't do it by wishing them dead, and Rusty wasn't paid. We are not guilty, and neither is he." Celeste called her back as promised. She hoped it would ease her fears.

"We will be looked at as though we didn't care about their deaths."

"And what does that mean and who else cares? You don't want to put yourself in the middle of this investigation. It's time to heal Janelle."

"I didn't know how much I would miss him. Who killed him, Celeste? I need to know."

"It wasn't Rusty."

"How can you be sure?" Janelle questioned. She was crying, trying to brace herself for the answer.

"Rusty is my lover. He has been for a few years now. He didn't have either of them killed. I'm sure of it."

Janelle couldn't respond. Celeste's words took her breath. Celeste had no reason to question who killed her husband. She had the love of another man to help her heal. Janelle, lost and confused, hung up the phone.

Chapter Forty-Five

Damien debated whether to arrive earlier then discussed the next morning. He couldn't wait to be parked in from of Mona's townhouse. He hoped she would be as excited as he was about the time they would spend together. He prayed whatever ailment she had the night before found its cure during her night's sleep.

He allowed his temptations to settle while he turned on the television, a morning ritual he purposely avoided on the weekend. He used the remote to surf the channels and paused as he saw the faces of Leon Bates and Kevin Styles on the screen. He turned up the sound and sat attentively as the reporter began the breaking news story.

"The police have decided to continue the search for The Resort murderer. Although it seems the evidence has led them to a dead end, there is a worker who claims she can identify the mystery woman."

Damien swiped through his contacts on his cell phone hoping he had the number of the overzealous reporter. If Ms. Sayers was looking to force his unit to give her information, she'd be the last to get a complete report. He dialed her number and waited for her to answer.

"Hello, who you looking for?"

Stunned, Damien compared the number on his phone with the business card he found in his wallet while waiting for a voice to answer.

"Uh, I'm looking for Ms. Sayers?" he questioned not sure he had the right number.

"Oh, hold on, that's my moms." The boy replied with less bass in his voice.

Damien didn't know why he was relieved. He never thought about the reporter having a husband or a family. Now that he heard her son's voice he wondered if she lived in marital bliss.

"Good morning, may I help you?"

"Good morning."

"Detective Tyson? Wow, this is definitely out of the ordinary. What brought on this call?"

"I hope I'm wrong, to be honest; I was watching the news—"

"Hmmm, you too?" she interrupted. "How is it they got information before I did. I guess someone couldn't keep his promise. Are you calling for me to forgive you? Go ahead, tell me how it was the Chief who gave them the information."

"Samantha, cut me a break. I thought it was you."

"Me, how? I've been waiting for you to give me something, a sign, something." She smiled understanding the position he was in. "So, I can print what I have?"

"I guess you can. After all, the news has spared nothing." Damien would have to look elsewhere for the person who leaked the information.

"Tyson, to be honest with you, I think when the wives offered a reward for information, it all went public. It's out now but you can give me what you have, the details, and we can clean up the mess that has been made."

"I don't know that there is a mess. Maybe this woman, this worker can identify the mystery woman and another door will open. Otherwise it's as we thought, a cold case."

"So will you be interviewing this woman?" The reporter took a place on her couch hoping for a lengthy conversation.

"Stop smiling. Of course I will, maybe Monday or Tuesday," he paused, "off camera." Her silence prompted him to continue. "Let me see if she's another dead end, no need to waste your time."

"Damien, it's news and you promised. Let me print a statement from you, something."

"Wednesday, I'll call you then or will your son be screening your calls."

His comment caught her off guard. "Who? Oh, you know teens, no screens. Just call me." She'd be sure to answer the next call from him.

Mona grew tired of the repeated breaking news. She needed to find Ms. Thurston. If she claimed she recognized her with the scarf, she may have seen her without it. Mona didn't need the extra drama, especially since she had her eyes on her next target. She packed her cosmetics, the basics of her overnight needs. Damien didn't tell her the plans for the evening, so she packed two outfits, both equally alluring. Finally an intimate night; she wondered had the three month wait been worth it. The phone rang, interrupting her daydream and packing.

"Hey girl. Are you ready for your overnight?" It was Candice.

"Been ready. I hope I'm not wasting my time." Mona replied as she put her pink camisole and thong in her overnight bag. The bubble bath, pink manicure, and pedicure would add a sensual overtone.

"Girl, I'd love to waste my time with a man like Damien. You need to hook a sistah up! I'm still waiting on his friend, James."

"Candice! His name is Jeffrey. You can't even remember his name, and I bet he doesn't remember yours."

"So you say." Candice replied, her excitement was quickly extinguished. "Well play nice, and call a sistah when you get home. Did you speak to Kendra? She's talking to a detective on Monday."

"Hey did she mention anything about installing a security system?"

"No, why would she need that?"

"I was just wondering. Maybe she wanted peace of mind or safety."

"No, she didn't mention it."

Mona kept her thoughts to herself. She'd talk to Kendra about Damien's number being on her phone. She was sure it had to be a logical reason.

"Listen, Damien will be here any minute. I'll call you when I return."

"Take that walk on the wild side girl. Make sure you loosen up. You know release that ten—" Candice didn't hear Mona say goodbye before the dial tone sounded in her ear.

Chapter Forty-Six

The drive from the city to the Delaware Water Gap was refreshing. Damien suggested the ride and lunch at a quaint restaurant along the way. Mona was surprised that the simplicity of the outing touched her emotions. They talked about anything and everything. They agreed not to discuss work. Damien planned the day hoping that being away for the day would be the beginning of many memories.

"I've never traveled this route to the Gap. It's beautiful." Mona exclaimed as she looked out the large bay window of the restaurant. "The food here is delicious. Now tell me you found this place while working too."

"No, no clients in this area. I don't think the home or business owners get many break-ins."

Damien prepared himself for the discussion. It would be easier to tell her he was a detective if she continued to ask about his "clients"." Mona didn't seem to be overly interested in furthering that conversation. They left the restaurant and before returning to the car, they followed the path marked "Nature Walk". The waitress told them it was a perfect day to take the walk.

The afternoon was completed after window-shopping at a few smaller stores and boutiques. Damien offered Mona the opportunity to go into the stores where the window displays teased her. As a lover of shoes and handbags, she didn't refuse what he called a gift. Mona felt like a child in a candy store.

"They look nice on you." Damien complimented every pair she tried on.

"I'll take these. I like them too. The handbag they have matches and that's what caught my eye. Listen to me talking; you don't mind my shopping do you? You've found my weakness." Mona laughed in spite of herself.

"If it pleases you, I'm good. I said a day of relaxation and enjoyment. You seem to be enjoying it."

She handed the box with the shoes and the handbag to the cashier and stepped aside. Damien's phone rang and Mona's eyebrow reacted.

"Hello, oh hey what's up? Hang on." He completed the payment, took the bag from Mona and followed her out the door. Mona couldn't believe he didn't think it was rude to have the person on hold or take the call after she got in the car. Damien stood at the rear of the car and finished the conversation.

"Kendra, I wouldn't advise you to contact Jay. Why would you want to?"

"Damien, you want me to talk to the police on Monday. I need him to explain his intent. What was he thinking? Giving me her address was a setup."

"Exactly why you shouldn't call him. Let the man explain his intent in court. You don't know how this will play out. Kendra, he's looking a way out of the charges. If he loved you this wouldn't be a conversation. Girl, c'mon you're smarter than that."

Mona tried to hear his end of the conversation. He was agitated, that was obvious. Questions without answers kept her from listening any further. Damien got in the car without saying a word.

"Is something wrong?" Mona asked. She could see the anger in his facial expression.

"Family, you know. You don't want to cross barriers; that thin line that says, caution mind your business. What do you have a taste for? There's a great seafood diner near my house. I thought we could have dinner and finish this beautiful date with an evening at my home."

"Wait, before we decide, is your relative okay?" The answer would calm her curiosity; she had no real concerns.

"They'll be fine, I'm sure of it."

Mona didn't believe herself. She allowed him to avoid answering the question. Smiling, she couldn't disguise her feelings. He was totally different and she welcomed his assertiveness. Unlike Kevin or Leon, he wouldn't permit her to be the lead in the relationship. They could have a real love, a real relationship, one without barriers or limitations.

"So am I to assume that you're smiling at the thought of our evening?" Damien kissed her hand before putting the car in reverse.

"Well in a way." She was blushing — she couldn't believe he had her blushing. Being vulnerable wasn't a characteristic she toyed with. Often it was the prelude to sex. *"If he mentions sex, I'll be done before we get to the bedroom door."*

Chapter Forty-Seven

Jeff dialed the number again. After speaking with Ms. Thurston, he was sure if they got a sketch of the woman a new lead would be revealed. He'd need approval or a quick email from Damien to start the process. He texted Damien, instead of leaving a message. He was sure the annoyance of the pager would distract him. It wasn't until he received no reply that he remembered Damien was attempting to begin a love life.

Jeff and Damien were close. Although there was a five year age difference, it didn't seem to damper their conversation or thoughts. Jeff, who was never married, helped his friend through what they both saw as a difficult divorce. They agreed the hours of an investigative detective played a major part in ruining one's personal life, especially if they had a family. It would take an understanding partner and spouse to ignore the late night hours, the impromptu assignments, and the danger that each case could bring. There were a few that could understand it was a job with benefits and sacrifices.

Sonya Tyson took her vows seriously on the day she and Damien tied the knot. After the birth of their two daughters, missed birthdays and celebrations, canceled vacations and empty promises Sonya looked for reasons to stay. She thought her husband's promotion to Detective would mean a raise and other perks that would benefit the family. Damien worked longer hours and was rewarded with the Cold Case Unit. Sonya wished she could brag about him and his cases, most highlighted on the front page or the evening news. He avoided the media at all cost. She and Damien would argue about his closed mouth agreement. He swore her to secrecy. The only conversations they had between them that didn't lead to a disagreement or argument was about their girls. She remained Ms. Tyson because it gave her an identity. Although she was a model with great potential, being a detective's wife meant a lot to the ladies in the community, even if she attended quite a few events without her husband.

Sonya offered an alternative he could change his job, give up his position and the unit. He ignored her and she began looking forward to her nights alone. Soon she found someone who adored her but respected the marriage. Sonya's interest and curiosity led her to another's bed. She feared her never at home detective would suspect her changes. He did, but never mentioned it to Sonya.

Damien told Jeff of the discord. He shared his fears. He knew he would lose his family. It was either the woman he loved or the job he worked so hard to get. Being a detective was his life's dream. His children were the only reason he stayed with his wife; his marriage was not a happily ever after. He couldn't pretend it was and Sonya no longer cared. His suspicion wasn't confirmed until they were close to signing divorce papers.

Jeff went through it all, as a friend would. Damien went through withdrawals, stayed to himself, and worried those he worked with. Jeff was the only one who understood his co-workers concerns and his friend's pain. It was during that time that Damien wouldn't answer his calls.

It felt strange, Damien wanting to share his time with someone else. He hoped it wouldn't be a setback. As a friend he would remain at a distance and keep it all in prayer. The four years passed quickly but he feared Damien was still hanging on. He hoped to prove to Sonya that she wanted the life he could provide, but didn't want to compete with his job for time. Damien wanted her to know he understood. He often mentioned he knew she loved him. She would ask if he had met another. Damien would deny it though he wished he could say "yes".

Jeff agreed. If another woman stepped into Damien's life, Sonya would be more than willing to be a threat to their relationship. They both concluded that sincere relationships would be another thorn in his side. Jeff hoped of all the women Damien had encountered; Mona was more like the rose than the thorns he had met. Now that Damien planned to tell her he was a detective, Mona would either blossom or wither. Damien would suffer once again.

Jeff called Steve. The conversation was short. Without an approval from Damien he couldn't call the artist in or bring Ms. Thurston to the station. It would have to wait. Neither Ms. Thurston nor Steve seemed to be disturbed after waiting for two hours for the return call. They seemed sincere when they promised to make time on Monday. Jeff assured them the sketch would take place then.

Jeff was tempted to question Ms. Thurston's motive other than the ransom that was being offered. He'd leave that for Monday when he and Damien would analyze her answer. He decided not to bother calling Damien again.

Chapter Forty-Eight

Damien melted a few of Mona's barriers immediately when she found out he was a cook, a good cook. He and the chef at Chelsea's Seafood shared talk of a recipe and the Chef surprised the couple with the dish as described. They talked over a centered candlelight and Mona learned more about her date than she could have imagined.

"Well, I don't cook like this, but I can cook." Mona smiled coyly hoping her embarrassment didn't show.

"I don't get to cook like this often. Another reason I become familiar with restaurants and the chefs."

"So it's not just your clientele? I was admiring how you've kept in shape always having the business lunch or dinner."

Damien laughed as he wiped his mouth. "No my dear, a lot of times I don't get to eat with my clients. Very seldom you could say."

He knew he had to explain his occupation before they got to his home. His man cave was decorated with awards, plaques and a few pictures and articles giving credence to his position in the Police Department. He had a scrapbook filled with thank you letters from families and other memories on his executive desk. He worked at home often. Late nights were spent researching and checking background documents that were on file cards. Not the typical man cave, but one would immediately know he was an officer of the law.

His pictures through the ranks were mounted on the walls, while his desk was filled with his daughter's smiles. He had a lot to reveal if he expected Mona to spend the night in his home. No woman would tour his home without questions of who he was and what was in his past.

"Two girls and a wife. If it's not prying, where are they?"

"Sonya, my ex, travels a lot. She's a model or she wants to be one. Anyway, she's out of town quite often. The girls live with her parents in South Jersey. They visit me often, usually during a school break or my vacation. Kinda hard to get them to class from here. They're teens with their own social life, and being girls, well their grandmother prefers them to be with her. It works. I send whatever they need, mostly money for clothes."

"What about their mother? How often does she come to town?"

"Here? Never, I mean, there's no reason for her to come here."

"No, I mean to her parent's to see the girls."

"Oh, yeah. I don't know. I don't ask. The girls seem to be okay and they haven't mentioned not seeing her or anything. To be honest between their visits with me, her parents and mine, I really don't think they miss her much. My youngest is thirteen and her sister is fifteen."

"Hmm, I remember those days. Just learning about who you are without parental guidance."

"Uh ... listen, my girls have guidance." He smiled to soften the statement. Mona was teasing and he enjoyed playing along. She didn't bother to ask how young he was when he started his family. She kept her questions to herself, hoping he would fill in the blanks.

The dinner was topped with desert. Mona ordered the recommended chocolate cake with coffee. Damien settled for the coffee and the check. The intimate talk continued in the parking lot on the way to his car. He opened the passenger door of his navy blue Cadillac, CTS and waited for her to get face to face to ask his next question.

"So what about you Miss? No marriage, no children? How did you outrun the men of your youth?"

"Just not willing to be caught by any of those who chased. To be honest most keep secrets and play games. You know, they want to share their lives between home and business, or home and play."

Damien understood immediately what she avoided saying. He dared not pick it apart as his curiosity rose. He learned a valuable lesson with women and he dared not ruin their perfect evening.

"So I need to reveal my soul, my inhibitions; those things that time would uncover? I mean if you told me you needed to know all there is to know about me…"

Mona silenced him by softly pressing her lips to his. She didn't want the fairytale. The misleading fantasy would lead her to her journal and the fine specimen of a man with her, to his grave.

"In time, but whenever you do, promise me it will be the truth."

The moment swept them away. Damien kissed her with passion he hoped it would lead to a night of ecstasy. They arrived at his home in enough time to see the sunset. Damien loved showing what he considered the best view in the state. From the deck of his Edgewater, New Jersey condominium one could see the New York City skyline and waterway. They stood there admiring the picturesque view. Mona loved it. She said a silent prayer of thanks. Damien had to be a godsend.

"Would you like a glass of wine?" Damien interrupted her thoughts of the hours she'd love to spend in his home.

"Yes, I'll come in with you. This is beautiful. Did you select this area because of the view?"

"That and after the divorce, I sold the house we shared. Too many memories — good and bad. Plus, I like the solitude. I spend a lot of time doing work, after work."

It was then he remembered his man cave.

"Security protection work, after work? Really?" Damien poured the wine and raised his eyebrows.

"Your eyes say there's more to it."

"C'mon sit down with me." Mona moved slowly. She wasn't sure what he was about to reveal.

"It's not bad, I promise. Sit here with me." Damien put his glass on the table. Mona took the subtle hint and placed her glass next to his. She sat back on the sofa and prepared herself.

"Don't look so worried, that's one of the reasons I told you I did security work."

"What's one of the reasons? You didn't even know me when you told me that? Apparently you tell that lie to everyone."

"You're right, I do. I'm a Detective in the Homicide Unit, in Montclair. I don't tell where I work to just anyone, especially women. It seems that the time that I have to put in is too much for them."

Mona hoped he couldn't see the anxious feelings that were taking over.

"The job I love broke up my marriage and a few good relationships. You okay?"

"Uh yes, just a little surprised. Most men would brag about a job like that?"

"Maybe fifteen years ago, but not now. I work with Jeff and I've got Amir and a few others that I rely on when we are involved in an active investigation. Nothing really to brag about."

"Hmm ... so are you on a case now and what do you do when you don't have a case?" It would calm her nerves if he didn't have anything to do with the Bates case.

"Well, I've made it a rule not to mix my job and the cases with my personal life. You know more now than most of the women I dated."

"I love a good mystery. I love when the bad guy gets away. That's what your unit does, right? I mean you investigate when the suspect gets away."

"Something like that. If you love mysteries, I'm sure you've seen enough on the television."

"Yes, I have. Are you guys handling that case with the mystery woman?"

Damien looked at her and shook his head. He avoided the question.

"Well, now that you know what I do, if you call and get the answering machine, you'll understand."

Mona had drifted into her own world. Her thoughts changed quickly. She had hoped he would say yes. Then she could follow the investigation closer. She'd journal for sure when she got home. *He was a godsend for sure, but a relationship? He had to be better than the others; but then again he's lying about his job.*

Chapter Forty-Nine

Damien was left with his own conclusions. Mona didn't seem upset that his job was more demanding and had been challenging in his relationships and his marriage. He wondered what was on her mind, but dared to ask.

"I've never dated an officer, I've thought about cuffs though."

Damien watched as she stood pretending to be handcuffed with her hands clasped in the center of her back.

"I can only imagine what it would be like in cuffs."

"Depends on who put you in them and why." Damien stood behind her holding her hands together and kissing her neck. "A pretty lady, such as yourself, shouldn't need to be cuffed."

"So you wouldn't cuff me, even if I resisted arrest."

"You won't resist, believe me, and I'm sure you'll surrender."

Mona turned to face him with a sexy smile. "I give up."

"Let me show you the rest of my home since you'll be locked up here for the night."

They walked through the condo hand in hand. Damien explained his decorative skills, something he took pride in. If he told Mona he learned color schemes by watching his wife as she decorated their home, he was sure the tour would end.

"This room is my solace." Mona stepped into the room and smiled. She knew it was his man cave. There was no doubt, all the accolades on the walls spoke loudly; he was one of the best in his field.

"You do your work here? I mean you definitely have enough room and books." She picked up the book from the desk.

"Let me show you the library, that's where the books are."

"A library?"

"Well, let's just say that's what the den has become."

Damien rushed her out of the man cave hoping she didn't notice she wasn't really welcomed in that room. Although he had cleaned up a few of the reports, articles and notes, he didn't want her curiosity to cause her to question his investigations.

Mona saw the papers on his desk and was certain she needed just one chance to browse through his paperwork. His pretending not to rush her along spoke loudly.

"No women in the man cave huh?"

"No women in my home period. It's been a while, and she was a detective, so I guess I expected her to ignore some of the things I had laying around. I'm trying to impress you. You don't need to see reports and pictures. Sometimes, well most of the time, my job is really ugly."

"Hmm, well look at this!" She was in awe of the books, magazines, and CDs that sat neatly on the walnut shelves. "Did you have this case put in the wall?"

"No, it was done by the previous owner. Have a seat. Do you want more wine?"

"Yes, that would be nice."

Damien poured the wine into the glasses adding a cube of ice to both. As he sat next to Mona on the couch, he tapped the remote to his stereo system.

"Nice touch. Yes, I'm impressed. Why would one care about your job if it offers all of this?"

"Not important to them, I guess. I hope it doesn't bother you or should I say us."

"Not in the least."

He saw his opportunity. He gently reached for her glass and placed it on the table. He pulled her close to him and kissed her softly. Mona's response gave him permission to fulfill his desire. As he kissed her neck, he allowed his hand to roam. Damien found the hooks to her bra.

Mona relaxed permitting herself to be led to her fantasized pleasure. His hands were smooth and comforting. She lifted her arms as her bra fell to her waist. Damien didn't wait for her to ease down on the couch. He kissed her between her breasts and began to suckle her nipples. Mona closed her eyes as he returned to her lips.

"Follow me." Damien stood and took her hand. She followed him into his bedroom. He led her to the bed. She wanted to say how beautiful it was as she laid in the center of the king-sized bed. The cherry oak frame and posters were stenciled with a unique design. The dresser and armoire matched perfectly.

Mona was falling for him quickly. His mannerism, his character, his designer touch, and she hoped his lovemaking wouldn't ruin her hopes for a lasting relationship. His being a detective could be her advantage.

He approached the bed without his shirt and pants. Mona disrobed watching him as he pulled back the comforter and the sheet. The freshened linen, like the day, was prepared just for her. She was pleased to see his physique had aged gracefully. It was obvious he kept himself in shape.

Mona's body glistened in the dim lit room. Damien dreamed of their first encounter. Now the thought of it made his nature rise. Head to toe she was beautiful. Her natural hair fell to her shoulders as she released the braids from the band that gave her a sophisticated look. He smiled. Knowing she would be more than relaxed, being herself with him made him want her more.

The music that played through the condo set an undeniable mood. There was nothing left to do. Mona mounted his protected erection watching for his expression. His eyes met hers as the ride began. As she began to tingle, Damien turned her on her side. He kissed her neck as he penetrated her from behind rolling her slowly on her stomach. Mona wanted him. She hadn't been with a man in months, especially one who held her interest. She felt free, even if it was from her toys. She raised her hips. Damien moaned in appreciation. He reached around her waist and fondled her clitoris.

Mona moaned. The pleasure was mounting for both of them. She began moving quicker and Damien tried to slow her pace. He didn't want to end the session; it was too soon. She eased into a slower sensual pace, one that did more to him than expected. The condom was filled as he took a deep breath. She increased the speed and found her own thrill. She knew it was the beginning of a memorable evening.

Chapter Fifty

It was Monday morning, and Damien couldn't seem to focus. He arrived early after speaking to Jeff. Ms. Thurston would be there at nine. He and Jeff agreed to interview her before she met with Steve. She agreed to give him the details for the drawing.

After Saturday night, Sunday was a blur. He remembered fulfilling their pleasures before breakfast and saying he'd call later that evening. The rest of the afternoon was spent on the couch with both eyes closed. He mumbled into the phone when Mona called later. She laughed and told him goodnight. Jeff called to tell him about the interview and nothing else registered.

He glanced at the file and interview questions Jeff left on his desk. They hoped this was the lead that would break the case. Jeff entered the office obviously irritated.

"What's wrong?" Damien frowned wondering what his partner's look meant.

"I told you she was about the money. Ms. Thurston doesn't want to talk to us. Something about her job. The owner of the resort threatened to fire anyone talking to the cops or the media without their lawyers being present."

"What the hell is that about?"

"Reputation and sales. I guess they don't want a black cloud lingering over the resort."

"I'd think they'd want this thing solved. They can't stand another murder."

"Or anyone talking about it. If we want to talk to her, it will be through a third party."

"I'll call the owner. I don't mind talking to the lawyers. Hell, we're just asking for a description."

"And in the meantime?"

"Go through that list of bookings. Cross-reference the names with the dates. Someone was there on all three dates. Check the bookings for each of the men. Was it in their name or someone else? We know the suite they occupied. That's where we'll start."

"This is bull, man. Why would they threaten someone who can help the case?"

"Protecting the business man, that's all. I'll get with the lawyers and explain what we want."

"So the wives are out of the picture?"

"No, but I don't want to keep pressing them if there's someone who could tell us more. Neither of them identified the woman. Still seems there's something going on with them and Bearman."

"Hey, let me call Ms. Thurston before you call the owners. She said something about the reward. If they don't broadcast who got the money, maybe she'll be willing to talk in private."

"They withdrew the money. I got the message this morning." Damien solemnly stated.

"What? So they're no longer interested in who killed their husbands? Well, that works for us. No one needs to know who gave us the description."

"If that was her worry, call Steve and let's get this drawing."

Jeff dialed the number and asked for Ms. Thurston. It didn't take long to convince her. "Ms. Thurston agreed to come in after her shift. What about Ms. Village Post?"

"What about her?" Damien stopped looking through the folder he held. "What's behind the scenes doesn't matter to her. She needs the facts to make a good story. We give her the composite; they run it in the paper, and the media coverage would follow, without Ms. Thurston."

"You know your girl, she'll want more."

"Jeff, stop it, man it ain't like that." Damien shook his head and continued his search. "Listen, did you see the folder with the information about Kendra's attack?"

"Leana is supposed to see her today right? No, I didn't know you had the folder."

"I wanted to see what the preliminary report had. I'm wondering did they talk to the girlfriend, the other one, at all. I know they questioned Jay."

"I don't think they did. Leana said they had a car going to the house."

"She works with the city, right? No one went to her job?"

"Maybe they did, I don't know."

"That's why we stay busy. Why wouldn't they talk to the suspect? Kendra told them who did it."

"Maybe they want to make sure. Kendra should have answered the questions when she was in the hospital. Listen, they may not believe it was another chick. They questioned Jay; maybe they think he did it."

"They didn't lock his ass up! Crazy man, this business is crazy."

The phone rang before the detective could continue his rant. "Hello," Damien answered. "Leana, just the person I need to talk to. Are you still going to interview Kendra? Yea, I know, but what about the other woman. Kendra did tell the officers at the scene who did it right? Okay, understood, no I'm good. I'll tell him."

Jeff waited a minute, giving Damien time to pass on the information. "Well, did they talk to his side piece?"

"They want a documented interview with Kendra. That's the non-sense that caused me to take the offer for this position. Too much red tape. Leana's going to check what they have. Kendra said who did it, and no one questioned, what's that girl's name?"

"Talia, Talia Simmons. Here's the folder you're looking for". Jeff handed Damien the opened folder. "Are you going to Kendra's?"

"No, I don't think so. I want to see this composite. I'm hoping I can retrace my steps with it. A better picture may jog a memory or two at the restaurant."

Chapter Fifty-One

"I told her what happened at the hospital. I don't have time for the fake investigation. They know who she is just like they know Jay. They know they both work for the city with the Mayor. They both came in here with the intent of finding out whether or not I was going to press charges." Kendra turned to look and Mona and Candice. The two stopped by after lunch.

"I'm not understanding. I thought the interview was a part of the investigation." Candice looked at her friends. "Well tell me, is it?"

"Yes Candice, it is, but they're not looking to help me in this investigation. They're looking to protect Jay and Talia. Did either of them get locked up or picked up, for that matter?"

"Okay, so what did the female officer say they're going to do?" Mona questioned, wondering if Jay would be locked up before her planned outing. "The male may not have thought it was a big deal."

"She said they would gather all the information and add it to the report. If I decide to press charges, it will be a part of the disclosure. I'm not stupid. The investigation is done. I'll be downtown in the morning, bandages and all. I already contacted a lawyer."

"What about your connects? You're always talking about who you know in the police department. Maybe they could get the charges moved on. You are charging them right?" Candice waited for Kendra's answer. "Tell me, Mona, she's not gonna give us a 'But Jay' explanation for not filing charges."

"No Candice, I'm not! Yes, I'm filing charges on Talia, for sure."

"And—" Both Mona and Candice chimed in.

"They'll let him off with the technicalities. He's apologized, more than once. I don't think they'll be seeing each other."

"You're right Kendra. They won't be seeing each other again until the smoke clears. Are you dumb or are the pain meds diminishing your common sense?" Kendra gave Candice a piercing look. Mona spoke before the argument could get started.

"Candice has a point. How do you know they're not seeing each other now? You suspected it before, and now you can ignore it?"

"Hold up sisters, I didn't say I'd get back with him. I'm just saying she's gonna pay for what she did. I don't believe Jay told her to do this and maybe it wasn't a set-up."

"Kendra, maybe you won't need surgery! Maybe, Talia can be your BFF after it's all over. C'mon don't you see it yet? Jay is a cheat and cheats ruin our lives, and they should lose more than just the relationship." Mona was beginning to pace. "They deserve to feel the pain they dish out without a thought. He didn't stop humping her the night you went over there. What does that say about his feelings for you? Caring may be sharing but not in the bedroom with another."

"Wait you caught them sexing it up in the bed? Whose bed?" Candice was lost.

"He's the nasty ass. He's man enough to play the game, hell change the rules. They never win when the tables turn. That bitch got him thinking he's worthy enough to have two women. He's met the right one!"

"Who, he met who?" Candice was trying to understand. She looked at Kendra for clarity.

"Candice, don't make me laugh girl, your face is so twisted right now. Jay cheated on me, and a few weeks ago I caught him and Talia at his house in the bed. Yes, they were getting it in. I told Mona about it after going to the hospital."

Mona was still pacing. "It's a done deal. Done!!" She stormed out the door, her jacket and purse in hand.

"What the hell was that about? Tell me what I'm missing. The way she walked out of here I'm thinking, Jay is her man!"

"One fact for sure, her man is dead." Kendra thought about calling Jay. As quickly as it entered her mind, she ignored it offering Candice a slice of pie and coffee.

"So what am I missing? Why would she run off like that?"

"Maybe Jay reminds her of Leon; the cheating and all. I just want this mess to be over."

"Kendra, seriously, you are pressing charges right?"

"Hell yeah, Talia ain't getting away with this! If I didn't think I face charges myself, I'd see her."

"What about Jay?"

"He told them he wasn't there, and he didn't tell her to do anything to me. She had his keys to my place, and if he wasn't there, she was to give them to me. I had his keys too."

"So he denied it all."

"Candice, he apologized. This is about her and me. She didn't want me there asking about him."

"Well, I understand that but damn if the keys were exchanged, no foul. Why was she so angry knowing that's all it was? Sounds like she didn't know he had your keys or that you had his."

"Well she knows, and she'll be charged. They won't be seeing each other, that's for sure."

"And that's okay with you?"

"It will be." Kendra picked up her cup signaling for them to retreat to the living room. She cut on the television.

"So I guess you and Jay will be back together huh?" Candice dreaded the answer.

"Maybe off and on. I call it pity sex. After all, he'll have to look in my face and see my sacrifice. My hurt and pain matters. After I'm done with him, I'll send him back to Talia or anyone that will have his sorry ass."

Kendra got comfortable on the couch and surfed through the channels. Candice recognized the move. Over the past few weeks whenever Kendra got comfortable it meant shortly sleep would follow.

"I guess I just ain't that much in love. I mean, seems like you're getting back at him either way."

"You're right. Mona said it the other day. He's no better than Leon and that other guy, Kevin. They cheat and still expect the best of both worlds. Talia and me? Neither! She is so mad at his ass she won't want him and I'll use him until I'm satisfied."

Chapter Fifty-Two

There was no answer, and the voicemail annoyed Mona when it stated the mailbox was full. Mona didn't have time to wait for Jay's return call. She dialed the operator at City Hall and asked for Jay Rands. Hours had passed since she left Kendra and Candice standing in the middle of the room.

The hysteria that was mounting while she listened to Kendra's reflection of her interview could not be controlled any longer. Now at her home she was still pacing. She promised herself that Jay would be dead before he got another chance lay next to Kendra again. He didn't deserve her love. She picked up her journal and began her own therapy session.

"It's always the sister with a little above the norm that gets screwed in the end. Kendra almost lost her life loving a man that would never see or understand her value. She still values him. Do I still value them? There is no value in a cheater. There is nothing that is genuine or one hundred percent with them. I know that, but Kendra is looking to 'fix' him. Mold him like putty into the man she would love forever. I've got another mold for bastards like Jay Rands. It's whatever they can put his remains in. Easier to cremate his ass, after all he burned my girl. He burned his girl, Talia, and the ass has taken up my offer to burn them both again. Kendra can't fix that, but I can."

Her phone rang; the unexpected sound startled her. She took a deep breath before answering just in case it was Damien.

"Hello?"

"Hey, did I catch you at a bad time?" Jay asked. "I missed your call."

"No, not at all. Yes, I was wondering if we can meet Tuesday, tomorrow night instead."

"Sure babe, that's better for me. Where are we meeting or do you want me to pick you up?"

"No, the same diner, about six is good."

"Perfect. I'll see you then."

"Oh and Jay. Watch yourself, don't call Kendra."

"That's a thing of the past. I'm good, but you got me curious, so I'm down with it."

"What are you talking about?" Mona was stunned.

"They don't have anything on me; that's all. So you and I can celebrate. I'll have to give her some time then...."

"Then you'll run your game on her again? What good is it for me to help you? You'll just do it again."

"Look you approached me, right? So what you want to do? You got some game with you girl. Kendra ain't pressing no charges on me. So your lame ass excuse is an empty threat. Now we can still have this romp, you know what I mean? We get busy; I satisfy your curiosity and mine. Your girl ain't got to know shit!"

"Tomorrow at six Jay. Don't stand me up!"

"I'll be there."

Mona scribbled in the journal, crossed out the vulgar thought, and threw the pen and journal across the room.

"BASTARD!"

Chapter Fifty-Three

It was close to nine-thirty when Steve called Jeff to say he got a call to report to Homicide and see Detective Sheers. The artist didn't understand what he thought was apparently a mistake.

"Hold on man. Damien, did Sheers call you about Steve seeing them? Is there another case we don't know about?"

Damien looked up confused. "Transfer the call. No wait, let me call them. Tell Steve hold on."

Kai walked in the room with paperwork before Damien could make the call. "You better read the one on the top. Your case has been pulled."

"Steve, yea man, looks like they pulled the case. Report to them and let us know what they got. It's obvious the assholes won't be giving us a heads up." Jeff hung up the phone and joined Kai at Damien's desk.

"It's the same shit, man. Thanks, Kai. Don't release any paperwork to them until I let you know. Kai that includes copies." Damien threw his pen to the center of his desk.

"No problem. Oh, and you know the routine. The Captain said to call him." Kai smiled knowing the two men wouldn't want to talk to the Captain.

"If he calls before I call him, I'm not here." Damien returned his secretary's smile as she walked out the door. They both shook their heads, having cases returned when the leads were closing in was now routine.

"They found a link?" Jeff asked sarcastically.

"No, they know we found one. According to this paperwork the case is reassigned to Sheers."

"He's working on Cold Cases?"

"C'mon Jeff, this case is still warm. If they gave him a cold case, he'd never know what to do with it. This is no different. Did Ms. Thurston call?"

"Steve said he called her and told her he wouldn't be able to make it today. So if Sheers takes over, he'll still want to talk to Ms. Thurston."

"Not if he doesn't know where we are in the investigation. Let them do what they do. I'm not filling out these reports thoroughly anymore. Let Sheers and his cronies dig a little." Damien's statement made it obvious he wouldn't be teaming up with Detective Sheers. "Jeff see if Steve wouldn't mind meeting Ms. Thurston later this week. Arrange that, I'm sure this case will be back on this desk by the weekend."

"Well Sheers was right about one thing; here's the folder on the teen that got shot. No weapon, no obvious clues. Forensic report is pending, same for the official cause of death." Jeff dropped the folder on his desk.

"Sheers' case. So they did a swap. Let's wrap up the Pine Ridge Resort murder first."

"Damien, they've got the information. The folder is in their hands. It was dead anyway and they'll see that once they look over the entire file."

"If they even look. I've got the information on the tape. We'll lay low with it until they throw it back at us. In the meantime, we won't lose time."

"Alright, well I checked old man Bearman out. He has no connection with the resort. Cross referencing names, there's a few. The personnel at the resort were willing to do that for us. We should have that list in a day or two. I told them we want to focus on the dates of the murders only.

Most of the employees thought they saw the "mystery lady" but none saw her without a scarf, except Ms. Thurston." Jeff's frustration was obvious.

"Okay, let's look at the obvious. This mystery woman has not resurfaced. Surveillance tapes would show the other two at the resort as well. Start with Styles; find out if there's anything on any of the tapes before his murder, then do the same for Murphy. If this is a woman who was at the resort with all of them, maybe she's not just a business acquaintance."

"Alright, so you're saying a woman murdered three men at the same spot and no one noticed her at all?"

"Ms. Thurston did. Check this out. I've checked the records for all three reservations. The reservation is under a corporation, a real estate company, seems to be a Pine Ridge Resorts membership. Now here's the catch the real estate company is in Rockaway, New York. We need to check them out, find out who works there, and if our mystery woman is connected to them."

"It's a far stretch Damien. I mean you think there's a connection there?"

"We need to find out before Sheers does. It may lead us nowhere but for now, it's a lead."

Chapter Fifty-Four

Celeste hoped Janelle hadn't caused suspicion by taking back the offer of the reward. The news reported it with another update of the investigation. She was certain that reward or not, the murderer would not be found. Whoever it was saved Rusty from spending more time in Jersey covering another disappearance.

The excuse would be abandonment. The two men were, after all, in the same business; partners one could say. They had been seen together on a few occasions dining and discussing business. Now it was public knowledge they both knew and met this woman at the diner in Jersey City. It was slowly unraveling. Celeste was sure that soon it would be said Kevin and Leon were sleeping with the same woman. Married men with the same desires, and the same deadly end.

Rusty planned to kill Kevin months before his death and before Janelle asked for help. He had one reason, his love for Celeste. Killing Leon would be a way to seal their fate, he'd do anything for Celeste. Janelle's call was her desperation. She and Celeste had met at a dinner, shared conversation, and realized their husbands worked in the same field. Throughout the evening, the two watched their husbands flirt and mingle. They left the wives with plenty of time to vent and share their discontent. Celeste mentioned her worries would be over soon. Janelle called her a week later and asked how.

Celeste never told Janelle who or how, just that it would be handled. After the reporter announced the reward had been retracted, Celeste hoped Janelle realized it was over. The difference was obvious. Janelle still loved her husband, or she wanted everyone to believe that. Celeste knew the truth. She had been there. Lonely nights, wondering about her husband's safety. Money was coming and going in their accounts without any justification. Then there were the phone calls and whispers; the mood swings, the anger, and the pain of losing all the promises made at the altar. Celeste couldn't explain Rusty. The love they had, or finally admitted to, after a year of her venting and him listening without judgment wasn't sexual. Rusty had baggage too.

Rusty was about making money that made money, legal and illegal. If there was a barrier, he destroyed it or had it destroyed. He owned property he took as payments for debts owed. He put his life on the line for his children and his wife, who died after a battle with cancer. Celeste was his comfort during her final stages. Their secret meetings became emotional support for the both of them. After her death, they knew it was more.

Janelle became a friend, another to comfort with conversation. She understood clearly what she was going through. Whenever Celeste came to New Jersey to visit Rusty, she'd contact Janelle. Rusty agreed to kill the husbands, but after Kevin was found dead, it delayed Leon's fate. No one thought Leon would die months later at the same place. Rusty teased Celeste about it for weeks. He told her he'd never cross any woman because of the two of them. He'd wait for their confession; in the meantime he'd continue to romance Celeste.

Her son, like Janelle's children, was away for the summer. It would give her plenty of time to think. She channel surfed for a movie that would ease her into slumber. She tried not to think; how they died or who lured them into the Resort? Questions about seduction, bribery, robbery, she had no clue; it was strange three men, the same fate. The chimes' sound was louder than the televisions murmurs. The tone rang out the eleventh hour; she'd slip into slumber soon. Rusty would move in, there would be no more nightmares. Janelle would have to find her own peace.

Chapter Fifty-Five

Janelle had questions; questions she couldn't ask. Celeste hadn't returned her call so she called the precinct and told them, "No reward, we've changed our minds." Before the officer could ask for reasons, she hung up the phone.

The hours passed slowly, and now at ten it was announced on the news. She asked herself questions that were nagging at her since her husband's death. *"When will this feeling of guilt stop? Who killed him? Why? What do I tell my children?"* She screamed, "God forgive me!"

She disrobed and threw her gown on her bed. She put on the clothes she wore earlier in the day. Janelle was determined to get answers. She drove in what seemed like circles. Usually the air from the open windows was refreshing enough to calm her nerves. Focusing on the streetlights glare, Janelle would rid herself of the flashbacks. Leon's smile, his kiss, and the good times would fade into the darkness. Usually she could go home and sleep through the night, but tonight was different.

She was a block away from the restaurant. The name needled at her since her conversation with Celeste. Rusty, Janelle remembered hearing people ask for him by name at the restaurant. She wondered if he would be there and would he remember her. She pulled into the lot and parked. She dialed Celeste's number again. *"Answer the damn phone!"*

There was a tap on her car window; she couldn't see the face of the man in the shadow of the evening light. He tapped again. She pushed the automatic button and the window descended slowly. Trying not to look surprised she smiled as she recognized the young bartender.

"Hi." She waited for him to speak.

"Hey, are you okay? You've been sitting here a while."

"Uh, yeah, uh do you know Rusty?"

"My dad? You're looking for my dad?"

"Yes, uh, yes. I need to speak with him. Is he here?"

"He's down … he's here. Are you coming in? Does he know you were coming?"

"No, not really." Janelle answered unsure if it would ruin her chances to speak with his father. She realized, the man she knew as a business consultant was Rusty.

"Well, c'mon in. If the cops see you just sitting here we can get into trouble. They may think you're drunk or something."

Scott waited for her to get out of the car. The two walked to the diner's side entrance. The crowd was loud, different for a Monday night. There was no great sport event on any of the plasma televisions, or live entertainment for the night. The regulars were having a great time celebrating someone's birthday. The pool tables were shut down; the area was being used for food and the birthday cake. Gifts were stacked in the corner. Janelle gave a sheepish grin, pretending not to be a bit confused.

"Is the party for an employee?" She asked Scott as they walked to the opposite side of the room.

"Yes, and my father is officially retiring."

"Retiring? What does he do for a living?"

Scott laughed. "You don't know him at all do you?"

The question scared her. Janelle didn't know how to answer it.

"Was he working here? Did he have another job? I guess that's what I meant." Scott pulled out a chair for her.

"He worked building this restaurant into a lucrative source of income. He's been in this business for over thirty years. Just before I was born. He worked hard, mostly by himself, it's time for him to enjoy his life."

"I see, well I wanted to ask him a question or two if he can spare a moment."

Scott left her with her thoughts. She could hear the conversation as he told his father it was Leon's wife waiting to see him. Janelle was concerned. She knew Scott from the few times she and Celeste ate at the diner, but Rusty was never there. They corresponded through e-mails and phone conversations. She tried to calm herself. The soft-spoken man she met to finalize paperwork didn't appear to be a hit man. The stairs creaked, an indication that she would or could ask her questions. Rusty Bearman stood in the doorway looking her over. Janelle felt like he was looking through her. She was beginning to feel uneasy.

From the shadow, he asked his questions. "We meet again. Should I be suspicious?"

"No, there's no reason to be." She answered trying to focus on his face. The lighting made it hard to see any of his definitive features.

"Why are you here? What business haven't we completed? I thought I made it clear that we wouldn't need to meet again."

"Well, that's why I'm here. I'm not sure if we've had… uh… other business or that I owe you anything." She whispered as though others in the restaurant may have been eavesdropping.

Rusty approached the table where she sat. Janelle let out a breath of relief. He didn't look like a killer. The older white man looked much like his son, Scott. Though his dirty blonde hair had strands of gray mixed in, he showed no other signs of aging. He didn't have the look of a murderer or one who would arrange the demise of others. He put out his hand to greet her properly.

"Ms. Bates is it?"

"Yes. I'm sorry, I don't want to be a pain, but I'm worried."

Rusty gave the rest of her words no thought. A worried woman could be trouble. He and Celeste were finally able to be together, and this woman could cause a ripple in his plans. He looked her over carefully, not quite understanding what the worry would be.

He leaned in and lowered his voice. "If you're wondering about blackmail, we have no business, no need to be connected to the fate of your husband at all. I'm sure you've been told that. You're stirring the curiosity of the police and that will cause them to seek information that need not be uncovered. There is nothing to implicate you, me, or your friend in this murder case. Leave it as that, and our business is done. I really don't know another way to tell you this. Please excuse me if I sound rude. You wanted this done and it is, your prayers were answered."

"But, what about the woman?"

"What about her? Do you know her? I don't. Listen, live your life lady. I'm sure you had plans for your life after his death. Live on, be happy, before you slip and have an accident of your own."

Rusty stood and nodded good night. Janelle watched as he descended to the lower level. Scott never returned to the table. She walked out after the waiter told her he'd be happy to get her a menu. She was sick on her stomach again. She hadn't eaten in what seemed like days.

Chapter Fifty-Six

Mona answered the phone while she continued to coordinate a seductive outfit for the evening. "Hello."

"Well hello, lady. I was hoping not to speak to your machine again. You've been busy, huh?"

"Damien, yes busy isn't the word." She looked at the clock. She'd be more than thirty minutes late if she stopped and talked to him. "You've caught me running again. Will you be home tomorrow? Maybe we can have dinner after work, my treat."

"That's tempting, but I was actually calling because I will be busy with this case. Longer hours, I'm working with another unit on this one so I can't pinpoint free time. I was thinking more like the end of the week. I'll call you though if that's okay."

Mona didn't have time to pretend she was annoyed. "That's good." She had to meet Jay, arrange to confront Talia and Ms. Thurston and put it all in her journal. She needed to be at peace by the end of the week. Kendra would appreciate what she had done for her and then she could concentrate on her romance.

"You know I could be that woman that needs a little of her man each night, a climax to the weekend." She teased.

"The anticipation will be my climax I'm sure. I'll see what I can do. Maybe lunch, but I still don't think it will be until the end of the week." She could hear the disappointment in his response.

Mona found the blouse she was searching for. She stood before her dresser admiring her body in the mirror. The lace teddy and thong set was the under layer that would clinch the seduction.

"I don't know detective. I may need a hit of that teasing before the week's end. How about a late night call. I'll call you and we can go from there. You have had that type of call right?"

"I'm not sure. I'll be ready to answer. Warning, I may have to restrict calls from you after that, though."

"It's all legal, I assure you." She cleared her throat playfully.

Damien laughed. "I'll talk to you later sweetie. Enjoy your evening."

"You too." She hung up the phone and continued to dress quickly. Her makeup and jewelry would add her personal touch. The perfume would immediately heighten his desires. The black outfit would serve dual purposes — a turn on for Jay and a cover up for his murder.

Jay dialed Kendra's number again. She hadn't answered but he knew she couldn't resist their love. He couldn't afford Mona overhearing his conversation while he waited for her. He stayed in his car, he'd end the call whenever she arrived.

"Kendra, it's me baby, pick up the phone please."

He hung up the phone. Well, she'd have to be told again that he was a man that was a sucker for variety. Talia was different, and Mona would be too. He was sure of it. He pictured him mounting her before she suggested they should get together. He was cautious, he always used protection but he just wasn't a one-woman man. He thought Kendra understood. He was sorry about her face. She was pretty, with a warm skin tone, caramel, and flawless skin. Talia had what he called, "peach fuzz" on her lips. Not enough hair to shave; just enough to be sexy with it. Kendra was shorter than Talia. There was no comparison in the bed, they both took him higher than he cared to be. He'd lose control before they seemed to get into the rhythm. If he were truthful, they were a challenge, one he was addicted to.

He'd consider himself a whore, but no one cared how many women a man laid. He loved the chase, pretending he wanted more than sex, but he fell for Kendra like no other. He did want to be committed to her. He couldn't explain it now that she had been injured. He looked up from his phone as headlights flashed from across the parking lot. Mona was signaling. He hadn't noticed she was parking. He got out, secured his vehicle and waited for her to give instructions.

"We'll ride in my car." She shouted from her window. "Lock yours up it should be okay. I'll drive you back, I promise." Her laugh was sexy with an eerie overtone.

He went back to his car and cleared the seats of the scattered paperwork. He tapped his remote lock. After the two beeps, he returned to her car. Mona watched his deliberate walk. She checked the surroundings. She thought about telling him to move the car to the side of the diner. A nosey owner may report the car in the morning.

"I didn't think about it but if we're not back when the diner closes, they may have your car towed."

"It's a twenty-four hour diner, right? I thought it was." He started looking around for the sign.

"Hmm, why not just follow me?" She hoped she hadn't sparked a debate.

Jay shook his head slowly, took a deep breath and smiled. "No problem." He didn't wait to hear her reasons or comments.

They arrived shortly after nine. Mona's plans had been changed a few times. She had been there earlier to check in and prepare a few things. It took longer than she expected; she was driving slower than normal, allowing Jay to keep up. She settled for a place in Pennsylvania close to the New Jersey state line. Now in the dark, the drive catered to the winding roads. The suite was quaint, but the amenities given were just what she needed.

She didn't want to seem as though she was anxious, so she parked and waited for Jay to pull into the space beside her. They both got out of their cars. Jay looked around, impressed by the manicured landscape.

"I'm so sorry you can't see the grounds here. It's really beautiful. Maybe you'll get an opportunity to come back with your next boo thing." She blurted her remarks before he could question her reason for the rush.

"Why not with you? I mean, don't leave yourself out. You've got my interest girl." He reached for her hand. Mona led him to the suite certain no one would realize he was there. She booked the suite for the week. She'd be sure not to be visible to the staff for the next few days.

Chapter Fifty-Seven

The wine, candlelight and jazz prepared Jay for the grilled salmon, salad, roasted potatoes and his choice of dessert. Mona served him after she changed into a black lace kimono. She told him there was loungewear for him in the bedroom. She knew he wouldn't bring an overnight bag.

Jay had been subtly teased and completely pleased since they arrived. He took his time in the master bedroom. Mona was right; the place was perfect for a weekend getaway. He flipped the pages of the 'welcome booklet' left on the nightstand. The room was large, more than he expected, as was the rest of the suite. The sage and mint décor was perfectly matched with the oversized pillows and comforter. The adjoined bathroom held a Jacuzzi and shower with Egyptian tiles, a distinct design. The gold trim and fixtures stimulated his senses. He imagined the two of them sitting in the Jacuzzi filled with oils and bubbles.

As she said, on the bed were satin pajama pants with a matching shirt. Mona was definitely no match in seduction. He had never been threatened and seduced. He put his suspicions aside, changed his clothes and returned to the dining area. The colors and coordinated accessories gave the suite an air of dominance. There were two bedrooms with a spacious living room, dining area and kitchen.

The second bedroom had not been prepared by Mona with candles and sweet smells. He wondered if she was always one step ahead. The rendezvous was deliberate. His ego began to inflate. Jay smiled imagining he would have to sleep there if his performance was inadequate. The table was set and Mona was pouring wine into the glasses as he stood admiring her body through her lace covering. He wouldn't be disappointed, he was sure of it.

Jay walked behind her and talked softly into her ear. "You're a good judge of size. Everything fits perfectly, including your preparation of the room and meal. Did you cater this or prepare it?"

"I can't tell you all of my secrets now. Let's just say, I pay attention." Mona turned and faced Jay. They kissed a passionate kiss. Jay stepped back and watched her walk away. She brought the salad back to the table. "I hope you're hungry. I'm starving. Let's eat before we play."

Jay was mesmerized. It couldn't be real. None of the fellas would believe that he scored again with little effort. He'd put this night, a booty call, in the book for all of them. He wouldn't forget the details. Mona's voice was melodic; he had no idea what she was talking about. Her breast spoke another language, one he was willing to learn. He ate slowly savoring every forkful. Her hardened nipples poked through the lace. Her breast and the black lace moved to a slow rhythm that seemed to match his breathing. It was then he realized; he was being seduced.

The food was delicious; the salad had a bitter, sweet flavor, one he never tasted before. The salmon, skewers of shrimp and the potatoes were garnished with herbs and spices perfectly. Jay ate everything including another serving of the salmon.

"How am I supposed to perform with this meal fit for a king? You know I'll be sleep before we get to a second round." Jay's ego reared its ugly head again. Mona tried not to reveal her annoyance with his failed attempt at being more than he was. Jay was from the streets. She had dated his type before changing her circle of friends.

"Before you became Mr. Big working with the city and all, what did you do?"

"Mr. Big? Who told you that? I do well for myself but…."

Mona was agitated. She'd enjoy killing him. "What did you do before all that wellness?"

Jay laughed as he wiped his mouth with his napkin. "A little of this, a little of that. I worked for a two-year college as a recruiter. It was okay but I wanted a stable position."

"You ran drugs on campus?" She was sure he would say he did.

"No, what you saying?" He leaned back in the chair. He was full and ready to lay down. He couldn't explain the rush that came over him. His limbs were beginning to weaken.

"Hey can we get comfortable? You filled me up with that food. Yeah, it was delicious. I hope you're as good." Jay mumbled the rest of his words. He was losing control of his thoughts. "Hey, what was in the food, or the wine? Shit, you slip me something?"

Mona continued to clear the table and clean up. She ignored his question and watched him walk to the couch. While he was slipping into a state that would leave him unable to fight, she'd got rid of the evidence. She closed the container filled with her special salad. The mix of traditional vegetables; romaine lettuce, cucumbers, tomatoes, shredded cheese, onions, and eggs disguised the deadly components. Castor beans, and crushed hemlock; the salad dressing was a wine mixture laced with hemlock water and belladonna. A well-mixed portion would eventually kill a healthy adult, leaving little or no trace. Jay was her fourth victim. She was sure just as in the past, the cops would overlook any evidence that would implicate her.

He would be too sick for sex, she watched her past victims try to fight it. She wouldn't stay during the days he'd vomit and go into convulsions. She'd check on him and clean up any trace evidence until his death. Jay would be lucky. Her plans were to snip him and prop the limp muscle in his hand. Mona wanted him to suffer as she knew Kendra would do each time she faced a mirror or someone's questionable scowl.

She packed the bags and sat them near the door. Mona returned to the couch, but Jay's stomach began to have violent attacks. He was making his way to the bathroom. He barely made it there before his stomach released what his system knew was poison. She stood at the bathroom door waiting for his plea.

"Bitch! What did you do? Is this some sort of a joke?"

"Laugh, if you can. Is that what you and that street urchin did when Kendra walked in? Did you laugh together when you talked about her permanent scars?" Her voice was no longer melodic. She no longer had that secret passion for him, only contempt. Jay realized their rendezvous was a setup. Tears slowly fell from his eyes. It was at that moment he knew he was a victim.

"Let me help you to the bed. Show me what you gave so much of that two women would kill over you."

"You're fucking crazy." Jay's words were inaudible, he attempted to speak again. He could only mumble as he tried to stand. "Oh hell no, the room, the walls, what did you do to me?"

"Just what you wanted baby," Mona said mockingly. "Just what every cheating man deserves. You poison our systems, and we fall in love. You cheat, and it kills us internally while we continue to smile, loving you more. Your egotistic ass took it a step further. This will be your last orgasm, Mr. Rands. C'mon baby let me help you."

Mona began tugging at his pants. Jay tried to hold them at the waist but fell back on the bed. She didn't want sex; that was obvious to Jay. Torture, he was sure that was what she was going to do. He could feel his stomach flipping again. His body was jerking; he was beginning to sweat.

Mona grabbed his neck and aimed his head at the bucket on the side of the bed. Again he puked until his insides began to burn. Mona slapped his face with a damp cloth. She cleaned him as she would until his demise.

She pushed him back on the bed and continued removing his pants. She smiled staring at his penis that was as limp as his legs and arms.

"Well, I will say, you had a gift here. Maybe I should have fucked you first. Jay, are you listening?" She questioned wickedly.

"Mmm… Fuck you." Jay responded barely opening his eyes.

"That's just it Jay. I don't fuck with someone who is in another relationship. You knew, you knew Kendra loved you. You could have walked away. Fuck me, fuck me Jay, really?" Mona left him lying on the bed naked.

Jay's body was trembling, as his stomach was about to explode again. He made an effort to move to the edge of the bed. He needed to puke. He hung his head over the bucket again. As he lifted his head in his blurred state, he saw Mona's nude body before him.

"I decided you'd watch." She pushed the button on her dildo and smiled as he rolled slowly on his back. "Have you ever watched a woman please herself?"

She climbed on the bed and straddled him. She handed him the vibrating gadget. Jay smiled, he thought he felt a rise, a slight pulse. He wanted to flip her over and force himself in her.

Jay's thoughts and the buzzing of the gadget were teasing his reality. Mona was holding his hand around the base of the sex toy while she inserted it slowly into her vagina. His penis began to react, and he felt a twinge. His stomach wouldn't allow him the pleasure. Mona quickened the movement of his hand as the dildo aroused her. She closed her eyes as her wetness covered the tip of the man-made penis. She moved away from Jay as his body began to jerk again. She didn't attempt to help him get to the bucket.

As he began to vomit, she shoved the moistened toy in his mouth. As he gurgled and began to choke, Mona knew she wouldn't return. She'd kill him and cut off his penis before the night was over.

Chapter Fifty-Eight

Mona was pleased in more ways than she could put in writing. She hadn't done any work all morning. She spent the early hours entering her victory in her journal. She avoided the minor details.

Although she was proud of her last quest, she preferred to elaborate on the techniques she perfected while killing. She was better than most. She killed without leaving a trace. Through it all she hadn't thought about her relationship with the detective from homicide. As she scrolled pass his name she noticed she was comparing what she deemed was just to what she knew was unjust.

Damien had called as he promised. It was the middle of the week, and she didn't want the thoughts of any investigation to disturb her triumph. She kept their conversations short. He said he understood. He had worked late hours over the past few days and was just checking on her. Mona listened but didn't delve any deeper for information regarding his cases. After all, he did say his work was a topic that was off limits.

Kendra and Candice called twice. She knew they would be ringing her bell before the week ended. She'd be prepared with her excuse for not answering their calls when they asked. She had loose ends to tie up that would ensure she would not be connected to the death of Jay Rands. Mona would explain the freedom she and Kendra now shared. "*The death of a cheating lover was no loss and should be celebrated."* Her thoughts were still irrational.

She closed her journal and looked at her calendar. She made a note on the side of the calendar to call Ms. Thurston. Mona had been following the Bates case on the mid-day news. Detective Sheers, a newly appointed detective was recently assigned to the case. He gave an update, stating he would decide over the next few days whether the case was at a dead end. It seemed obvious that no other witnesses had come forward.

Mona wondered if Damien was working with Sheers. Then it would be understandable that he had to work late. Maybe Kendra would be able to tell her where Damien Tyson worked within the department. She still had questions regarding his number being in Kendra's phone. Rekindling her new relationship was next after silencing Ms. Thurston. She needed to be able to trust him, and she wanted his love. She didn't need any detectives questioning her, especially Damien. She questioned herself, *"Would he be my character witness if I got caught?"*

She began tapping the pen nervously on the table. If it came to it she would have to kill him. She opened the journal again waiting for a solution to her predetermined dilemma. *"WHAT WILL I DO?"* She threw the book across the room. She'd handle it one way or another. She picked up the phone and dialed The Pine Ridge Resort.

"Hello, I'm looking for a Ms. Thurston. May I speak with her?"

The woman on the other end didn't ask any questions or tell Mona to hold on. She heard the phone drop as though it hit a desk or podium. The representative at the front desk didn't transfer the call. Mona wondered if Ms. Thurston was the voice that answered.

"Good morning, Ms. Thurston, may I help you?"

"Yes, how are you, Ms. Thurston. I am an attorney working on the Bates case. I'm checking into your statements regarding the woman you've said you can identify. Is this a good time to talk?" Mona waited for a response knowing she had stunned the woman.

"Uh, now is not a good time, no not at all. I haven't talked to anyone regarding any woman." Ms. Thurston lied, hoping the conversation was not recorded. The conditions of her return to work prohibited her to make any statements regarding the murder or any of the guests.

"Ms. Thurston, I've spoken with Detective Sheers and he's said he's waiting for you to come in and speak with him. I wouldn't advise you do that at all." Mona's lie was convincing.

"I don't know a Detective Sheers, did you say that was his name? I spoke with a guy named Porter who came here. What is your name?"

"Ms. Thurston, if you're doubtful about this woman's identity, I feel obligated to tell you not to get involved. You wouldn't want to be a part of any litigation would you? False identification could cause you to lose your job, money and even property you may own. The woman you implicate could sue you."

Mona hoped this would scare the woman into not talking to anyone. She was sure the resort wouldn't want her in the middle of the investigation either. There was a long pause. Mona thought the woman had hung up.

"Ms. Thurston, are you there, do you understand what you may be getting yourself into?"

"No, I haven't and won't be talking to anyone. You're right, I don't have much and I don't need to be in any investigation. Besides, I only saw her once without that scarf. Usually, she comes with a scarf; I think she's Muslim."

"What do you know about her other than her clothing? Do you know or remember her checking in or a room number? Who was with her?"

"No, she checks in by herself. I've seen her come down to the bar area here in the lobby, but even then she's alone. I think she comes here to do work and leave. What did you say your name was?"

"As I said I represent a client in the Bates case. Ms. Thurston, I want you to understand that I am looking out for you as well. The detectives are looking to blame the resort in some way. You don't want to be a part of that. Saying you can identify people who may be involved says that you may have had some idea that the murder was to take place. Does that make sense to you?" Mona knew the woman would be confused. She spoke fast and confident, as though what she said were facts.

"No, I don't know that at all. I just saw the woman on the television and thought I could help. They think she can help. How would that be a problem?"

"Well if you believe that fine. I must tell you though that I would be doing a disservice to my client if I didn't call you. If the case takes a bad turn and the officer's focus on that woman instead of what's in front of them. ... Well thank you, Ms. Thurston. I'm sure we'll be in touch."

Mona hung up before the woman could make a comment.

Chapter Fifty-Nine

Ms. Thurston was upset. The reservationist asked if she could help. Ms. Thurston bolted to the ladies room. Her fears had begun. The manager told her to *"stay out of it."* Now an attorney had given her the same advice. Porter and the artist were expecting her to meet with them. The call changed her mind.

Jeff was waiting for Steve's call. They both avoided Sheers, hoping he wouldn't ask if they had any information that would help the case. Damien was right, they could continue their angle for self-satisfaction. They knew the case would be thrown their way once Sheers and his boys found themselves at a dead end.

The phone rang and Jeff signaled to Damien he'd pick up. He was sure it was Steve. "Hello."

"Good morning, this is Ms. Thurston. Is Jeff Porter there?"

"This is Jeff, Ms. Thurston. How can I help you? I believe Steve will be calling you this morning for our meeting."

"Uh, that's what I'm calling about. I left a message on his phone and now I'm calling you. I won't be able to help you with that woman. I'm not sure we're talking about the same person. I've been warned by my job and now a lawyer that I need to be careful of identifying anyone."

"No one will know that you spoke to us Ms. Thurston. Detective Tyson will speak with your boss. Who is this lawyer?"

Damien put down the material he was reading. The call, although one-sided, gained his interest.

"Mr. Porter, or Detective Porter, I can't. Please understand I just can't."

"Ms. Thurston, who was the lawyer. Did they give you a name?"

"No, she said she was representing someone in the Bates case. I asked her name, but she never told me. Suppose it's the woman, or maybe even the killer, or the wife? That's too much to worry about, I can't. I'm sorry."

"If you feel threatened we need to know that. I can get you protection."

"No, no that won't be necessary. Once I hang up this phone, I'm done with it. Can you please let Steve know, he was so nice."

"Thank you, Ms. Thurston, yes I'll let him know."

"And Detective can you leave this discussion off the television?"

"Yes, ma'am."

The phone went dead. Jeff stood with the receiver in his hand not believing what he had heard. The detective turned to his partner shaking his head.

"Ms. Thurston, man someone called her and scared her. A lawyer representing the Bates case? Who is that? Janelle got a lawyer, for what?"

"Wait, what? A lawyer called Ms. Thurston and said what?"

"Man I don't know. Something about she'd been warned by her job and now this lawyer. She did say something that may give us another angle."

Damien didn't comment. He waited for Jeff to finish his thought.

"She said she feared it could be the wife, the mystery woman or the killer. If the killer's the mystery woman, maybe she would want to send a threat."

Damien leaned back in his chair. Neither man said anything allowing the silence to help them sort out her words. Damien picked up the phone and quickly dialed a number.

"Hey, I'm going to need a warrant. Yea, for phone records. Pine Ridge Resorts. I know Sheers is on the case; he can have it. I just need this last bit to tie up my loose ends. I'll give him a complete write up or lead. Yea, I'm asking for one more day."

Jeff smiled knowing the Chief would give Tyson what he needed. Damien hung up the phone and clapped his hands as though he made the winning point in a game.

"So we're going to Pine Ridge Resorts?" The two put on their suit jackets.

"You know it. Sheers will have to wait another day."

The drive to the resort seemed shorter each time they rode the highway, even though the travel time didn't change. The detectives made casual talk about everything other than the case until they reached the parking lot. Porter grabbed the manila envelope that contained the warrant.

"Damien, how do we keep Ms. Thurston out of this? I mean if they ask why we need the phone records."

"They can't be that dumb. I mean if the woman calling is the killer, she may target any of their staff. That's what I'm going to tell them unless you have another angle to throw at them."

Tyson thought about it during the drive. He was sure the caller wasn't a lawyer, the mystery woman, or Janelle. He was hoping the phone records would show the same number connected to the reservation. He was sure Porter hadn't thought about that being a possibility or a connection.

The two detectives introduced themselves to the manager for the day. The young man knew they were coming. He explained that the resort kept the records for reports and training purposes. He was willing to share what he thought would help. Tyson and Porter sighed both would agree he was a bit too willing.

"I've worked here for three years, never, never gentlemen have we had murders here. I mean, you know the first one was at our romantic suites. It's located in the most remote area of our property. Secluded enough for a murder, not that we needed that for publicity. Follow me, we can talk, and I'll show you whatever will help. Put that paperwork down, your Chief called and asked for Mr. Lyons. He's not here, but you wouldn't have gotten much from that stiff."

Porter wanted to wait in the lobby. Tyson was good with not saying what he thought. Porter knew he eventually would have told the younger man to speak only when questioned.

Reggie Ward was the favorite. Both staff and customers loved the fact that he was direct and a lot more personable than Mr. Lyons. The detectives learned that the resort was a family property and Reggie, considered himself a member of the family although he wasn't a Pines. The resort was managed by Mr. Lyons during the day, usually six in the morning until three or four in the afternoon. Reggie came on duty from five until he felt like leaving. Although Mr. Lyons an older distant cousin of the Pines didn't care for Reggie's character, his wardrobe, or his voice, all had to admit he handled the customers with care.

His wardrobe for the day was casual. Gold pants with a printed shirt, accessorized with pink and gold striped socks. His pink t-shirt and belt were what he would call his personal touch. His voice was an octave below soprano, and his flamboyant character kept his information about the resort amusing.

"Ease up Detectives. I mean if you can't love what you do, why do it at all? This mess is serious, but the Pines is about relaxation and enjoyment. Can I get you a drink, water, I know you're on duty?"

"No just the records for now, thanks." Porter quickly answered as they entered the office.

"How about you? Are you considered the lead on this? I can't imagine him being the lead? He's too self-absorbed." Reggie looked at Porter and winked.

Tyson spoke before Porter could respond. "We share the duty of the lead. It's just been one of those cases. I guess it's Mr. Lyons that told the staff that if they got involved they could get fired. You know that can be looked at as interference with an investigation?"

"He said that? What an ass? Excuse me, whatever I can do I will."

"What about Ms. Thurston?" Porter questioned Reggie and caught a sideways glance from his partner.

"It wouldn't matter. If she knows something, she better speak up. Someone's life has been taken, what's wrong with Paul, I mean Mr. Lyons? Well here, let me show you how this computer works."

The men went over to the computer, which didn't take long to load pages of information. Reggie explained each step as he pulled up the calls for the day.

"We can get the same information for any day this year. Now if you need to look into last year or any other year, I'll have to pull up the files for them. If you're looking for just one phone number, just put the number in and search. It will bring up any call with that number. Do you know the number or the date?"

Tyson had tired of Reggie as well. Porter handed him the folder. He was a bit much as he pranced from the computer to the printer giving the detectives more than what they needed. Neither of them had the nerve to stop his rhythm or question his reason.

"Hey, did you guys look at the cameras for the reservations?" Reggie questioned, looking at the pictures in the folder. "Yes, the cameras may have a shot of this diva, that scarf is hot!

"No one mentioned that cameras were used for the reservations." Tyson and Porter put down the data sheets they were reviewing.

"Of course they wouldn't; we review them when there's a problem or complaint from the guest. Some of our representatives forget who really pays their salary. Give me a minute I'll set you up with a review for your dates."

Reggie left them looking at each other bewildered. Neither wanted to speak too soon.

"Go ahead man say it." Porter stated as his laughter chimed in with Tyson's.

"It ain't over until—" Tyson began.

"That fat woman sings." Porter finished.

Chapter Sixty

Talia hadn't returned to work, too embarrassed to become the subject of the whispers. She resigned. She left messages on Jay's cell, but he hadn't returned her calls. She was going crazy. She finally used the keys Kendra left to let herself into his home. She left her apartment and stayed with a relative after the incident. It wasn't home; she felt she wore out her welcome there. She needed her things from Jay, since she was moving as soon as possible.

Her cousin was right Jay "owed" her big time. She'd have Jay and a few of his friends put her things in storage. They'd have to remain there for a few months until the "heat" was off her. Jay could put the bill in his name. She was certain after the police gathered the facts, she'd do time or pay a hefty fine. It wouldn't be long before Jay would weasel his way out of the entire incident. Once again the thought crossed her mind. It was a set-up.

She couldn't argue with her cousin, but she didn't want Jay to be in trouble. Everyone she told about her situation, wanted to stay out of it for obvious reasons. They volunteered to handle the storage fee and get her out of state, if she couldn't contact Jay.

Talia turned the key to his front door after calling him again. When the voice indicated to leave a message, she hung up. She didn't see his car, and there was a stench of old garbage that permeated the air. She could tell he hadn't been there over the past few days.

She checked all the rooms. Nothing seemed unusual or out of place. She pushed the message button that was blinking. As the messages began to play, Talia noticed Jay's scribble on the notepad near the phone: *Diner 7 p.m.*

She stood at the kitchen island trying to remember her last conversation on Sunday with Jay. He didn't mention a diner, and there was no date, just a time on the pad. She flipped through the other papers near the phone. Talia didn't want to second-guess herself; something was wrong. The messages were still playing back, she heard a woman's voice telling him to call her back. Anger was her first reaction. She knew about Kendra. She refused to dwell on the thought that he was cheating. The message was short and to the point, maybe it was business. She shrugged her shoulders and continued to look for clues of his presence.

The garbage hadn't been emptied since the weekend. She remembered the containers of the takeout food they ate Saturday. Jay was somewhat of a neat freak. The sink held a few dishes, the garbage and mail in his mailbox brought her to the conclusion that something was seriously wrong.

Talia called his office. It was early afternoon; she'd talk to the receptionist and find out if it was a chance he was out of town. She suppressed her desire to call the police and report him missing. She wasn't sure that Kendra hadn't pressed charges on both of them. As soon as one thought left her mind, another would enter. There was one thought that delayed her phone call. *"Maybe he's with Kendra."* She put the phone down.

She took out the garbage and cleaned up the kitchen. The odor had her gagging. She was glad there were no bugs in the plastic receptacle. She sprayed the kitchen and lit scented oils to replace the remnants of the week old garbage. That's when she realized, he hadn't been home for a week.

She went upstairs to the bedroom. She checked his closet for missing suits, garment bags, and suitcases. She went into the bathroom where she found his toothbrush, razor and colognes in place. Everything was in its proper place. She teased him often about his neatness rituals, but now tears began to run down her cheeks. Talia feared the worse.

She entered his den searching for his laptop, his pride, and joy. It was there, on the coffee table. She wouldn't get much from his emails or latest correspondence, both were password protected. She shut off the computer and decided it would be best to call the office.

The receptionist, a co-worker of both Talia and Jay's, wanted to talk longer. Talia politely explained he was missing and she was debating about calling the police. The receptionist convinced her to wait until he called her.

"Girl, Jay frequently disappears after breakups with Kendra. It really doesn't matter who else his sorry ass is dealing with on the side. He'll call, still have a job, and you probably won't talk to his sorry ass again. I wish you would have told me you were dealing with him. I could have given you enough of his shit to make you puke."

Talia couldn't be mad with her honesty. She thanked her before she was asked what her plans were. She hadn't planned the last couple of weeks. It was clear. Her stop at Jay's would have to be temporary. She hung up the phone and called her cousin.

＃ Chapter Sixty-One

Kendra dialed the number again. Damien told her he'd be in his office and if not she surely knew how to reach him on his cell. Neither of the connections was working, and she was aggravated. She couldn't reach Mona, and Candice was her last choice. She was tired of being confined.

Her phone rang twice before Candice blew the horn signaling she was outside. She thought one of the calls was Jay with his morning check-in; looking at the number was a disappointment. It was Leana. She didn't need another session filled with questions the police had already asked. Kendra repeated the story, her intentions to press charges and her need to be left alone to each officer that called or stopped by. She wanted Damien to tell them to stop. They obviously found out she was his cousin and wanted to impress him. Their answers to her questions let her know it wasn't genuine concern. The second call was strange. She dialed the number that flashed on her cell, but the recording told her to re-dial. There was no need to repeat her actions. She had become frustrated. She was more than happy when Candice finally arrived.

"Look, don't blame me," Candice spoke before Kendra gave her a stern stare.

"You called and well, I had company to put out. Just think, I gave up my morning desert. We both were too tired to romp and play another round last night." Candice smiled as her thoughts of the previous night gave her a tingle.

"Stop your shit girl, you and who? I thought we told you about the pickups. You won't be satisfied until your ass catches something."

"I caught it alright and for your information he is not a pickup. I mean, he was, but this has been pretty steady for a few months. I just don't talk about him much."

"That's cause' he ain't much. Let's check out Mona first, maybe the chick will grace us with her presence today. I don't have much to do anyway." Kendra pulled out her cell and dialed Mona's number. "Did you speak to her lately? She hasn't been around much." "Not since she stormed out of your apartment." Candice didn't show any concern.

"Hey chick, you know the routine. We know you're there, and we're on our way." Kendra put the phone back in her handbag. "So is this a delayed reaction to Leon? I don't get it; why would she be sulking over Jay?"

"Maybe she's not sulking. I don't know, it was like she was mad for you. Don't get me wrong I was pissed too, but she was overboard."

"I guess you could be right. Anyway, let's go see. She's a good friend Candice. Losing a love to death or another woman can carry the same pain. Maybe Jay's actions reminded her of Leon's lies."

"What lies?"

"He obviously didn't tell her he was married with children. That in itself is a stab in the heart; then she had to be in the background for the funeral. Yea that might bring on some withdrawal."

"So you think she's grieving for you as well? I don't buy it, but yes, she's a friend." Candice turned up the radio and focused on her driving. Kendra understood the silent message. They rode enfolded in their thoughts.

The ride was long enough for both women to prepare themselves for what they thought would be a stern lecture on cheating men. Neither questioned the other about their individual thoughts, but each knew the truth; Mona was a realist, they loved the happily ever after.

Candice parked across the driveway blocking Mona's car in. There were no other spaces, and she'd ignore the ticket.

"Candice, what's wrong?" Kendra questioned when she noticed Candice looking back at the vehicle.

"I hope I don't get a ticket. Shit, I'm gonna have to tell Mona pull up so I can park behind her." Candice replied giving a second thought to ignoring a ticket.

"Girl please, I'll pay the ticket. Hell, I'll use that shit against them too. They don't do their jobs, and they've got the gall to give us a ticket. It's Mona's driveway. C'mon!"

There weren't many cars parked in any of the other driveways. Candice followed Kendra after observing how others were parked. She shook her head and said a prayer. They reached the porch and rang the bell. Kendra reached in her handbag for her cell phone. As she began to dial Mona's number the door opened. They had to push it to get in, but they knew that Mona's ritual had begun and as always would lead to deep conversations and suspicions.

Mona had been waiting for them. She prepared herself and her home for the guests. She completed the writings in her journal before they arrived. There were still a few things that needed to fall into place. Candice and Kendra had a role to play once Jay's body was found, and she needed to prepare them. She'd explain it all if she could trust them. The media would be airing Jay's misfortune soon, and she didn't need them linking the murders. She didn't know what she'd do if they wanted to turn her in.

"I knew the two of you would be here sooner or later. I made some lunch, you hungry." Mona yelled back from the kitchen

"Well, you didn't call or return my calls. Damn, you cooked for us knowing I can't eat like I want to?" Kendra poked her lips out as much as she could and then grinned.

"Be careful. That smirk had to hurt. How is it healing?" Mona was glad that they were there to chat. She let her guard down.

"It's coming along. The meds are the worst. That's why I've got Candice my chauffeur with me. Right girl?"

Candice seemed to be in a daze. She was watching Mona closely. "Mona, what's irking you? You stormed out of Kendra's the other day and then we don't hear from you for more than a week. I hope the love bug didn't bite you already? How's that hunk you're dating?"

"Hunk, where did you get that word from? We haven't been out lately. We're good with that though. I wanted to talk to you guys about what I've been doing." Mona paused, as she noticed their expressions change. "Damn, what's wrong with you guys?"

"Really Mona what's going on with you?" They joined her in the kitchen. Mona was stirring the iced tea. She put the platter of chicken wings on the island. They each took a stool.

"Nothing, really, damn! Listen I needed some time to think things over. I've been dating, working, and between the two spending time with you guys. I needed a few days to take it all in, that's all."

Candice and Kendra listened as she explained she didn't want to fall in love with Damien. She feared another failed relationship would ruin her hopes for her future. Mona played the pity party song while they ate. She placed the potato salad and chips in front of them.

"You do understand where I'm coming from Kendra, right? I mean I didn't have a violent relationship, but it's still a love lost."

"Well just like you told me. It's better that you know than to see it over and over again."

Candice's cell rang. She excused herself from the conversation to answer it. Kendra wanted to talk more about Damien, but she decided to talk to him first. If he was serious about a relationship with Mona, as a friend she'd let Mona know Damien was close to perfection. She didn't want either of them hurt.

His career and dedication to it was his only downfall. She was sure Mona wouldn't have any problems with a notable man.

Candice returned to her seat. "Hey do you guys mind? That was an important call. I've got to leave and get some business straight. Mona would you mind dropping Kendra off if I'm not back? Kendra, call me first I'll let you know if I'm on my way. Sorry I'm gonna miss the juicy parts." Candice grabbed a paper towel and two chicken wings.

"What juicy parts? Sit down and eat, you've got a minute." Mona was lost as usual when Candice talked in circles.

"I don't really. Like you, I've been busy, other than driving Ms. Daisy around. Juicy, as in you and the guy, what's his name, the one with the fine friend? I know you got busy. You can't hide this one from us. I gotta go; I'll be back. Call me Kendra." Candice rushed through the hall to the front door. Kendra and Mona were left alone. They preferred it that way.

"I didn't want to say much while she was here. I think we're both grieving in a way. I guess you're right Mona, we've lost."

"I've been thinking over the past few days. Leon wasn't the first man that cheated on me. I had to put a stop to my fantasies. I was lying to myself while he was lying to his wife and me."

"You think he told his wife about you?"

"I don't know. I never met her, and he never mentioned her."

Kendra was deep in her thoughts while Mona moved the food from the area.

"I made a cake. Do you want a slice?"

"It'll take me forever to eat it, what the hell, a small piece. Why do they treat women that way? I mean there's enough chick's dying for a booty call. Why mistreat those who fall in love with their asses?"

"I don't think I loved them enough, you know? I didn't tolerate their shit from the door. I think, if I gave in a little, wasn't so demanding, then maybe." Mona waited for Kendra's comment.

"That ain't love Mona; it's called being blind and dumb. I should have told Jay like you told Leon. If either of us cheated they wouldn't love us more, that's the fantasy. Have one main dude and a few on standby." Kendra smiled as the cake plate caught her eye.

"Listen, they don't deserve us and they want us to feel undeserving. I mean none of them did anything for me. I think it's the curse of the successful woman. We've built the pedestal and we sit high. It's a matter of not getting off our high to satisfy them. We've got to attract a man that is on his own pedestal, you know. One that can handle a successful woman without comparing us to them."

"So were the others different from Leon?"

"No, they cheated too. They all have someone or are involved with someone later in the relationships. That's what they do. They all deserve what they got."

"Who are we talking about now Mona?"

"The Leon's, Kevin's, Joe, Harry, Bob. Does it matter what their name is?" Mona was dodging the point she wanted to make.

"I guess not, you're right. I don't know if I would want to wish death on them. I mean I thought Jay and I were a match, in love, nothing between us."

"Hold it girl, Jay cheated a few times didn't he? Are you still defending his actions? Death is too good for some of these cowards. I guess that's why I stay suspicious. First it's the no calls, no show; then the excuses; then the make-up sex; then it starts all over again. I'm too old for that shit. I told Leon and the others the same thing. The love died and so did they. Couldn't have happened better than that. Karma has found a partner, me."

Kendra felt uneasy. She couldn't digest the arrogance Mona displayed. She talked like she had got away with murder. Kendra was intrigued by her confidence but cautious. She was acting as though she was on drugs.

"So Karma was the cause of Leon's death?"

"They can't live and love two, think about it. When you're loving one the other is starving for your attention and your love. I longed for Leon some nights. He'd lie and I'd listen, clinging to his promises. Tell me you didn't do that with Jay."

"No you're right. I guess my thought of Karma getting his ass is an STD or erectile dysfunction. Either of those would put a cramp on his lifestyle. Jay's a good man gone astray; not a mature thing to do in a committed relationship. He'll grow up and wish for me."

"Stop dreaming, besides I wouldn't count on him becoming mature or growing up. I know you've attracted others."

"What?"

"The other day your phone rang while you were in the shower.

A special man calling I would imagine."

"Can I get more tea?" Kendra asked as she headed for the kitchen. "If anything it was some nosey ass trying to get me to let them visit. I had a few of those calls. There's one guy though that I love hearing from, but he's always busy. I've watched him for years. He's a little older, though, but hey I may have to push up now that Jay and I are done."

Mona's thoughts went quickly to the phone call she saw on Kendra's phone. It was Damien's name that appeared. She pushed her mind to think harder, but she couldn't remember the number. It may have been the office.

"Really? You never mentioned you had eyes for another. Must not be much if you were settling for Jay."

"Well I think he's in a relationship. I don't know how serious. He's been around awhile. He's a friend of a relative. I've just always been curious."

"Curiosity killed the cat, be careful."

"Girl, I know that's right. I don't know now with this relationship signature on my face. I pray my face will be decent once it heals." Kendra bowed her head trying to hold back the tears.

"Well, if he knows you, he knows what you've been through. Is he a looker? Jay was one."

"Jay is girl; I think that was the instant attraction, kept me coming for more. I don't know, this guy is a detective, but I think he's dealing with someone there. I'll have to do some investigating."

"Well, you know what I say about cheaters." Mona had no way to question Kendra about her admiration. "I've got to make better choices too. I think I have and even if I haven't, I've found a way to get rid of them."

"Get rid of them?" Kendra watched Mona as she seemed to be a little antsy. "What if they're like Jay, you know persistent?"

"Jay won't bother you again, don't worry about it. Just like Leon and Kevin, cheaters, they had to learn a lesson. They don't understand until it's too late. I don't blame Talia and Janelle, that's Leon's wife, they are just like us in a way." Mona turned and faced Kendra as she leaned on the counter.

A feeling of fear came over Kendra. She wanted to leave but didn't know what to say without Mona becoming suspicious.

"Talia is nothing like us." Mona was confusing Kendra. "I feel sorry for Janelle though. Did you speak to her after the funeral?"

"No, why would I? He cheated on her and me. I doubt if she knew how much her husband hurt me or how much Kevin hurt me, or how much Jay hurt you."

"Hey, let's change the subject. It's depressing me talking about these damn losers. So how was your weekend away? I haven't talked to you since you were away? What's his name and where did you go?"

"Hmmm. You sure you don't want to talk about your lost love. You over him now?" Kendra had that bad feeling again. She pulled out her cell phone.

"Candice said she'd be back when? I ain't sitting with you alone on the pity pot. You got some issues that are beyond the therapy I know. I thought I went through it." She dialed Candice's number. "Girl, you can come on back and get me. Mona needs some time to herself. Can't do therapy when you're in therapy. Yeah, I'll be ready, blow the horn."

"Look baby, I did for you what I did for myself. Set you free. You'll grieve a little but Jay understands now. Who's your new friend Kendra?" Mona put her hand on her friend's back rubbing it slowly as though she was consoling her.

"What new friend?"

"The cop you like. He called you. Is his name Damien?"

"Damien? Girl, please, he's my cousin. I like Amir, his partner at times. Damien is like a brother to me."

"So he calls you all the time?"

"Yeah, but like I said he's a cousin. My mom's sister is his mother."

"Does his wife know about you?"

"They're not together, and there's nothing to know. He told me he was dating you. I didn't say anything just in case it didn't work out. I didn't want you or him to feel you had to give it a try because you knew me."

"So you came between him and his wife?"

"Mona, please! What kind of question is that? Hell no!"

"A man spending time with a "cousin" could be looked at as a special relationship. One that would cause trouble. You did mention curiosity, maybe you're a little too curious."

"Girl you're losing it."

The sound of the horn allowed Kendra to release a deep sigh. She left Mona standing in the kitchen. She grabbed her purse from the couch and let herself out the front door without a goodbye. Mona walked to the front door, which Kendra left ajar. She watched as Kendra hurried, slamming the passenger door.

"What's done in the dark baby?! Let me find out!" Mona returned to her journal hoping not to fill the next few pages with new victims.

Chapter Sixty-Two

Kendra was too nervous to talk. Candice kept looking at the passenger seat waiting for her to get settled. Kendra put back the seat and closed her eyes. She didn't want her intuition to take over common sense. Mona couldn't be a killer. She'd talk to Damien as soon as she got home. She pulled out her cell phone checking for Jay's call.

"He didn't call me. He hasn't called in days Candice. Something is wrong!" Kendra turned down the radio so she wouldn't have to shout.

"Who? What happened between you and Mona?"

"Jay and Mona, well she implied that he deserved what happened to Leon and Kevin. Who the hell is Kevin?"

"Leon and Kevin? Leon Bates, her old boyfriend? Isn't that the guy that they're investigating?"

"Wait so is Kevin. So did she date Kevin too? Maybe she knows what happened to them."

"What did she say happened? Or what did she say would happen to Jay?"

"She said he'd wind up dead like them."

"Kendra, calm down, that just means they got what they deserved. You know, Karma is a bitch." Candice shook her head knowing Kendra wouldn't let it go. "Mona doesn't know anything about the murder. How could she? Who did she say Kevin was?"

"She didn't. It's just that she talked like she did know and she included Jay. Candice, he has been calling me every day since I was injured. I haven't heard from him in three days."

"Maybe, he gave up. Hell, maybe he and Talia realize you are serious about the lawsuit. He could do some serious jail time. I know I wouldn't be calling you and hanging around."

"He has nowhere to go Candice. I know too much about him, his family and friends. He was just begging me to think about it. I didn't even tell the cops where I thought he could be or where he could go."

"What about Talia? Did you try to get in touch with her?"

"Candice, why would I call that bitch?"

"Cause Jay is missing."

Kendra couldn't answer. The feeling of fear took over as tears rolled down her face. She turned up the volume on the radio and closed her eyes. Jay's face appeared and slowly faded away.

Chapter Sixty-Three

Celeste answered her phone. She was in a rush with only fifteen minutes to be at the airport. It would be her last trip to New Jersey and she'd be returning with Russell Bearman. She saw Janelle's number and said a prayer. She thought after Janelle spoke with Rusty she'd leave the "case" to the detectives. Celeste was ready for a new beginning with the man she loved.

"Hey, I'm running late. I'll call you from the car." Celeste didn't wait for Janelle to respond. She hung up the phone. She was turning into the extended parking lot when her phone buzzed again.

"Yes, yes Janelle. Can this wait? I'll be in New Jersey tonight."

"Celeste, I know who she is. Well, I don't know her but I've got a picture of her without the scarf."

"What? Who?"

"The mystery woman. I've got a picture of her. I thought I knew her features. It's the real estate person, the one who sold us our home and the office space here."

"Are you serious? Was she sleeping with Leon?"

"Celeste, I don't know but this is the mystery woman. Listen call me when you land. Before I go to the police with this do you think Rusty knows her?"

"Police! Janelle why? Let it go. This is what we wanted and if she did it, oh well. My plane is boarding in a few. Don't do anything until I look at the picture too. I'll call Rusty."

Janelle spent the time going through more of Leon's personal items. She found pictures and papers hidden in a chest drawer in their guest room. She never went in the room and often wondered why Leon found comfort there instead of the den he called his 'man cave.' The room with its darkened borders, was complimented with lighter ivory walls and window décor. Janelle never thought about the hidden corners of the closets or the trunk under the bed. There were business papers, insurance policies for older family members and other memorabilia that meant nothing to Janelle. Her name wasn't on any of the documents, and they were of no value to her children.

She considered dividing the papers so she would be able to send them to the beneficiaries and those whose names appeared on handwritten notes. After coming across pictures, articles and magazines that included Leon she decided to burn it all as she had the others. It was then that she found the pictures of the women he met while in business, some in travel, and others in the bed.

There were tapes, video recordings, and letters. Janelle couldn't listen to the tapes or view the videos, but she read a few of the letters. She found them childish. They reminded her of grammar school notes from boys to girls. It became obvious that Leon's intimate thoughts were his childhood fears.

Janelle knew little about his youth or adolescent years. He only talked about college and beginning a business. Reading more of the contracts, she learned he knew as much about business as he did love. There were many women who seemed to enjoy being with her late husband. Leon was no Adonis, yet he had women with him on every business trip and vacation. No pictures of family or his wife.

She flipped through each picture, now more carefully. She was looking for more of the woman the police thought could lead them to the killer. Tyson and Porter had one thing right; the woman knew Leon. She wondered if she knew Kevin as well. There was a video with her name on it. Janelle couldn't watch it.

Four hours had passed before her doorbell rang. Rusty and Celeste didn't look pleased, but the change in the schedule was necessary. Neither wanted to have to look over their shoulders once they settled in Texas.

Celeste made herself comfortable as Rusty went through the pictures. Janelle placed all the pictures on the dining room table. She made them coffee and offered them something to eat. Rusty looked each of the pictures over without giving a thought to any food or drink.

"I know a few of these women, but not her. I've seen her at the diner. Before you ask Janelle, she has been there with more men than just your husband. Seemed to be business, she had paperwork, briefcase, calculator, always business. The police want a killer. They won't find it with her. I don't think this is the killer."

"Rusty, how do you know?"

"She's still in town. Why would the killer stay in town?"

Janelle didn't wait for him to answer his own question.

"She's not finished. She's still killing." Celeste's response sent a chill down Janelle's spine.

"I'm calling the police. This is not what we wanted. I can't sleep. I miss him so, and I can't forgive myself for wishing, no wanting him dead."

"You're going to tell the police what we wanted to do?"

"No, but, Celeste you've got Rusty. I've got two children that need to return home to a stable home. I can't get my stability back without forgiving myself. If they find the killer then maybe, I won't feel like I helped kill him."

The trio sat and talked, laughed and cried. They understood their tie to each other would be forever. Once Rusty and Celeste left Janelle's home, she called the police and left a message for Detective Tyson.

Chapter Sixty-Four

Candice watched Kendra as she frantically dialed numbers and slammed the receiver into its cradle. After a third attempt, she dropped to the couch in tears.

"Kendra, just wait for your cousin to return your calls. I'll drive you to the precinct if you want me to."

"I need to be here. I'm safe here." Kendra began to fiddle with her cell phone. "Why hasn't he called?"

"You're no longer with him remember? Why would you want him to call? Who are you afraid of? Him?"

"Candice, have you been listening to me? Jay is missing, or something is wrong. Mona is talking murder, and I can't reach Damien. It may not add up to you, but something is wrong."

"Okay, I get it detective. So what do we do? Nothing that you've told me is conclusive; it's all speculation. I do know something about detective work."

Kendra knew Candice was right. She just needed a call from someone to confirm her suspicions. She wanted to warn Damien, and she wanted her feelings about Mona to be wrong. She couldn't have been friends with a serial killer. She prayed not.

"How's your face? Have you taken your medicine today? You're doing a lot of talking and movement and…."

"Candice! Mona killed Leon. I know it. I don't know if she's killed before but Jay or Damien may be her next victims."

Candice went to the kitchen and got Kendra's medicine. She stopped at the kitchen table. The words had an effect on her. It suddenly hit her. Mona spoke of cheaters and what they deserved often. Candice never thought Mona was expressing her own actions.

She walked back into the living room. Kendra had turned on the television. As she flipped through the channels, she paused long enough to take the pills Candice gave her.

"No news is good news huh?" She asked with tears streaming down her face. "Candice please call Jay's number for me, please."

"I've got Jeff's number. Have you tried calling that woman that was here?"

"Yes! Call Jeff and I'll try her and Amir."

The two dialed and listened as the answer machines of the intended parties chimed in promising to return their calls. Just as they turned to talk to each other, the television announced why most of the homicide unit would be busy.

The words "Breaking News" flashed boldly across the fifty-four-inch screen interrupting the scheduled program. The newscaster on the six o'clock evening sat waiting for his cue to speak.

"Just in, a man's body has been found at the Springs Lake cabins in Monroe County. Personnel at the cabins discovered the body after the keys had not been returned. Police are not sure how long the man had been there. The man's identity has not been verified. We'll have more at six."

"Oh, my God! Candice, it's Jay. I know it is."

The phone rang, and the two women panicked. They starred at the phone as it blared its familiar tone.

"You answer Candice."

"Hello. Yes, this is Candice. Kendra is resting. No, we won't. Okay, I will. Yes, as soon as she awakes." Candice hung up the phone. "That was Detective Sheers; he wants to talk to you. You're to call him as soon as you get up."

"Call Damien." The medicine was beginning to work. Kendra lay back on the couch with her cell phone in hand.

"Damien? Why not call Leana?"

"Damn Candice, keep up. The dead man in that report is Jay Rands. Why else would they want to ask more questions? They probably think I did it."

"They think you killed him?"

"Just make the call!"

"What are you going to do?"

"I'm calling Talia."

"Why her?"

"Candice, make the damn call!"

Candice did as she was asked. Damien's voice message caught her attention. She thought about the networking event where she and Mona met. She remembered the two men realizing Kendra's cousin and his partner were the men they met that evening. That was more than three months ago. She had so many questions to ask. She looked back at Kendra. Her friend was beginning to nod. It was obvious she had not reached Talia or never really meant to contact her. She had begun to feel the effects of the medicine; Candice was left to sit with her thoughts.

Her mind raced swiftly, without answers or anyone to discuss it with, she turned her attention to the news. It was six o'clock, and the reports held no other information than what was reported in the brief earlier. Candice remembered when the news of Leon's murder aired. Mona became distant just as she had with Jay's disappearance. She didn't want to think Kendra's assumptions were right. Candice chuckled to herself, *"Only Mona would be bold enough to date the detective investigating the murder of her ex-lover."*

Candice decided to cook a little dinner for herself and Kendra. She was sure Damien or Jay would contact her before the night was over. She wished Mona would call. She would always make sense of the irrational. Mona would put to rest Kendra's suspicions. Candice pulled out the pots she needed for the vegetables. She'd make broccoli and corn with the chicken Kendra was thawing out. The smell of the food would awaken Kendra, and they could talk.

Mona never spoke much about her relationships. As Candice reminisced, she tried to remember if she had ever mentioned a Kevin. Candice whispered her thoughts aloud. *"The police were trying to connect the two murders. There had to be a reason. Kendra thought Mona was the killer. Did it mean she killed both men and now Jay?"* Candice returned to the living room hoping Kendra was coherent.

The doorbell rang causing Kendra to stir and Candice to jump.

"Kendra, someone's ringing the bell." She whispered hoping the television wasn't loud enough to be heard.

"Hmmm, get it. It's probably Jay or Damien."

"Are they ringing right here or do I buzz them in?"

"Candice, damn girl! Buzz, push the buzzer." She barked as she turned to get comfortable again.

"Who is it?" Candice yelled into the intercom box on the wall.

"Damien." The answer eased her mind. She felt safe again now wondering why she had a sudden rush of fear.

"It's Damien, Kendra. Now you can explain all of this to him."

Candice went to the door with her belongings in hand. She opened the door and spoke quickly.

"I don't want to be a geek, less than a friend or anything but I don't want to have to worry about who's looking for me. It's obvious that this will not end well, if it ends at all. I'm Candice I don't know if you remember me but me, Mona and Kendra are friends. Well me, and Kendra are; Mona may be in trouble. Do you remember me? I met you the night you met Mona. I'm sorry Kendra's on the couch and I've got to go."

Damien listened as he tried to close the door. Candice wouldn't allow it. As she spoke she positioned herself in the doorway. He wondered what she knew or what she saw. She was clearly shaken.

"I'm sorry Candice, yes I remember you. I can't let you go out the door without some questions. C'mon back in, let me clear up the questions and you can leave. You answered the phone when the Detective called right?"

He gently closed the door and guided her back to the living room. Kendra sat up when she heard his voice.

"What do they want now?"

"Kendra, they found Jay. He's dead. They wanted to ask you more questions about that girl and of course your whereabouts. I told them I'd come and talk to you. You'll still have to go to the precinct."

"Oh my God Kendra. What if you're right?"

"Right, right about what?" Damien asked as he took a seat at end of the couch.

Kendra's eyes were fixed. Tears dropped down her face.

"They think I did it don't they?"

"Yeah, I'm sure the possibilities crossed their minds. Even if they do, I told them I would bring you back for questioning."

"You've got to tell him Kendra."

"Tell me what?"

"It wasn't me. It was Mona."

Chapter Sixty-Five

Mona's plans were unraveling. She watched the six o'clock news and smiled after hearing the body was discovered. It was the news that followed that disrupted her temporary joy.

"An anonymous caller has contacted the police. They may have the answer they've been looking for. Let's go to the precinct where our correspondent Sherri Fields has more on the story."

Mona fell back in her chaise chair. The caller claimed to have pictures of the mystery woman. Mona slammed down the journal and her pen. She'd have to confront someone else. Mona never planned on killing to protect her identity. In her warped state of mind, the killings were warranted. She was saving the wives, herself and now Kendra.

She had to ask herself who had the pictures. It was close to eight o'clock before she decided to question Kendra. After leaving as she did and the announcement of Jay's body being found, she may have told the police she suspected Mona. She put on her jeans and a sweatshirt. She reached deep into her closet to grab her jacket, her handgun, and keys. Mona would explain how she couldn't sleep knowing Kendra was alone. She had questions and she understood Kendra could need persuasion.

Mona and Kendra had been friends for more than ten years. A network event in New York was where their paths crossed. Kendra seemed a little shy or what she called reserved. It was a part of her nature to scan the room, and watch the body language as the crowd mingled. Since she was an observer as well that night, Mona noticed Kendra and sparked a conversation. They laughed together as they pointed out the masked business owners and the serious corporation leaders. Both groups overreacted with gestures and comments. It was obvious they were seeking more than business deals. Kendra, at that time, was a Secretarial Assistant and Office Manager for an insurance company. She told Mona she loved the job so much she couldn't remember the names of the personnel or their titles at the end of the day. She took the job to move away from an oversexed roommate.

Mona had just moved to Jersey escaping a money driven relationship in New York City. She often thought about him and wondered what he was up to but dared not contact him. As an afterthought years later Mona knew he wasn't cheating but she wished he had. She and Kendra agreed a clinging man was indeed a pain. The women exchanged numbers and that's where their friendship began.

Candice was more Kendra's friend than Mona's. She was into Zumba, Yoga, nutritional foods, and exercise. She met Kendra at a Zumba event and became her partner in a few of the fundraising events for the city. She wasn't as outgoing as Kendra or Mona but her personality added balance to the trio. She, unlike Kendra and Mona, wanted to start a family and that alone often ended her relationships. Candice had a list of requirements she'd present to each new beau and after a few deep conversations she would find herself writing a new list.

The three shared past experiences and never pried into matters they hadn't shared. Mona's love life was a topic that was off limits until she began dating Leon. Kendra would talk about Jay and others only to compare a man's thoughts or actions. Candice, the least experienced, would chime in hoping to be recognized as an equal. None of them were materialistic. Their relationship with men was purely emotional and whenever their emotions weren't pleased they would have an impromptu meeting of the minds. Mona became the advisor, and she felt compelled to see them happy.

Mona didn't notice Damien's black BMW parked across the street from Kendra's apartment. She rang the bell hoping Kendra hadn't taken her medicine and fallen to sleep. She needed Kendra's full attention. She pushed the bell a second time and got the responding buzz for her to enter.

She climbed the two flights of stairs not wanting to wait for the elevator. She shook her head as she thought of her regular visits. She always took the elevator. The complex was small, three stories high with six apartments on each level. The appeal of the units kept a waiting list, but Mona wasn't impressed until she walked into Kendra's home during her first visit.

The door was left open for her. She didn't knock thinking Kendra was alone. Mona heard his voice and instantly put her hand in her jacket pocket. She didn't understand why he was there. It was too late for official business.

"Mona, hey I was going to call you." Damien said as he stood to greet her. Mona was confused but she took her hand out of her pocket and allowed him to kiss her on her cheek.

"I didn't expect you but I'm glad you're here. You can tell Damien that I was here at home all week." Kendra was nervous and Mona didn't know why, unless she had been trying to convince Damien she was Jay's abductor and possibly his killer.

"Really." Mona replied too soft for either Damien or Kendra's comfort.

"I didn't know you were one of the friends Kendra talked about all the time. She never mentioned names."

"Mona, are you okay? Damien is my cousin. My connect, as you and Candice tease me about. They think I had something to do with Jay's—"

"Death. That's why I came over." Mona lied. "I thought you'd take it kind of hard, hearing it on the news like that. I found out about Leon that way." Mona cut her eyes to Damien for his reaction.

Kendra had filled him in with as much information as she knew about Mona. She broke down in tears by the time she concluded that Mona was crazy. A psychopath on a mission, was the description she gave Damien.

Damien's phone rang. He quickly glanced at Kendra and turned away from the ladies as he answered an anticipated call. Sheers had called earlier hoping Damien would convince Kendra to come in and make a statement. They needed to tie loose ends. They didn't think the same person killed Jay and Leon. She simply needed to clear her name.

The call was from Jeff. He was looking at the pictures sent to the unit from Janelle. The sealed envelope, with scribbled notes indicating dates and time, was proof that Leon was aware of the danger Mona presented. Janelle highlighted the date that matched the photo aired on the television. A message addressed to Detective Porter was taped on the outside of the envelope.

"You and Inspector Gadget may need this to pinpoint your mystery lady. I heard the case was re-opened under another detective. Here's a bonus for you. She was working with my husband day and night. I don't know her name. I hired someone to catch him in his indiscretions and this is what was brought to me. Good luck."

"Damien, you won't believe who this woman is."

"Yes, I don't know. I'm trying to convince her to come to the office."

"Who, Mona?"

"No, Kendra. She needs to make a statement."

"What the hell are you talking about man? Oh, oh shit. Is Mona with you guys?"

"Yea, we'll be there shortly. Kendra's a little shaken about all this, but that's why I'll be with her when they ask all their questions."

Damien spoke a little above a whisper. He didn't want Mona to think Kendra mentioned Mona as a possible suspect in any of the murders.

"She might be armed. Do you want a unit there?"

"She is. I'm sure of it. She saw the news. Okay, look do that, and we'll be there soon."

"So do you think the killer is—"

"That's it. I'll need to refer to the notes the cops on the scene have. She's not over it yet. We'll be there, for sure."

Damien felt the muzzle of the handgun pressing on his back.

"Hang up the phone and save two lives."

Chapter Sixty-Six

Jeff made the necessary calls. He didn't give details but the officers were ready to move. He explained there may be a hostage situation developing. The S.W.A.T. team was on standby and would be strategically placed.

The neighboring complex and the others residing in Kendra's unit were told to evacuate. The movement was done quickly as not to alert anyone in Kendra's apartment. Jeff waited to hear from Damien. It would only be a matter of time before the media would send their correspondents to cover the story. They needed a sign that everyone was okay.

After fifteen minutes Detective Sheers agreed, Leana would make a follow up call to Kendra. It wouldn't seem strange that she'd call since the police were requesting Kendra to come to the precinct. Jeff told him about the picture and the possibility that the mystery woman was with Damien.

"What proof do we have that this woman killed anyone?" Sheers wanted a debate. "I need more information than Damien's cousin blaming another woman. What motive would she have to kill the Rands guy?"

"We can argue about this later. We got two calls one about this picture that arrived and another about Kendra Lewis and Mona Mandell. This is Mona Mandell!"

Sheers took the photo in hand. He remembered the photo of the woman and the scarf. It was the closest they got to the mystery woman. It may have been a long shot but it was the closest they had.

"Alright, she may be this woman but that's not explaining a murder."

"Look, Damien is on it. That's why he's there in the apartment with them. He went to talk to Kendra and bring her to the precinct. Mona showed up and pulled a gun on the two of them. Call it what you want man, but if Leana can't talk her out of there we're going in."

"It ain't my call and your boy took the case back, this mess is on him and you. If she killed Rands, then thanks for the help. You guys have stepped out of your lane once again. Your paper trail speaks for itself; boxes of guess work leading nowhere. I assume you called me to clean up this mess too."

"You got called 'cause you're so far up the Chief's ass that you heard the phone ring before he did. I don't know how you got the information. We didn't need you and your guys, and still don't. Do me a favor. Stand down."

Chapter Sixty-Seven

Talia was packing frantically when she heard the news of Jay's body being found. His identification, credit cards and cash in his wallet verified who he was, and his death didn't seem suspicious. There was no robbery. The news didn't have a complete report from the active crime scene, but he had been dead at least forty-eight hours. The staff at the cabins didn't remember the woman who booked the cabin. Jay was not with her at the time of the booking.

Talia sat staring at the screen crying silently. She didn't know what to do. The police would return in the morning hoping to catch her leaving for work. She was sure they would be at Jay's apartment looking for clues.

She called her cousin who agreed to meet her. She needed to pack as much as she could. He'd be sure to put the rest in storage. There would be a train ticket to New York for her. She could stay with family there until they set her up in another state.

The news continued with other events of the day, nothing that held her interest. She focused on the stories only to keep her mind off the reality that Jay was dead. There were no reports indicating how he died. Jay was healthy. Talia often admired how well kept he was. He didn't look his age. Close to forty, he didn't exercise regularly. He played basketball once or twice a month with the men at the job. He was active enough to keep his heart and blood pressure stable. He wasn't on any medication. His sex drive was healthy, and he wasn't a smoker or drinker. He never showed signs of fatigue or illness.

The relationship began after a luncheon held to recognize a new program. Talia's office worked with the City Council to complete the project and she was assigned to work with Jay. They worked diligently together. Focused on the project, they met the deadline and reaped the rewards. Once the program started they were given another project and another deadline. The two worked a few days a week and got closer than either of them expected.

Jay never mentioned a relationship and since Kendra no longer worked at the Office of Planning and Development, he saw no reason to mention her. Kendra's office was moved to another location a few months after the second project began. She never suspected Jay and Talia worked together day and night.

When Kendra showed up and caught them in the bed, Jay explained she hadn't taken their break-up well. He hadn't taken the keys from her. He promised he would; his excuse was all she needed. They fell into each other's arms and continued to satisfy their desires.

She didn't understand women like Kendra; pushing themselves on men that no longer want them. There was no need for Kendra to show up at her place. Jay didn't warn Talia she would be dropping off the keys there. When Kendra arrived, Talia didn't know what to expect. Kendra wanted to rush in the apartment. When she invited Talia outside she didn't dare go outside without protection.

Anger and fear caused her to slash Kendra's face. She regretted it the moment the blood began to flow. She had no idea how bad the cuts were or if Kendra had a weapon of her own. She wanted everyone to know she was scared, but she didn't stay to tell her side of the story. She ran in and got Kendra a damp towel. She grabbed her keys and fled from her own apartment. Kendra attended to her wounds, never noticing the blue Sonata pull out of the parking lot.

Talia wondered if Kendra knew he was found dead. It was the second time she thought about calling her. It wouldn't be a welcomed call, she was sure Kendra would be too angered to share any information. She whispered a prayer, hoping it was natural causes and not foul play. As an afterthought, she prayed it wasn't Kendra who killed him. Her thoughts scared her. She zipped another garment bag. She sat on the bed; she had got a lot done. She called her cousin again.

"It's me. Yes, I'm almost ready. I was just wondering, could they really accuse me of killing him?"

Chapter Sixty-Eight

"Mona, you're making something out of nothing. Damien is my cousin, my first cousin. You're…."

"Shut the fuck up." Mona yelled at Kendra. "What do you think? I'm stupid!! Why is he here Kendra? I noticed his number on your phone while you were in the hospital. I thought it was in connection to the assault. Get over there with her." Mona waved the gun in the direction she wanted Damien to move. "Fucking cheaters. You never quit. You push up on us and we give in and you ease your way into our hearts. Well this is what a fucked up heart will get you!"

Damien walked across the room. His eyes met Kendra's. She was fighting back the tears. He reached out to touch her.

"Wow, you want to try that eye to eye connection with me standing here?"

Damien turned to face Mona. "What don't you get woman? She is family. I can't prove that to you with that damn gun pointing at us. Put the gun down, Mona. Let's talk and clear this up. The police want to talk to her; that's why I'm here."

"The police, why Kendra? Did you call them to tell them it was me they've been flashing across the news? After all, I've done for you?"

"What have you done for me Mona? I'm staring at the end of a gun and you want to shoot me and my cousin, what the hell have you done for me?" Kendra cried out hysterically. Damien sat on the couch and pulled her to sit down with him.

"Put the gun down Mona. You're not a killer."

"Yes I am! You didn't tell him Kendra? Isn't that why he's here? Is he your knight in shiny armor? I told you don't worry, I'll take care of things and you called your man? The one who told me he could see a future in us, but he's here with you. Kendra don't you see, he's just like Leon and Jay?"

The doorbell rang and Damien rushed Mona as she turned toward the door. They wrestled and the gun went off and the bullet pierced the window. Damien managed to overcome Mona. He secured the weapon and put her in handcuffs.

"Are you okay?" Damien asked Kendra.

"Yes, are you? Did you get hit?"

"No we're good. Call Jeff, tell him to send a car." Damien headed to the door with Mona. She seemed to have settled into a drunken state of mind.

The bell rang again. Kendra pushed the buzzer and opened the door. Leana and two officers entered. Mona was escorted out with them.

"What the hell happened?" Leana looked at Damien and Kendra as the pressures of the past hour were lifted.

Damien told Leana the details as he knew them while Kendra answered her questions. They walked out to the crowded street filled with flashing police car lights and reporters. They were escorted to a waiting car. Damien smiled when he saw his partner waving at him to come to his car.

"Hey man, you alright? Is Kendra okay?" Jeff was worried.

"Yea, we're good. She's with Leana on her way to the precinct. My car is here, I'll follow you."

The cars proceeded to the precinct leaving the sea of reporters scrambling as they retreated to their vans. Their destination was obvious. There would be a statement by Detective Damien Tyson and the spokesperson for the police. Samantha Sayers watched from a distance. She directed her cameramen and the rest of the crew to meet her at the rear of the precinct. She had the inside story, one she was sure Detective Tyson wouldn't want told.

Chapter Sixty-Nine

Mona was certain her lawyer would laugh at the charges. After all, the death had no traces of murder. The words of a distraught woman recovering from a traumatic situation would be her best defense. Kendra was on heavy drugs and her claim that Mona confessed would be inadmissible once her medication and situation was mentioned in detail.

The gun was a legal possession. She owned the gun, and a rifle, neither was a new purchase. She carried often when she had late night meetings or appointments. Passion driven, she would admit she had been hurt in past relationships but never by a friend. She would attest that Kendra was like a sister to her. In fact the only friend she truly had.

Yes, the image in the picture was her. Mona couldn't deny either image. The scarf was not an attempt to hide her identity. Ms. Thurston in her own words stated she had seen her often with the scarf. It was merely an accent to the outfits she wore. She had no idea that she was being photographed in the other pictures. It was her but she couldn't remember a date or time. Yes, she was with Leon, however she was crushed when she found out he was dead.

Walter Reed, a prominent lawyer in Essex County, read over the statements she made prior to his arrival. He smiled. She had not been read her Miranda Rights, however she answered willingly. It may help her prove how unstable she was at the time she made the threats.

The charge, aggravated assault was severe, even without any suggestions of the murders. The deadly weapon charges would be enough to give her jail time. However, she threatened to shoot; she never pulled the trigger. All would agree her state of mind was definitely altered. She was acting on damaged emotions. It would be a fight but it would be his only angle. One that would pierce the hearts of a jury if pitched right.

The officers were cordial and very cooperative, they always were. They led the gray-haired man into the waiting area. He smiled as he had each and every time he visited a client behind bars. His session with Mona would be the same as theirs, brief but necessary.

Her bail would be set and she would be free only to come back in two weeks. Mr. Reed explained the procedure to her. The time frame for her release and the hearing may be subject to change. Mona didn't ask any questions. She had been silent for hours, the officers informed the lawyer. He looked at her distant stare. He began to repeat his strategy to her as though she were his child.

Chapter Seventy

Ms. Sayers entered the Homicide unit looking for Tyson or Porter. Officers were hanging out chatting about the arrest. The gist of the conversations indicated there was a reason to celebrate and it was moments away. The reporter hoped they were right. She'd get the front page article and become a thorn in Detective Sheers side. Her conversation with him was short and through his arrogance she could see he didn't care if Detective Tyson solved the case, he would get the credit.

Looking beyond, the crowd she could see the door to their office was partially opened. As she got closer, she could hear Tyson and Porter discussing the evidence found during the last few hours. She entered the office interrupting their thoughts and conversation. Porter spoke hoping he wouldn't offend her.

"You're not supposed to be here. The interview will be held outside. Someone should have stopped you as you came in."

"Jeff, I mean Detective Porter. I came to see if you guys are alright. This is awful. I mean Damien are you okay?" Samantha asked pushing her way past Jeff.

Damien finally sat down. He wore the trauma of the day on his face. He had been pacing and sorting notes since they got back from

Kendra's apartment. He looked up slowly and responded as though he was a fog.

"Ms. Sayers, yes, yes, I'm okay. I'm mentally preparing for that mess you came through. You know, trying to be ahead of the B.S. they're gonna cause."

"I can imagine. I know, as Jeff said, and please call me Samantha. I should be with the other reporters, but I didn't come for a story. I came to offer my help if you allow me to help you."

"Help? Help with what?"

Jeff took a seat. He didn't want to interfere. Samantha Sayers was one in a million. She'd get the best out of any interview. The intimate details that no reporter seemed to pay attention to would be aired in a professional, but blunt manner. He hoped Damien was prepared for her questions. If not, he would read about it in the next issue of the Village post.

"You don't think they'd find out and attempt to ruin you do you?"

"Samantha, who, find out what? I've had a hell of a day and…."

"You were sleeping with the killer." She said what he had been thinking since Kendra told him that Mona confessed to killing Leon Bates.

"If they question her about the murders she may or can implicate you. Damien, that's headline news. Sheers would eat it up. He's after your unit. I know you know that. If what you say about the evidence in the murder of Leon Bates doesn't point to her, can she be convicted or even indicted?"

Jeff waited for Damien to answer. It became obvious that the murders were still unsolved. The coroner's report was inconclusive. The blunt force was on both reports but there were no fingerprints or weapons found. The premises appeared to be clean.

"One thing for sure, we've got more information than Sheers and his boys." Jeff handed Damien another folder. "That's all the information Leana gathered on your girl; she's clean. Her business is Real

Estate Investments Plus; she's the listed owner and CEO. She's had the business for fifteen years. Not much here about her family. She has nothing in her records that would lead one to believe she's a killer."

"Well guys, the media won't wait for an investigation to make an overall statement about today's incidents. Someone will add who she is, who Kendra is, and who they are to Damien. Whatever can't be proven will be assumed. She may even use your relationship as her defense."

Damien took a deep breath. What he considered a romantic start, once again, led to him being in the spotlight on his job. He and Sheers had been the top candidates to run the Cold Case Unit. Sheers was involved in an investigation that could have resulted in his termination, but instead the Chief declined his application for the unit. That was six years ago, and Damien had been the target of rumors, innuendos, and a few smudge campaigns. His subordinates, including those who worked with him, often understood his frustrations. Sheers was waiting for mistakes, botched investigations, or anything negative that would cross the Chief's desk with Detective Tyson's signature. Both detectives knew it would change the leadership of the unit. Sheers would be a candidate in good standing. He had his team ready to take over.

The news correspondents were being organized in the outer office. Each wearing their press tags with their names and the newspaper or television broadcast station they represented. The makeshift staging area was surrounded with lights and a podium with three microphones. The reporters were preparing their notepads. There were a few who were talking into their recorders, a prelude to the reports they would share.

"So let me tell them the truth. Allow me to take the blows and respond with your words." Samantha looked at him with raised brows.

"And how do you propose to do that? Write rebuttals, or corrections to what they say?" Damien stood up and reached for his suit jacket hanging behind him. "I meant to change this suit before going out there. Damn. Jeff, go see how long I've got. I can change in the office."

Jeff left hoping his partner would be able to make the quick change. He looked disheveled, and everyone knew Damien kept everything, including himself, in order. He needed a moment to take it all in.

"Ms. Sayers, I didn't want to talk about this while Jeff was here. This woman, Mona Mandell, can't be the killer. I've been dating her for months; she's not that kind of woman."

"Detective, your emotions have blinded you. Think about it as you would an investigation. As I said, you're the best at what you do. There's a reason the chief appointed you. I don't want to believe you got the job because Sheers was in trouble. Are you going to console her when she goes to jail? Like I said when I walked in, I'm here to help you. Give me the exclusive. I will interview you and the unit. I'll set up an interview with your cousin, Kendra, that's her name right?"

"Kendra, yes that's her name."

"Well, I'll talk to her and Mona. There's bound to be information that's deep seeded and caused Mona's action.

Jeff returned. Seeing the two standing face to face, he didn't want to interfere. He waited outside the door.

"Tell your partner his girl made bail. Looks like he screwed up in more ways than one." Detective Sheers made his sarcastic remark kept and walking through the crowd.

Jeff rushed in ignoring what seemed like a secret conversation. His thoughts were it was more than a conversation. He hoped Damien wasn't being suckered into more than he could handle.

"Hey, she made bail. How could that be? You're a detective, and she held a gun on you. What the fuck does that say to the media? Explain it!"

"What did they charge her with?" Damien hoped it wasn't a trumped up charge. He needed time to connect her with the murders.

"I don't know man, but how the hell does she pull a gun on you and make bail before a press conference."

"Who's her lawyer?" Samantha asked.

"What difference does that make?" Both Jeff and Damien responded and looked to her for the answer.

"Lawyers have connections too. Let me step out. I'll see if my people know anything."

"Sheers is celebrating. He says you screwed up. I guess they know you were dating Mona."

"Jeff, there's no way anyone knows anything unless Mona told it. When Kendra tells what Mona told her, it won't take a genius to know she's trying to get out of it."

"Wait, man, wait. You're not going to say you were dating her?"

"No, why should I? If they ask, I'll tell where we met; we went out to dinner a few times; and—"

"You had sex with her; that will definitely raise eyebrows."

"Why? Grown folks have sex. None of this has to do with me knowing she was a killer. I still don't know, or believe it. Man, she was different."

"Yeah, and Sheers is waiting for you to try to lie your way to that other side. You'll have his desk, and that ass will be in here with me. Tell them, man, don't wait for them to ask."

Samantha knocked on the door and entered the room. She closed the door as though the chattering crowd would notice she slipped into the office.

"Definitely a problem. Not a big one but the media vultures will eat it up."

"What you're not that type of bird?" Jeff didn't understand her alliance.

"Jeff, she's going to help put this straight."

"Okay, enlighten us."

"They have her on aggravated assault, for now. No other evidence is available to get her on anything else. It seems the problem is that they don't know if your visit was while performing police duties or personal duties. They didn't have her bail set. Someone's trying to stir your emotions. She's still in custody."

"Damn! I knew it man. I told you. Anything to get you out of this position." Jeff began to pace the floor.

"I asked the Chief, would they be letting her go? He said Walter Reed is her lawyer; he'd eat the Department alive if they didn't offer bail. She told them the two of you were lovers. Your cousin is being held for questioning."

"Held longer than the suspect? They can't be letting her go." Damien couldn't understand them holding Kendra and considering to release Mona. "Look, I've got to change clothes. I'll talk to the Chief after this press mess. Samantha, thank you."

"I'll do what I can to give you a chance to recant some of the questions. The article will clear it all and tell it all if you allow me to print it."

"Wait, what article?" Jeff questioned. He waved Damien on who stopped at the office door. "Go ahead man, get changed. I'll reject this proposal if it's part of the set up."

"You don't really believe I'd set you guys up do you?" Samantha asked with a smile. "I like the dynamic duo, as you're called. I like Damien even more. I wouldn't set you up. Now I can't say what I'd love to do to that damn Sheers, though. I don't want your team to lose, especially when I'm the only cheerleader."

"Whew, excuse me, I didn't know you felt that way. Well, yeah, Sheers has had it out for this unit since it started. The Chief could care less as long as we solve more than we toss. This mess would toss us for sure. So what can the pretty reporter do for us?"

"Not us, baby, Damien. I've got a few secrets up my sleeve about Sheers and the boys on his team. The Chief can spare me the fence because he's riding on either side. He knows Damien's character and those who work with him sit higher than most. Sheers has got something more in his jacket, and that's the news I'm after. It may even include the Chief. This report, the cold cases you've handled have been a shoe-in for me. The closer I get, the closer I want to be."

"Sounds personal. What did or didn't Sheers do to you?"

"They're positioning." She cut their conversation short. "I've got to get out there with my people. We'll talk before print. I'll see you guys in a few."

Samantha Sayers hurried to the outer office where the photographers had begun snapping pictures of the Mayor and the Chief. Jeff didn't bother to move. He flipped through the pages of queries and the evidence reports that were on his desk. His thoughts weren't detailed enough, and he knew that was the problem. Somewhere he missed the evidence that pointed to a woman. It never failed, the evidence never lied, and it was always visible, just overlooked. There was evidence that would prove Mona Mandell was a murderer.

Chapter Seventy-One

Damien smiled as he stepped off the stage. Sheers had put his foot in his mouth twice during the questioning. Samantha kept her promise. As the top in her field, she was respected and allowed to step in with the questions others wouldn't ask. Sheers had stepped near the edge of a cliff with his snide remarks and she let him beg for rope to regain his footing.

"Man, you should have been out there. That damn Sheers, man you would have thought he was a reporter. He fed that weasel from the Daily the questions, but Samantha knew they were from Sheers." Damien was in a much better mood than when he left the office.

"So she kept her word?" Jeff rolled his chair away from his desk, avoiding the small pile of paperwork. It was obvious he had been working.

"You found anything?"

"No, just can't make heads or tails of it. How did we miss the murderer being a woman?"

"That may be the denial that Sheers was eluding to?"

"What? Oh, and just so you know Mona is still here. She's been granted bail, though, just like Ms. Sayers said. Two Hundred and Fifty thousand, cash, you think she's got it?"

"I hope not. It will give us a chance to rethink this investigation. We've got the possible killer. There's something in those reports that points to her."

"So what did old boy have to say?"

Damien went into the bathroom, but left the door open to continue their conversation.

"His first question shook me. He asked how long I knew Mona Mandell and did I know she was a friend of my cousin? I didn't know he knew they were friends. Then I thought about it; he talked to Leana or he spoke with Kendra.

"So you answered him?"

"No, Samantha blurted her question over his. She asked were they friends long and did my cousin introduce us. I understood then she would soften whatever they threw at me."

"Okay, but what shook him. You do realize he won't stop. He'll get someone who is just as hungry as Samantha for a story."

"Well, he asked was this the first time I was involved with a suspect? I knew he'd try that. He did his suspension last year for dealing with a CI."

"The informant in that case was dealing with him?"

"Man, where have you been? Anyway, Samantha asked, what was the connection between Mona and the murder? I had to be honest. We don't have a connection, but if the information we gathered today proved that she was connected, we would pursue it." Damien returned to his seat. He took a deep breath with less stress.

"I know you were glad to get out of the spotlight. Even if that suit looked good on the tube." They laughed. Damien rolled up his sleeves. His freshly pressed white shirt and suspenders that matched the tie was a few steps above the office norm. He kept two suits for instant media interviews. What he claimed was a wardrobe nightmare would never happen to him again. He'd be ready head to toe for the unsuspected spotlight shots. Now that spontaneous answers were no longer required, they could concentrate on proving Mona's guilt.

"Sheers is dirty man; it's only a matter of time. Listen, I want to see what's going on with Kendra. They can't keep her without cause."

"I'll meet you here. A few things in these files may look different since we know Mona may be the killer."

Damien didn't agree. He wanted anything other than Mona being guilty of murder.

Chapter Seventy - Two

Kendra asked when she would be able to leave. The female officer gave her a stern look and kept pushing the buttons on her cell phone. The detectives entered the area, and the chatter in the office stopped. All eyes were on the two men who made their way over to the desk where Kendra sat.

She didn't recognize the office, the officers or the detectives. She reminded herself that her entrance was from the rear of the building. There were no numbers in the elevator to indicate the floors and with no sound indication,

Kendra had no idea what floor they were on. She didn't understand why she and Mona were brought through the same entrance. She was brought into the office and told to sit. It had been an hour before she saw Mona through the stenciled glass. She was handcuffed and being escorted to another area. It was then that Kendra realized she was being held for what she thought was questioning.

After three hours of sitting, her face in pain, and the fear that she was not there to give a statement, it became obvious there was another reason she was being detained. She watched the detectives as they made themselves comfortable with coffee and the paperwork that had been computer generated. Kendra knew they would run a background check on both her and Mona. She sighed in frustration. The chair she had been sitting in was beginning to numb her thighs and buttocks. The younger of the two detectives came over to her. Kendra smiled hoping his attitude was better than the officers who gave her the cold shoulder.

"Ma'am, follow me, please." The young man's badge and nameplate was easy to remember. Kendra didn't know why, but she had made a mental list of all the officers she came into contact with from the time she left her apartment.

"Where am I going and why?"

"They're ready to take your statement ma'am." The officer replied without any expression. "Right this way."

Kendra followed his lead without any other questions. She entered a room with a table and three chairs. She knew the area, as described in books and seen on movies. She had no idea why she would be interrogated. She waited for the men to enter the room.

Detective Sheers entered the room alone.

"What no partner? I'm surprised Sheers. That's your name, right? I'd like to see my cousin, Detective Tyson."

"I would think you've had enough of him. Seems as though the connection between you two has caused you more trouble than he's worth." He opened a folder and took the seat across from her.

Kendra had choice words on her mind, but she held her tongue with a prayer to God. "Why am I here? I was assaulted no one cared, now this and you're overly concerned? I'm not buying it, Sir. Why am I here?" She asked again.

"Well, I'm sure you're aware that your statement has to be documented. I'm here to read you your Miranda Rights, and then I'll take that statement."

"I gave your people a statement over four hours ago. I gave your people a statement over a few weeks ago. I'm done giving statements without understanding why? Nothing has been done nor does it appear that it will be done. I—"

"Ms. Lewis, I assure you this is all a part of our protocol. Yes, you were assaulted twice. We'll be talking about that as well."

"What else is there to discuss? I'm the victim." Kendra passed on the stare the female officer gave her earlier.

Sheers laughed. "I wonder what look you gave your boyfriend before you killed him."

"Me? Killed who?" She braced herself as he said the name.

"Jay Rands, Ms. Lewis. Jay Rands was your boyfriend, am I right?"

Kendra nodded her head. It was official. The words she wanted to be confirmed were said. Jay was the body that was found dead.

"And you think I killed him?"

"Well let's just say you're a suspect. So we need to know a few things about your relationship. We'll need you to stop with the wounded victim, the emotional lover, or the scorned woman antics. We can serve you better if you just confess to what you and Ms. Mandell plotted for Mr. Rands."

"And just how does that help me any. If you believe I am the killer, I guess after all of these questions it will support the evidence for an arrest. Interesting I get slashed across the face and threatened in my home, yet I'm a part of the plot for murder. I need to see my cousin. I know you know who he is. Maybe this is your lame attempt to get his position. Yea, asshole I know who and what you are. You want to ask me questions about a murder and my involvement? Talk to my fucking lawyer. You better hope you've got a spot out there with your homies 'cause you'll never have an office."

"So you're not willing to cooperate?"

"Let me talk to my cousin and a lawyer. There's your cooperation."

"I'll get the phone so you can call your lawyer. Your cousin will have to search for you, there's your cooperation. Thank you, Ms. Lewis. Just what I thought, you and your damn cousin are from the same family tree."

"And you're looking for a place to tie a noose. Sorry, I've got a little more education in the law. The statement…right back at ya." Kendra could feel the tears seeping out of her eyes.

The door closed behind Sheers as he left the room. It wasn't long before Leana entered with Kendra's cell phone.

"How'd you get my phone?" She asked as though she was aggravated. Softening her words she asked again.

"They haven't turned your items in yet. Just what you weren't allowed to bring in this area. I told the officer I was working with Damien on this case. They don't know their asses from their elbows, so I took your phone. I signed it out as evidence." Leana shook her head realizing Kendra wasn't aware they were processing her. "Girl don't ask. Listen, Damien had to do a press conference but he'll be here after he changes his clothes."

"Thanks, I need to call my lawyer. I'll wait for Damien if you're sure he's coming. His asshole co-worker Sheers was here. This is a setup Leana. I wouldn't kill anyone." She paused, "To tell you the truth, I still loved him. Mona thought he deserved what the others got. That's what she said. Wow, what am I thinking, you're investigating aren't you?"

"No, I came to tell you Damien was coming. They've got Mona. Tell them what you know about her, when you met and anything she told you about since you've been close to her." Leana walked toward the door, and the Officer, standing by, let her out of the room. "Oh, Kendra. You can talk to me, Jeff and Damien. Beware of the others."

Kendra looked up from the table. She still had her cell phone. She dialed the only support she could trust… Damien Tyson.

Chapter Seventy-Three

Kendra sat waiting. Damien promised he would have the answers to her questions and the lawyer to get her released if they needed one. No one came to check on her during the wait. She was grateful they didn't put her in handcuffs. The thought of being locked in a cell for whatever the police thought she had done was causing anxiety. She called Candice to ease her nerves.

"Hey, are you home?" Kendra asked trying not to sound nervous.

"Yes, where are you? It's all over the news that the police have made an arrest for Jay's murder. They haven't said who it is. They had a breaking news clip with more details to follow."

"Mona's being questioned, and so am I."

"You. Why? What did you do?"

"Listen, I don't know. They probably think it was revenge."

"Kendra, no, I'm so sorry. Is there anything I can do?"

"Well, if they ask for a character witness it will be you." Kendra began to cry. "I didn't want to breakdown again, but Candice, how could Mona do this?"

"Has she confessed?"

"I don't know; we're in separate areas. I thought we were coming here because she pulled a gun on us?"

"Huh, a gun? Mona has a gun?"

"Listen, Candice, I'm being questioned. I don't know if it's for Jay's murder or Mona's outrage."

"Kendra? Do you think Mona did it?"

"Yes, I do. All that talk about what cheaters deserve, well, in her mind Jay deserved it too I guess."

"Kendra. Be careful don't say much cause you said he deserved it too."

"I didn't say it because I would kill him, or tell Mona to do it."

"So what do I say if they question me, Kendra? You and Mona sounded crazy with that shit. How can I lie about that?"

"Has anyone questioned you?"

"No, not yet."

"Well let's not talk about it. You know I wasn't saying I would kill him right?"

"Yea, but. Okay Kendra, I get what you're saying."

Kendra hung up the phone when she heard voices in the hall. The conversation was muffled, but the few words she could put together were about Damien and the power he had to pull a case out of the rafters and solve it. The officers that spoke believed Damien knew Mona and Kendra were planning to kill Jay. They wondered why he didn't pass the case to someone else knowing he was personally connected. They thought Porter should have taken over. After all, they were partners.

She wanted to know who was doing the talking and were they for or against Tyson. She heard them greeting Damien. She put her phone in her pocket just as her door opened. She watched as the small group of five walked past the large glass window. She tried to match the voices with the faces, but without knowing them at all she would only be able to repeat what she heard.

"Are you okay?" Damien held an envelope in his hands. He gestured for Kendra to join him at the table. He placed the envelope between them.

"I want to know what's going on Damien or are you Detective Tyson now."

"C'mon Kendra, I've never been Detective Tyson to you and never will. They need to clear up a few things and your name was put into this mess."

"By who, Mona? They can't trust her word."

"In a case of murder, until it's solved, all who are named…"

Kendra finished the sentence for him. "I know, all who are named are suspect until cleared. So what am I suspected of?"

"Conspiracy. They seem to think you and Mona killed Jay. She confessed but said you wanted her to kill him. You couldn't do it by yourself and Mona understood you needed revenge to move on. It's a theory, but a good one."

"When did he die? I mean they found him today. Did she kill him before she came to my place?"

"Well according to the preliminary reports, he's been dead a couple of days. We'll know more once the autopsy is done." Damien pushed the envelope to Kendra.

She opened the envelope and put the pictures of Jay on the table. He looked like he was sleeping. She ran her finger across his face.

"What is the cause of death? I mean, was there a weapon, blood, contusions or signs of a fight?"

"No, there were no signs at all. That's what prompted an autopsy. Nothing obvious just like…"

"Yea, that's what I'm telling you. Mona admitted to killing before. Is it the same as the murders you're investigating? Leon, Kevin, Raymond, all of them were her lovers. She found out they had wives or someone they were committed to, and she killed them. We talked about Jay often. Our relationship, the ups, and downs but she never mentioned the men in her life until recently. We went with her to Leon's funeral. I think that was the one that sent her overboard. Then I told her about Jay and Talia."

The door opened, and the two were silenced by the lawyer, Jacob Wynn, as he thanked the officers. Mr. Wynn was the family's lawyer and lifelong friend of Damien's father. A well-dressed man, in his late sixties, who professed he would retire at seventy. He was greeted with a smile and a firm handshake from Damien. He turned his attention to Kendra.

"Ms. Kendra, it has been years since I saw you and your mother. I am so sorry it is here that we meet again. How are you holding up?"

"I'm not understanding any of this. Why am I here? This woman has killed again and threatened to kill Damien and me, but I'm here. Can I leave? I've been here longer than I expected, and I haven't had my medicine. I just want to leave."

"Well, I'll have to see what they're holding you for."

"Damien just said conspiracy. Where did they get that from? The woman that killed four men that I know of."

Mr. Wynn moved the empty chair so he could sit next to Kendra. "My dear, how do you know that?"

"She told me, Mr. Wynn. She kept hinting to what could be done. No, what needed to be done to cheaters, men that couldn't be honest when meeting a woman they claimed they wanted to be with. She had deep seeded problems with men who loved women only to betray them. Mr. Wynn, she told me in so many ways, and I just thought we were venting. I didn't realize she had killed her ex-boyfriends."

"Who else did she speak to about this? Do you know if she has any other friends or relatives?"

"No. Just me and Candice. Candice is my other friend. She's been with her often. She and Mona have a schedule, well kinda, to help me. Candice has been driving me around and Mona has been cooking for me and sitting with me and how could she kill Jay? How?" Kendra began to cry.

Damien held her hand. "We're going to find out exactly what went on with Jay. If what you're saying is true we may have solved those cases too."

"What happens to me? I can't stay in here. They can't make me, will they?"

Wynn pulled out a steno pad and scribbled information he would need. Where does Candice live?"

Kendra gave him her information and told him about Talia and Jay. Kendra hoped he would connect the dots as she had. Damien and the lawyer left Kendra waiting again.

Chapter Seventy-Four

Candice didn't want her testimony to cause Kendra any problems. She came to Damien's office with the letter from Mona's lawyer in hand. She never spoke to him and had no intentions of bringing attention to herself. She couldn't understand why he selected her to be a part of Mona's case.

It had been three months since the murder of Jay Rands and Kendra had not been in touch with her friend who simply told the truth. Candice was questioned, as Kendra requested, but her answers didn't clear Kendra. It seemed that her answers gave the credence to what Mona's statement read. The two of them were guilty of Jay's murder. Kendra would be released on bail, but she had to return for the trial.

Damien and Jeff worked hard to connect Jay's murder to the Pine Ridge Resort murders. Sheers hung in the background waiting for what he considered a drowning man's last plunge. He was certain the Cold Case Unit would be appointed new personnel. Tyson and Porter would be out, and Sheers, and his boys would be in. It was just a matter of Candice Miller telling it all in her innocent way. He knew what she meant when she said, *"Kendra was angry and wanted Jay to suffer. I've been in that situation before. Yes, the three of us spoke about Jay. Mona misunderstood what we were saying. She stormed out of the apartment that day. I don't know if she spoke to Kendra later. I guess Jay's no longer the issue now that he's dead."* It didn't matter what he thought or what she meant. What mattered was the jury would convict both Kendra Lewis and Mona Mandell for murder. Tyson's association with two females who committed murder wouldn't get him fired, but there would be a shuffle of positions.

Jeff told Candice to stop by and see them whenever she felt she needed to. Today was the first day she felt the pressure taking over. Sheers and his boys had threatened her off and on since her questioning. Her statement was what kept Kendra in jail that night. Now she feared her testimony would give her a lengthy sentence. The indictment hearing was set for Monday. Candice didn't want the weekend to be filled with more pacing and crying. Kendra didn't speak to her much. She used the excuse that there was apparently a conflict between the two of them. Candice was losing herself in guilt.

She found a parking space close to the municipal building. She was glad she didn't have to pass the parking attendant who flirted with her too often. She told Mona and Kendra he was a pervert with a job. Just the thought of being alone now, the closer they got to the court date, was annoying. Candice didn't have many friends, and now two of the closest were at odds with each other. There was nothing she could do but tell the truth or so she thought. The truth had set no one free.

It was ten o'clock, and she was sure both Damien and Jeff would be in the office. There seemed to be a lot of foot traffic in the halls, but Candice didn't bother to ask what was going on. She got into the elevator, and as the doors opened, she could see there was a press conference being held in front of the very door she had to enter.

She spotted Jeff and Damien near the makeshift platform. The reporters were yelling questions regarding the indictment and the assumed related cases. Everyone wanted to know if there was indeed a connection between the Pine Ridge Resort murders and Jay Rands. There were no answers that would suffice the media or the crowd that was increasing in size.

"Will you be able to connect Mona Mandell to the Bates and Styles murders?" The man held his microphone higher to get the anticipated response.

"Are you sure Kendra Lewis wasn't involved in the other killings?" A voice yelled.

"There was mention that it is their friend that confirmed their involvement. Is she speaking up to keep the eyes off her?" The question sparked whispers and grumbling from the attentive crowd.

Candice moved quickly through the crowd hoping no one was in Damien's office. She was glad her name was being held until she took the stand. She didn't notice Samantha Sayers following her.

"Ms. Miller, Ms. Miller, can I talk to you a minute?"

Her raspy voice was an attempt to whisper. Samantha didn't want the others to notice her speaking to Candice. The two women went into the office without the paparazzi's cameras and questions. Candice took a seat immediately to avoid collapsing. The pressure of the crowd and the ordeal was overwhelming. She hadn't imagined the reaction from the media or the effect the case would have on her.

"Is this how it is around the courthouse during trials? I've seen them on the television. I can't imagine going through this badgering and yelling day after day. Oh my, God I can't do this."

Candice began to rock back and forth in her seat. Samantha had seen this reaction during interviews. If asked, she would tell anyone that Candice was not ready to take the stand or face an audience that would include her friends. The badgering questions from the prosecutor and the defense attorneys would cause her to have a breakdown during her testimony. She left Candice, who was apparently rattled, to get her a cup of water. Samantha returned hoping to have a few minutes to give her words of advice. Showing immediate gratitude, Candice drank the water down quickly but shook her head "no" to the offer of a refill.

"Thanks, I'm sorry. I've never seen anything like this." Candice admitted reluctantly. "It's a little much."

Samantha got a chair from behind the desk and sat silently with Candice as she regained her composure. The silence was good for the two of them. Earlier Samantha spoke with the other reporters who worked with her at the Village Post. It was obvious that the story would attract an audience once Damien's relationship with the suspects was dragged through the media. She had her own shadows of love gone wrong and if the media only knew, she'd be looking for new employment. She was an emotionally driven woman, and although she never expressed it openly, she had strong feelings for Detective Tyson.

The business connections kept them mixing in the same circles, and she was sure that Mona Mandell was a temporary fix for any man. There would be an internal investigation. The Cold Case Unit would lose the reputation and the team that hadn't failed in years. Damien's demeanor captured Samantha upon their first meeting. She was still in a trance. One she couldn't see ending with Detective Sheers' jealousy and confusion.

Samantha decided after Mona's arrest she would ruin the intentions of bad press. Candice would be their first target. Unknowingly she had disclosed enough information to spark an internal war in the Homicide Unit; she unknowingly gave them another piece of priceless news.

Candice put out her hand. Samantha held it for her. "You'll be fine. All of this is a bit much. I'm sure it's taking a toll on all of you. It's difficult to see those you love go through things like this."

"I can't testify against my friends. They took what I said and twisted my words, what I meant, Ms. Sayers they added assumptions! They told me I could speak freely and when I did, I got this." She handed the summons to Samantha.

"Really? The defense wants you to testify for them?" Samantha wanted to talk to her about being on the stand for Kendra, not Mona.

"It's Mona's lawyer. He seems to think I can help prove Mona and Kendra killed Jay. I asked him how that helps either of them. I don't understand the strategy. Kendra won't speak to me, and Mona, well, I can't talk to her."

Samantha was puzzled. She thought the prosecutor would be interested in what Candice would have to say. The news broke when Candice volunteered to talk to the police.

"I would have thought he'd be scared of your testimony. After all, as a friend you've had many conversations you could have shared."

"Well stupid me, I chose the wrong one to tell him. I tried explaining what happened but… Ms. Sayers you're not here to get a story are you? Maybe I should wait for the detectives and speak to them."

"Ms. Miller, I assure you our conversation will remain between us and in this room. You can trust me. I want to help this case, for Damien and Kendra. I won't print anything unless you agree."

Candice needed an understanding ear, so she continued.

"I guess Mona was more than secretive about the men in her life. We knew she dated, but she never shared information about who they were or what they did. You know, girl talk about relationships. Kendra and I would talk about our feelings what we thought were their feelings, girl talk. Kendra was with Jay off and on for a couple of years, so he was often who we compared others with, at least I did. Mona would chime in never mentioning her man's name. We'd listen intently, she seemed like such an authority in relationships and the main reason for breakups being cheating. She said men put us in categories. She said she was tired of men thinking they had the perfect side piece. I told the police Mona convinced us that they deserved whatever they got when the wives or the girlfriend found out what was really going on."

Samantha listened as Candice continued to explain Mona's theories and solutions for cheaters. The story was more than what she expected. It became clear that Candice was the key that could open or lock the cell door for Kendra. Candice was right the lawyer could twist her words and pitch a case for some of Mona's freedom. She wondered if there was any evidence that would prove Kendra may have been involved.

"So did Kendra ever mention she told Mona she wanted Jay dead?"

"Ms. Sayers after her accident or the assault on her face, she would say that Jay and Talia would pay. But who wouldn't want them to pay; have you seen her face? Kendra has more surgeries to suffer through. Mona said she killed him! Why include Kendra?"

Chapter Seventy-Five

Samantha didn't have the answers Candice needed to settle her thoughts. Damien and Jeff entered the office and the women ended their conversation. Samantha stood to leave the trio to sort out details. She gave Candice her card and told her to call if she wanted to.

The women hugged goodbye as though they had been friends longer than their hour-long encounter. Damien was pleased to see Candice accepted their invitation to talk at the office. Candice repeated her story to Jeff and Damien, both assured her she hadn't done anything wrong. They were still collecting evidence at the crime scene, Mona's apartment and taking statements such as hers.

"Candice did you know Leon Bates?" Damien laid the pictures on his desk. Jeff brought over the pictures of the other Pine Ridge Resorts murder victims.

"Or either of these men?" Jeff pulled the pictures from an envelope on his desk. "Or is this woman familiar?"

The sketched image was complete without the scarf. It was Mona. Jeff laid the sketch next to the photo marked "mystery woman".

"Oh my God!" Candice picked up the sketch. She never mentioned her thoughts of the "mystery woman" aloud. "I said the woman had features like Mona. Did you recognize it?" She looked to the detectives for nods of agreement. "You didn't?" She was surprised.

"We just got the completed sketch. We needed someone who had seen her without the scarf." Jeff stated firmly not wanting Candice to think they ignored the resemblance.

"She did a good job of disguising herself. But usually when she wears her scarves like this, she wears shades. I recognize both the scarf and the shades."

"Candice, did Kendra recognize her with this scarf?" Damien doubted his cousin missed this clue.

"We talked about this so-called mystery woman, but neither of us dared to say Mona fit the features. She didn't even mention it; now I know why."

"With this picture and your testimony we can link her to The Pine Ridge Resort murders. They're bringing her journal from the house and checking her cell phone. They think with what they've found she will be put away for years. Amir called just before they left her home."

Damien sat in the chair closer to Candice. "Listen, I know this is a tight spot to be in. You've got to mention your conversations about the murders, her attitude, and how you and Kendra talked whenever she wasn't around. You've got to convince them that—"

"Mona is and was crazy enough to kill all of them, by herself" Jeff injected. "We can handle the rest. There will be enough evidence to bury her. Look the toxicology report is here. Shows levels of toxins in Jay Rands stomach. Man, she may have poisoned him. She mentioned poisons in her journal."

Damien stood slowly. "I missed the clues trying to secure a relationship. Damn."

Jeff patted him on his back. "Sometimes we're blinded by that thing called love. We got her now; that's all that matters. Sheers didn't pull it off, and that's what he was after."

Candice was lost, still gazing at the pictures. "I'm going to get going. You guys helped me. You and Ms. Sayers. She's a good person. Damien, she likes and respects you and your team a lot. Don't be blind twice. When this is over maybe, the four of us can go out or something huh, Jeff?"

Jeff smiled and shook her hand. She gave Damien a hug. "Call me if you need to before Monday. Please tell Kendra to call me too. She won't accept my calls. I know what she thinks, but it's not what it looks like."

"I'll tell her. I'll contact and thank Ms. Sayers too. Don't be a stranger." Damien walked her to the office door.

"I won't, I promise."

Chapter Seventy-Six

"So how can I handle the discovery for the murders if his people are at the scene picking over what could be evidence?"

Sheers was pleading with the Chief and had been for the past thirty minutes. He, Tyson and Porter were called in the office after their outburst in the hall. Chief Michaels was playing referee as usual.

"Listen, you boys already know where this is heading. The papers will eat this squabble you guys have and spit out all kinda shit that this department doesn't need. Sheers, you can't expect me to tell Tyson's team to back off when you haven't done a damn thing to move this case off the shelves. You had your chance when the case was assigned to homicide. The unit shelved it. Tell me you're closer now because it's with Tyson, and I'll have your ass for sure."

He paused to look over the papers and reports Tyson brought to him regarding the new evidence.

"We got this in the search or did you know about this before?"

"Sir? What do you mean before?" Damien didn't like the implication of the Chief's question.

"While you were laying up with the murderer; how far back doesn't make a difference, it's my case!" Sheers blurted out sarcastically.

"Really Sheers!! What the hell is wrong with you?! You deserve a fist in your mouth, and I think I'm the only one standing in the way of that! The sign of a coward Sheers. Know when to pick your fights. Shut the hell up! Tyson, I mean was this evidence found earlier. Maybe right after the arrest, before an official search was requested. I'm looking at reports concerning a journal, phone records, and what's this, oh business reports. Did you have access to this before? Did you go back there before the search?"

"No, I didn't."

"Tyson, these are questions they'll ask. I don't want them throwing out evidence because of your relationship."

"Understood. No, I haven't been there since the arrest."

"Good, now how do we get you and your cousin, is it, out of this mess. Any suggestions, Sheers? News for you Sheers, if Tyson doesn't get out of this, you'll answer for anything that springs up. So if you know anything that would damage him or this unit speak up, or shut up!"

The conversation ended. The Chief wasn't open to Sheer's ranting without any proof of what he was saying. Tyson didn't smile until he closed the door of his office. He came through the ranks with Chief Michaels. They had their differences over the years, but he knew the value of having the team and Tyson's reputation with the media. Sheers hadn't changed over the years, and his walk through the ranks was always on thin ice.

There was a note on Damien's desk from Jeff. He was with Amir getting a statement from Scott Bearman and Jessica. Now that they had Mona's sketch it would be easy to get someone to say they saw her with Leon Bates and the others. They would meet him at the resort if he wanted to be in on the questioning. Damien decided he'd visit Ms. Sayers at her office instead.

The Village Post wasn't far from the police station. On a good day, one could walk from the station to the offices that told the stories that fed the community. It was those stories that Damien was worried about as he walked toward the parking lot to take the short ride to meet Samantha.

Sheer's was parked close to Damien's vehicle, and he grinned as he saw the detective approaching. It was an opportunity to dig in, but he had been warned.

"I must admit you wear it well Tyson. Through the thick, thin and shit, you have a way of maintaining a clean appearance." Sheers yelled over the hood of his car.

Tyson ignored the comment as he had so many of Sheers' sarcastic remarks. He opened his door then turned toward Sheers. "I never asked you, I mean I just assumed you and that pretty CI, the one that ruined your career, were an item. Did you know how deep she was in the thick and thin of shit? Naw I didn't think so. You know us men we investigate the ones that are in deep. Hey, let's compare notes. You lost the evidence, the perps, and your mind, but you were in so deep you traveled with her. I heard you brought her to a few of the community functions. That's when the Chief saved your ass and your manhood. If she would have invited you into the shit she was in; you'd be doing time. Did you know there was a hit out on you? Shit, that would have saved the department the embarrassment each time you show your hate for me. They remember; you lost it. It won't happen Sheers. The Unit is mine."

Sheers got into his car and slammed his door. Tyson won another round. He was sure their fight would continue another day. Fifteen minutes later Tyson was offered a seat in the waiting area of the Village Post. Samantha was finishing on the phone in her office. The receptionist gave him a subtle glance, obviously aware who the handsome detective was and why he was there.

"There's coffee made, or if you prefer tea, we have that as well."

"No thank you." He picked up a copy of the Post that was in the rack near where he sat. The headline was as was expected. *"Mona Mandell, a local businesswoman, was arrested today for aggravated assault."* There was no mention of Jay Rands or Kendra Lewis and no mention of the Detectives name.

"That's not a final copy detective; we put those in the rack just to provide reading material in the waiting area. Ms. Sayers will see you now."

It wasn't considered procedural for a detective or any law enforcement personnel to have a meeting with a member of the press in their office. If necessary, the reporters would hound the department for a meeting. Damien stayed clear of the temporary celebrity status both written and taped for viewers. He walked into Samantha Sayers' office and felt instant relief.

He prepared himself for file cabinets, unfinished projects lying around, piles of paperwork on her desk and all sorts of organized chaos. He understood, sharing an office with Jeff, that it was functional for those without a need for a system.

Samantha stood as he entered the room. Her smile always weakened him, but her beauty was equally stunning. He couldn't deny Jeff's consistent reminder, she didn't hide her admiration for Detective Damien Tyson.

"Good morning Detective. I love your suit. You look rested. Are you getting some rest? I'm sure it's not easy."

"I'm doing my best. I came to thank you for the diversions and keeping your word."

"Damien, they'll use you. The media, your department, your colleagues, and even your so-called friends, will watch as this mess unravels and offer you no assistance. I'm true to my word because I believe in you and what you do. Let's sit in here."

He followed her to an attached room. He assumed it was a small conference room. An oval table sat in the middle of the room. The four chairs matched the carpet and window décor perfectly. Damien smiled to himself as his minute knowledge of interior design nudged at him.

"We need a room like this." He continued to look around. The shelves were stacked with magazines and what he was sure were outdated Village Post papers.

"I often come in here, close the door and get into a zone. I want to write the articles with the truth. Some of the people or stories we write about have a background story. Most reporters don't want to delve into the history. Damien, that's what's important. Why? Why does one victimize another? I don't know; it's always been more than just what we see on the surface. Your incident blew me away."

She paused as she noticed his look. He was definitely paying attention, but she wasn't sure he heard what she said.

"Damien, are you okay?"

"To be honest, no. I want to break the rules. I want to talk to Ms. Mandell and Kendra before this hearing. Samantha, my cousin, is being set up. She's back in the County. Something about undisclosed evidence. They revoked the bail. She's been there since Friday."

"What about evidence? What have they found? Listen, the underground whispers are they won't get Mandell for the Pine murders. She confessed and included Kendra in the Rands murder. Now the aggravated assault, well if they pursue it, you'll be the topic. Your boys at the top don't want that. It opens too many avenues of misbehavior that would, of course, be tabloid worthy."

"Not much. We have the toxicology report and the findings prompted another search. I'm sure the lawyer will find a way to get her out of the Rands murder. We've got people that can identify her as the mystery woman, but there's no connection between her and the murders. I'm sure with the picture circulating through the media; she has a concocted story prepared. Mona's not a stupid woman. I can't say what went wrong or why she did this. I need to talk to her just to give me peace of mind."

"So my dear detective is that what brings you, for the first time I must add, to my office?"

"I'm sure you know. You can do an interview; get the story. I've only got a few questions. They're not about me or our relationship if there was one. Samantha, as a man, I need to understand if I provoked this last killing."

"How? She's obviously killed before. She told Kendra and Candice that men like that didn't deserve to live."

"Exactly, I need to be sure I'm not that kind of man. She came to Kendra's home for two reasons. She thought we were lovers, and she wanted to shut Kendra up. Maybe she'll open up, give a clue that we can link to the Pine Murders. She's a killer. I finally convinced myself of that. Now I need to know she won't get away with it."

"Revenge for your frayed emotions?"

"If I told you no would you believe me?"

Samantha smiled and then laughed. Her laughter caused him to relax. He shook his head realizing he didn't need to be on edge.

"Of course I wouldn't Damien, you're human. If you told me your emotions were in order after finding the woman you were in a relationship with was a serial killer….. yea, right. Listen, I don't understand how or why but I do know that you are not that 'kind of guy' she described. Shame on her or any other woman that doesn't recognize you."

"Samantha, remember when you labeled us in your article as Batman and Robin? Jeff and I often thought it was to heighten your popularity. I never gave it much thought. Well, I'm lying, I thought you were trying a ploy for more information, stories. Today, I thought about it again. You're not that kind of reporter, and I want to apologize for thinking that way."

"Some of us want to do our job. Then there are others who have more than a business interest in the detectives we write about. So let me make an appointment to visit Ms. Mandell and Kendra. Visiting the two of them for a story won't seem odd. I can't guarantee the lawyers will allow it, but I'll do what I can to convince them it's to their advantage. Batman can't continue to wear his emotions on his sleeve and solve crimes."

They stood; a silent understanding preceded the handshake and embrace. Damien would let Jeff know Ms. Sayers was more than just a reporter; he hoped she was a friend.

Chapter Seventy-Seven

The bleak walls of the County Jail changed many, even the visitors who entered its doors. The reporter was well aware of the routine. The search, the stares, the makeshift identification that was worn throughout the visit, it all made it evident outsiders were not welcomed, especially the media.

Ms. Sayers' contacts gave her an open invitation to visit whenever she called. Once again her fairness in reporting the truth allowed her more than normal access. She didn't wait long and after a few greetings she was escorted to the small room where she waited for Kendra Lewis. It unnerved her as she heard the heavy doors clicking open and slamming shut.

She never knew how long the maze was from the units to the conference area, but she counted eight doors slamming each time she visited. The plexiglass window was never smudge free or cleaned. She sat in a plastic chair that would soon become uncomfortable.

There was a phone that she would take some time to clean with a paper towel and anti-bacterial wipes before using. The lights were bright and somewhat annoying, but they served a purpose. There was no sign of cleanliness anywhere. The walls were painted gray. Samantha would always say that the dirt would blend in if evenly smeared. The tiled floors were polished over the permanent stains and dirt.

Although everyone held in the County were not convicted felons, where they sat was no different. The seat that awaited Kendra was a steel stool. She wouldn't be given an opportunity to clean the area where she sat or the phone she would need to use. The officer would wait at a podium located at the entrance. There were portioned walls on each side of her seat to give each visit a bit of privacy.

Samantha was offered a conference room a perk that was offered to authorized visitors. She declined. The entry ritual was more invasive, one she avoided at all cost.

Kendra entered the area wide-eyed and apparently scared. Her hair was pulled back, an obvious attempt to make it acceptable. Her clothes were neat but in need of changing. Samantha wondered if she had received any care for her scar that was still healing. Kendra took her seat faintly smiling as she recognized the reporter before her.

"Hello, Ms. Sayers. My lawyer said to expect your visit. It's been a rough week, but I've been praying, and here you are."

"Well I'm certainly not a savior but I'm hoping this visit will clear up a few things for my readers and maybe even your case."

The interview was an hour long. Kendra admitted to having the conversation that Candice had revealed.

"It was no conspiracy or plan to have Jay killed. Ms. Sayers, it was merely a conversation among friends or those I thought were my friends. I was frustrated with the relationship. How many women have said it over coffee or during a night out? He was cheating; a cheater, and I felt stupid for being in love with him. I took him back over and over. I was fed up, and I didn't know how to handle it. Killing him wasn't an option for me. I like my freedom."

"What about your suspicions? You mentioned you knew immediately that Mona killed Jay. Was that because of the conversations you had in the past? Did she ever say she killed her past lovers because they cheated?"

"No, not in so many words. Ms. Sayers, she's smooth. I would have alerted Damien as soon as I thought she was a killer. I called him that night to tell him what I thought. That's when I knew. I wish it had been sooner."

"Do you have any questions for me?"

"Am I going to be sentenced? What's your opinion? Why would they revoke my bail?"

"I don't know. I'm hoping this will put some questions in the minds of the citizens. Your cousin sends his love, and I'm leaving you with prayers. Oh, Candice mentioned Mona storming out of your place when she found out Jay was calling you. Did you think this was odd?"

Kendra hesitated as she remembered Candice's reaction to Mona leaving. "Yes, Candice said something about the way Mona left being strange. I wonder if she began setting him up that day. There were times Jay called, and I didn't answer. He was constantly calling and then suddenly the calls stopped. Until she came to my house, I hadn't heard from Mona since the day she stormed out. I guess with my face healing and trying to keep calm about our breakup, I didn't put it together."

There wasn't much more to say. Samantha would revise and complete her notes while waiting for the officer to return with Mona Mandell.

Mona didn't recognize the name when the lawyer told her there was a reporter from the Village Post that wanted to speak with her. She was advised not to speak with any media without him being present. Mona didn't want him there. She agreed to the interview and waived the right to have the attorney present. She needed a message to get to Damien.

Samantha heard the motors to the first door, the clicking and then the slam. She put the pad she'd been writing on in her satchel, leaving a few blank sheets in front of her. She pretended not to be stunned by Mona's natural beauty. She'd have fun describing the woman who no one would suspect as a murderer. Mona's braids were up in a perfect bun. Even without a touch of makeup her skin had a glow. Samantha wondered what products she used that would leave flawless skin without a blemish after days without use. She wasn't much taller than the reporter, and her weight evenly proportioned. A twinge of jealousy caused Samantha to sit up straight as though she wasn't getting enough attention. The officer smiled at the reporter and once again he returned to his podium. Mona took her seat and picked up the phone.

"Good afternoon Ms. Mandell," Samantha spoke into the receiver hoping she didn't sound like she was screaming.

"Good afternoon."

Samantha continued hoping Mona's mood would change. She didn't care for the fake professional air Mona mastered since being arrested. Her sarcasm could be detected immediately.

"Well, I'm Samantha Sayers from the Village Post. I'm sure you've heard of our paper. I want to give the people, the readers a clear look at who you are and why you're being charged for murder."

"That's simple Miss, what is your name again?"

"Samantha Sayers."

"Nice to meet you. Who I am really doesn't matter, Ms. Sayers. People will think what they want. I'll be that women who killed Jay Rands, the woman who held a gun on Detective Tyson and his so-called cousin. They'll call it what they want, and it doesn't matter."

"So you pled guilty to killing Jay Rands?"

"Kendra and I did kill him, together. If she hadn't given me his address, phone number or said she wanted him dead, I would have been home."

Samantha looked into Mona's eyes as she told her of the conversation that she claimed led her to release the pain her friend held.

"She wouldn't move on. He had shown her where he stood in the relationship. He had that woman cut her. Kendra was caught in his web of deception."

The reporter wanted to stop her, but she was sure she would tell the entire story. Her plot, how she made the plans, and how she murdered a man that had no attachment to her.

"It's no secret. I've been released from them all. Cheaters get what they deserve."

"Is that why you went to Kendra's home that night?"

It was as though Mona snapped out of a trance.

"Who are you? I thought you wanted to know about me, my case and explaining my actions. Are you here for Damien Tyson?"

Mona's anger rose. She clenched her teeth as she whispered harshly spitting on the Plexiglass.

"You tell that bastard that I know a cheat when I see one. They claim they're cousins? Where was he when she was bruised and damaged? Where was he when half her face was cut? Wait, you, are you here to protect him? Tell him he's no better than the rest. They got what they deserved."

With her last words, she dropped the receiver and walked away. Samantha had to repeat the last thing she said aloud. *"They got what they deserved."* It was then she understood Kendra's statement. Mona spewed it with such vengeance, even without evidence, Samantha knew she was the killer that had committed the Pine Ridge Resort murders.

Chapter Seventy-Eight

Damien didn't make a habit of visiting the scene of the crime often. His expertise was putting the gathered evidence together. It often reminded him of puzzle pieces. He would examine each piece, keeping it until he solved the crime. The walls of his office were filled. He hadn't left Friday night until late.

It was early Saturday morning. The hearing was set for Monday morning. The detectives were determined there had to be something that was overlooked. Jeff and Leana arrived ten minutes after him. Their first stop was where Jay Rand's body was found. Damien had his bathroom dusted. He remembered days after the murder that she had been through his condo. He hoped the fingerprints they found were good enough for comparison.

It would have been easier if the arrest was for the murder instead of the aggravated assault. The team would have to prove she killed Jay Rands with solid evidence. The responding police took pictures, lifted prints, and in the written statement they wrote the evidence was inconclusive. They still needed more.

"No murder is perfect. It's overlooked evidence, the lack of paying attention to detail." Damien stated as they turned the key to the cabin.

The manager at the hotel told them he hadn't allowed anyone in the cabin since the yellow tape was cut earlier in the week.

"Leana, start wherever you think she may have slipped up and left something or left her prints. Look for traces of food particles."

"I thought you said they dusted for prints." She looked for either of the men to answer. She didn't wait for them to answer. She put on her rubber gloves and continued to the bedroom.

"I don't know if they cleaned that room thoroughly. Be careful in there." Jeff called out to her.

"Did anyone check this furniture?" The men joined Leana in the bedroom. "Did they check for his last meal? This stuff on the bed and the nightstand indicates someone vomited. We may not need the food particles."

"They checked the contents of his stomach. Scrape it and bag it. The lab can tell us what it is. I requested skin and hair samples after reviewing their initial report."

Jeff and Damien inspected the side of the nightstand. Jeff cut a piece of the rug that held the hardened remains of what they concluded may have been food. The trio continued their search. It seemed that once again the place had been carelessly checked over after the killing.

"Jeff, put a call in for the hazmat crew. Tell them the scene is ready to be cleaned. Have them bag and tag anything they find." Damien took off his gloves and headed to the door.

"Wait." Jeff was on his knees looking under the bed. "There's something here. Let's just hope it matches."

"What is it?" Leana and Damien asked in unison.

Jeff pulled out his flashlight to give the area the needed light. "The match to the earring turned in by Ms. Thurston from Leon Bates room."

Damien nodded his head. "We'll have to question her again. You guys can take off. I'll call the resort and make arrangements to speak with the manager and Ms. Thurston."

"Man you ruined my Saturday already, I'm with you for the day."

Leana didn't answer. They knew she'd be with the two of them. She suggested they stop by the evidence lab first.

Leana led the detectives to large cabinets that were labeled according to date and a number that corresponded to the log book she stopped to look in. "Fifty-five, twenty-one," She said to no one. She found the cabinet with the same number posted on the clipboard attached by a cord. The physical evidence they wanted to see was found labeled and tagged Pine Ridge Resorts with the other physical evidence found in the room.

"Well, how do we link the missing earring to the crime? We know she's a member at the resort, but it's still not murder." Jeff signed the log book after checking the box for any other evidence they may have needed.

"Let me talk to her. I'll add what she's been missing, her jewelry. Let's see if that will rattle her. They're beautiful and often beauty is expensive."

Chapter Seventy-Nine

It wasn't the norm, the pressures to "wrap up" the case were heightened. The unit needed hard evidence for the prosecutor to charge Mona Mandell with The Pine Ridge Resort murders. There was no need to contact the Chief or anyone who could push the paperwork through without a confession or facts.

The trio decided to separate. Porter would stay on the evidence. He needed to include anything that would link the findings with their discovery, possible poisoning. Tyson would wait until Leana drilled Mona and then his plans would fall into place.

Time was not on their side. Tyson stood at his desk staring at the post-its. There was nothing they excluded or so they thought. The lab results were being run on particles in his stomach; the tech confirmed it had to be in the food. He called back with a list of things that wouldn't be easy to detect. The test would take time, and there would be no way he could sign papers stating the results could be the same in the previous murders. Tyson knew they would be the same. They needed time.

Leana arrived at the County Jail and surrendered her credentials. She prepared a story in case she was asked for the letter that normally proceeded outside law enforcement visits. She emptied her pockets, which included the earring that was found and paperwork. She took a chance and watched as the officer searched through the forms. "I need Ms. Mandell to sign those before court on Monday." The officer smiled and processed her without any questions.

Leana had been working in the homicide unit, mainly cold cases, over eight years. She was the balance when Amir wasn't around, often the reasoning voice that spoke louder than Jeff or Damien. She loved chasing evidence and ultimately catching the criminal. After talking with Kendra, she too felt a twinge of anger toward Jay and men like him. She hadn't detected a killer instinct in the young woman who lost part of her face because she chose to hold on to love. This case was more than catching a killer. Leana had many thoughts as she followed the officer to a conference area. She wanted to understand what would push a woman to kill in this manner. Mona Mandell practically got away with murder. She confessed to killing Jay Rands. Leana wondered why Mona confessed. She may have gotten away with his murder as well. There were no obvious connections. The challenge for the homicide unit was to have her confess to the Pine Ridge Resort killings.

She wasn't the detective chosen to speak or question Mona during the initial interrogation. The case was active and after all she worked with Tyson. The gossip and rumors touched the four of them; each had their point of view. Leana's was simple. Tyson was a good man and supervisor, which was all that mattered. He was just too close to the case to see the small connections. Amir and Jeff would agree they all were chosen to bring the dead cases to life, but this case was different. Leana knew Damien wanted this one to die quickly.

The officer's pace quickened as they approached the first door. "I'm sorry there's a movement coming through this hall. I didn't want you to have to wait." Leana hurried her steps grateful the officer was considerate. The rooms hadn't changed since she'd been there a year ago. She remembered the stench in the air. She wondered how many inmates recognized the difference or just wanted a breath of fresh air. They passed two doors before the officer opened the door to the conference room.

"She'll be here shortly. Would you prefer her to remain in handcuffs, Ma'am?"

"No, you can remove the cuffs. She's got to read and sign a few papers. If that's okay with you."

"Uh, no problem. We have to ask, though." The officer's response hinted that Leana might have a problem. Leana hoped it would present a problem, one that would lead to another confession.

The room was a step up from a window visit. There was a table that would separate them. They had wooden chairs, similar to those in a courtroom. Leana took her seat recognizing that the arms had been scratched, a pen etching. She wondered if her seat should have been on the opposite side of the table. She ignored her assumptions, sat down, and emptied the large envelope on the table.

Moments before she heard the final door opening she turned the papers for Mona to view. She put the evidence bags and their contents back into the larger envelope. The stage was set. Mona Mandell would play her role, and as Leana hoped, the curtain would fall. This would be Mona Mandell's last performance.

Leana had her visions about cheating men or women. It often included murder, victims such as Kendra, even suicides. The results were never positive if the police had to be involved. There were many Mona's and Kendra's that suppressed their anger and simply moved on. Leana put her pad and pen on the table just as Mona and the officer entered the room. Leana stood and introduced herself. The exchange of words was colder than she expected.

"How are you feeling? Are you okay with this?" Leana asked as a courtesy. She really didn't care.

"Does it make a difference? Detective Wilson, that's what you said your name was?"

"Yes, I just need your signature. If you can identify a few smaller items we found at the scene, you can sign for them as well. We can't turn anything over to these authorities without your signature. It's routine Ms. Mandell."

"It can't be mine, but I can write that as well, correct?"

"Yes. The papers are there for your review."

Mona took the time to read the documents. There was nothing unusual about her transfer to the County Jail. She signed the papers and gave the information requested. It was Leana's cue to put the plastic evidence bags on the table that now included the earring. She waited for Mona's reaction. Mona pushed the signed papers to Leana with the pen resting upon them.

"Are these the items that are thought to be mine?"

Mona's question was her feeble attempt to gather her thoughts. She looked through the clear plastic bags tagged with taped labels. Clearly she could see the items that were Leon Bates. His business card, one cuff link and what she thought may have been a napkin. She didn't understand why the napkin was there.

Leana put the second envelope on the table. It contained one earring and Mona's journal. She stood and took the other from her pocket and placed it on the table between the two bags.

"It seems you've been collecting items from my home."

"Not without a warrant Ms. Mandell. Let's do this, I need to keep the paperwork separated. These items are from one of the Pine Ridge Resort murders. We have what we think is enough evidence to confirm you were there the night and some days prior to the murder of Mr. Bates. The items in the bag on your left are from the Jay Rands murder."

"My journal is not a part of any investigation. It's personal writings!" Mona was apparently agitated. Leana needed her to identify with the earrings.

"Ms. Mandell I understand, and there is a space on the form where you can indicate any discrepancies. Is there any other item that shouldn't be placed as evidence from the scene of the crime?"

"My journal never leaves my home! Detective, you tell that bitch ass Tyson that's a dirty defense!"

"Defense? What do you mean? You weren't dating him when Leon Bates was murdered were you?"

"No," Mona replied calming herself.

She hadn't taken the bait. Leana let the silence speak as Mona eyed the earrings.

"I loved him. I began to feel like I was loved. Damien is a good man, and I couldn't love him the way he would love me. Funny how bad relationships linger in your emotions. I was still hurting. Jay Rands hurt Kendra, a friend, my friend. I needed to put him out of my mind, out of my thoughts. Please tell Damien, I did love him, I do love him."

"Did you love Leon Bates?"

"Why is he a topic? He was murdered, and the case has been considered cold right?"

"They have a way of resurrecting themselves. This earring was found by the staff at The Pine Ridge Resort. The match was found in the cabin with Jay Rands. Are you claiming them as yours? We haven't run any test on them to be sure it isn't just a coincidence that the same earring was found at two murder scenes."

"Hmmm… well, Leon and I were at the resort that week. I left him there after our last romp. We agreed we wouldn't see each other again. I may have lost the earring there."

"And the match at the murder scene of ……"

"Okay, what about Jay. What are you implying? I commit murder and leave an earring? Please, if anything I didn't notice they were missing."

The earring was in Mona's jeans. She noticed she didn't have the match when she got home after leaving Leon gurgling in the suite. She wore the same jeans the day she helped Jay vomit until he passed out. She attempted to clean the floor and the side of the bed where he made a mess. She thought she heard the teardrop earring fall, but she didn't find it. It never crossed her mind that the two earrings would be brought together as evidence to have her convicted of two murders.

"So to pin Leon's murder on me you need me to sign that the earring is mine?"

"No Ms. Mandell, we just need to know that we can put them with your property that was collected when you were arrested."

Mona signed the forms and stood, ready to leave.

"Detective, I'd hate for your unit or Tyson, as you call him, to fall apart. The Bates murder is cold and finding a killer now is impossible." She laughed loudly. "An earring. Wow, yeah take that to the prosecutor and see how far that gets you."

The officer placed the handcuffs on Mona's wrist. The two began to walk toward the door.

"Oh, Ms. Mandell, officer please wait a moment. Ms. Mandell, so that I'm sure. You did initial next to the journal as it being yours correct?"

"Yeah, it's mine, and you'll hear from my lawyer. There was no probable cause to search my home."

"Yes, file what you believe is necessary Ms. Mandell. Your lawyer can explain it to you."

Leana packed the envelopes. She was pleased with her pursuit. They had her acknowledgment of the earrings and the journal. The journal in her handwriting told it all.

Leana got to her car. She called the office. "Hey Tyson, make the call. We got ourselves a gold medal."

"She confessed?"

"No. Her journal did, and the earrings helped us get the permission we needed to search her home. Oh, she said to let you know she did truly love you."

"Just like a black widow. I'm glad I didn't get caught in her web."

Chapter Eighty

Monday morning the courtroom was filled. The clerk of the court made it known that any outburst or disruptions would not be tolerated. The press took over the first few rows while others complained the court was too small for such a controversial case. Tyson and Porter had grown accustomed to the grumbling audience and would often offer their seats. Today was different; they would be in court for the entire proceeding. The Village Post had the story printed in Sunday's news. Samantha Sayers had done it again. She had the updated report and the story of the evidence linking Mona Mandell to The Pine Ridge Resort murders.

Although the proceedings of the morning would not include The Pine Ridge Resort case, there were many in the audience who wanted to bear witness to the unfolding drama. Kendra was released that morning and wanted no part of the proceeding or the press. She called Candice for a ride home. Candice was pleased to hear from her friend. They agreed the trial would be enough for either of them.

Janelle phoned Celeste and updated her with the tangled suspicions and conclusions. She was worried they may have to testify. Celeste laughed but told her she'd make the trip to New Jersey if she were summoned. She and Rusty were sure it wouldn't come to that. Janelle sat in the courtroom with a picture of Mona and her husband in her purse. Janelle's memory was nudged, and she found the pictures Leon had stashed in his home office. She needed closure. She needed to hear the voice of the woman who called her home many nights looking for her husband.

Talia took a seat in the back of the court. She sought to put things together or to finalize them. Either of which would give her peace of mind. She couldn't stay in New Jersey and not worry about pending charges. Although she wanted to tell Kendra how sorry she was, she was sure her presence wouldn't be appreciated. She would have to be a shadow in the courtroom and at Jay's funeral. Her cousin agreed to accompany her. They sat together with no one noticing her tears.

Leana and Amir stood in the rear of the courtroom. They would leave once the court date was set. Samantha Sayers entered the court waved in their direction and took her seat in the front.

Everyone stood to their feet, respecting the entrance of the judge as she approached the bench. Tyson smiled as he found comfort that Judge Matilda Hennings was the presiding judge for the case. The District Attorney's office was confident that The Pine Ridge Resort Murders would be enough to put Mona away for life. Their first hurdle was the murder of Jay Rands.

Charges were read, and a plea of not guilty was entered by Walter Reed, Mona's attorney. The moans from the court got the response of the gavel by Judge Hennings.

"Quiet! Quiet! I will not have that. Mr. Reed you have entered the plea of not guilty?"

"Yes your Honor. My client's plea is not guilty. We have evidence that she was coaxed into entering the guilty plea."

"I see. Ms. Mandell, please stand. Do you understand what is going on in this proceeding?"

"I do your Honor." Mona responded as though she was a student in a class.

"So be it. Enter the plea as stated by the attorney for Ms. Mona Mandell. The court date is set for October 21st."

"Your honor may I ask that there be a bail reduction."

"Objection your honor."

The voices in the audience got louder. The gavel slammed three times. "Order!!"

"Your Honor, Ms. Mandell is a flight risk. In light of new evidence where Ms. Mandell is again the accused in one maybe two other murders, the State of New Jersey asks that bail remain as is."

"Mr. Reed are you aware of this evidence?"

"I am your Honor. However, one case has nothing to do with another. Since my client has cooperated, we feel…."

"Objection! Her cooperation your Honor is to get the least of the penalties from the state. She has manipulated the system, your Honor."

"Mr. Reed, after looking through your petition to the court for a bail reduction, I have to agree with the state. There will be no reduction. Am I to understand there will be no charges presented for Ms. Kendra Lewis?"

Mona's lawyer and Mona took their seats. Mona surveyed the room. Her eyes met Damien's who hadn't taken his eyes off her. She tried to smile, hoping the tears wouldn't fall.

"Your Honor, the state has dropped the charges against Ms. Lewis."

Damien heard what he needed to hear. His stare was cold as he kept focus on Mona. The message was clear he had the evidence he needed to solve The Pine Ridge Resort murders.

The court was adjourned, and the reporters surrounded Mona, the lawyers, and the officers. Mona watched Damien as he approached Samantha Sayers. Damien extended his hand, and Samantha grabbed it smiling. Damien hugged the reporter and shook hands with those who accompanied her. It was then that Mona couldn't hold her tears any longer.

Other Novels by Nanette M. Buchanan

Family Secrets Lies and Alibi's

A Different Kind of Love

Bruised Love

Skeletons Beyond The Closed Door

Gossip Line

Bonded Betrayal

Scattered Pieces

The Stranger Within

The Hustler's Touch

Duplicity

The Corner Pew

Purchase Your Copy Today

www.NanetteMBuchanan.com

Books are available in Kindle, Nook and other ebook formats

www.ingramcontent.com/pod-product-compliance
Lightning Source LLC
Chambersburg PA
CBHW070048120726
47909CB00002B/321